TROUBLED WATER

ROBERT T. SCHUETZ

outskirts
press

Troubled Water
All Rights Reserved.
Copyright © 2025 Robert T. Schuetz
v3.0

This is a work of fiction. Names, characters, businesses, places, events, locales, and incidents are either the products of the author's imagination or used in a fictitious manner. Any resemblance to actual persons, living or dead, or actual events is purely coincidental.

The opinions expressed in this manuscript are solely the opinions of the author and do not represent the opinions or thoughts of the publisher. The author has represented and warranted full ownership and/or legal right to publish all the materials in this book.

This book may not be reproduced, transmitted, or stored in whole or in part by any means, including graphic, electronic, or mechanical without the express written consent of the publisher except in the case of brief quotations embodied in critical articles and reviews.

Outskirts Press, Inc.
http://www.outskirtspress.com

ISBN: 978-1-9772-7799-2

Library of Congress Control Number: 2024922300

Cover Photo © 2025 www.gettyimages.com. All rights reserved - used with permission.

Outskirts Press and the "OP" logo are trademarks belonging to Outskirts Press, Inc.

PRINTED IN THE UNITED STATES OF AMERICA

*For Mom & Dad.
I mean, where would I be without them?*

"Perhaps the truth depends on a walk around the lake."

– Wallace Stevens

Chapter 1
Last Kiss

"Well, where oh where can my baby be?"

A silvery mist shimmied and grimaced in the twin beams stretching beyond Lilly LeBlanc's fogged windshield. The August drizzle cast a slick sheen across the winding stretch of two-lane, draping a veil of suspicion between the humpback peaks. The driver, after rubbing her fatigued, bloodshot eyes, peered into her rearview mirror and watched a pair of headlights gain ground on her with each passing second. In the mirror's hazy reflection, dread moistened the young woman's weary eyes.

Although she had no one to call, Lilly reached for her cellphone as her truck careened along a shadowy, twisting stretch of Spearfish Canyon Highway. She bit her lower lip and squirmed in her seat, then clawed at her splotchy throat. After a tricky hairpin turn, she tugged at the seat belt stretched snug across her waist. Lilly's truck was as old as her, but rolled on newer tires. Bud Wolcott replaced the truck's brake pads and rotors a month ago.

A stubborn sliver of sunlight clung to the western reaches of the Black Hills. The winding parkway featured narrow shoulders and infrequent guardrails, very few places where vehicles can pull over.

Spearfish Creek churned seventy-five feet below the driver's door. The rocky drop-off on her right was much higher and twice as steep. Nightfall chased the shadows from the deep crags of this rough canyon and Lilly feared she'd entered a most formidable gauntlet.

Pesky drizzle spotted her windshield and dampened the narrow highway the locals often called 14A. Lilly's cell phone squirted from her grip as she reached up to trigger the windshield wipers. The phone tumbled between the seats, and she scowled, wringing her palms against the steering wheel.

Folks at the hospital said Lilly had watery, expressive blue eyes—pretty, but tinged with sadness. In the mirror, those eyes tracked between her windshield and the revenant lurking somewhere behind her. She remembered traffic was sparse along this desolate track, especially after dark. Her clammy hands trembled as she dabbed beads of sweat from her face with a rumpled fast-food napkin. Lilly didn't know where she'd picked up her threatening tail. Maybe the chase began up north, perhaps all the way back to Interstate 90.

The posted speed limit signs read forty-five, but thirty-five flirted with peril even under ideal conditions. With eight miles of curves before Victoria Junction, Lilly gripped the wheel with both hands and pressed her foot on the gas pedal. She squinted her eyes, surveying ahead as far as the bends and the gloom would allow. Her truck leaned into the corners and drifted around the curves. Lilly downshifted up the inclines and coasted the downhill runs. Over and over, she checked her mirrors while humming along with the radio.

Lilly, a certified nursing assistant, stopped at the Spearfish Walmart following an emotional road trip to Minnesota. She purchased several frozen meals, a case of bottled water, and an assortment of feminine products. She told Sam, her boss, she planned to stay put for a few days, binge-watching Netflix, and awaiting further instruction.

Lilly never considered house-sitting to be a dangerous side

hustle. She liked the scenery and the lavish accommodations. Her compensation was generous, bordering on ridiculous. The recent, crazy drama was another matter. She didn't have time, nor the emotional capacity, for creepers and stalkers. After rounding another curve, she muttered a few affirmations while drumming her thumbs on the steering wheel. "I did the right thing," she said, combing a lock of hair away from her eyes. "The boy is safe."

With darkness taking hold, Lilly glanced back at the empty booster seat and wiped a tear from her cheek. She dabbed her eyes before adjusting her mirrors. Then she exhaled a heavy sigh, noticing her chaser's eerie headlights disappearing behind a gloomy saw-toothed hillside. Lilly's little four-by-four gained some precious ground, and she patted her hand on the dashboard while affording herself a small grin. The FM radio, with regrettable timing, played a somber oldie about a young couple torn apart by a fatal car accident.

The melancholy melody faded just as the twin beams reappeared in Lilly's mirrors, closing fast. She jabbed at the radio knobs to quiet the noise. Her tires whined on the wet pavement as the truck streaked through the fog wafting from Bridal Veil Falls. Just ahead, Cleopatra Place veered sharp to the left. Many travelers regarded this secluded passage as the darkest and most rugged within Spearfish Canyon.

Rain or shine, swinging the tricky left turn was a risky measure because Cleopatra split north-south, just west of the intersection. The southern leg came to a dead-end less than a quarter mile from the highway, hundreds of feet above Squaw Creek. Lilly knew she'd get caught in a pickle if the chaser saw her attempting an evasive maneuver.

Again, the threatening headlights faded from her mirrors. Lilly saw her chance and pressed on the accelerator, racing for the upcoming exit. She stabbed at the brakes and jerked the front wheels hard to the left. Her rear tires began drifting to the right. Lilly cranked her steering wheel left and right with frenetic hand-over-hand movements, trying to over-correct for the skid. But she soon realized it was too late. The dark canyon swirled, becoming a tangled blur. Lilly screamed as her little four-by-four spun in two complete circles. Then, in a split second, her rear bumper clipped a boulder, catapulting the small pickup into a catastrophic barrel roll.

The rainy night exploded with the groans of twisting metal and the shatter of busting glass. Like an abused toy, her truck spiraled towards certain destruction. The mangled wreckage landed bottom up with a final thunderous slam. Lilly's gnarled truck scraped and screeched to a stop at the road's edge, high above the fork where mercurial Squaw Creek cascaded into bubbling Spearfish Creek.

Suspended upside down and cloaked in total darkness, Lilly lost all perception of time and space. She blinked her eyes and warm, syrupy streams trickled across her face, sopping her curly blond hair. The seat belt bound Lilly's shoulders and tightened across her neck. She fumbled and flailed for the release, counting her gasps and trying to fend off a panic attack.

Lilly couldn't move her hands, and she couldn't kick her feet. Each time she tried to move one of her limbs, painful sparks jabbed at her spine. She grimaced and shuddered, spending the next moments pleading through her sniffles. "Help. Somebody, anybody. Help me. God, please."

Lilly's blackout may have lasted seconds, minutes, or perhaps hours. She had no way of knowing. Her mind, absorbed in this ravenous shadow, floated in waves of fluctuating consciousness. Her crusted eyelids wouldn't open and she exhaled, only to confirm she was still alive. Despite her dire straits, Lilly didn't fear the scabrous face of death, she'd seen it many times. But she wondered who would mourn for her. She was alone.

From somewhere across the murk, Lilly heard a vehicle approaching, its tires crunching over the loose gravel and broken glass. She tried to scream for help, but not a peep came forth. The mysterious auto skidded to a halt and a pair of doors slammed shut. She heard two pairs of feet scratch along the ground. Heavy-soled footfalls walking, not running towards her sissing wreckage.

Lilly held her breath, her mind continuing to drift in and out of a groggy soup. Above the sound of the waters rushing below, a voice, deep and gruff, spoke with a slight Canadian accent. "We're wasting our time. Look at this fuckin' mess. Nobody survives a wreck like this."

A second man coughed, then said, "That would be just our luck. C'mon, we gotta check it out. We've got no other leads, and the chiefs will want a detailed report. Ya know. Ten million is a boatload of money. Pay dirt for both of us, if we play our cards right."

"Cards? The hell you sayin'?"

"I'm talking about the golden rule. Finders keepers."

"That ain't the golden rule, dumbass," the first man spouted. "You better get that greed outta your head right now. Remember what happened to Hammer? Steal from the snakes, my friend—you'll twinkle among the stars."

"I s'pose you're right," the second man said. "And don't forget about that witch he was riding with. She's a slippery one. Goes to show, you just can't trust anyone these days. It's blacker than coyote shit up here. Grab your phone, wouldja? We need more light."

Lilly hung like a dripping slab of meat in a steaming, mangled oven. She heard the men's conversation echo along the rocky ridge as their footsteps scratched closer to the edge. She smelled their cigarette smoke, and subtle vibrations told her the strange men stood within a few feet of her shattered windows.

After some shuffling and panting, the first man asked, "Well. Is she dead?"

Lilly felt the second man's breath puff across her face.

He pinched his nose and said, "Can't tell. Blood everywhere." Soon, after a weighty sigh, he tugged at his chin. "Shit. She's breathing."

Lilly smelled the pungency of the two men and sensed their callous eyes upon her. She heard them whispering, assessing her desperate situation. After another minute, the second man reached in and peeled the seatbelt from Lilly's severed throat. "Yo, Lilly. Ya hear me?" He shook her car seat, then grumbled as he turned to his partner. "Her neck's fucked up. She's not dead, but she will be soon."

The first man, the one with the deep voice, asked, "What about the kid?"

Lilly felt her truck jostle from the second man's crawling and pawing. He shouted from the back. "There's an empty booster seat. Groceries and food wrappers scattered all over. No sign of the kid."

The first man explored the grounds surrounding the wreckage, shaking his head. "Hey, what about her cell phone?"

The second man huffed as he crawled out. "I didn't see one." The rain stopped, and he looked up at a clearing, starlit sky. "My DNA and fingerprints are all over this fuckin' mess." He shook his head and motioned back to their truck. "We gotta finish it, man."

The first man nodded, twirling a key fob on his finger as he trudged away.

The second man stood and stretched his back. He lit a cigarette, inhaling a full drag. He puffed his smoke into the sky, then shouted to his partner. "Shit, man. We're no closer to catching the witch, and no closer to finding Hammer's truck." He took another drag from his cigarette, then glanced past his shoulder, signaling the first man with a thumbs-up.

Lilly heard a door slam. She listened to the starter whine, and soon the pickup roared to life. She listened to the second man's boots grinding on the pavement as he pivoted and stepped away. Then he whistled and shouted. "Let 'er go, man." He waved his arm and pointed towards the river. "This bird's done flying. Time for her bath, partner."

The first man, the driver, spoke with cruel satisfaction in his voice. "Step aside, little man. Watch this shit." He inched the dark pickup forward until the push bar pressed against the side of Lilly's upturned four-by-four. In a last fit of clarity and anguish, Lilly mustered a feeble screech as the driver feathered the gas pedal. The engine labored and the rear wheels slipped. Soon, the off-road tires found their grip, and the mighty truck plowed the twisted wreckage over the edge.

The second man took one last drag of his cigarette, puffed three smoke rings to the sky, then flicked the butt, sending it sparking and tumbling over the craggy ledge. Stepping from the truck, the first man blew a kiss towards the array of stars twinkling overhead. The two natives slapped high-fives. They listened as Lilly's crippled truck smashed through the trees before splashing into the rapids below. "C'mon, asshole," the first man said, before exhaling a sigh. "I'll buy you a beer, two if you're lucky."

The second man scratched at the back of his neck. "You're on, shithead. Ya think we should call 9-1-1?"

The first man shook his head and gave his partner a shove. "Shit, no! You're kidding, right?"

The second man flicked his lighter and cupped his hands in front of his face, sparking another cigarette. "Shit, what are we gonna tell the chiefs?" He closed his lighter with the flick of his wrist. "We've got a lot of nothing going; no witch, no kid, and no leads on their goddamn money." He exhaled his smoke and scrunched his face into a grimace. "We're kinda screwed here."

"Hey, don't get your undies in a bunch," the first man said. "We'll figure something out." He picked up a jagged piece of broken taillight and pitched it into the gorge. "Let's go. I could eat a fuckin' horse."

Her pain diminished as her resignation took hold. Lilly soared through the canyon, spiraling, diving, and cornering against heavenly thermals. At last, she withdrew her wings and plunged into the river, a noble bird diving among the fish. Cool waters bubbled around her, cleansing her feathers and purifying her soul. Soon, a divine radiance surrounded her face and Lilly LeBlanc donned an angelic smile amid her last earthly thought. *"The boy is safe."*

Chapter 2
It's Late

"It's late. We've got to get on home."

Five hundred miles northwest of Devils Bathtub, Dean Rivers spit a sloppy plash of brown juice at a grasshopper sunning itself on a flat rock. His partner, the agitated shooter, said, "There's little to no wind, and I'd say we're ninety-five yards out, favorable downhill angle." The shooter shifted his weight, snugging the rifle's shock pad into his shoulder. "I've got center mass in the crosshairs. Should I take him out?"

"Jeez, Manny," Rivers said, shaking his head. "You sound like a fucking ignoramus. What's with all the hard-ass sniper mumbo-jumbo?" Rivers propped himself up on his elbows and adjusted his binoculars. "Hold your water there, G.I. Joe. How the hell do you know what he's doing over there?"

Manny Rodriguez, casting a hard stare, made a farting sound. "That's always been your problem, man. You're fuckin' soft—a skinny-ass redneck pussy."

"What's the matter, honey?" Rivers asked, turning from his binoculars and giving Rodriguez a demeaning pout. "You missing your rump rangers from the can?"

Manny kicked a dusty lump of brush at Rivers. "I should do the Normans a solid, by shooting your sorry ass and feeding you to the fishes," he said in his fractured, uneducated English.

"Okay, Capone, that's very fuckin' original." Rivers shook his head and rolled his eyes before leaning into Manny's face. "Like the Normans could give a shit over a two-bit vagrant like you. So bring it on, tough guy. I'll stick that muzzle so far up your ass, you'll be scratching your nose for a month." Rivers spat another glob of chewing tobacco in Manny's direction, then returned to peering through his binoculars.

Rodriguez fumed, tracking his unsuspecting target through his rifle's scope. He muttered some Spanish gibberish, vowing to deal with Rivers later.

The two sweaty ranch hands lay stretched out on their stomachs upon a rise overlooking the cracked, muddy banks of the Red River. The late afternoon sun blazed orange through a hazy western sky. From their dusty perch on the North Dakota side of a sizable oxbow, they watched a tall blond-haired man step from his truck and stretch his arms and legs.

The agent wore blue jeans, a sweat-soaked khaki shirt, and a maroon baseball cap. He surveyed his lonesome surroundings, lowered the tailgate, then lifted a pair of toolboxes from the back. After checking his smartphone, he sidestepped his way down the bumpy slope that stretched below the overpass on the Minnesota side of the river.

"Shit," Rodriguez said, rolling to his side. "That asshole's gone under the bridge. There goes my clean shot. Thanks a lot, man."

Rivers stood and brushed dirt and grass clippings from his pants. "Blind, stupid, and judgmental, that's some combination. No wonder the prison gents keep falling for you. C'mon, let's get our asses over there, see what's going on. Our moody boss hates surprises."

Two minutes later, with the state worker concealed below them,

Rodriguez and Rivers leaned into the truck's open windows. Large decals on either side of the yellow pickup displayed the Minnesota Department of Natural Resources shield. Rivers pointed his thumb over his shoulder and said, "Manny, make yourself useful and check the bed."

Rodriguez flashed a mocking salute and trudged away while Rivers reached through the passenger window and opened the glove box. The farmhand discovered a state-issued handgun sheathed in a black holster. The leather sleeve had MN-DNR embossed on the flap.

Dean Rivers stood tall and angular, a weathered forty-six years old, with high cheekbones, dimpled chin, and deep-set blue eyes. He peeked over his shoulder to see that his Mexican toady was still working behind the truck. Rivers trained his eyes northwest along North Dakota Highway 5, then southeast down Minnesota Highway 175. After scanning the western fields, he grabbed the holster and tucked the agent's handgun into the back of his pants.

Manuel Rodriguez stood a foot shorter than Rivers. His tanned brown skin stretched tight across his shaved head and tattooed muscles. Manny smoked marijuana and tobacco every day, leaving his crooked teeth and calloused fingers stained. A decade younger than Rivers, Rodriguez worked the previous two years as a grunt laborer for the Normans. This was after serving a five-year stint in a maximum-security North Dakota State Penitentiary for armed robbery and aggravated assault.

Rodriguez pushed aside a pile of tarps and two coils of rope, finding nothing of interest in the truck's bed. Like Rivers, the twitchy Mexican stood on the shoulder looking northwest, then southeast—no traffic, and no witnesses. He sneered at his intolerant partner. "I'm going down there to see what that gringo's doing. No matter what we do, Ed's gonna be pissed," he said, scowling at the yellow truck. "That ugly asshole don't like gophers as it is—wait until he finds out a goddamn tree hugger is fishing 'round his property." Rodriquez splayed his fingers and said, "¡Auge!"

"Well, look at you and your robust vocabulary. Prison GED comes in handy, doesn't it?" Rivers spat onto the crushed gravel shoulder. "Wait up. I'm goin' with you. And for Christ's sake, let me do the talking."

Rodriguez rolled his eyes and cursed under his breath. The two dusty men side-shuffled and high-stepped their way through the tall weeds and prairie grass blanketing the rutted slope.

At the bottom, they stopped to let their eyes adjust to the darkness, then slogged along the rank, sticky riverbank into the shadows of the overpass. Ten degrees cooler in the shade, they discovered the DNR agent wearing camo-colored waders and squatting near the river's edge. The pair watched him fill small plastic vials with water.

Rodriguez shouted before Rivers could utter a word. "Hey, conservation man! The hell ya doin' down here?"

"What the…" the startled agent said, spinning on his heels and standing to face the two interlopers. "You guys scared the bejesus outta me. Have you boys ever heard of knocking?" Silhouetted against the bright opening under the overpass, the agent pointed at the shorter man, the indignant one, clutching a rifle. He reached for his belt, then pursed his lips as he shook his head.

Rivers said, "No need to be alarmed, mister. We saw your truck up on the road and thought you might need help." Rivers motioned for Rodriguez to lower his gun. "This uncivilized ruffian is Rodriguez. I'm Rivers. We work for the Normans. They've got twenty-five hundred acres a stone's throw from here." Rivers wiped a brown dribble from his chin, then pointed a thumb over his shoulder. "Dairy's a tough go these days, pushing only a few head this summer. Our operation's 'bout a mile past that rise."

The agent took a deep breath as he dried his hands on a shop rag. The two curious farmhands inched closer, and the agent reached out to shake Rivers' hand. "Tom Fulgham, conservation officer, Minnesota Department of Natural Resources."

Rodriguez didn't offer his hand, huffing his displeasure instead. "Topos."

Fulgham dropped the towel into one of his open toolboxes. "What's that?" He asked. But Rodriguez stood glaring at him without answering. Fulgham stretched his back and locked eyes with the defiant farmhand. Then he shifted his gaze, examining the roughnecks standing in their sweat-soaked, filthy clothing. After another minute of forced conversation, Fulgham said, "Sure is hot up there. What brings you guys down to the river?"

Rodriguez uttered something derogatory, but Rivers cut him off. "Ed Norman thinks a bobcat, maybe a wolf, killed one of his calves. Thought we might find footprints in the mud down here, set a few traps," Rivers said, motioning to the muddy banks. "Ya seen any large animal tracks?"

Fulgham wiped his brow, then shook his head. "Just got here, haven't really looked around. But I'm warning you. This area is a popular spot for kayakers and fishermen. Setting traps down here is a bad idea. I can't let you do that, not on this side."

Rodriguez stared at Fulgham, rotating the Browning rifle in his hands. Rivers glanced over and watched his partner attempting to intimidate the young DNR officer. The lanky farmhand looked up and waited for a noisy westbound eighteen-wheeler to rumble across the overpass. "If you don't mind me asking, what are you doing down here?"

Fulgham crouched, reading his container labels, then organized the bottles at the bottom of one of his cases. He stood and held a jar in front of his eyes. "I'm gathering samples, recording the depth." The agent turned and pointed. "You can tell by those marks the river's pretty low. We've received reports of foul odors and fish kills near Hilltop and St. Vincent. The Canadians are up in arms. They claim the water's fluctuating more than it should, especially considering our drought. Long story short, they're blaming Minnesotans for their water being outta whack."

Rivers swatted at a horsefly, then rubbed the back of his neck. "Have you checked between Two Rivers? I've heard there's been some shady irrigation practices up that way. A few of the farmers got fined a couple years ago for pumping wastewater into the watershed. Don't have to tell you, greywater can include some nasty shit." He wiped a line of sweat from his forehead and pointed east. "The McFarlands have a big place where the branches converge. It might be worth your time to check 'em out. Heads up for the chicken man. He's a shifty one."

The agent looked over his shoulder and nodded. "Good to know. We plan to test all the confluences in the valley. But the thing is, we're finding elevated bacteria and nitrates in this area between Drayton Dam and Golden Grain. I'd sooner eat road kill than drink from this river. Just take a sniff. Smells like liquid death, right?"

Rivers nodded but said nothing. Rodriguez, snooping, stepped closer to look into the DNR agent's toolboxes. Fulgham wedged the last water sample back into the box and shut both cases with an emphatic slam.

Fulgham stood and jotted a few notes into a small spiral notepad. "You guys said you work for the Normans. That right?"

The pair exchanged sideways glances in their devious silence, and beads of sweat appeared on their sunburned faces. Crickets chirped and cicadas buzzed, drowning the faint melody of the muddy water as it oozed north towards Canada.

Muttering to himself, Fulgham scribbled their names. "Rivers and Rodriguez." The two farmhands rocked on their heels as Fulgham glanced down at the hunting rifle gripped in Manny's hands. "Mr. Rodriguez, that's a nice rifle. I'd hate to see it confiscated by the man. There's no license required to carry a gun in North Dakota, but that's not the case over here. If you don't have a permit, you can purchase one at the sheriff's office in Kittson."

Fulgham pulled his phone from his shirt pocket. "How about I call to let them know you're on your way?"

Rodriguez stood puffy-chested, close enough for the officer to see his dingy teeth. He scowled at the agent, his veins pulsing in his neck and fury smoldering in his eyes.

Rivers knew Rodriguez hated people, especially white guys with badges, talking down to him. Rivers waited for another truck to pass overhead, then broke the contentious stalemate. "Alright, we get it. Back on our side. Ain't that right? We'll let you get back to your work, then pray for rain. How's that sound?"

As the farmhands backed away, Fulgham tapped his phone's screen, snapping their picture. Then he tapped the screen, speed-dialing his office. Before the call could connect, Rodriguez raised his gun and fired a .223 round through the officer's neck.

Fulgham staggered, dropping his phone as he reached for his spouting throat. Rodriguez aimed and fired a second shot that exploded dead center into the officer's chest. Fulgham dropped to his knees, then flopped to his back, laying motionless except for his heaving chest and one quivering foot.

The lanky farmhand covered his ears as the thunderous blasts echoed off the underside of the concrete bridge. "Why the hell did you do that?" He asked with a snarl, shaking his fists. "What the fuck is wrong with you, Manny?"

Rodriguez stepped over and stared down at his victim, watching life seep from the young officer's eyes with each passing second. "Fuck him," he said, spitting into the river. "I didn't like the way he was talking to me. Smug-ass punk can take his permit and shove it up his ass."

The cold-blooded farmhand knelt and started rifling through the dying man's pockets. Rodriguez found the truck keys and stripped sixteen dollars from Fulgham's hand-tooled wallet. He smashed the agent's phone with a craggy chunk of riprap, then tossed the pieces into the river, along with the dying man's billfold.

Rivers stomped around, waving his hands like a petulant child. "Nice going, dipshit. This place'll be crawling with cops when he doesn't report back. When Edward finds out, he's gonna have the Snakes skin us alive."

"Fuck him. How about you quit your whining and help me dump this stinky mess into the river? This asshole's heavier than he looks. Ah man, I think he jus' shit himself."

As Fulgham exhaled his last gurgling breath, Rivers fixed an angry stare into Manny's eyes and shook his head. "You're fuckin' stupid, man. Ballistics will match your rifle and your hands were all over that guy. Now what are you gonna do?"

Rodriguez kicked a few pebbles into the water, then unzipped his pants to take a piss. "I need to think. Gimme a fuckin' minute here, wouldja?"

After more arguing, the two hayseeds dragged Fulgham's bulky body up the bumpy slope towards the truck. Rivers, panting, stopped to stretch his achy back. "Okay," he said. "Here's what we're gonna do. We'll drive the DNR truck back to the farm, park it inside the second barn at the north end of the Holstein pasture. You, mister crazy-ass gunman, will chop up the body and run it through the waste grinder. We'll burn his clothes with the other dirty stuff. After dark, Skinny Pete's gonna run the truck through a car wash and drive it over to Lake Bronson, park it at the visitor's center. People will assume that a nosey operative's gone missing. It wouldn't be the first time a tree hugger's gone off the grid."

Again, Rodriguez checked to see if anyone was driving along the highway. He and Rivers strained as they hoisted Tom Fulgham's lifeless body onto the truck's open tailgate. After wiping his brow and catching his breath, Rodriguez lit a cigarette and blew a big puff of smoke at Rivers. "Skinny Pete, the retard?" He asked, wearing a furrowed brow.

Rivers waved the smoke away and raised an eyebrow. "Well, that's rather insensitive."

"You just asked me to chop up a dead guy and run him through a goddamn meat grinder. Stop bustin' my balls, asshole. I'll give you fuckin' insensitive." Rodriguez wiped his brow, then swatted at the flies hovering around his head. "Why Pete?"

"We'll make sure his fingerprints and DNA get plastered all over this truck. If an investigation leads to Norman Farms, he's too stupid to understand questions and too honest to come up with a good alibi. He'll get baited into a confession. That beanpole is our patsy if things get dicey."

Rodriguez huffed as he folded and shoved Fulgham's long legs into the truck bed. "Okay, I'm with you now. I'll get a migrant to pick him up at the Cenex station."

"Now you're thinking. Hop up there and grab his arms, wouldja? We'll wrap him in one of these tarps. I'm gonna run back down and grab those boxes." Rodriguez flicked his cigarette butt into the weeds, then set his rifle on the tailgate. He swore under his breath as he crawled into the truck and began tugging Fulgham's stiffening arms.

Rivers slipped the pistol from behind his back and checked for passing cars. He clicked the safety off and said, "I'm tired of cleaning up your goddamn messes. I'll see you in hell, Manny." Rivers pulled the trigger three times, shooting Rodriguez twice in the chest, then once in the man's brown, creased forehead.

The killer surveyed the area, then climbed into the truck's bed and covered both bodies with towels, tarps, and ropes. "I'm doing you a solid. You'd be dead from lung cancer within five years. And let me tell you, that's one miserable way to go. Gettin' late. Sleep tight, you stinky wetback."

Rivers shuddered and pinched the bridge of his nose. He remembered it had been years since he'd killed anybody. After climbing into the cab, he twisted the key and checked both directions for traffic. Then he adjusted the rearview mirrors and cut a wide U-turn before heading west. West, away from the winding brown river. West, towards a blood-red sun sagging beyond the Badlands of North Dakota.

Chapter 3
Fire Lake

"Who's goin' to ride that chrome three-wheeler?"

Dale Sommers trimmed the yoke, adjusted his baseball cap, then glanced over his shoulder at John Thompson. The pilot's anxious passenger wore a fatigued, sober expression on his face. He caught Sommers' eyes, then cleared his throat and mustered a tenuous grin. "The last time I flew commercial, it was out of Boise. I asked the ticket agent to send one of my bags to Atlanta and the other one to Phoenix. She said, 'I don't think we can do that.' So, I said, 'Y'all did it last week when I flew to Minneapolis.'" Thompson coughed, then forced a chuckle at his tired airport joke.

The ardent cowboy was tall and handsome, like his older brother, Jim, the retired U.S. Senator. His shoulder-length hair, bushy eyebrows, and thick mustache were white as driven snow. His wrinkled and weathered skin wore like the tanned leather of a timeworn saddle. Thompson, backed by family power and wealth, lived proud and prominent, but not pretentious. Sommers viewed Thompson as the embodiment of unrefined prosperity, an authentic man's man, and a living relic of the old west.

Thompson sat slumped in the first-row passenger's seat opposite the pilot. Apprehension returned to his face as he examined the charred expanses of the Panhandle National Forest. He told the pilot the vast stretches of scorched mountain tops looked unearthly. A strange black terrain with nary a living thing in sight—a stark contrast to the year-round greenery provided by endless stands of spruce and fir. The cowboy ran his fingers through his hair, replaced his hat, then shared what was troubling him. Thompson Mill and Lumber, the largest employer in northern Idaho, sat head-on in the path of a raging wildfire.

Thompson tucked a pinch of chewing tobacco into his lower lip, then spoke in a western drawl accented with a hint of a whistle. He leaned forward and tapped Sommers on the shoulder, then pointed at the windshield. "Lots of smoke out there, 'eh?" Then, after several seconds of clumsy silence, Thompson changed the subject. "Brother Jim says you're a natural at this whole flying thing."

Determination flashed in Sommers' eyes as he put the Cessna into a sharp, plunging turn. "Well, I had a patient instructor. It took us flying together every day for a year before I felt better about landings. About four hundred hours of flight time. But don't go throwing too many bouquets my way. This trusty bird almost flies herself. My friends would tell you I'm just a slow learner."

Thompson wiped his mouth and shifted in his seat, pulling a harmonica from his hip pocket. He launched into a few of his favorite tunes. Sommers caught both the fit and the irony of the man's song choices. He grinned and bobbed his head, humming along with "Ring of Fire".

Sommers peered out his side window while banking hard to his left. The sharp turn gave him a bird's-eye view of the ground. At five hundred feet above the blackened tree-tops, the air was thick with the smell of charred wood and smoldering brush. He pointed with his thumb. "How 'bout we circle around, see how things are looking at the sawmill? Your Hotshots mentioned some festering flames south of their firebreak line. The boys said they had 'em contained, but you know how fast things can change."

The pilot looked over his shoulder at Thompson to see a brown dribble of tobacco juice trickling down the cowboy's chin. Sommers rolled his eyes and shook his head, sporting a grimace that showed his disgust. "Chewing tobacco. For the life of me. I'll never understand the compulsion." He shrugged and studied his radar screen. "NWS pulled the rain from today's forecast, but the westerlies are gonna pick up again. That could spell more trouble."

Thompson cocked his bushy eyebrows and puckered his lips. Then he spit another gooey strand into his empty aluminum can. He wiped his chin on the back of his hand and peered ahead, studying the gauges strewn across the instrument panel. "I agree. It's a nasty habit. But I can't smoke at the mill. You know how that would go down."

Sommers shifted in his seat and nodded while his passenger sat and reflected. "Sorry," Thompson said. "Poor choice of words." He turned to look out the side window. "I tend to worry about things outta my control. The occasional pinch smooths some of my roughest edges."

Thompson tapped his finger on the window, gazing out at the smoke hovering above the treetops. "It could be worse. We could be in California. The late, great golden state is a revolting dumpster fire right now." Thompson spit again, then changed the subject. "How do you like flying this thing?" He asked. "Jim hated to part with it, but he wanted more range and more payload. He knew you'd put 'er to good use and treat 'er with kid gloves."

Sommers' thoughts drifted to northern California. He pictured Andie Hansen hiking among the giant sequoias, searching for her twin sister who'd gone off the grid years before. After a few seconds of guiltless fantasizing, he snapped back to the present. "A few years ago, I was in the middle of a romantic interlude with a beautiful mermaid when your brother swooped in on us like a kamikaze fighter. She's somewhere in the Cascades while the two of us are high over these Bitterroots. Maybe it's fate."

Sommers sat quiet for a lengthy moment, recalling The Beach Boys, Independence Day, and the bizarre events of a latter-day summer. Blistering hot, bone dry, and on the brink of danger, very similar to these present-day Rockies. Once the turmoil stopped, he thought life would return to normal. But years of hardship reminded him there was no normal.

Word travels fast in a small town. Sommers' skeptics claimed he'd changed, that his heart had hardened, and he'd become jaded. The big lumberjack had to admit, life became more complicated since taking a steamy swim with Andie, then more so since taking flight with a dangerous bird of prey.

Sommers felt he'd been under a witch's spell since the day Senator Bradly-Doyle died. That event changed his life's trajectory. Three years had passed and even the brightest folks around Lac Clair knew little of it. He peered through the soupy haze ahead, trying to rationalize his past, trying to visualize his future.

Inspired by the swashbuckling Big Jim Thompson, the fifty-two-year-old lumberjack earned his private pilot's license in thirteen months. Sommers, his mother Gracie, and his Uncle Grumpy swapped thirty acres with the farmers across the road. The plot gained from the Peterson brothers created the space to build a simple Quonset Hut airplane hangar. The Ormond Brothers paved a three-thousand-foot heated runway running parallel along DeRoxe Road. Flying was more than an expensive hobby. Sommers had at least two important reasons for needing to travel hundreds of miles unencumbered at a moment's notice.

Most days, Sommers felt trapped between two worlds. There was the comfortable simplicity of northern Minnesota, and the adventurous uncertainty of the Black Hills. He drummed his thumbs on the yoke, then leaned back towards Thompson. "When Grumpy told me your brother was selling this bird, it got me thinking. His asking price was pretty meager, especially in this market. Jim could've made two or three times what he got from me."

"My brother must've given you his friends and family discount. Like I said, his priority was for this plane to end up in a good home." He paused for a moment. "I also think he's trying to close the gap between Idaho and Minnesota. Jim and I were never especially close—we're buckaroos of a different color. He thinks of Gracie and Grumpy as kin, the only family he's got left outside of me. He's taken a shine to you, too. I gotta say, you and Jim have a lot in common."

Thompson reached ahead and tapped Sommers' captain's chair. "You know what keeps me up at night?" Sommers shook his head and Thompson asked, "Why on earth would a millionaire like yourself, flying a half-million-dollar airplane, continue to drive that rusted-out piece of shit Chevy? Baby-poop yellow to boot. I mean, wow."

Sommers smirked, adjusting his headset. "Millionaire? If that were true, and I'm not saying it is, it's just on paper. You can check my wallet. If there's ten bucks in there, then yes, I'll admit to being a rich man. But full disclosure here, counselor. Phelps the Wonder Pup has the passenger seat, and the radio presets adjusted just as he wants 'em. He's figured out how to lower the windows, and he knows there's always at least one biscuit in the console. That slobbering beast would never let me scrap ol' yeller." The two men plunged into a fit of contagious laughter.

With the single-engine turbo humming in the background, the pilot let his mind wander. This time to his friends and family back at Lake Victoria—an uncommon stew of misfits. Sommers sighed, enjoying his daydream. Then, with his fingers, he flashed a V for Victoria sign.

Sommers peeked at his wristwatch and nodded his head. "I'm sure you've heard the expression; money isn't everything," he said.

"That's more than just a passing fancy with my family. Uncle Grumpy spent decades living off his poker winnings and whatever loose change he found under his couch cushions. Maybe that frugal lifestyle fuels his crankiness. Lord knows, Grumps lives on his own terms in that little ol' cabin with his little ol' fishing boat on that little ol' lake. And all the while, he and your brother turned a few hush-hush investments into millions. I've watched him wear that same ratty flannel day after day, but I don't think he'd have it any other way."

The pilot tapped the fuel gauge with his finger, then looked over his shoulder at Thompson. "Henry David Thoreau said, 'wealth is the ability to fully experience life.' Kinda puts it into perspective, doncha think?"

The two men sat in silence for a few minutes, staring out the windows into the haze. Sommers interrupted the heavy silence. "When's Jim getting back from Alaska?"

John worked up another spit, then counted on his fingers. "Nine, no ten, days. His clients paid up front for the entire two weeks. He said the fishing's been decent." The cowboy waved his hand at the smoky slopes. "Not much for him to do about this mess, anyway. It'd break his heart to see these forests going up in smoke, and over what, a climate cultist striking a box of matches. Go figure."

Sommers dropped the small airplane low over the original firebreak line. It was a yellow-beige strip of bare ground, two football fields wide and two miles long, located just south of Thompson Mill and Lumber. Out of habit, he tugged at the bill of his baseball cap, then pointed. "I'm no expert at this. But here's what I'm thinking. You have some protection from the state highway to the west and Canyon Creek on the east. Those peaks above the tree line guard the north. I say we clear-cut another break line about a half-mile south of the first one, then do a controlled burn of all the grass and brush between the breaks. That way, the mill's protected on three sides, and we'll build you some cushion to the south. You should be able to get your water trucks down there once we've finished. What do you think?"

Thompson unfolded his arms and smoothed his mustache. "Makes sense to me. I mean, what've we got to lose? I'll kick Cappy in the ass after we land."

Sommers peered down through the smoke. "One more thing. Ask Cappy if we can get started tonight. The guys will get more done without the afternoon sun beating down on them—finish first-thing in the morning. Besides, we should torch the debris before the updrafts get to howling."

"Good idea," Thompson said. "I'll cut the guys loose to rest up—get back at it after dinner." He puckered and spit into his aluminum can, then turned to gaze out his window. "Game on. Lord knows, I can't afford to lose this one."

Later that evening, an apricot sunset flushed the jagged peaks of the Bitterroot Mountains. Sommers, along with Thompson's team of young firefighters, took to digging, chopping, and clearing a second firebreak line. Excavation equipment felled trees, and dragged away stumps, stripping the earth of anything flammable.

Pesky bugs and the late-night darkness hampered their progress. Sommers' small group of laborers cut saplings and brush tucked into recesses the bulldozers couldn't reach. The brawny crew worked through the night in a synchronized line of destruction that would've made Tecumseh Sherman proud.

Nine exhausting hours later, with sunrise peeking over the eastern ridge, thirteen sweaty men gathered along the bank of Canyon Creek. They exchanged high-fives and chugged water from their gallon jugs. His face blackened by dust and soot, Sommers stood hunched over, hands on his knees, fighting to catch a breath. The smoke and elevation threw unwelcome challenges at the big Minnesotan. Sommers muttered as he gasped for air. "Father Time, you're one prickly pain in my backside."

From out of the smog, one of the older, more experienced firefighters patted him on the back. "Yo, lake lover. You okay?"

Sommers stood tall. His layers of clothing soaked in sweat. He stretched his arms out in front of his broad chest, then removed his grimy yellow hardhat. He had a wheeze in his voice. "I haven't slept in two days, and my lungs are burning from smoke inhalation. My back feels like a stampeding herd of buffalo ran roughshod over it. But I'd say I'm fair to middling. How are you holding up?"

The muscular firefighter gave a thumbs up, then reached out with his gloved hand. "Danny McBride—my bros call me D-Mac. My family's chock full of loggers from Wisconsin. They told me stories about a Dale Sommers who threw axes like nobody's business. He said the nimble giant was a man among boys at the Hayward Games. Sound like someone you know?"

Sommers caught his breath, cleared his throat, then kicked a burnt pine cone into a gully. "You know, I can't recall. But on the off chance it was me, that was another time, and another place."

McBride grinned, then pulled a tomahawk from his tool belt and presented it to the exhausted lumberjack. "How's that old throwing arm? Think you still got it?"

"I can't even raise my arms over my head, and my competitive throwing days are long gone." Sommers coughed as he waved McBride off. "No offense, but I'll pass."

McBride sputtered a filthy noise and pressed Sommers. "C'mon, old-timer, let's see that championship form. I'll bet you five bucks you can't hit that tree right over there."

Sommers shook his head, then turned to look upon a blackened spruce trunk a foot in diameter standing twenty feet away. The other Thompson Hotshots, hearing the challenge, gathered around, egging Sommers on. McBride tapped Sommers on the shoulder with the ax handle, pushing him. "C'mon man, what do ya say? It's just a fin."

The circle of grimy men closed tighter. "I'm serious," Sommers said, inspecting the blade. "I ain't much of a gambler. Besides, this isn't an ideal throwing ax."

The group let out a loud chorus of boos and heckles. As the sunrise melted the mountainside shadows, Sommers scanned the bloodshot eyes of his bunkmates. Then he removed his leather gloves and grasped the American Tomahawk by its polished hickory handle. Turning it in his hand, he felt the weight and craftsmanship seep into his fingers. He recognized the hatchet as a model favored by American soldiers. The hand-crafted tool provided both utility and protection, weighing only twenty-four ounces. It had a four-inch blade at one end of its forged steel head and a rock hammer at the other. Each of Thompson's soot-covered firefighters had one looped inside his tool belt.

Sommers ran his thumb along the blade, admiring its meticulous sharpness. He looked back at McBride, who shrugged his shoulders and raised his palms. Sommers turned to face the target, then adjusted his stance by sliding his left foot forward twelve inches. He inhaled a deep breath and extended the tomahawk up and back beyond his shoulder. Next, he brought his arm forward in a smooth downward motion, sending the blade firing like a twirling, sizzling bolt of lightning.

Thwack! The blade struck a small, blackened tree two feet to the right of McBride's intended target. The tomahawk hung dead-center, head high from the hapless trunk. The Hotshots let out a collective groan. McBride laughed and tossed his helmet into the air in a mocking, overzealous celebration. "Nice shot, dude. Wrong damn tree. But hey, I give you credit for trying. You brought some serious heat on that throw." McBride looked the big man over, then patted him on the back. "Hey, don't worry about the bet. We're good."

Sommers shrugged his shoulders and dropped his chin in feigned defeat. McBride strutted around the group, clapping his hands and taunting the humble lumberjack. A murmur of disappointment ballooned from the gathering. From out of nowhere, the raucous clatter of two water trucks laboring up the steep canyon road interrupted the clamorous firefighters.

Soon, John Thompson emerged from the fog. He wore a chocolate-colored Cattleman's hat, western boots, and a wide belt featuring an oversized silver buckle. He was there to check on the team's progress and oversee the controlled burn. The boss man tucked a pinch into his lower lip, then tipped his hat towards Sommers. Thompson asked, "What's going on, fellas?"

Cappy stammered, trying to explain the impromptu competition. But McBride interrupted him, criticizing Sommers' errant throw.

Thompson took a moment to assess the scene, then looked his friend in the eye and flashed him a wink. Big John pursed his lips as he studied the peculiar inaccuracy of Sommers' throw. The crew rocked in their boots, twirling their hardhats in their hands. Thompson looked them over, then grinned as he pulled a thick roll of money from his vest pocket. "Let's raise the stakes, shall we? Who's feeling lucky?"

The Hotshots cheered and Thompson counted a stack of one-hundred-dollar bills. "I will pay one hundred dollars for each ax that sticks in the same tree our friend Mr. Sommers just hit. The throw must come from this distance. It's what, 'bout twenty feet? He asked. "Your choice. Either the highfalutin Danny McBride tosses your ax, or the flying lumberjack gives it a fling. Best think about it and choose wisely, gentlemen."

Sommers looked down at his boots, his face flush with

embarrassment. Thompson barked, "For Christ's sake, Danny. Wipe that shit-eatin' grin off your face and go fetch your blade."

After a brief hesitation, McBride yanked his tomahawk from the tree. A tenderfoot firefighter wearing smudged glasses stripped his ax from its sheath. "Here you go, Mr. Sommers," he said, handing over his ax. "No pressure, but I could sure use that hundred bucks."

Sommers waited for McBride to join the throwing line, then turned and fired the young man's tomahawk. He struck the same four-inch tree trunk in the exact location as his previous throw.

Thompson shouted and clapped his weathered hands. "You're a winner, Timmy!"

The circle of Hotshots pumped their fists and cheered as their boss handed the smiling firefighter a crisp one-hundred-dollar bill. The others began pulling their axes from their belts and formed a line behind Sommers. One by one, the merry firefighters retrieved their axes and extended their hands to receive the unexpected windfall.

Spectacular theater for everyone but Thompson, Sommers split that narrow trunk dead center with each one of his powerful throws. Last in line, McBride stood embarrassed. Everyone could tell he was trying to decide whether to attempt his own throw or swallow his pride and accept the reward courtesy of the man he'd ridiculed.

McBride handed his tomahawk back to Sommers. "Go ahead, mister. I deserve this beat down."

Sommers nodded at Thompson, who pulled an oversized handkerchief from his pocket. He used the plaid cloth to blindfold the mighty pilot. The circle of firefighters closed in as he pivoted towards the target, gripping McBride's ax in his calloused right hand.

Thompson's troupe chanted in unison, "Sommers, Sommers, Sommers!"

The big lumberjack inhaled, then stepped and fired. His ax exploded like Thor's mighty hammer. Sommers stuck the sharpened blade handle deep, dead center of McBride's original twelve-inch trunk.

With an air of mysticism and impeccable timing, a thunderclap boomed from beyond the northern peaks. The firefighters ducked and looked around as lightning flashes and dark clouds rolled in from the northwest. Thompson slipped the remaining bills back into his pocket. "I'm sorry, Danny. Sommers missed." The crew laughed and cheered as a torrent of large raindrops cascaded from the heavens.

Thompson stood grinning ear to ear as Sommers returned the bandana. To show there were no hard feelings, McBride shook hands with Sommers, then turned and shrugged to the group. The mythical Minnesotan pointed his nose skyward, allowing the cool shower to rinse his blackened face. Thompson's firefighters watched him with slack-jawed amazement.

Before long, the heavy rain drenched the mountainside, and the team let out a raucous victory cheer. Thompson broke out his harmonica and the Hotshots clapped and sang while they packed away their gear. Dripping in satisfaction, Sommers stood with his arms crossed like a triumphant totem. He couldn't help but laugh out loud at the rowdy spectacle.

Thompson finished his tune and slapped his pilot on the back. "That's great work, partner—can't wait to see your encore."

Sommers stuffed his work gloves inside his hard hat. "Show's over," he said, examining the stormy sky. "Time for me to get on home."

Chapter 4
Problems

"Problems, problems, problems all day long."

An off-duty cop limped like a peg-legged sailor as he pushed through the doorway at Casey's Corner Market. Spatters of rust-colored dirt covered his jersey, pants, and cleats—residue from a disappointing game. Captain Gregory O'Leary stopped for his usual post-game remedy: a large sausage pizza and a twelve-pack of ale. The Everly Brothers' brooding harmonies flowed from the store's overhead speakers. O'Leary reversed his baseball hat and muttered to anyone within earshot. "Ol' Casey's messin' with me again." He and his collection of bruises lingered in the beer cooler's frosty draft.

The surly third baseman hobbled down the aisle and lifted his chin at the attractive young woman working behind the counter. "Losing feels worse than winning feels good," he said. "Vin Scully said that. And I gotta tell ya, sugar. He was goddamn right."

She turned from the cigarette rack, wincing as she looked O'Leary up and down. "That bad?" She asked, while gnawing on her bubble gum.

O'Leary hefted his beer onto the counter. "Lost to Davenport in extras," he said. "Went one for four. My throwing error allowed the winning run. How's that for a steaming pile of cow poop?" The bubbly brunette chuckled and shook her head, scanning the barcode into the register with a beep. He nodded and reached for his wallet. "The guys went out for wings and beers, but all I want is a back rub. What time do you get off?"

The clerk just giggled and flipped her hair to the side. O'Leary pouted and said, "I'm serious."

Greg O'Leary, a reputed ladies' man, and a decorated Army Ranger, had many pelts on his wall, confirming both his toughness and his marksmanship. After a decade with the Fargo PD, the city council passed him over for a prestigious promotion. The superintendent washed his hands of the issue, hiding behind red tape and DEI quotas. Word on the street was Deputy Jerome Blackmon, a street cop with only four years of experience, was the council's choice for chief.

The flirtatious clerk returned to stuffing cigarette cartons into the display rack. O'Leary waited for his pizza, flexing his aching knee. "There's no shortage of problems out there," he said. "Maybe I'll take early retirement and go into business for myself. Heck, maybe I won't work at all."

The clerk popped her head up from behind the register. "Sounds pretty chill to me. You should go for it."

A grizzled Latino man wearing a hairnet and a scowl stepped from the kitchen and slid a pizza box across the counter. O'Leary tipped his cap. "Thanks, Carlos."

Carlos lifted his chin, muttering something in Spanish, then slinked back into his scullery.

The busty clerk leaned in and wrote her name and number on the box using a black Sharpie. She drew a little heart next to her name. O'Leary slid forty dollars towards the register, before rotating the box to read her message. "Thanks, Ashley. Keep the change." He grinned, limping for the exit, then winked as he backed his way through the door. "I'll call ya."

Gray clouds gathered overhead, obscuring the moon and stars, and the night air grew thick with humidity. Channel four meteorologists mentioned a line of thunderstorms forming between Minot and Bismarck. The decreasing barometric pressure inspired mayflies by the thousands to dance in the overhead lights—pesky bugs getting in their last late-summer flings.

Following a car wash, O'Leary parked his shiny Durango, now free of bug guts and road dust, near the outermost gas pumps. He watched three suspicious teenagers hanging out around the corner of the convenience store. Two Latinos and one white kid, all wearing the uniform of street punks: steel-toed work boots, baggy jeans, and dark hoodies. They snuffed out their joints and stepped from the shadows, approaching him from behind. O'Leary realized his preoccupied hands and profound limp characterized him as easy prey.

O'Leary set the case of beer on the ground near his feet and lifted the rear gate on his black SUV. He'd folded the rear seat down so his warm pizza box could sit flat on the floor. He'd locked his service revolver in the center console, but his twenty-eight-ounce softball bat rested in plain view, its tape-wrapped handle jutting from his oversized gear bag.

The off-duty officer heard their footsteps come to a stop behind him. Before he could turn, the lanky white kid said, "Yo, rookie. Nothing stupid. Drop the key on the ground and take your walk. Me and my boys have got the munchies—leave the pizza and beer, too."

O'Leary smelled their sweat, and the cannabis on their breaths. He peeked under his arm and watched the bossy teen stretch a neck gaiter up across his face, then draw a small handgun from the pocket of his hoodie. The two Latino sidekicks followed suit. The detective, following a momentary hesitation, did as the white kid asked. He exhaled a heavy sigh, then dropped his key fob on the pavement near his feet. "Tonight," he said. "I couldn't hit a cow in the ass with a banjo. But as far as you *mariquitas* are concerned, I'm the Sultan of

Swat. You can bet your asses in about thirty seconds I'll be swinging for the fences. Fair warning, I'm a cop with a shitty attitude. *Ustedes están cometiendo un gran error.*"

The shorter of the two Mexicans kicked O'Leary in the back. "¡Cállate estúpido! Put the beer in the back. Get on the fuckin' ground. ¡Ahora!"

O'Leary reached down and grabbed the handle of the case with his left hand. Then he exploded. He launched and twisted, slinging the box in a speeding orbit, smashing the bottles alongside the mouthy kid's head. The brutal swing flipped the belligerent teen to the pavement in a spray of foaming beer and burnished blood.

Then O'Leary snatched the softball bat with his right hand. He flicked the stick with surprising speed and power. It cracked against the white kid's gun-toting hand, breaking bones and triggering shrieks of agony. O'Leary fought to maintain his balance, his sore knee and slippery cleats throwing him out of whack. He finished his awkward rotation in time to find a second punk six feet away, gun drawn and pointed at his chest.

The masked teen glanced at the ground, seeing one of his comrades knocked out cold, his twisted face gurgling in a puddle of reddish foam. Their leader tried to escape by crawling away, his mangled hand dragging at his side. The remaining punk snapped at O'Leary, slobbering through his Latino accent. "You asshole! ¡Est*a noche, te mueres!*"

O'Leary wiped his brow and smirked with the slightest hint of pity. The defiant thug stood shaking in his sagging jeans and greasy work boots. O'Leary saw the boy's face scrunched with fury, but his eyes were moist, brimming with fear. "So, *chico duro*," the officer said with a smirk. "You're willing to throw your life away over convenience store pizza and a few Wisconsin ales?"

The kid flashed a look of confusion while O'Leary spun the bat handle in his right hand, keeping his grip relaxed. Sirens blared in the distance, and the teen shifted his eyes in their direction long enough for O'Leary to flip the bat to his left hand. He snapped the handle across the unsuspecting teen's wrist, knocking the gun from his grip with a vicious crack.

O'Leary, with a growl in his voice, said, "That's right, muchacho—switch hitter. Now that I've leveled the playing field, let's do something about that foul mouth of yours." The detective fired a savage blow using his right elbow. He caught the stunned teen across the face, breaking his jaw, and doubling him over in pain. He finished the punk off with a knee strike to the head, crushing the kid's nose, toppling him to the ground in a suffering heap.

As blood flowed from the kid's battered face, the white gunman staggered across the highway and tumbled into a ditch. Seconds later, O'Leary saw a police cruiser's flashing emergency lights reflecting off Casey's front windows. He also saw Ashley standing in the doorway, shaking her head with her arms folded across her chest.

O'Leary grabbed a seat in the back of his Durango. He leaned to the side, slipped his cell phone from his back pocket, then checked his recent messages. He'd missed a call from his attorney, Jack Hughes, and one from his ex-wife, Amy. The detective twisted the top from one of the two surviving beer bottles. He tilted his head back, guzzling the frosty cold brew. It was then his eyes caught sight of a security camera tucked between the light fixtures above the gas pumps.

Three squad cars sped in and screeched to a stop. The beat cop leaped out and inspected the two bleeding Latinos sprawled on the pavement. O'Leary sipped his beer and mumbled to himself. "Welp, maybe Hughes can save my pension." Then he peeled a rubbery triangle from the pizza box and chomped a bite as the arriving officers approached O'Leary with their guns drawn.

The first cop, grinning and looking amused, shook his head. "Cap, if you could hit a softball as hard as you punch gangbangers, we'd be league champs right now."

O'Leary plucked a thread of cheese from his chin, ignoring the cop's accurate, but insensitive comment. He washed his pizza down with a gulp of his beer, then belched and wiped his mouth on his sleeve. "Strange, these Latinos are pretty good ball players. Too bad these assholes never learned one of life's important lessons."

The second cop twirled a set of handcuffs on his finger. "Oh yeah, what's that?"

O'Leary tossed his bat into the back of his Durango, then turned and glared at the pathetic carjackers. "Sometimes you're the Louisville Slugger, and sometimes you're the ball."

The first cop swatted at some mayflies, then sang out. "Sometimes you're the windshield, sometimes you're the bug."

The shorter of the two Latino boys, the one with the shards of broken glass stuck to his face, began stirring. O'Leary kicked the kid's handgun aside and poured a splash of beer across the boy's bleeding lips. Then he crouched down, leaning into the kid's face. "Hey Poncho, you owe me ten beers. Your chicken-shit leader has hung you and your amigo out to dry. What's his name?"

The boy sputtered and shook his head without answering. Captain O'Leary stood and stepped on the boy's chest with one of his metal cleats. "Couldn't quite hear you. Come again."

The hapless punk choked, then shook his head and spit three bloody teeth onto the pavement. Then, with bloody lips and watery eyes, he said, "*Reeevers.*"

Chapter 5
What Is Life

"Tell me, what is my life without your love?"

A few early morning hikers watched a small, single-engine airplane complete a series of tight, low circles above sleepy Spearfish Canyon. Sunrise, glowing fiery red, bloomed beyond the eastern hogbacks, dismissing the overnight fog while warming the Black Hills. Sommers recalled the age-old saying about a sailor's warning when a red sky appears in the morning. He'd heard forecasters predicting a rare late summer clipper could swoop in from the Canadian Rockies. Sommers knew he'd have to land soon, whether that was near Rapid City or home in Lake Victoria.

The pilot scrutinized his hodgepodge assortment of analog gauges and soon realized he'd flown from Idaho against some stiff crosswinds. There was no chance he'd make it to Minnesota without stopping for fuel. GPS navigation showed Clyde Ice Airfield thirteen miles away. The flying lumberjack calculated he could have wheels on the ground in five minutes. He radioed ahead to secure a grass runway, then prepared for landing.

Sommers circled Devils Bathtub, and then Pettigrew Gulch, seeing no obvious signs of life at Samantha's mountain-top retreat:

no movement, no lights, and no cars in the driveway. He pursed his lips and shook his head, acknowledging it wouldn't be the first time she'd run off on a last-minute trip without calling.

Renowned as a seductive and confident woman, many of her professional endeavors remained shrouded in mystery. From day one, she warned her smitten partner. "My secrets are as dark as they are deep. It'd be dangerous for you to know everything about me."

It didn't take long for Sommers to accept the fact that the boy had complicated things for Sam—made life more challenging for both of them. Lilly LeBlanc's nurturing skills helped their makeshift family maintain some semblance of normalcy. She was the glue holding their reticent arrangement together.

It was a strange and complex world for Samantha Stevens and Dale Sommers. Despite their contrasting histories, unique political entanglements, and secretive financial boons, they tried to make things work. It took a high-minded effort by the three adults to create an anchored home life for the boy.

Sommers scanned the eastern horizon and wondered if normal family life might be an old wives' tale. Besides, what right did he have to expect normalcy? Their Black Hills guise, perhaps it was nothing more than picking nits.

Dale Sommers, a boyish-looking fifty-two-year-old, was a giant of a man in every way. He could've played either professional football or major league baseball. Standing six foot five and weighing two hundred and fifty pounds, he possessed a unique combination of strength, speed, and agility.

The venerated embodiment of Paul Bunyan chose a life of seclusion and conservation. On indefinite leave from the Minnesota Department of Natural Resources, Sommers volunteered as a researcher and sustainability advisor for the U.S. Forest Service.

When not flying out to South Dakota, or parts beyond, he spent his days fishing, carving tree stumps into animal sculptures, or hiking the woods around his family's homestead. Standing at ease inches above the water at the end of his wooden dock, this is where he found serenity. This is where he sought spiritual clarity with his receptive ears trained towards God.

On the ground at SPF, it didn't surprise Sommers that Sam's phone went straight to voicemail, same as Lilly's. Next, he tried connecting with his friends at home, Jack, Jenny, then Moon Deer. Again, no answers, just their humdrum voicemail greetings. He adjusted his baseball cap and scanned the horizon, searching for a cell tower, and not understanding why, today of all days, he didn't have service.

The imposing pilot, with concern scrawled across his face, paced in circles around his airplane, holding his phone overhead, trying to get more bars. Nearby, appearing focused on mechanical things, Otto Schuler observed Sommers' angst from the corner of his eye.

Otto wasn't much to look at. Most said he was rather homely with his concentration-creased forehead and gray flattop haircut. His wistful blue eyes, always focused behind his tinted aviator's glasses. If not for the mechanic's jumpsuit and greasy smudges, the nerdy man could've passed for a bookish librarian or a rumpled pharmacist. A distinguished graduate of the Air Force Academy, Schuler was a bona fide savant when it came to flying objects.

As a former aerospace engineer at NASA, he found enjoyment tinkering with anything that could overcome the forces of inertia and gravity. Otto Schuler was standoffish and always preoccupied. Few people realized he might also be the planet's smartest living person. Sommers often wondered why someone with an IQ approaching two-hundred would land at a tiny airport in South Dakota. When asked about this, Schuler would wave it off and grumble about it being a long story, then return to his pop rivets and pressure gauges.

With a yellow number-two pencil tucked behind his ear at all times, the senior mechanic at Black Hills Aero was never much for needless conversation. On this day, Schuler fueled the small Cessna in the shade of a single-bay hangar. Next, he ran a series of safety checks while Sommers fiddled with his cell phone. The pilot scrunched his face and asked, "What the heck happened to the reception 'round here?"

Schuler wiped his hands on a shop rag, then stuffed the oil-stained cloth into the back pocket of his greasy overalls. "If you're talking about cell phones and whatnot, I gotta tell ya, that's not my calling."

Sommers nodded to confirm he'd heard the crusty war-horse's silly pun. Schuler's expression made it apparent their conversation about mobile technology wasn't going any further. He crouched near the front wheel, checking the tire pressure. Then, following an absorbed moment of silence, Schuler turned and peered at the western sky. "You plan on sticking around for a few days?" He lifted his nose to sniff the breeze, then glanced at his wristwatch. "NWS Doppler shows one hell of a storm blowing in. Maybe eight to ten inches of blowing white stuff on August 19th. Can you believe that nonsense?"

Sommers looked out at the clouding sky, then adjusted his baseball cap. He asked, "You're telling me to take off, right?" Schuler appeared fixated, but shook his head. He slipped the pencil from behind his ear and dabbed the point on his tongue. Then he checked a few boxes on a page affixed to his dog-eared NASA clipboard.

Without warning, Sommers' phone started chiming, and text messages began streaming in one after another. The first was from his friend, Schmitty, the eccentric drone pilot. His cryptic message made little sense to the pilot. *Your mom wants you home for lunch. Trouble brewing up north. Call me.*

Sommers made a mental note to call Schmitty, but he tried Sam's number first now that his phone had gained a signal. He scraped his boots and kicked at the gravel while he waited. Then he listened to a generic voicemail greeting and left a brief message. The pilot also left a message on Lilly's phone. Next, Sommers tapped his screen, dialing Schmitty's number. "Schmitty, Sommers here. What's goin' on?"

The modern-day tech hippy picked up after the second ring. "Dude, how's it hangin'? Where the heck are you?"

Sommers, influenced by Samantha's clandestine activities, had become cautious about providing his exact location. "Hanging low and inside. I'm in South Dakota—wanted to see the cleanup effort in Sturgis after the biker rally."

Schmitty snorted through his laugh, then said, "That's kinda weird, man. Hey, I've only got a few minutes here. I'm driving out to Itasca to shoot aerials of the headwaters—super overrated, if you ask me. Anyway, I stopped by your place on my way. Those feisty Peterson brothers are like a pair of rabid elephants, long memories and short fuses. They smell about as bad, too. Just a couple of crazy old crackers, eh? And what's up Grumpy's ass? It's like the entire world's developed anger issues."

Sommers cut off his drone-flying friend. "Hey, no offense, but I'm kinda on a schedule, too. Mind cutting to the quick?"

"Sorry, man. Your mom wants you home ASAP. Something about a package arriving for you."

"Package?" Sommers asked, watching a hawk circle high above a distant ridge.

"Yea, well. I didn't catch her drift. Say, you remember Tommy Fulgham? I think he was an intern when you were working outta the Brainerd office."

"Name rings a bell. Tall drink of water, baseball player?"

"Yep, that's him. He's been gone 'bout a week. They found his work truck at Lake Bronson, but the kid's nowhere to be found. His last check-in was six days ago. He was supposed to be taking water samples north of Hastings Landing. The BCA's got agents snooping around, searching the valley. They asked me to grab some hi-res footage of the boat docks on the north end of Drayton, near the casino. I don't think they've got any real leads. Seems to me they're grasping at straws 'cause Tommy's never struck me as much of a gambler. Anyway, one of the BCA investigators said he'd be calling you. His name's Vernon or Vincent, something with a V."

"You mean, Virgil?" He asked, trying to keep Schmitty on point. "Tommy's folks must be worried sick. Good people, supportive of our conservation efforts. Why would the BCA be calling me?"

"Straws, man. They're leaning on local professionals. I told them nobody knows northwest Minnesota better than Dale Sommers."

"Thanks for the endorsement, but I can't imagine being much help."

"You're right about Tommy's parents, they're pissed. I ran into Ben Fulgham outside the car wash over at Gary's Place. He's fed-up with how the investigation's being handled. The cops aren't telling him shit. Ben knows you're a well-connected go-getter and an expert tracker. He's hoping you can pressure the DNR into coughing up more information, maybe apply some heat to a trail that's getting cold."

A brisk, northwest wind picked up, and Sommers felt the first few drops of rain. He also felt the familiar trappings of being caught between two worlds. "I need to finish something out here," he said, gazing up at a darkening sky. "The weather might ruin my plans, but there's still a chance I'll be back in a few hours. In the meantime, give Julie Hughes a call and fill her in on the situation. You know she's a badger, she'll burrow into places the BCA hasn't even considered yet."

"You're talking about the former Julie Barnes, right? Honey badger's more like it—smoking hot secretary with a sweet pair of…"

"Whoa there, Sparky. That's my buddy's wife you're talking about. Been a few years, but I'm sure you remember our dustup on Blackhawk Road. Best tread light, my techy friend. She's an investigator who's always ready for a fight, and besides, her jealous husband carries a grudge and a large caliber weapon. Know what I mean?"

"What I remember most about Blackhawk Road was that crazy-ass convict almost blowing my brains out. And don't underestimate the hidden powers of us irresistible nerds. I've been told I pack a pretty big weapon, too." Schmitty belched a hearty laugh before signing off. "Text me when you get back. I want to hear more about this mysterious package."

Sommers heard his friend laughing as the call disconnected. Next, he tapped his phone to call Bud Wolcott at Sturgis Harley Davidson. "Hey Bud. Sommers here. How you doin'? Hope I'm not waking you."

After a momentary delay, Bud said, "Sommers. No problem, man—don't open for another thirty minutes. How's your lady, and how's that nutty little crumb-cruncher?"

"Well, I was hoping you might tell me. From up high, it appears no one's around. Sam's phone keeps going right to voicemail. Have you seen her around?"

"We worked the Junction Avenue booth together during the rally," Wolcott said. "Not our usual crowd. Go woke, ya go broke, man. Anyway, Sam's a thing, you know that. She posed for a bazillion selfies and got cramps in her hand from signing autographs. To answer your question, I haven't seen her since the last day of the run."

Sommers scratched at the back of his neck, pacing around the hangar. "Hmm, what about Lilly? Seen her around?"

"Nope, can't say that I have."

"Well, I'm in a pickle this morning. I need to get back—trying to stay ahead of the weather, but I'm concerned about the radio silence up on the mountain. Did Sam mention any business trips? She meet anyone at the rally? My apologies if I sound out of sorts. I've been spitting on wildfires in Idaho for the past week. Too much smoke, I guess."

Wolcott snickered before he said, "Bro, I'm all about the smoke. Sorry. I shouldn't laugh. But, like I told ya, you should've rolled into the rally. Nothing like it anywhere, man."

"Sorry, not my thing. Got no patience for crowds. I'd rather play with chisels and chainsaws. I'm sure it was quite the scene—sounds like you guys did okay."

"We did alright. Ya know. Now that you mention it, I remember Sam having lunch with a couple of guys last week. Dudes looked like her people. You know, natives. They dressed like bikers, but they weren't bikers, if you know what I mean. One guy was tall like you, the other shorter than me. I think they wanted to do a feature piece about two-wheel tours of the Dakota reservations, but I'm not positive about that."

Sommers checked his watch, then asked, "Were these guys legit? Did you sense they were dangerous?"

"Nah, nothing like that," Wolcott said. "The dudes acted like posers, that's all. Listen, man, I must've met a thousand bikers last week, so my recollection is fuzzy at best. I remember these guys asked to see Hawk. It's been forever since I've heard anyone call her by that name. Maybe they were old friends, former business associates. perhaps."

Sommers heard the shuffling of papers, then Wolcott exhaled and said, "Hey, I'm leaving for Cabo tomorrow morning, going deep-sea fishing. Gonna unwind with a few of my buds, maybe get lucky with a couple of senoritas. It sounds like you've got to take off. But tell you what, I'll ride out to her place this afternoon. I'll call you later with a status report. How'd that be?"

Sommers thought about Bud's offer, then looked over at Schuler, who signaled ten minutes with his fingers. The pilot pointed to his phone and signaled one minute with his index finger. "That's an hour each way, you sure? Look, I don't want to impose, but I'm kinda stuck here. Shoot, I'd appreciate your help."

Wolcott said, "No problem, man. If it snows, I'll wheel over in the Jeep. It's a sweet ride either way. Take a chill pill, man. Sam's a big girl, she can take care of herself. I'll call you tonight."

"A clipper's gonna be whipping in any minute. Be careful out there. I've got a spooky feeling about this. The garage code is the same, but bring your key, just in case. You're a good man, Bud. I owe you one." Sommers' phone cut out before Wolcott could sign off.

Ten minutes later, following Otto Schuler's advice, Sommers was in the air, sailing for Minnesota. An arctic blue sky with a smattering of billowy clouds lay ahead of him. The pilot leaned against the side window, admiring the patchwork quilt below—fields rolling like an ocean of ambers and greens as far as he could see.

Then he peeked over his shoulder to see threatening clouds filled with darkness and uncertainty. He turned up the music and wondered if the weather gods were trying to tell him something, sending the big man some kind of insidious warning.

The pilot hummed along with the chorus, squinting at the salmon-colored horizon. He recalled a sunny evening in the yard, firing fastballs into his father's catcher's mitt. The battery struck out hitters until daylight ran out. Had Sommers realized that would be their last game of catch, he would've never stopped throwing.

His memory lingered, then floated away, just like the mysterious shadows of the Black Hills. Sommers adjusted his baseball hat and checked the gauges strewn across his instrument panel. With a bit of trepidation, he glanced over his shoulder, then shook his head. Those dismal storm clouds were gaining on him.

Chapter 6
Fantasy Girl

"Lately I'm learnin' that so many yearnings are never to be."

Dean Rivers clapped his dusty gloved hands together, then folded his arms across his chest. He leaned back and watched the roaring flames swell towards a flawless sapphire sky. The farmhand lifted his chin at the smoke and said, "Well, that's about it. One of you assholes is heading north, the other south." Billows of black soot peppered with flakes of white ash twisted higher, then floated east towards the Red River. Rivers nodded and sneered at the appropriateness of this. "Back whence you came, fellas."

From around the corner of her faded yellow two-story farmhouse, Susan Norman raced over, seated behind the steering wheel of her orange all-terrain vehicle. She skidded to a stop inches from the farmhand's grimy work boots. After climbing out, she waved a woven floppy hat in front of her face. "Phew, hot one today. That's quite a fire ya got there—stinks something awful, don't it?" Rivers watched Susan pinch her nose, then dab a trickle of sweat from between her ample breasts. "How's it goin', Mr. Rivers?"

Rivers wiped his brow with his shirtsleeve, trying to hide his eyes while staring at Norman's chest. "Going okay, Ma'am. Name's Dean, 'member?" He shrugged as he pointed at the fire. "There's a nasty jumble of crud buried in there, oil cans, and prob'ly a skunk or two. Smell will let up once the flames kick into high gear." From the corner of his eye, he looked her over like an ogler with a metal detector spies sunbathers at the beach.

Rivers earned a far-reaching reputation for bird-dogging the tramps, but Susan B. Norman was different. Sexy and in her mid-thirties, everyone found her captivating. She was spunky, independent, and even the highfalutin city women, green with envy, said she was soft on the eyes. Kansas-born and farm-raised, Rivers thought she was better suited for South Beach or Rodeo Drive based only on her racy strut and her coquettish smile.

His mind deep into his fantasy, Rivers watched the tantalizing woman tie her blond hair into a ponytail, revealing her slender neck and her freckled shoulders. She nestled her hat atop her head, shaded her eyes with her hand, then studied the swirls of smoke sailing off towards Minnesota. With the curve of her hip leaning against the ATV, she caught Rivers amid a lustful stare and smiled. Then she twirled a wisp of her blond hair. "Save it for the grannies, Dean. Sue or Susan, if you please."

She gave him a wink and clapped her hands, then shifted her attention back to the crackling fire. "Shame that the old barn had to come down. The siding had such unique coloring and old-world character." She pouted and kicked at the dirt with the toe of her boot. "Well, anyway, Edward agrees with you. He told me we should've demolished this relic years ago, said we're lucky it didn't collapse on somebody—could've gotten our asses sued off."

Rivers nodded, leaning his lanky arms over a rake's wooden handle. Susan's joyless demeanor hinted at what the townsfolk were whispering. Her pizza-faced man couldn't come close to satisfying her. Rivers stepped close and put forth his manliest smile. "Chin up, Susan. Before striking the match, I pulled the best planks and several of the beams. Reclaimed wood is fetching a pretty penny these days." He cocked his head towards a nearby pole barn. "I stacked the boards behind the old man's machine shed. They'll plane up nice, make a sweet feature wall for somebody."

Susan brushed flakes of ash from her shoulder and flashed her trademark alluring grin. "Well done, Dean." Rivers watched her walk with a bouncy, determined gait towards the back of her ATV. "I've got some old boxes and papers back here. Would you mind helping me toss 'em into your fire?" Rivers cinched his work gloves, trying to appear cool, but leapt into action like an eager puppy.

The searing heat kept the pair away from the popping and crackling of the growing inferno. Susan grunted, heaving a paper box containing old notebooks towards the burning rubble, but landed with a thud, short of the mark. Rivers bounded over and kicked the carton, somersaulting it into the flames and sending a burst of orange embers fluttering skyward. Susan giggled as Rivers, looking like a gangly scarecrow, staggered back to the coolness at her side.

Susan patted his back and rubbed his shoulders while he caught his breath. Then she winked at him. "Sure beats a shredder, right?" Rivers nodded and smirked, brushing ashes from his hair. She turned to examine a plume of dust tracking along Valley Road. "I've got a job for Manny, but I can't find him anywhere. Have you seen him around?"

"Manny Rodriguez?" Rivers wiped his forehead with his shirttail, then shaded his eyes and surveyed the north pasture. "I haven't seen that smelly bum for days. He's gotta be on a bender with a few of them immigrant fags."

Susan shot him a frosty scowl, so he turned away and stared into the dancing flames.

Rivers grabbed his rake and pushed some stray clinkers into the festering pile. As she turned to walk away, he said, "Mrs. Norman, I gotta be honest with you. Rodriguez got out over his skis, asked a lot of suspicious questions. I mean, how far should we trust a convicted felon?" He watched a plume of black smoke spiral away and cleared his throat with a cough. "I asked your husband to take Manny off the payroll. He's nothin' but a low-rent drifter, everyone knows that."

Rivers watched Susan shake her head while watching the paper boxes burn. The sweaty farmhand said, "He won't be coming back." He felt Susan pat him on his backside and watched her turn away just as her husband rolled up in his dusty pickup truck. Cigarette smoke and the twang of hillbilly bluegrass wafted from Edward's open windows.

Susan and Edward exchanged piercing, frigid glares. Then, without saying a word, she climbed back into her four-wheeler. Rivers watched the irritated woman crank the steering wheel and stir a cloud of dust as she sped away.

Edward Norman stepped from his truck, glaring at his lanky laborer. He grabbed a crumbling wooden skid from his truck's bed and flipped it like a matchbook into the crackling fire. Then he turned to face Rivers, sizing him up. "Sorry to interrupt your enchanted moment." Norman pivoted towards the burning debris and scrunched his nose. "Reeks of coon shit out here. I could see your goddamn smoke from the Interstate—the hell you guys throw in there?"

Edward wasn't as tall as Rivers, but thicker and stronger, with broad shoulders and muscular arms. A middling bull-rider back in his day, he had deep, puckered scars on the left side of his face, the result of one too many rodeo spills. He tried to hide the damage with his long hair and a scraggly beard.

The offish farmer had trouble turning his head, and he tottered along with a pronounced limp. Everyone, including Rivers, wondered what Susan ever saw in Edward since the hardass wasn't much to look at. Her gimpy cowboy wasn't much of a dancer either. The whispers from town suggested the beauty was on a mission to fleece the beast of his money.

Hardened from having lived a tough life, Rivers wasn't prone to intimidation. The gritty farmhand stripped his gloves from his hands and inspected his gnarled, calloused knuckles. "Mrs. Norman wanted help with some old boxes." He pointed a thumb towards the fire. "Manny was out here shooting gophers and skunks last week. You know damned well the sonofabitch is too lazy to bury his kills. Sure as eggs are eggs, that dumbass tossed the varmints into the hayloft."

Norman nodded, accepting Rivers' explanation for the rancid odor. Rivers watched the man's eyes shift from agitated to determined. Norman slipped a folded sheet of paper from his shirt pocket and handed it to his sweating grunt. "What's this?" Rivers asked.

Norman leaned in and pointed at the illustration. "Bought it two days ago. It's a Ford F-150."

Rivers rolled his eyes before spitting into the fire. "I can see that. What's this got to do with me?"

Norman folded his arms across his chest, hitting Rivers with a hard-nosed stare. "It's been in storage for two years," he said. "The guys at Wenner's prepped it for us yesterday, replaced the belts and hoses. With all the supply chain shit going on, there aren't any car haulers available. Anyway, I need you to get your ass down to Fargo and pick 'er up. Jerry can drive you this afternoon. Wenner's place is east of the zoo—truck's inside. Big Bill's expecting you. On your way back, stop at Halverson's in Grand Forks. Kurt's gonna take care of the striping and lettering. Should only take a few hours. Think of it as a relaxing road trip on my dime."

Rivers squinted, studying the creased paper. "I think I've seen this truck." The pictured Ford had chrome wheels, tinted windows, and a two-inch lift kit. Rivers pinched a clump of chewing tobacco and stuffed the canister into his back pocket. Then he tucked the shreds into his lower lip and cocked his head towards Ed's current ride, sputtering as he spoke. "Black's a god-awful choice for 'round here. Skinny Pete will have to wash it every ten minutes." Rivers spent another moment scrutinizing the picture, then locked eyes with Norman and sniffed the air. "Ya know what? This deal smells kinda shitty to me. Why don't you get 'er yourself?"

Norman cracked his knuckles and got up into Rivers' face. "Adjust your attitude. I'm not asking here. The sale is contingent on us picking it up today. I've got a meeting in Devils Lake, not that it's any of your goddamn business."

Rivers shook his head, then crumpled the paper into a ball and tossed it into the fire. "Not interested." He kicked a glowing ember into the crackling flames. "Shame, you've gotta go so far to close your deal," he said. "The boys are sayin' this place is going down the fuckin' tubes. You're selling out to the Snakes, aren't you?"

Rivers tossed his rake aside and thrust his finger at Norman's face. "You pay me fuckin' peanuts to keep this leaky barge afloat. How am I supposed to do that when you're always flushing us down a shit-stained bowl?" Rivers spit a sloppy plash near Norman's feet, then wiped his mouth with the back of his hand. "Get yourself another lackey."

He turned to step away, but Norman stopped him, clamping hard onto Rivers' arm. The farmhand saw the boss man's face grow slick with sweat. He glanced down at the meaty hand gripping his elbow, then locked into Ed's bloodshot eyes. "Well, shit. You wanna take it there?"

Rivers jerked his arm free and snarled at his boss. "Been waiting years for a chance to kick your ugly ass. I'm wearing the proper boots, and you know it. You're a lily-livered cock sucker. I can see it in your eyes. I can smell it on your skin." Rivers scrunched his nose and balled his hands into hardened fists. "C'mon rodeo clown, walk or shoot."

Rivers watched Ed Norman glance over his shoulder to see his wife standing on the top step of her wrap-around porch, her fisted hands digging into her hips. Rivers tracked the man's stare and from across the field, he could feel the woman's emptiness. Susan's defiant posture spoke volumes. She'd pay through the nose to see her husband suffer.

Rivers lowered his hands as Norman stepped back to his truck. Edward sparked a cigarette and leaned against the rusty fender. After blowing his smoke at Rivers, he said, "I'm willing to forget about your little hissy fit. Susan wanted me to send Manny. Honestly, she thinks this is her deal, but she's pretty naïve to Big Bill's crooked ways." Norman brushed gray flakes from his shirt sleeve. "Shit, maybe you're right. We're putting you in a tough spot. But tell you what, since this isn't your usual detail, I'll pay you a thousand dollars for your confidence and your time."

The lanky farmhand peeked over his shoulder at the farmhouse, then spit and shook his head. Norman reached into his crusty pickup and pulled out an envelope thick with cash. He flicked his cigarette towards the burning rubbish, then started counting hundred-dollar bills. "How about twenty-five hundred? I'll also give you some pocket money for food and expenses. Enough for someone to fluff your pillow, perhaps?"

Rivers licked his chapped lips and stepped closer to the barbaric cowboy. "Make it five, and I won't bat an eye. I won't say a goddamn word."

Norman, thinking it over, kicked at the dirt, then turned to face Rivers. "Okay, deal. Here's half. But just so we're clear, leave the others outta this. Like you said, not one damn word."

Rivers hesitated, then nodded. He grabbed the stack of bills and folded them in half, then held the cash under his nose. Seconds later, he stuffed the folded wad into his front pocket and crossed his arms, waiting for his boss' next move.

Norman turned and hobbled away, climbing into his truck and pointing his thumb towards the farmhouse. "From now on, you answer only to me. Susan's papers are none of your goddamn business." The driver hesitated, then slid his holstered Colt 357 onto the dashboard. He glared through his smudge-streaked windshield without turning his head. "You'll receive instructions and another fist of cash from Wenner." Then he shifted the truck into drive and nodded towards the house. "Expecting to see that Ford parked in Jerry's shop tomorrow night. Follow the posted speed limit and for cryin' out loud, don't go doin' anything stupid."

Rivers, flush with sarcasm, saluted him and said, "Aye, aye, captain. Enjoy your party in the viper's nest."

Norman sped off towards Highway 5 with a clay-colored dust cloud rolling in his wake. Rivers shook his head as he stretched his work gloves over his sweating, shaking hands. Ten yards away, the torrid blaze continued to snap at him, and the impetuous farmhand stood motionless, leaning on his rake and letting his adrenaline rush pass.

Rivers peered into the dancing flames. They conjured gruesome images of blood-stained faces. He saw Manny's seedy grimace, and he saw an oozing slash across his wife's severed throat. Then he saw a third figure, cloaked and obscure, summoning him with a bony finger. Rivers shook his head, trying to clear the ghastly visions. He coughed and gasped for air before speaking to the phantoms in the flames. "Why me, you heathens?"

Rivers used his rake to shove wood scraps into the pile of orange clinkers, trying to erase the inferno's evil flares. With Edward's truck out of view, he turned to watch Susan toss her hat aside and unfurl her long blonde hair. Her yellow wisps shimmered like corn silk. He watched as she sat and rocked on her porch swing, looking back at him. Rivers spat another brown glob into the fire, then whispered to the flames. "Well, shit. Why not me?"

Without warning, Rivers' phone vibrated, and he dug it from his pocket. He heard a woman's voice, soft and sultry. "Dean, it's Susan."

Then, following a deliberate pause, she said, "I could tell your conversation was getting heated out there. What's Edward up to?"

Rivers sputtered through his lips and scratched at the back of his neck. "Not much. Just two dudes working through a disagreement. He wants the old man to drive me down to Fargo this afternoon."

"Fargo. What on earth for?"

"Can't say. That's between him and me."

"Really? Listen, Dean. You've always been special to me. I've got big plans for you, big plans for both of us." Then she exhaled a breathy sigh. "I hope you're not gonna let that bulge in your pocket cloud your thinking."

Rivers watched Susan Norman stand from her porch swing with her shapely figure silhouetted against the midday sun. "Plans?" He asked, watching her kick off her boots. "What plans?"

"Come on up to the house. I'll pour you a cold drink." She smacked her lips, then caught her breath. "Later, I'll fix you a hot plate and we'll see where things go from there."

Chapter 7
Gone

"This ain't no temporary, typical tearful goodbye"

What should've taken two hours had already surpassed three. Jerry Reynolds sat beaming in the driver's seat, his age-spotted, wrinkled hands gripping the oversized steering wheel of his 1966 Chevrolet Impala. He hadn't uttered but two words the entire trip. If the turquoise two-door broke fifty miles per hour, it was from sheer luck, and a gusty tailwind propelling the old car down a hill. Dean Rivers, sitting shotgun, could've blinked and missed this welcome burst of acceleration.

Instead of taking Interstate 29 south to Fargo, Reynolds' restored Chevy meandered along rural country two-lanes. He stopped every thirty minutes, stepping out to pee on hapless weeds withering on the chalky shoulders. Hazy, late afternoon sunshine warmed his back, so Reynolds took his sweet time pissing on the Highway 4 signpost outside of Warsaw.

Rivers studied the lettering, then grumbled after checking his watch. "You know, considering the time we've spent on this deserted trail, we could very well be in bloody Poland."

Reynolds zipped his fly and pointed south. "Nope, but soon

enough. Past those hills." He wiped his hands on his pants, gazed at the cracked, graying ribbon of pavement, and smirked. "Back in the day, a Polish friend of mine got hired to paint the yellow lines along this road. His first day, he painted ten miles, impressing his boss. The second day, he painted five, and on his third day, he painted only one mile of this track. His foreman asked, what's the problem, man? My buddy says, sorry boss, but with each passing day, I have to walk farther and farther to get back to that blasted paint bucket."

Rivers shook his head, then downed the last gulp of his Dr. Pepper. "Whatever, old-timer," he said, before dropping a resounding belch. "That's just stupid." He tossed his empty bottle into the weeds, scattering a band of grasshoppers. After swatting a few of the bugs from his face, he stretched his arms high over his head. "Hey Pops. How 'bout you let me take the wheel for a while? Give them old bones a chance to rest. You can just sit back and enjoy this breathtaking scenery."

Reynolds blocked Rivers' insolence with a snort. "Nah."

Rivers kicked at a stone, then tramped around in the middle of the lonesome highway. He inflated his defiance, tucking his fingers into the front pockets of his tattered jeans, scanning the horizon with his lips puckered. The farmhand slumped his shoulders, which were draped beneath a sweat-soaked Farmall t-shirt clinging to his ribs. With his face twisted into a pout, he said, "You know, if I get to walkin', you may catch me in The Forks by sometime tomorrow afternoon. What do you say? Wanna meet at the Blue Moose for early bird supper?"

After allowing his sarcasm to percolate, Rivers raised his face to the sky. "Norman's punishing me for something, isn't he?"

Reynolds let out a groan as he climbed back behind the wheel. "Don't know. What do you think?" He twisted the key, and the starter carped for two seconds before the throaty big-block rumbled to life.

"Is this about Susan?" Rivers asked, rolling his eyes and scrunching his face into a scowl. With hesitation, he slid back onto the sun-scorched passenger seat. "Shit ol' man, why black?" Then he huffed as he scooched his backside across the hot vinyl. "The engine's got a ballsy sound. No puny little six banger, is it?"

"427."

Rivers slapped his thighs and bobbed his head. "Hot damn! She fast?"

Reynolds spun the wheel, easing back onto the highway without signaling or checking his mirrors. "Very."

"Back to short answers, eh? No more of your hilarious jokes?" Rivers sputtered and pointed to the large, damp blotches under his arms. "Shame the A/C's busted."

Reynolds tapped the dashboard with his scrawny fingers. "Ice Cold."

"Well, fuck me then. How 'bout sharing some of that frosty goodness?"

"Nope."

"Why the hell not?"

Reynolds shifted in the driver's seat, gazing through the bug-splattered windshield without responding. Rivers dabbed his sweat-slicked forehead, then folded his arms across his chest and closed his eyes. He muttered something about Canadian blizzards before drifting off.

A short time later, a hapless dragonfly the size of a walnut ricocheted off the windshield, causing Rivers to awaken with a start. "Shit! The hell was that?"

"Bug," Reynolds said through his scowl.

Rivers shook his head, then faced the driver. "Nice fuckin' timing. I was in the middle of a dream. Susan Norman was running along a white sand beach wearing nothing but a skimpy bikini."

Reynolds cocked an eyebrow, then nodded his head twice.

After shaking his head and chewing his bottom lip, Rivers said, "Okay, Pops. I've only got one left in the chamber. Radio play?"

Reynolds reached down and turned a chromed silver knob. "Like a puppy with two peters." The Delco AM radio belched some static, then a local DJ blabbed on and on, reeling off the daily ag report in a stodgy midwestern voice.

"Ah, hell no." Rivers covered his ears and shook his head. "I'm surrounded by fuckin' clodhoppers."

Reynolds drummed his thumbs on the steering wheel. "Want some music?"

Rivers clasped his hands together in mock prayer. Then he watched his chauffeur stuff an oversized cassette into an eight-track tape player mounted below the dashboard.

Rivers let out a feigned whoop. "Alright Pops, now we're talking. Crank that shit up!" Jay and the Americans made their drive through Poland, North Dakota, almost tolerable.

Jerry Reynolds worked as a handyman at Norman Farms. Edward's father hired him way back in 1965. Reynolds, a civil engineer in the Army, had just returned from Vietnam. Jerry saved his pennies and his dimes, special-ordering his prized Impala direct from General Motors in early 1966.

Folks said ol' JR could fix anything that rolled on wheels—a magician wearing a tool belt instead of a top hat and cape. With no wife and no family, nobody knew much about the reclusive veteran. Many thought he might be the oldest living person in Pembina County. For the next hundred miles, Reynolds' guttural sounds and short answers confirmed many of the rumors swirling around Edward and Susan Norman.

Reynolds explained, on most days, Ed popped antidepressants and opioids by the handfuls, most often Percocet. He had always been abusive, unstable, and ill-equipped to run the family farm. The pensive driver went on, verifying Ed was a master at cutting corners, looking to make a quick buck. But his schemes always seemed to end in disaster. It took almost two centuries, but the Dakota Sioux were taking their revenge on the Normans, especially the pizza-faced bull rider.

Every one of Edward's drug runs to Devils Lake cost him thousands of dollars. During the last few years, Norman Farms careened towards financial ruin. This was because the dairy industry was in steep decline, and also because the gimpy addict couldn't find other ways to manage his ceaseless aches and pains. The Normans were in negotiations with both Big Bill Wenner and the Dakota Sioux Syndicate, trying to secure their financial backing. Their grandiose plan was to transform the struggling family farm into a swanky golf and casino resort.

Jerry Reynolds said he could see through Susan's dumb-blonde schtick better than most. He said she earned her accounting degree from Kansas State University in three years. Savvy with numbers, she had a good head for business. For three years following her graduation, Susan managed a successful bordello in KC's unheralded red-light district. That's where young Ed Norman, a cowboy looking for more than eight seconds of hard bucking, stopped by to proposition her.

Despite years of abuse, Susan held the slimmest thread of loyalty to her husband. He got her off cocaine, got her off the streets. He helped her through tough times when the world turned its back on her. Reynolds let out a sigh and said, "Susan's as sharp as a tack, but bad choices follow her like an orphaned calf." He scratched at his chin before shifting in his seat. "One thing's for sure, the Normans aren't in Kansas anymore."

Over time, Susan grew tired of Edward's moodiness, his insulting remarks, and his complete lack of business acumen. The crux of her marital dissatisfaction lay with their inability to have children. She and Ed had stopped trying years ago, and now slept in separate farmhouses. Adoption, because of her checkered past, was impossible, and Susan researched alternative pregnancy programs. But her husband was a miserly traditionalist devoted to his narcotics. Reynolds shook his head and predicted the farm wouldn't survive another two years, even with Susan Norman at the helm.

Rivers fanned his face with a folded road map. "That's a crazy barrel of monkey piss, Pops. How do you know all this shit?"

Reynolds glanced over at Rivers. "Got fifty years in at Norman Farms—got one mouth and these two big ears. You do the math."

Two hours and four pit stops later, Reynolds turned and parked in front of the tall service door at Wenner Motors. Rivers checked his watch and snapped at the old-timer. "Nice going, man. They've been closed for two fuckin' hours. Ed told me the deal had to go down today. Now what the hell are we gonna do?"

Reynolds looked around, then scratched at the sunburn on the back of his neck. "I've heard you've got a son—lives somewhere around here, right? You should drop in and check on him."

No sooner had the words left Jerry's mouth, the large overhead door rolled open. Big Bill Wenner stood wearing a menacing frown on his blubbery, round face. He looked like a slobbering bulldog, quaking in front of the glossy black pickup. The enormous man had a smoldering cigar jutting from the corner of his mouth and a blue key fob dangling from one of his chubby index fingers.

Big Bill's neck and torso were so big, his necktie could only reach the middle button of his sauce-stained dress shirt. Rivers waved, then peeled himself from the vinyl seat, stepping clear of the idling Impala. A split second later, he wheeled and watched slack-jawed as Jerry Reynolds cut a raucous U-turn, smoking the rear tires before rocketing east on Highway 52 without saying goodbye.

Wenner grinned through his swirling cloud of cigar smoke. "Bitchin' ride, 'eh? That there was zero to sixty in seven seconds. Five hundred horsepower. We tricked out the transmission and installed the four-ten gears last summer. That old bastard didn't let you drive 'er, did he?"

Rivers yammered as he rocked back and forth on his heels. "Fuck, no. We spent the last five hours zigzagging across North Dakota, never cracking forty. The last hundred miles was nothing but some sixties band singing the same goddamn songs over and over. If I hear *Cara Mia* one more time, I'm gonna fuckin' puke."

His voice hoarse from years of chain-smoking and snarling at his employees, Big Bill studied his gold wristwatch, then spewed a slushy cough. He wiped his mouth with the back of his hand and said, "Damn. Where's that grisly old boss of yours? Kinda expected him three hours ago." Rivers shrugged his shoulders and tried to explain, but Wenner cut him off, handing the driver a manila envelope and two key fobs.

Wenner slogged back to the garage door's control panel. "The registration's in the glove box, and the tank's full. Kurt's expecting you tomorrow morning, eight o'clock, sharp."

Rivers raised his hand, wanting more information. But Big Bill, once again, waved him off. "This goddamn truck has got a curse on it. The sooner you get her outta my sight, the better off we'll be."

Big Bill's jowls shook like the floppy ears on a hound dog. He coughed, belched, then pointed his cigar towards the highway. "You tell that hot number we're square. And tell that ugly peckerhead he owes me one, a big one." He swiped his meaty palms together, then raised his empty hands for Rivers to see. "Don't let the door crack your ass on the way out."

An hour later, Dean Rivers had five thousand dollars burning a hole in his pocket. His stomach grumbled like an angry yard dog. To satisfy both, he spent the evening on the east end of Fargo at Wenner's other profitable establishment, the Silver Wolf Casino.

Ted Lindstrom, a long-time security guard who looked and sounded a lot like Sam Elliot, leaned against a quarter slot machine with a toothpick jutting from the corner of his mouth. He smiled and waved at Rivers as soon as the dusty hayseed stepped from the chrome-plated revolving door.

"Sonofabitch! Dirty Dean Rivers, long time no see," Lindstrom said, extending his hand. "How the hell are ya? Staying outta trouble, I assume."

The farmhand shook hands with the former sheriff while surveying the rows of noisy gaming machines. Their flashing lights floundered in the dense cloud hanging over the lobby. Rivers made a farting sound and said, "Always, but you know what they say."

Lindstrom laughed as he slapped Rivers on the back. "Right, ass out of you and sometimes me. How about that boy of yours? Is he keeping his nose clean?"

Rivers latched his eyes onto a sexy bartender he hadn't seen before. After gawking at her shapely figure for several seconds, his attention drifted back to Lindstrom. "Oh, Duane? Wouldn't know. Haven't seen him in years. Got any food 'round here? I could eat a horse." Then Rivers turned and pointed at the enticing bartender. "Hold that thought and tell me that sweet angel's name."

Lindstrom peered through the opaque fog of cigarette smoke that surrounded the casino bar. "That, my friend, is Angie, the assassin, McCormick. She's hotter than a blowtorch and twice as deadly. If you've got your insurance paid up and you're feeling snappy, I can introduce you."

Rivers punched Lindstrom in the shoulder. "Insurance? You're fuckin' kidding, right? Let's go, man. I haven't sniffed a pair of teats like hers since sunup this morning."

Lindstrom let out another hearty laugh. "Okay, cowboy. But don't say I didn't warn you."

Rivers spent the next two hours wearing out the paisley carpeting between his bar stool and the hundred-dollar blackjack table. Lady Luck, ever elusive, smiled at him on this night. He gobbled a medium-rare twenty-ounce T-Bone while guzzling four bottles of Spotted Cow. Then the prickly farmhand tripled his money in short order by doubling down and hitting twenty-one on three consecutive hands.

The fortuitous gambler spent most of the evening chatting with Angie. He gawked at her augmented thirty-four double Ds and told her about his lucrative adventure with the mysterious black pickup. Long after the senior crowd left on their bus, Rivers, feeling salty and playing with house money, slid from his barstool after leaving a two-hundred-dollar tip for his enchanting server.

He turned back and doubled-down again. This time, by asking the assassin for her phone number. "What a night," he said, following a cough and a belch. "No doubt about it, you're tender on my tired eyes. But it's been a long day, and this goddamn smoke's bested me. What I need more than anything is a hot shower and a cool pillow." Rivers grabbed Angie's hand and unfurled his neediest pout. "Who's got the most primo bed 'round here? As you can see, I'm in no condition to drive tonight."

Angie twirled the ends of her strawberry-blond hair and leaned her top-shelf melons out over the bar. She wore a playful grin and purred like a cat as she spoke. "Well, to tell you the truth, my four-poster is kinda worn to the nubs, but there's a Courtyard and a Days Inn near the university." Then she gave herself a slap to the forehead. "Shit, what am I saying? You can walk right across to the Radisson. Pricey, but it's a classy place, only two blocks away. Don't ask me how I know, but they've got free Wi-Fi and a tasty breakfast buffet. My shift ends at midnight," she said, nibbling the fingernail on her pinky finger. "Would you like some company for hotcakes and sausage?"

Rivers ran his fingertips along the back of Angie's arm as she tapped her number into his cell phone. "Most important meal of the day," he said, staring deep into Angie's tantalizing cleavage. "Give me a little time to check in and freshen up. I'll text you my room number." McCormick winked and nodded, then stretched across the bar and planted a moist kiss on Rivers' neck.

The lucky gambler scanned the casino floor as he backed away from the bar with a silly grin plastered across his face. He spotted Lindstrom, smiling like a cheshire cat at the opposite end of the lobby. The cordial security guard flashed a thumbs up, then patted himself on the chest. Rivers saluted and nodded his appreciation before locking eyes with the two natives seated at the opposite end of the bar.

The pair dressed like bikers, and they'd been sipping beer and downing whiskey chasers from the same barstools the entire night. Rivers muttered as he shook his head. "Drunk-ass rez monkeys." The three exchanged prolonged, posturing stares before Rivers broke the standoff by flipping double birds at the two boozers. He waved as he backpedaled towards the exit, inviting their next move.

Five minutes later, Rivers sat at a red light, staring into space and mumbling to his steering wheel. "Too many beers, too much second-hand smoke, something doesn't feel right. Things never come this easy for me." He drove north to 5th Street, caressing the truck's leather-appointed seats and swiping through the music menus on the infotainment screen. He found an oldies station he liked and turned up the volume.

Rivers made a series of turns and parked on the top level of a parking garage across the street from the Radisson. Then he called in a reservation requesting two rooms on the fifteenth floor, one facing the river, the other facing the street. He texted a message to Angie, giving her the street-side number. Then he tucked a pinch of chew into his lower lip and waited. With the city lights twinkling all around, the quiet coolness of the rooftop washed over him. Dean Rivers sang an old refrain he couldn't shake from his head.

"*Cara Mia, mine. Cara Mia, mine. Cara Mia, mine.*"

Just after midnight, the cowboy's blood boiled, and his heart sank. He leaned against a post in the garage overlooking 5th Street, watching the two Snakes from the bar park their truck around the corner. The pair, one tall man and one short, jogged towards the hotel vestibule. Rivers thought they moved with confidence, like cops, not clumsy drunk bikers.

The two men stopped behind the valet's station, checked their handguns, then continued into the hotel. Rivers tapped himself along his beltline, feeling for a holster he wasn't wearing. Buying more time, he texted Angie again, sending her a different room number, claiming he'd splurged on a jacuzzi suite. After that, he called the hotel front desk to cancel his reservations. Before hanging up, he reported a suspicious odor clouding the fifteenth-floor hallway.

Rivers climbed back into the truck and pounded his fists on the steering wheel. He shouted a series of muddled obscenities, then turned left onto 7th Avenue, wheeling towards the Interstate. His good fortune long gone, he checked the speedometer and said, "That fuckin' fat man called it right, this truck's snakebit."

A long row of orange road construction barrels slowed Rivers' progress as he curved the ramp onto northbound I-29. In a flash, he slammed on the brakes and skidded to a stop, almost hitting a worker staggering along the shoulder. He flashed the high beams and honked the horn, alerting the laborer of his presence.

Rivers lowered the passenger window and leaned out. "Drunk-ass motherfucker, watch where you're walking! I almost snuffed your lights out." Then he realized the wobbly man wasn't a careless worker, but a stoned hitchhiker wearing a filthy, blood-stained hoodie and muddied work boots.

The shrouded pedestrian extended his left middle finger. "Fuck off, asshole."

Rivers stomped on the gas pedal and fishtailed past the grubby jaywalker, wheeling onto the highway. He adjusted the rearview mirror in time to see the stumbling bum take another two steps before collapsing into the sticky muck clogging the bottom of the roadside ditch. Rivers nodded and said, "Serves you right, putrid piece of shit."

Chapter 8
Highway Patrol

"I got a star on my car and one on my chest."

Ted Lindstrom exhaled a sigh of relief after seeing Rivers and his two shady adversaries leave the casino without incident. He'd broken up a fight the previous night and his battered knuckles were sore. Angie McCormick sent a tray of dirty tumblers off with the busboy, then began singing to herself as she wiped down the bar with a damp towel. Lindstrom winked at her, then shuffled off to the security office.

A few minutes later, he plopped into his desk chair and initiated the backup of the security camera recordings. Still clinging to past habits as a county sheriff, he pressed a button on his police scanner and listened while munching on a tray of pretzels he smuggled from the bar.

The radio transmitted a burst of static, so Lindstrom leaned in and stopped chewing.

"Car thirteen to dispatch. Is this a clear channel? 10-52, 10-5-2. Transport needed to Sanford General. Location, 7th avenue and the northbound I-29 entrance ramp. Subject is a white male, age undisclosed. Possible hit and run. Fractures, maybe internals. Subject's

unresponsive—name could be Winters, Ridders, or Rivers—under the influence, couldn't make heads nor tails over what he said. Thirteen over."

"*Copy that, thirteen. Channel's clear—EMT's in route.*"

"*10-4 dispatch. Thirteen out.*"

Lindstrom scattered his pretzels as he dashed from the office to find the assassin. He caught her gliding towards the staff exit. "Whoa Angie, wait up!" After catching his breath, he asked, "Dean Rivers, you get his cell number?"

McCormick shot him a quizzical look while she fumbled for her phone. "He texted me about twenty minutes ago. Sup?"

"Get him on the horn. I heard an emergency call on the scanner—just wanna make sure he's alright."

McCormick made a few swipes and taps on her cell phone, then put it to her ear and listened. "He's not picking up, might be in the shower."

"Try again."

McCormick exhaled an overly-dramatized huff, then tapped redial. After six rings, she held an index finger in front of Lindstrom and said, "Rivers. Angie. Just confirming our breakfast plans. Call me, okay." She looked up at Lindstrom and shrugged her shoulders. "Don't get your undies in a bunch, sweetie. Nobody skips town on the assassin before sunup."

Lindstrom smoothed his mustache. "Yea, but I know what I heard. He left here with fifteen grand in his pocket and I've got a bad feeling. Did you guys make any plans, other than knocking boots and cracking eggs?"

McCormick rolled her eyes and flipped her shoulder-length hair away from her face. "Nah, he mentioned something about delivering a truck to Grand Forks tomorrow morning." She paused and scrunched her face as she processed the evening's provocative conversations.

"What is it?" Lindstrom asked, grabbing her shoulders.

"The two biker dudes seated at the end of the bar took no interest in my boobs—which is kinda weird. They were very curious about Rivers, though."

Lindstrom peeked down at Angie's chest. "They're gay." Then he shook his head and tugged at his whiskers. "The scanner mentioned northbound 29. Rivers could be on the run. C'mon, let's get our boy."

"You go ahead," McCormick said, fidgeting with her arms folded across her chest. "I get motion sickness at the drop of a hat." Then she flipped her hair and placed her hand on Lindstrom's shoulder. "Dude, I hate to break it to ya, but your crazy scanner calls are a bunch of hooey." She pointed her thumb towards the door. "I'm heading over to the hotel. I'll text you a selfie from our hot tub. If you're lucky, it'll be a shot of the twins bobbing up for air."

McCormick cupped her chest with both hands and licked her lips. Then she folded a piece of mint chewing gum into her mouth and strutted away. Lindstrom rolled his eyes, then turned the opposite direction, jogging for the staff parking lot.

Thanks to a six hundred horsepower Hemi and a stroke of good luck, Lindstrom caught up with Rivers on I-29, two miles south of Argusville. The black pickup was easy to spot behind the red and blue flashes of a state trooper's light bar. Despite the cop's frantic waving and his insistence to drive ahead, Lindstrom pulled to the shoulder. He parked behind the police cruiser, then stepped out, holding his security badge above his head.

Lindstrom took two steps before the trooper stomped his foot and shouted at him. "Sir, get back in your vehicle. Unless there's nukes in the air, best be on your way. Don't push me—I've got a second set of cuffs just your size."

Lindstrom pointed to his badge. "This is an emergency. I'm a retired sheriff. You can haul me in. Just let me explain first. Your driver's an acquaintance of mine." Lindstrom watched and waited as the trooper held up an index finger, then gave terse direction through the Ford's driver's side window.

The trooper was a middle-aged man, average height but thick, sporting a beer belly that sagged over his belt buckle. He had a bald, wrinkled head stuffed into a campaign hat, and his face featured a bushy mustache and two bushy eyebrows, all salt and pepper in color.

The trooper lumbered towards Lindstrom, requesting some identification. Then, after scrutinizing the driver's license, the officer said, "First off, Lindstrom, your casino badge don't mean shit to me. I asked you to get back into your car—you hard of hearing, or just itchin' to spend a night in the hoosegow?" Lindstrom held his ground, not responding. The trooper waited for a pair of eighteen wheelers to roar past, then pointed at his name badge. "Okay, then. Name's Mauch. Let's have it."

Lindstrom folded his arms across his chest and shook his head. The two men locked eyes for a few seconds. Lindstrom broke their stare-down, turning to watch the orange running lights of semis parading south towards Fargo-Moorhead. He took a deep breath, then raised his chin at the black Ford. "I caught a PD report on my scanner about fifteen minutes ago. If that's Dean Rivers up there, then his son was just taken to Sanford General. He's not answering his phone. I wanted to catch him and point his ass back to Fargo."

Mauch glanced at his watch. "Fifteen minutes from Fargo? You must've been hauling ass, boy. Speed limit is seventy through here." Again, the two exchanged hard stares.

"Considering the circumstances..." Lindstrom paused, surveying the endless darkness of the surrounding countryside. "Why'd you pull him over?"

"Funny you should ask." Mauch mulled over Lindstrom's question, tapping the man's ID on his chin. "Not that it's any of your business. But I stopped him because his temporary plate is hanging by a thread." The officer turned and pointed his thumb at the truck.

"I ran the VIN, and guess what? Salvage vehicle. Rivers stole it and slapped a hijacked temp tag on the back. That truck's headed to a chop shop."

Lindstrom peered through Mauch's flashing emergency lights. Before he could appeal, the trooper bared a devilish grin and said, "Your boy has alcohol on his breath. You stickin' around for the sobriety test? C'mon, this should be fun." Then the smirk drained from the officer's face. "Can you confirm your whereabouts this evening? I've got a feeling this is a team effort and I have half a mind to run you both in. Grand theft auto carries a one year minimum sentence in this state, but you already knew that, being a security guard and all."

Lindstrom's slow burn didn't last very long. He blurted out a laugh, then leaned into the trooper's face. "Shit, Kojak. You got all that from a dangling plate? That's fuckin' impressive." Lindstrom tucked his badge into his back pocket, then poked Mauch in the chest with his index finger. "You gonna bet your job on an obsolete database and a stupid hunch?"

Lindstrom poked the trooper again, harder. "Rivers picked up the Ford from Wenner Motors earlier this afternoon—paid cash for it. I've been pacing the casino floor since four o'clock and my goddamn feet are killing me. The only connection you'll find between me and Dirty Dean Rivers is my boss, Big Bill Wenner."

Lindstrom smoothed his mustache, then held his wrists out to the trooper. "Best get to work with those cuffs, mister. Won't make a damn bit of difference. I'll still kick your pudgy ass way into next week."

Mauch glared at Lindstrom, then chewed his lip as he looked over his shoulder at the shiny black Ford. He dropped his right hand down to his belt holster as his eyes returned to Lindstrom's face. He spent the next few seconds kicking pieces of gravel into the weeds. "Big Bill's your boss, ya say? And that truck's from his lot?"

Lindstrom crossed his arms and nodded his head, flashing a knowing grin. Mauch said, "Fuck this shit! You boys got bigger problems than this state's penal system." The trooper tossed Lindstrom's ID license at his chest, then turned for his cruiser. "I suggest you follow Mr. Rivers to the hospital. Honor the posted limits, because I guarantee the next flatfoot won't be so understanding." Mauch trudged to his cruiser, slammed the door and killed the flashing lights. Seconds later, the cruiser roared away, leaving a spray of shoulder gravel and road dust in its wake.

Rivers stepped from the pickup. "What the hell are you doin' here? And what the hell was that about?"

Lindstrom rolled his eyes and shook his head. "Long story. Nice truck. Trooper wanted to slap you with GTA and a DUI. Are you drunk?"

"Hell nah," Rivers said. "That tub of lard is a grade A asshole." Rivers touched his nose and recited the alphabet backwards just to prove his point.

Lindstrom grabbed Rivers by the elbow and spun him towards the truck. "Stop being a smartass for one minute and listen. You need to get over to the hospital and check on your son. I'd go with you but I just got an emergency call—a missing persons thing in Devils Lake. If I don't get shot, I'll be back around noon tomorrow. Call me. We'll grab a beer. You better get going."

Dean Rivers parked in a secluded spot near the emergency entrance to Sanford General Hospital. Inside, the receptionist hit Rivers with a scrutinizing look, but confirmed Duane Rivers as an admitted patient. She said, "They just finished x-rays. Techs fit him with an air cast. Surgeon's evaluating the images." She handed the disheveled father a stack of forms to be completed while he sat in the waiting area.

Rivers studied the wall clock as he paced the floor of the emergency wing. After several failed attempts to get more information from the receptionist, he stepped outside for a smoke. He cupped his hands around the lighter, watching the hypnotic flame dance in front of his face. Then he snapped the lighter closed without lighting his smoke.

Rivers raised his eyes and stepped back from the curb as a white Taurus with Wenner Motors placards on the doors rolled along the emergency drive. He saw the bleary-eyed hitchhiker from the entrance ramp seated in the back. His grim face stared back at Rivers from under the shadow of his filthy hood. With a cigarette hanging from the corner of his mouth, Rivers eyeballed the Ford until it rolled out of sight.

He rushed back to the receptionist's counter, demanding to see his son. After several phone calls and a few frantic exchanges with the hospital staff, the receptionist, with worry moistening her eyes, said, "I'm sorry, sir. We can't find your son anywhere." Rivers slipped the medical forms from his shirt pocket and shredded them in the receptionist's face. He sprinkled the shreds across the counter, then turned and stomped out without saying a word.

Dean Rivers' cell phone vibrated as he climbed back into the pickup. He rejected the assassin's call, then blocked her number. After a minute of staring through the windshield, he twisted the key. The truck's starter whined, and the mysterious four-by-four growled to life.

Three miles away, at his small condo in West Fargo, Greg O'Leary tossed a lump of pizza crust back into the box. He jabbed his greasy finger at the TV remote, killing the late-night news. Following his frequent habit, he turned up the police scanner while he brushed his teeth and stripped out of his grimy softball uniform.

O'Leary ran a shower, then listened to the 10-52 call as steam clouded the vanity mirror. He glanced out to his living room and muttered at the half-eaten pizza resting on his bruised coffee table. "Reevers." He scrambled for his socks and stumbled while pulling up his pants. O'Leary cursed, then grabbed his keys from the end table and bolted out the door.

A freight train cooled his momentum, but thirty minutes later, the sleepy cop parked under a tree in the hospital's visitor's lot. He sipped black coffee and spied the emergency entrance. His patience running thin, he called the hospital and told the chief of staff to hold Rivers in recovery and to not allow him any visitors. The administrator told O'Leary that Rivers was sleeping through his evaluation, so O'Leary sat and waited.

After another thirty minutes, O'Leary watched a dark pickup leave the lot just as a matching black pickup pulled in and parked in front of the emergency entrance. Two Native Americans dressed in motorcycle leathers climbed from their truck and rushed into the hospital. O'Leary slipped his service revolver from the console, checked the safety, then held it in his lap. He drove across the lot and parked in front of the black Ford, blocking its escape.

Seconds later, the two shifty visitors exploded from the exit, charging for their truck. They surveyed the parking situation, and the taller man pointed at O'Leary. "Hey asshole, move that piece of shit!"

Officer O'Leary stepped from his SUV with his hands behind his back. "You boys seem to be in a hurry. Where's the fire?"

The shorter man, the one with hostile eyes, stepped closer. "Get the fuck out of the way before somebody gets hurt."

O'Leary grinned, pulling his badge and his thirty-eight from behind his back. "I'd say you're in luck, fellas," he said with a confident grin. Then he pointed up at the emergency room sign, glowing red above the hospital vestibule.

Chapter 9
Learning to Fly

"Well, I started out down a dirty road."

Sommers sailed northeast, thirty-five hundred feet above the golden waves of the Sheyenne National Grassland. Then, a short time later, he flew over the slow-moving, caramel-colored Red River. The topography change comforted him like an old blanket as he drifted into Minnesota's welcoming airspace. The patchwork quilt of forests, prairies, and fields stretched as far as he could see. But now the green and gold contours lay accessorized by hundreds of lakes sparkling like sapphires in the midday sun.

The pilot glanced at the array of gauges strewn along his instrument panel, then surveyed the countryside below. He watched fluffy cumulus clouds cast drifting shadows. Sommers imagined the dark splotches as dinosaurs roaming across the land. After a short time, he took a break from admiring the colorful panorama to scrutinize his cell phone. No messages from Sam, Lilly, or Bud. No texts from Jack Hughes or Joy Moon Deer.

Sommers shrugged and shook his head, trying to ditch his feelings of uncertainty. Despite his feeble attempts to distract himself, the pilot became contemplative while his airplane flew snug against the heavens. He heard only the hypnotic hum of the eighty-inch propeller, and the easygoing flight allowed Sommers to consider his life's undulating odyssey. At some point, middle-age wisdom overwhelmed his depression and guilt. He chalked it up to unfamiliar optimism and realized he'd spent too much of his emotional currency rationalizing ancient tragedies.

He recalled just turning ten when his father died in a suspicious fire at S & E Lumber. Later, in his early twenties, his inconsolable two-timing wife took a fatal leap off Victory Bluff. This was minutes after she discovered their infant son was lifeless in his crib. For years, the reclusive giant immersed himself in solitary professional pursuits, spending his days wallowing in anguish and detachment.

A decade later, Sommers' life took another dramatic turn. His mother, Gracie, the longtime family pillar, battled profound dementia. Her only child, on the brink of fifty, navigated a turbulent summer when organized crime and political corruption chased him down. Only three summers had passed since greedy shysters schemed to steal his family's homestead right out from under their feet.

Ten miles out, Sommers shook himself back to the present, spotting Victoria's unique circular shape among the countless other lakes. He'd made this arrival many times and still felt the warm flutter of anticipation when his beloved home came into view. The big lumberjack felt his geographic and emotional centers align each time he returned home.

Again, the pilot checked his gauges, then pressed the yoke forward, putting the plane into a gradual descent. He goosed the throttle and tapped an audio button on the instrument panel. Songs from one of his favorite playlists poured from the speakers, and soon, cowboy guitar chords and vocal harmonies filled the cockpit. He turned up the volume and grinned, flashing a peace sign with his fingers. V for Victoria.

Back in the day, Big Jim Thompson taught Sommers how to lean into his landings and enjoy the thrill of buzzing the tower. Sommers puckered his lips and nodded, recalling the day Thompson, a retired U.S. Senator, put the Cessna into a sheer dive just beyond the rocky edge of Victory Bluff. Thompson's plane streaked across the lake mere inches above the waves, before scattering the startled crowd gathered along the western shore. Forgotten by many, Sommers knew the barnstorming senator changed the course of history for the entire nation.

Senator Trish Bradley-Doyle's political supporters called Big Jim's impromptu airshow a reckless insurrection. However, months after the senator's fatal stumble from power, the FAA cleared Thompson of any wrong-doing. During his sit-down with Tucker, the candid cowboy from Idaho condemned the unelected bureaucracy and the political puppets. He wagged his finger in front of the camera and said, "To a crazy ship, all winds are contrary."

The locals had grown accustomed to Sommers' dramatic landings, and many were eager to take part. As his plane soared in at one-hundred-fifty knots, the pilot announced this day's arrival in roaring fashion. People who knew Sommers best realized these raucous entrances ran contrary to his humble nature. Those who misunderstood him thought he was a foolhardy show-off. The truth, as is often the case, lived somewhere in the middle. Simple as pie, Sommers just liked to celebrate his homecomings with family and friends.

Down at the intersection of Highway 5 and Route 11, Sommers spotted Gary Johnson power washing the picnic tables behind his popular convenience store. The famous artisan waved, then sprayed a stream of soapy water fifty feet into the air. Seconds later, Sommers swooped low over the Peterson Brother's southern cornfield. Al leaned out of the combine harvester and waved his baseball cap. His brother, Bob, rolling alongside in the off-load tractor, looked up and shook his fist. Since their birth, sometime around 1950, Bob had always been a tick or two slower than his older twin. The oft-repeated wisecrack at the DeRoxe Club was, you gotta keep looking out for number one because Bob Peterson's always stepping in number two.

Sommers recalled there was a time when flying low over Peterson Brothers Farm was a foolhardy stunt. Everyone knew those crusty ol' boys had itchy trigger fingers. The lifelong farmers would trample one another to see who could fire off the first shot. To reduce his risk of being blasted from the sky, Sommers glued a pair of giant PB Farm decals to the underside of his Cessna's wings. Later, after some arm twisting and two fifths of Kentucky bourbon, he took the guys up for a few laps above Lac Clair. It took Sommers sixty minutes and ten gallons of one-hundred octane to convince the militant hayseeds he wasn't moonlighting as a Canadian drug mule.

Sommers craned his neck, looking down to make sure the runway was clear. He tugged at his seatbelt and spied the orange windsock drooping from a pole above his hangar. Soon, he veered north and backed off the throttle, coasting above the north woods cemetery. The pilot tipped his hat to Pop Sommers, then punched the throttle, taking the Cessna higher and faster around the rugged north shore.

Moments later, just like Thompson, he put his airplane into a steep dive past Victory Bluff's salmon-colored face. His Uncle Grumpy, eighty-something and ornery as a snapping turtle, trolled the weed line along Townsend Drop-off. As the plane plunged towards him, the crusty bloke waved his sun-faded baseball hat, then flipped his nephew the bird for disrupting his walleye fishery.

Sommers streaked westward across the lake less than one-hundred feet above the sparkling ripples. On this warm Saturday afternoon, the pilot smiled, seeing many of his favorite people enjoying the summer sunshine. He spotted C. J. Hunter and Scooter Carlson cruising on the bartender's pontoon boat, tinkering with their depth finder again. Sommers knew their adjustments were flimsy excuses.

From behind their dark sunglasses, they liked to sip beer as they ogled the female sunbathers. The tipsy pair laughed and toasted Sommers with their beer cans as his plane zipped over their floating catbird's seat.

Sommers sped towards the southwest cove and trained his eyes on Jenny Roarke and Joy Moon Deer. The pair lay stretched out on a pair of loungers, catching rays from Hansen's dock. They wore nothing more than dark Ray-Bans, teensy-weensy bikinis, and a shiny layer of tanning lotion. Jenny raised her frosty tumbler in a toast, but Joy turned over on her chair, hiking up her thong. Sommers considered it a contentious gesture and wondered why Joy hadn't replied to his phone messages, asking himself, "I wonder what put the burr under her saddle?"

Jenny and Joy lived together, renting Andie Hansen's lake house for a pittance. Jenny worked as a shift nurse at Lakes General Hospital. She also provided in-home care for Sommers' mother. Under Jenny's care, Gracie's health improved. Her promising treatments included holistic meds, a regimented sleep schedule, and a judicious diet.

Jenny's spunky roommate, Joy Moon Deer, had worked as a detective with the Bureau of Indian Affairs. These days, she served as a deputy sheriff for the local county. Folks speculated the two libidinous women were more than just friends. But that wasn't any of his concern. Years earlier, he'd learned to distance himself from people's personal matters. Sommers, private as he was, always seemed to provide endless fodder for the area rumormongers.

Sommers pulled back on the yoke, and the plane climbed a lofty arch. He backed off on the throttle and aimed the nose north, fixing to double back to his favored southern approach. Sommers saw Rosie Carlson sweeping the patio at the DeRoxe Club. She waved her broom in the air as he zoomed overhead. Gracie Sommers, always busy, stood in the front yard, hanging laundry on a clothesline.

The pilot noticed her hair had turned white. He saw a clothespin hanging from the corner of her mouth as she twirled a small black t-shirt above her head.

At last, Sommers looked down to see Phelps, Grumpy's loyal mutt, jumping and barking along the sandy shoreline. A toddler wearing nothing but long curly hair and cut-off jeans ran in circles, splashing water at the playful pooch. The boy's outstretched arms looked like the wings of a spirited bird, like the wings on his father's small airplane.

Sommers took a deep breath and blinked the emotion from his eyes. He silenced the music and took another lap around the lake to absorb the scene. Soaking in deep sentiments, he watched with a full heart as Phelps and Noah danced and splashed in the shallows between the docks. Sommers doubted he'd ever view a scene as splendid as this, so close to perfection and aligning with his concept of heaven. The emotional pilot adjusted his baseball cap and lifted his eyes skyward. *"Our boy is safe."*

Following a supper that included grilled burgers, sweet corn, and watermelon wedges, Gracie scooped ice cream for dessert. Her son tucked Noah in for the night. The day filled with fresh air and fair water took their toll on the energetic youngster. Gracie caught her son on his way to the kitchen, handing him a chilled dish. "Bet it was lights out right when his head hit the pillow. That boy has only two speeds, neutral and full steam ahead. Any word from his momma?"

Sommers checked his phone, frowned, then shook his head.

Gracie bit her lower lip before licking an ice cream dribble from her spoon. She mustered a smile, then gushed about her grandson. "I knew he was a Sommers the moment I laid eyes on him—toughest rug rat I've ever seen. Smart as a whip, too. This morning, he dug a hole in the sand, filled it with water, then poked little sticks in the ground all around it. He said it was Noah's little lake."

Gracie clinked her spoon on the dish and stared out at the bluff. "Wish your father was here to see all this." Then, following her moment of wistful reflection, she snapped back. "Yep, that boy's a chip off the old block, no doubt about it." Then her expression turned serious. "So, mister. When were you planning to tell me I was a grandmother again? I'm not getting any younger, ya know."

He shrugged his shoulders and shook his head. "It's kinda complicated, Ma." Then he changed the subject. "How did Noah get here? I mean, who delivered the package?"

Joy sat on the screened-in porch, watching the sunset cast orange glints across the water. She ate vanilla ice cream drizzled with chocolate syrup. After slurping a milky bite, she raised her spoon in the air. "I brought him in the cruiser. He thought it was cool when I tooted the siren. Anyway, the clerk at the courthouse said a young woman dropped him off at the front desk. She mentioned you by name, then took off before they could question her."

Sommers swallowed his spoonful of chocolate, then rubbed his temples. Joy's story was the first sliver of acknowledgement he'd gotten from her in months and he tried hiding his surprise behind his headache. "Woman?" He asked. "Didn't you get a name? What did she look like?"

Gracie waved her spoon in the air, shaking her head as she turned to join Grumpy in front of the TV.

Moon Deer stepped into the kitchen and took a seat at the table, her bare arms and legs tanned from hours in the sun. She licked chocolate sauce from her spoon. "No name, young, with curly blond hair. Oh, I almost forgot. There's a duffle filled with the kid's clothes and shit. I stuck it in the closet behind you."

The description left little doubt in Sommers' mind. It was Lilly

LeBlanc who brought Noah to Lac Clair. He rummaged through the bulky duffle, searching for clues. Soon, he came across a picture postcard that had slipped into a crease hidden near the bottom of the bag. The front of the card featured a stylized photograph of Grahams Island, a trendy tourist destination within Devils Lake. The back was blank except for the words *"Time for Me to Fly"*, written in artistic calligraphy.

Sommers, brimming with curiosity, held the card to his nose. Then, with a single sniff, those ominous storm clouds from the Dakotas rushed forward and absorbed him. With his hopes dashed, and his future blurred, Sommers' heart sank like a boat anchor wrapped in a tangle of mucky weeds. The intimate fragrance, wood-sage and sea salt, hit him like a tidal wave. There was no mistaking her calling card. The calculated message from Samantha showcased her penmanship and her unmistakable scent. Sommers knew, deep down, the cryptic note was also her casual way of saying goodbye.

Sommers slumped to the floor. Phelps sat beside him and lapped the melting ice cream from the jolted man's dish. He caught Joy scrutinizing the troubled look on his face. He felt himself drifting back into familiar waters as he stared into the bottom of his ceramic dish. Once again, trying to rationalize the inexplicable.

Sommers, his sullen trance broken by Grumpy's cursing and Gracie's laughter in the next room, glanced at the dusty old clock hanging above the stove. Then he looked across at Joy. "I'm meeting Julie and Jack at the club in a little while. How about if you join us?"

Moon Deer, never one to hide her emotions, pointed her spoon at Sommers' nose. "Hell no! You ghost me for three fucking years, and now you want a goddamn shoulder to cry on? Let me tell you, buster. It's pretty shitty always being the consolation prize."

Nurse Jenny, her fair skin sunburned pinkish red, placed her empty bowl and spoon in the kitchen sink. She grabbed two oatmeal cookies from a Mr. Potato Head pottery jar, then tip-toed to the front porch, avoiding eye contact with the quarreling pair.

Sommers stood and adjusted his baseball hat. He studied the postcard again, then slipped it into his back pocket. "I'm not sure what you mean by ghosts, but it's… It's just complicated, that's all." Then he made a sour face, feeling a twinge in his gut. "I'm sorry," he said, with all the meager emotion he could muster.

Sommers waved goodnight to his mother and uncle, then stepped into the yard. He trudged along the trail through the south woods, pondering how he'd gotten into such a predicament. An obsessive planner, he tried, but couldn't seem to focus on his next moves. It wasn't intentional, but his philandering and secrecy alienated those closest to him. He looked out across the glossy lake, then glared at Victory Bluff. Sommers wagged his finger and warned the phantom, known by very few as The Watcher.

Soon, the sound of footsteps interrupted his thoughts as Joy came jogging up the trail to meet him. She punched his good shoulder, then stood with hands on her hips, catching her breath. "On second thought, I could use a fuckin' drink. You're buyin', kiddo."

She examined his hands, and Sommers knew Joy was searching for a wedding band. She looped her arm under his and looked up at the stars. "Seems to me we've been down this path before. How 'bout you start at the beginning? And try not to say anything stupid. You'll leave me no choice but to shoot your sorry ass."

Before Sommers could answer, Joy stopped, took a deep breath, and then glanced over her shoulder at the haunting face rising from the eastern shore. After several seconds of heavy silence, she slapped the big man's backside, then tugged at his arm. "Let's go. I'm fuckin' thirsty."

Chapter 10
S.O.S.

"Where are those happy days? They seem so hard to find."

Nestled on the western shore of Lake Victoria, the DeRoxe Club bustled with a balmy summer energy. Some in the exuberant Saturday night crowd watched the Vikings game showing on the big screen TV while many patrons were there to eat, drink, and socialize. Sommers plopped eight quarters into the jukebox as Joy Moon Deer huddled a round of beers from Scooter Carlson at the bar.

The pair met near the bar entrance, then shuffled through the crowd, sharing greetings and making small talk about the weather. After a few minutes of mingling, they slid into a corner booth, joining their friends, Jack and Julie Hughes. The two women clinked their bottles, sipped their beers, then joined the crowd, singing along with a catchy ABBA song pumping from the Wurlitzer Bubbler.

Rosie Carlson brought a nacho platter to their table and gossiped with the ladies. When the girls got together, their conversation always devolved into a steamy debate. Who possessed the firmest buns and which of the three featured the nicest bosom? Their lewd discussion sent Sommers into a fit of nervous laughter. But not tonight. His eyes were distant, his mind somewhere else. His grim thoughts jumped forward and back, and from place to place.

Jack snapped his fingers to get Sommers' attention. He cocked his head towards the TV and sputtered through his lips. "Looks like the Vikings are committing to mediocrity early this year."

Sommers glanced up at the TV while drawing a swig from his Coca-Cola bottle. He belched, then wiped his mouth with the back of his hand. "Yep, sure looks that way, leaky offensive line." The big lumberjack watched Rosie skip away to another booth, then he lifted his chin at Julie. "Did Schmitty get ahold of you?" He asked, spinning his empty bottle on the table. "Any updates on the Fulgham kid?"

Julie Hughes, an aspiring lawyer working as a private investigator for her husband, set her beer down and shook her head. "I'm driving up to Kittson County tomorrow. I got his phone records and GPS data from our BCA contact. Fulgham's boss sent him out for water samples. Tommy was parked along the Red River north of Drayton when he last checked in." Julie poked around the nacho platter, digging for chicken and cheese with a tortilla chip. "The strange thing is, the truck sent overnight pings from Pembina County hours after his cell phone went dead. What the hell would Fulgham be doing in North Dakota at 3:00 AM?"

Sommers pursed his lips and scratched at the whiskers on his chin. "I'd go with you, but I need to fly out to Spearfish tomorrow morning."

Moon Deer shot Sommers a flinty look, downing the rest of her beer in a single gulp. She burped and pointed the empty bottle at Julie. "Shit. I'd like to tag along. But only if you plan to rattle cages and bust heads."

Sommers tapped Moon Deer's shoulder and held his finger in front of her face. She shouted as she brushed his hand aside. "Don't fuckin' shush me! If Jules wants a ride-along, then I'm going, damn it."

Jack lifted his chin at Sommers and chimed in, interrupting the fray. "You know we've got a clipper blowing in, right? I don't think you're getting outta here for a few days." The table fell silent, then Jack cleared his throat and asked, "How 'bout you tell us what's going on? The last time you pulled us all together, we started cracking safes and mobilizing forces against an evil red-head."

Sommers adjusted his baseball cap, then tapped the tabletop with a bottle cap. "Y'all know that Noah's here at the lake. My mom's watching him down at the cabin." After a lengthy pause, he took a deep breath, then exhaled his heavy sigh. "Sam's gone missing and I can't reach Lilly. Could be trouble. Big trouble."

He searched his friends' faces, looking for their backing. "We have a friend in Sturgis. He told me he'd drive out to check on things at the lodge." Sommers stared into his pop bottle, then shook his head. "I haven't heard back from him since early this morning." Sommers, the consummate servant to others, glanced out at the lake and realized he couldn't fix everything himself, not this time. "I need answers and I need some muscle to help me get 'em." He chewed on his lower lip, then shook his head again. "Noah."

Julie dabbed cheese sauce from her lip and said, "You could also use someone to look after things here at the lake."

Joy slammed her bottle on the table. "What the hell do I look like, fuckin' chopped liver?" She crunched on a chip, then spewed crumbs through her profanity. "Shit, Dale! Why didn't you call the sheriff's office or the fuckin' feds?"

Sommers tried calming Joy, then thought better of it. Instead, he pulled the cryptic postcard from his pocket and slid it across the table to Jack, his trusted friend and attorney.

After looking around the barroom, Jack flipped the card over twice, examining each side. Then he held it to his nose and took a sniff. "Yep, that's her alright," he said with a nod. "If I'm reading this right, she's long gone. Back to being Hawk and trying to cut her ties with the syndicate." Jack pointed his beer bottle at Sommers, then locked eyes with Moon Deer. "Let's assume I'm right. That means he can't go to the cops. Sam's trying to eradicate her nefarious past. Out of necessity, she's gone rogue."

Moon Deer waved her hands in the air, then covered her ears. She leaned in closer, nose to nose with Sommers. "Is that why you didn't marry her? Sam's a money-laundering, drug-trafficking mob boss. Even a dumbshit like you should know that. What the hell have you gotten us into? Looks to me like you rolled out the red carpet and invited the monsters to destroy us. Thanks a hell of a lot, man."

His eyes sank to the floor. Jack grabbed Moon Deer's arm just as she wheeled to punch Sommers in the chest. The quick-witted lawyer took a drink, then tapped his finger on the table. "Look, their arrangement is complicated. There's no denying that. We can blame political entanglements, financial complexities, and even their geographic challenges. But I can assure you, there's no lack of commitment. As the big guy's legal counsel and financial trustee, I advised him not to marry Samantha, even though that was his intent."

Jack shifted in his seat, then tapped his index finger on the table. "She knew he wanted a child. She knew damn well the big guy's roots were planted deep, right here. So, their unusual agreement was her idea. It's not Ozzie and Harriet, but under the circumstances, it's legally and financially prudent."

Moon Deer's mouth hung open as she turned to face Julie. "Prudent, my ass! Were you aware of this bullshit?" Julie shrugged her shoulders and nodded. Then she stuffed a tortilla chip into her mouth before excusing herself to fetch another round of drinks.

Moon Deer stood to leave, but Sommers snatched her arm, holding her back. "I need you to fly to Spearfish with me." He watched the anger drain from her face as she sank back into her seat. "If there's a better tracker than you, then I haven't met 'em." He cleared his throat and fiddled with the bill of his baseball hat. "I realize it's awkward, but I sure could use your help."

Julie came back to the table carrying three beers and a Coke for Sommers. She was about to speak, but Jack kept talking, trying to persuade the big lumberjack. "C'mon, man. I just cleaned and calibrated my .38. You realize I have a history with Patricia Hawkins. Why can't I go with you?"

Julie cleared her throat and grimaced, her disapproval obvious to everyone seated around the table, even Jack.

Sommers took a sip, then set his bottle down and began counting on his fingers. "First, I appreciate your offer. But I've seen your itchy trigger finger in action. And to be frank, your aim ain't all that great." Sommers kept counting as Julie and Joy nodded in agreement. "Second, I need you here at the lake. I think you'd agree. It's just too risky for both of us to go."

Jack pouted while tapping his fingers on the table. "If you're gonna be pigheaded enough to leave me behind, then let me suggest a manhunter for you, a detective with the Fargo PD, and a former Army Ranger. You remember Greg O'Leary? He spearheaded the Potter investigation." Jack sipped his beer, dabbed his lip, then said, "Got himself into a bit of hot water, a hush-hush excessive force incident. I'm negotiating the terms of his termination. Both sides want the incident to go away without creating a messy standoff." Jack dug his cell phone from his pocket. "He doesn't look like much, but O'Leary's an ass-kicker, and a marksman to boot—perfect for your expedition. I'm texting you his contact card."

Sommers nodded and said thanks. Then Julie asked to see the postcard. After studying the picture, she snapped photos of the front and back with her phone. "You're gonna need more than Moon Deer and O'Leary. Grahams Island is off the beaten path, pretty deep into Native territory. And with Sam on the move, you're gonna need another tracker."

Moon Deer asked, "How the hell did you know all that? You ever been to Grahams Island?" She swirled her beer and inhaled a deep breath as she gazed up at the rafters. "How about Ted Lindstrom?" She asked the big man.

Sommers shrugged, lifting his palms in the air.

Moon Deer scowled and waved him off. "Ted's a good dude. Works security at the Silver Wolf in Fargo. He's looking for any old excuse to get outta that shithole. Ted's got first-hand experience with the whole Hawk and Hammer thing. He's a retired sheriff with BIA connections—got a nose like a fuckin' bloodhound. Ted rolls old school. Trust me, he's the right man for you." Moon Deer's thumbs started tapping her phone with a flurry. "Another bonus, he's made a small fortune as a badass bounty hunter. I'm shootin' him a text right now."

Julie said, "Good thinking, sis. Send your dog straight to Devils Lake while y'all check on things in Spearfish—cast a wider net."

To those outside her inner circle, Julie came across like a blonde-haired bimbo with ADHD. But Sommers knew she possessed a genius-level IQ and a photographic memory. Hardened by abuse and ready for a fight, Julie had a black belt in Jiu-Jitsu, and a concealed-carry gun permit.

Sommers finished his soda, then stood and fished some change from his pocket. "Okay, then. Guess that settles it. Since the weather is working against me, our little posse will reconvene here tomorrow night." Then the exhausted man tipped his hat and pivoted towards the jukebox, where he dropped his last eight quarters into the glowing contraption. C.J. Hunter, a retired firefighter, snuck up behind him and slapped him on the back. Sommers gasped, almost jumping out of his boots.

Hunter erupted with a booming laugh. He'd been drinking since noon and his words slurred through his woozy smile. "Captain Sommers, how the hell are ya?" The two exchanged a handshake, then engaged in small talk about boats and motorcycles. Hunter wobbled and scratched at his beard, looking as though something profound was about to escape his lips. "Say, here's one from outta the blue," he said, wiping his mouth after belching a wet hiccough. "A couple of Indian fellas came by the store last week asking about Hank. They were dressed like bikers, and I wondered if Halloween came early this year. Anyway, one was a tall drink of water, the other was a little wise ass with a Napoleon complex. You remember Henry Two Horse, doncha?"

Sommers felt for the nasty scar running down his left side. "Hammerin' Hank, how could I forget?"

"That's right. Anyway, these guys wanted to see the upstairs apartment—said they were old friends looking for his belongings. They kept asking about that fancy truck of his."

"Interesting. They ask about me?" Sommers turned and pressed a few buttons on the jukebox. "What did you tell them?"

"I told 'em to fuck off, that's what I told 'em. Pickup's long gone, and the apartment's been empty for two years—just storage nowadays." Hunter sipped his draft beer, then wiped the foam from his mouth before burping. "Shit Sommers, you're a goddamn phantom. We never see you. How the hell would those Indians know you even exist?"

Hunter chugged the last of his beer, leaned in closer, then shared the rest of his story. "Funny thing is, no sooner than those two posers leave, a couple of badass cops come strolling in, asking the same stupid questions. If they wanted intel on Hank's truck, the dumbasses could've run the VIN through the DMV database. It wasn't all bad, though. One of 'em got eyes for that bass boat sitting in the front window. Maybe they were just trying to feel me out, seeing if I was involved with Hank's friends. Anyway, I thought you'd like to know, since you've always thought Hammer's pickup had a whammy on it."

"No worries there," Sommers said. "C'mon buddy, you think

Hank had any real friends?" Before Hunter could answer, Sommers patted his jolly friend on the shoulder and winked. "I plunked two dollars into this thing. Here, pick a couple of songs you and Doris can dance to."

Hunter's laugh rumbled like the V-twin engine on his Harley. "Shit. If I want to frost Doris's twinkie, all she's gotta do is straddle my hog." Sommers shook his head, smirking at his friend's crass humor. Then his thoughts shifted to his son. Sommers tipped his baseball cap to Hunter and turned for the door without saying goodnight.

An hour later, after checking on his sleeping boy, Sommers and Moon Deer rested at the end of Hansen's dock, dangling their toes in the water and staring at the macabre moonlit face of Victory Bluff. Sommers skipped a flat stone across the glassy cove. "There's no logical reason, but I think there's a connection between Sam's exodus and Tommy Fulgham's disappearance."

Moon Deer shifted closer and pointed to where Sommers had skipped his rock. "Trouble ripples like water," she said, slipping her arm around his waist and leaning into his side. "I'm gonna request some time off. You know this is gonna get messy, right?"

Sommers stared down into the blackness of the water. "Yep."

"You're never gonna see her again. You know that, right?"

"Yep," he said, tracing circles in the water with his big toe.

Joy exhaled a heavy sigh. "Someday, you're gonna wake the fuck up and realize everything you need is right here."

"I've always thought that. Maybe this is just a strange dream, some sort of misunderstanding." They sat together in dense silence. Sommers cleared his throat and lifted his face towards the waxing moon. "Got anything else on your mind?"

Joy shoved Sommers and slapped him on his back. "Shit, man. You don't wanna know. When you're fresh outta options and desperation has chewed your ass raw, then I'll tell you what's on my mind."

She reached up and kissed him on the cheek, then wagged her finger in his face. "Soon enough, ya big lug, soon enough."

Moon Deer gathered her shoes and socks, then stood to leave. "I'm fuckin' beat. I'll see you in the morning." Then she danced away, drifting into the shadows of the south woods. "That's one terrific kid you got there," she said over her shoulder.

Seconds later, Sommers heard Moon Deer singing one of the popular songs from DeRoxe's jukebox.

The big lumberjack closed his eyes and tuned in to the tiny waves lapping against the sea wall. A gentle breeze sent the puzzled father a message strung out in musical code. He could've sworn he heard Carl Sandburg's voice echo from the bulrushes. "*A child is God's opinion that the world must go on.*"

Chapter 11
I'm Movin' On

"That big eight-wheeler rollin' down the track…"

The filthy, battered teen cracked his crusty eyelids open enough to peek at a peach-colored sunrise beginning to kindle. "Where the fuck are we?" The boy's words sputtered from his mouth, garbled and sleepy, and he struggled to prop himself upright in the F-150's passenger seat. "Ah shit. What time is it?" He asked, rubbing his face and peeking through his fingers at the driver. He let the musky smell of leather flow into his nostrils. "Sweet ride. Fuckin' stole it, didn't you?"

The boy's father, Dean Rivers, put the Ford in park, then pointed at the revolving door leading into the emergency room. "Hospital," he said. "Almost six o'clock. Truck belongs to my boss."

Duane Rivers blinked his sleepy, bloodshot eyes. "Too fuckin' early, man." Then he smacked his parched lips. "How the hell did you find me?"

"Passed out in Wenner's parking lot, reclining against a white Taurus." He pointed with his chin and changed the subject. "Your hand looks pretty jacked up. You need to get it looked at." The driver stabbed at buttons, unlocking doors and adjusting the mirrors. He started the emergency flashers and asked, "Who the hell did that to you? You still runnin' with them beaners?"

"Don't be such a fucking bigot," Duane said with a huff, working a kink out of his neck. "It's a long story. Besides, what the hell do you care?"

The boy's father rolled his eyes and raised his palms. "Hey, just tryin' to help, here. You've got my ear. Why can't you tell me what happened? And if it was those shithead gangbangers, I swear to God...."

"It was a cop, alright!" Duane shifted in his seat and stared out the passenger window, avoiding eye contact with the miserable man behind the wheel. "A fuckin' pig beat me with a baseball bat," he said, resignation seeping through his sigh. "Ya fuckin' happy now?"

"Cop? Gimme a name. We'll sue him into oblivion." Rivers shook his head and lowered the driver's side window. He lit a cigarette and sat squinting at the sunshine blooming in his rearview mirror. Then he sniffed and said, "Stinks like a wet dog's ass in here." He blew his puff of smoke out the window. "So, what'd you do?" He asked. "Cops don't go around beatin' on white kids for no reason."

"I ain't got time for this." Duane fidgeted, picking at the dried mud on his boots. "Don't know why you brought me here. I ain't got no money, no goddamn insurance either."

Rivers stared at the steering wheel, squeezing its leather grip with his tanned, calloused hands. After a moment of quiet that lingered too long, he shook his head and tossed a thick envelope into his son's soiled lap. "That's ten grand. Now get in there and get your hand fixed before you end up disabled for good. Gotta phone?"

The fusty teenager lifted his mangled arm and laughed with a note of resignation. "Can't reach it. Phone's dead, busted to shit, anyway." He stuffed the cash into the front pocket of his bloodstained hoodie, then strained to open the door with his left hand. Duane turned back and asked, "Where the hell are you going? You're not coming in?"

The boy waited for an answer that wasn't coming. Then he shook his head and groaned as he stumbled into the parking lot. "Guess it don't fuckin' matter, right?" The battered teen slammed the truck's door and stared at his ghastly reflection in the glossy black finish.

Dean Rivers lowered the window and leaned over. "I gotta get this truck to Grand Forks by eight—another five grand is riding on it. They're gonna keep you here for a day, maybe two, because of the drugs. I'll circle back to check on you. How 'bout I bring you a new phone?"

The staggering teen flipped his father the bird and shouted over his shoulder. "Don't fucking bother. I'll be long gone by then."

Rivers sat with the truck idling and watched his wounded, bitter son wrestle with the revolving door. He felt bad, but not that bad. He recalled his own rough upbringing in rural North Dakota. The beatings, the emotional abuse, and the persistent neglect never drifted far from his consciousness.

Rivers closed the window, cranked up the AC, then put the truck in drive. The coldhearted loaner had no intention of ever returning to Fargo. He shrugged his shoulders and muttered to himself. "Some folks just gotta learn the hard way."

Minutes later and miles from the hospital, Rivers checked his rearview mirrors. He considered the previous night's drama and stuck to the back roads. The grizzled farmhand tapped through the radio presets, turning left onto Minnesota 75. He'd already seen the North Dakota side in slow motion. Now he made tracks up The King of Trails, a somewhat scenic leg of America's original highway system. The rolling meadows and the jutting escarpments provided a vivid contrast to the camel-colored prairies of Pembina County.

Rivers tapped the screen on his phone and discovered he'd missed three calls from Ted Lindstrom. He snorted like a crimped hog, then deleted the messages without listening to them. Rivers crossed a narrow bridge over the lazy Buffalo River, then lowered the driver's window and fired another cigarette. He turned up the radio and thought about Jerry Reynolds driving through Pleasant Valley without a care in the world. Johnny Cash legitimized what both men had long known. Life without strings was a darn good way to roll.

Four cigarettes later, Rivers drove along the northern reaches of what the locals called The Forks. He zig-zagged his way through a decaying industrial park near English Coulee. The boarded-up, graffiti-sprayed buildings, cracked sidewalks, and mucked-up streets hinted this area was past its prime. Rivers shook his head, believing it was unlikely the crumbling neighborhood ever enjoyed an actual heyday.

Halverson's was a seedy hole-in-the-wall auto body shop nestled between Mill Road and Business 81. Rivers, tired and hungry, reeked of smoke and three-day sweats. He arrived a few minutes early and felt desolation and suspicion hanging in the morning fog. He cruised around the block, scouting the rutted streets for serpents. Next, he turned right onto Bacon Avenue and parked in a rail yard where he could spy the humdrum garage from an inconspicuous distance.

Rivers flicked his cigarette butt out the window, then silenced the radio. "Well, I'll be damned," he said as he shifted in his seat. Sitting in the alley opposite him was the truck he'd seen the previous night. The black F-250 looked very similar to the F-150 he was driving. His two Indian friends from the casino sat inside, gnawing on breakfast sandwiches. "Shit," he said, rubbing his growling stomach. "I could devour a whole sack of them McNothins in 'bout five minutes."

Rivers leaned forward against the steering wheel and watched as the two men stepped out and tossed their trash into a rusty dumpster riddled with dents. The short man sipped coffee from a paper cup while the taller man performed half-assed gunslinger tricks with his revolver. Time passed, and the men sagged against their Ford's fenders, yawning and checking their cell phones. Rivers cracked his knuckles, feeling this rendezvous had all the earmarks of a setup. He whispered and shook his head. "Ed Norman, you hideous bastard. You had me duped from the get-go."

He put his truck in reverse and inched around the corner of a loading dock, where he could observe the oblivious hunters. After fumbling with his phone, Rivers dialed Wenner's number. No answer. Then he dialed the number posted above Halverson's garage door. Again, no answer, but a recorded message said the shop's number was no longer in service.

His skepticism billowing like a storm cloud, Rivers sent a roguish text message to his back-stabbing boss. *Shop closed. Heading back on 29.*" Then, a minute later, he watched the short Indian splash his coffee on the ground and begin tapping his phone. Soon, the two ruffians jumped into their truck and sped west on 24th Avenue, racing for the Interstate.

Rivers chuckled to himself, turning left on Washington Street with no workable plan. He licked his lips and scanned the roadside advertising, seeking a pair of golden arches. The musing driver pointed his truck south and lamented his dicey return to Fargo. Lady Luck, so tantalizing the previous day, abandoned him hours ago. He rapped the steering wheel with his thumbs and caught his sunken eyes in the mirror. Rivers mumbled at his drawn reflection. "That blubbery beast was right, this goddamn truck's snake-bit."

One hundred miles west of The Forks, perched on a ridge overlooking Black Tiger Bay, a cunning bird of prey watched Conrad Kelly prepare for his morning swim. For the past three days, Samantha Stevens, Patricia Hawkins, a.k.a. Hawk studied the man's early morning ritual.

Kelly would strip out of his slippers and robe in the predawn darkness, then swim the half-mile strait to a tiny island in Devils Lake. After twenty minutes of yoga poses, he'd stretch out on the granite slab and meditate until the sunrise warmed his skin. Then he'd swim back to the forested peninsula, dress, and hike home. Kelly's routine lasted sixty minutes.

Hawk appreciated the man's commitment to his physical wellness. His propensity for dramatic machinations was another matter. She whispered as she swiped the zipper closed on her tactical pack. "Soak it up, Chief. Gonna be your last dip for a while."

Conrad Kelly, one of five DSS Chiefs presiding over the Dakota Sioux Syndicate, was enjoying the height of his power. The other leaders, lacking his sway, gave Kelly a wide berth. Known as Snakes, the DSS functioned like any other consortium of organized crime. They engaged in drug trafficking, racketeering, and prostitution—cannibalizing their own to make a buck. A far cry from revered tribal elders, The Chiefs were mob bosses ruling the largest reservations sprinkled across the Upper Midwest. Conrad Kelly and his ruthless minions controlled the sleazy underbelly of the Spirit Lake Reservation.

Hawk, dressed in a form-fitting camouflage running suit, climbed down from her lookout and jogged through the woods. She paused and checked her watch, listening to the faint splashes of Kelly's breast strokes. Soon, Hawk arrived at a lakeside picnic shelter where the swimmer had stashed his robe and sandals. After scanning the area, she slipped the belt from the robe and tucked it in the front pocket of her hoodie. Next, she emptied the pockets, finding two condom wrappers and a house key tied to a floaty fob.

The crafty woman located a chunk of limestone riprap the size of a bowling ball and wrapped it in Kelly's robe. Then she hid the garments under a nearby spruce tree. Hawk slipped into the shade below the evergreens, where she waited, listening. No hikers or fishermen yet, just predator and prey.

Before she assumed her identity as Samantha Stevens, Patricia Hawkins led a sophisticated double life. By day, she worked as a nerdy, mild-mannered paralegal in the law offices of Doyle and Hughes. By night, she was a seductive, cold-blooded enforcer with the DSS—a sexy serpent armed with sharpened teeth and deadly venom. But that was years before Samantha's romance with Dale Sommers, years before Noah arrived out of the blue.

A coral-colored slice of sunshine climbed above the horizon beyond the lapping shore of Devils Lake. While Hawk studied Kelly, she considered her current situation and sat, unconvinced. Any expectation of peace was unrealistic for her and her loved ones, especially with a wicked past continuing to nip at Hawk's wings.

Like clockwork, Chief Kelly emerged from the bay naked as the day he was born, dripping wet. The dark-skinned, muscular man shook the water from his long hair, then froze when he realized his clothes were missing. Kelly searched the area, moving like a panther. He crouched among the trees, scanning his wooded surroundings.

Hawk outflanked him in the dim light, circling back to the shelter, where she replaced the Chief's balled-up robe and sandals. She cleared her throat and said, "Delightful morning for a swim. This summer's been a scorcher. Hard to imagine the lake being cold, but from the looks of you, it must be."

Conrad Kelly wheeled, self-assured, gazing upon the sharp-tongued woman. Their staring match lasted several seconds before he laughed with a huff. "Well, well. If it isn't my old flame, swooping in to crap all over me."

Troubled Water

Kelly stood tall and sturdy, his tattooed arms folded across his thick chest. "Care to take a swim? I remember how I used to warm your cockles." He waited for her reaction, dabbing at droplets clinging to his chin. "You're not dressed for the beach. What brings you to Spirit Lake?" He asked.

The sunrise climbed higher behind Hawk's back, making it difficult to see the details of her silhouetted face. "Warmth, she asked. "Even on your best day, you never came close to finding my cockles." Then she turned and gathered the Chief's heavy robe, holding it scooped in her arms. "I'll cut to the chase. Your Snakes are on my ass, following me all over the Dakotas. I came to find out why?"

Kelly inched closer, nodding his head. He asked, "What? No hello? No, hey how's the family?" She stood firm, not amused or intimidated. He shook his head and sputtered through his lips. "Snakes?" He asked. Then, after an extended pause, he flipped his hands above his head. "Okay, I'll play along. Your boy, Hammer, disrespected the nation. He bit the hand that fed him and disgraced Chief Barnes. Our scouts claim the big guy bought the farm a few years back. Shame, if that's true. They say his farewell tour was aboard a Harley with a long-legged woman straddling his waist—a woman matching your lithe description."

Hawk laughed, trying to disguise her duplicity. "Hammer, huh? Haven't seen that moocher in years. What'd he do? Drink himself to death."

"Don't know. Maybe he just rode off into the sunset." Kelly counted on his fingers as he spoke. "But before he burned rubber, he embezzled millions from member casinos. He was under contract to trim some fat from the syndicate. Since you're standing here gawking at my member, I'd say he never pulled his knife. Did you know he tried to blackmail Chief Barnes? Even an idiot knows that's a big fuckin' no-no. And you remember Stewbie, down at Lake Traverse? He's one twitchy ol' boy—got no sense of humor. Anyway, Hammer's disappearance has caused a bunch of three-letter agencies to crawl on us like ants on a Snickers bar."

Hawk bit her tongue to keep from laughing. She cocked her head, scrutinizing the naked man. "Believe me, your member's nothing to chirp about—I've ridden better. That said, your other shortcomings have nothing to do with me. Why don't you just tell the feds the truth? An operative went rogue, took some money, then flew the coop."

Chief Kelly squeezed water from his long, dark hair. "C'mon, sugar. You know it doesn't work like that." Then he cracked a wry grin. "We have to give them something to get 'em off our backs." Kelly crossed his arms and rocked on the balls of his bare feet. "Good guys, bad guys, what's the difference? They're all trying to find Hammer's truck. So, what can you tell me?"

Hawk took a step towards Kelly. "Black F-150 with chromed wheels and tinted windows? Hmm, I haven't seen it. Why don't you try the DMV? You know this has nothing to do with me. What crazy shit are you trying to pull here?"

"Listen. We know the two of you took a ride out to Crazy Horse. No one gives a shit about that asshole—we want our money and we want the feds off our backs." Kelly turned and glared at the water. "He was very protective of his truck. My scouts believe it's the key to putting closure on a series of embarrassing incidents. Personally, I think the syndicate is only looking for your help."

Hawk huffed, then shook her head. "Don't know what to tell you. Life is good, and I prefer to keep it that way."

Creases appeared on Kelly's forehead as he pursed his lips. Then he cocked his head to the side. "I see. Well, I told the boys it was a longshot, anyway. Can I have my robe back now?"

Hawk glanced over her shoulder at the lake, then turned back and said, "Some might assume I killed Hammer before he could fulfill his contract—that I took his money. That's what you told your lieutenants, isn't it?" After a few seconds of posturing and silence, Hawk became more deliberate and direct. "Henry was a dead man walking. He killed himself on that monument. Call off your boys and point them elsewhere. I'm worthless currency to the syndicate, and the feds won't touch me."

The two adversaries engaged in another staring match. Then Hawk said, "I've never been the patient kind. You know damn well I'll take care of things myself if the Snakes force my hand."

Kelly glared at Hawk. He stepped closer and snapped his fingers. "Okay, I'll call off the dogs. But speaking of boys. How's your little one? He doin' alright?"

A smoldering intensity ignited inside Hawk's chest. She stood silent for a long moment, plotting. Her fiery gaze sliced into the arrogant mob boss. She crept closer. "He's fine. And he'd better stay that way."

Still exposed, with trickles of water running down his neck, Kelly stood firm. He licked his lips, then smirked. "Are you sure about that? I got word of an accident in Spearfish Canyon. Well, naturally, my thoughts went to the boy."

"What the hell are you talking about? What accident?"

"Oh my, you haven't heard. LeBlanc's Subaru took a header into Squaw Creek. Spine-tingling, from what I've been told." Kelly rocked back and forth, sporting a sly grin. "Sorry, that's in poor taste. I'm just the messenger here."

Hawk choked back her emotions, but her arms trembled from the weight of the stone wrapped in red terry-cloth. Kelly extended his arms, and Hawk jumped at her chance. With all her might, she fired a basketball chest pass at Kelly. The jagged rock caromed off the man's forehead with a deadly crack. Then she sprang from the ground, unleashing a powerful kick that struck Kelly in his midsection.

The sudden jolts sent the Chief crumpling to the ground,

knocking him senseless. Hawk leaped on top of the stunned warrior, wrapping the belt around his neck and mouth, then binding his wrists. Kelly, bleeding and dazed, tried digging his feet into the sand as Hawk dragged him by his belt, face first, into the shallows of Pelican Bay.

Sixty seconds later, the frenzied flailing stopped, and Chief Kelly lay unresponsive, his body floating in three feet of ruddy water. Hawk unfurled the cloth belt, seeing no abrasions and no bruises. She nodded and said, "A diving accident. Now that's unfortunate." Then she shoved Kelly's body off and he drifted like a fallen log towards the granite island.

Hawk brushed over the footprints and blood spatter along the shore, then stood, soaking wet, catching her breath. She checked herself for injuries, then turned to take one last look at Conrad Kelly's suntanned ass sticking up from the water. She pondered the naked man's last words, then hissed at the floating corpse before ducking into the forest.

Soon, sweating and out of breath, she arrived back at the Black Tiger Campground. Satisfied by the lack of witnesses, she hustled into the rented RV and dug a burner phone from a hidden storage niche. She confirmed a weak signal, thought for a moment, then sent a cryptic message to Sommers. *"Is the box builder cutting gopher wood?"*

While waiting for a reply, she stripped out of her wet clothes and rinsed herself off in a hot shower. Then she rocked in the captain's chair while twirling a plastic spoon in her yogurt parfait. Twenty minutes passed, then, without warning, the cheap phone vibrated in her hand. Samantha took a moment to compose herself, allaying her fears. Curiosity overtook her anxiety, and she turned the phone to reveal the reply. *"Not today. Bird watching out back."*

Samantha exhaled an enormous sigh of relief and considered

calling her sturdy lumberjack. Instead, she plucked the SIM card and cracked the phone into pieces, tossing them into a nearby dumpster. Still coming down from her adrenaline rush, she climbed up into the cab and steered the rented motorhome onto Highway 20, aiming her rig for Lake Traverse. Samantha fluffed her damp hair as she bobbed her head in time with the music. She flashed a determined grin and thought, *"My boys are safe."*

Chapter 12
Straight Shooter

"Don't get me mad, don't tell no lie."

Greg O'Leary twiddled his fingers as he gazed out the small side window. He peered through a silvery veil of condensation; his view streaked by dozens of quivering raindrops racing across the tinted glass. "Let me get this straight," he said, chewing on a thin plastic straw. "You live in Minnesota, but Samantha lives in Spearfish. The two of you have a son and an au pair, and you bought this airplane so you could fly out to see 'em whenever you want." Then O'Leary scratched at his chin and nodded with cocked eyebrows. "Very unconventional."

O'Leary leaned back and examined Joy Moon Deer from the corner of his eye. "Listen, I'm in no position to judge. I'm divorced. Not all that recent, but my ex insists on a weekly booty call. Chinese takeout, craft beer, and some hanky-panky on the couch. Go figure, right?" He sipped his beer, then said, "I gotta say, the sex is hotter than when we were married. I think her lawyer included date nights as a stipulation in our dissolution agreement. Never read the damn thing, so who the hell knows?"

O'Leary gulped the rest of his beer, then muffled his belch.

"No matter how you slice it, I'm still paying for that damn couch. We should've avoided the solid color and kicked in for the Scotch Guard." He glanced across the narrow aisle at Moon Deer and smirked. Sommers watched her flash a grimace enhanced with an eye roll, disgust beaming like neon across her pouty face.

Sommers and O'Leary hit it off from the start. The big lumberjack appreciated the veteran's honesty and his no-nonsense, take-it-or-leave-it attitude. He estimated O'Leary stood five foot ten and weighed one hundred eighty pounds, built sturdy with the slightest hint of middle-age pudge showing at his beltline. He wore his thinning, light brown hair very short, and his hazel eyes were bright and alert. Even without knowing his history, Sommers saw O'Leary had ex-military splashed all over him—upright posture, observant senses, and a quiet confidence showing a readiness to take swift, aggressive action.

Moon Deer scrutinized O'Leary with a sideways glance, shaking her head. After shifting in her seat, she broke her silence and wagged a finger in the detective's face. "You come across like a dipshit ground pounder who can't get out of his own way. Jack built you up into some sort of heroic ass-kicker, but I gotta say, I don't fuckin' see it." She kicked off her shoes and folded her arms across her chest. "And you've been ogling at my boobs for the last forty-five minutes. Don't fuckin' deny it, cowboy."

Sommers grinned, listening to Joy's rant, and feeling relieved she wasn't directing her angst at him for once. He said, "Joy, anyone with a lick of sense knows you're a tease. You invite attention like a cow patty draws houseflies to a pasture."

She flipped him the bird, then closed her eyes, grinning as she settled in for a nap. The two men smirked as they exchanged looks of skepticism, then shrugged her off.

The elite team of trackers had spent their first hour after takeoff discussing the purpose of their mission. While O'Leary and Moon

Deer snoozed in their seats, Sommers let their strategies cycle through his head. First, they'd make a covert approach and search for evidence of foul play. Was Samantha on the run? Did she get abducted? Why hadn't they heard from Lilly or Bud?

Next, the team would compare their findings with Ted Lindstrom's report from Grahams Island. Knowing Sam as he did, Sommers knew she was in hiding, and it would be a longshot picking up her trail. He assumed they'd never find her, not unless she allowed it to happen. The pilot's mind tumbled like a clothes dryer full of mismatched socks. He thought Moon Deer was right about his situation, and this bothered him. How would he explain things to his wide-eyed son if things went off the rails?

After thirty minutes of contemplative silence, Sommers' little airplane hit a bouncy patch of turbulence. O'Leary and Moon Deer rubbed the sleep from their eyes and stretched their arms as the plane jounced against the gusts. The pilot looked over his shoulder and reported to the others. "I know it doesn't feel like it, but we've dodged the worst of the storm. I think Lindstrom's gained a few hours on us. He told me he'd check in from Devils Lake. We should arrive at Sam's place in time for his call." Sommers, feeling drained but determined, shifted in his seat and glared at the distant peaks, biting into a deceitful rose-colored skyline.

An hour later, after taxiing to a stop at Black Hills Aero, Sommers introduced Moon Deer and O'Leary to his petulant mechanic, Otto Schuler. Schuler hummed and grunted while he tinkered with a Beechcraft Bonanza parked on the hangar's apron. The brooding technician, operating at a snail's pace, shifted his attention to the small Cessna. Otto inspected the landing gear while fuel sloshed into the tank.

O'Leary and Moon Deer transferred bulky duffel bags from the plane to their rented SUV, while Schuler crouched near the plane's front wheel. He summoned the pilot by drumming his pencil's eraser on the plane's nose cone. Sommers nodded and said, "You've chewed the guts right outta that pencil. Everything okay?"

Like a pensive sloth, Otto took his time making a few notations on his clipboard. "Does the front end shimmy during takeoffs and landings?"

Sommers frowned, adjusted his baseball cap, and nodded yes.

The mechanic pointed his number two pencil at one of the aluminum arms supporting the front suspension. "This is a torque link." Then he grabbed the rod and shook it until it went clackity-clack like the wheels on an old locomotive. "The bushings have worn to the nub. And your bearings, they're shot too. I'll have to order the parts, and with all this supply chain shit going on...."

"I get it—gonna take time, and it's gonna cost me." Sommers looked over his shoulder, watching O'Leary and Moon Deer. He saw them leaning against the black Tahoe, sharing some laughs and munching on protein bars. He turned back and rapped his knuckles on the propeller. "Is she safe to fly?"

Otto tapped his chin with the pencil while staring at the front wheel of the plane. "She might have one or two more landings in 'er. But you gotta go easy. The front wheel's gonna shake and moan like a Crook City whore."

Sommers rolled his eyes and shook his head. "Anyone ever told you that you have a unique way with words?" Then he shrugged his shoulders and clapped his hands. "Welp, order the parts and work your magic. We'll hitchhike back to the lake if we have to."

The search party's seating arrangement stayed consistent as Sommers steered their black Chevy along the rocky escarpments of Spearfish Canyon. He always admired these rugged surroundings, taking in the lofty trees, the frothy waters, and the distinctive geology. But Sommers feared this trip would be different, the scenic backdrop contaminated by unforeseen troubles and dangerous complications.

A single-lane tunnel, followed by a narrow bridge, carried the crew high above churning Spearfish Creek. O'Leary and Moon Deer sat in the back, comparing their arsenals and cracking jokes about the dumbest criminals they've collared. At first blush, Sommers thought the two officers clicked, having a lot in common. The driver swiped through the radio presets, trying to find a song to drown his concerns. KZMX, out of Hot Springs, spun up an oldies mix that worked for this occasion. Somewhat.

O'Leary leaned over towards Moon Deer and tugged on his earlobe. "Doesn't he listen to anything from this century? You know, I could use some AC/DC or Pearl Jam, just to get my heart pumping."

Moon Deer burst out laughing and punched him in the shoulder. "Shit. I'm with you, man. Give me some *Thunderstruck*, like right fuckin' now!" She bobbed her head and pointed at their driver. "When it comes to music, the big lug only wanders into this millennium as a last resort. Or if I threaten to beat his ass." The two enjoyed another laugh as their chauffeur scowled at them in the rearview mirror.

Sommers felt like a bus driver chaperoning a third-grade field trip. Any second, he'd be hearing snapping bubble gum, farting noises, and more giggling. He thought about changing the station to quiet their laughter, then reconsidered. He turned up the volume and hummed along with the tunes. In between Buddy Holly and The Monkees, Sommers muted the radio and said, "Tough luck kiddies, my charter, my music."

O'Leary leaned forward in the back seat and took advantage of the commercial break. "Hey partner, what's up with your mechanic? He's orbiting on a different plane, wouldn't you say?"

Sommers chewed his bottom lip and nodded. "That's an interesting way to put it," he said, glancing into the rearview mirror. "Don't let his sullied look throw you. He used to work for NASA— aerospace engineer. No joke, people in the know say Otto Schuler's smarter than Elon Musk."

Moon Deer chimed in. "Creepy fucker's what he is. I'll bet he's in witness protection for selling secrets to the Chinese."

Sommers scrunched his face and shook his head, not appreciating her judgmental tenor. Still, he considered her rant as a plausible explanation for the mechanical genius landing in remote South Dakota.

"Saddle up, gang," Sommers said, checking his watch, then pointing at a brown road sign. "Next stop, Devils Bathtub."

Chapter 13
Livin' Thing

"Sailin' away on the crest of a wave, it's like magic."

Thirty minutes after leaving Otto Schuler sulking in the hangar, Sommers' troupe turned left into the wayside above the Devils Bathtub Trailhead. Sommers parked the Tahoe behind an island of evergreens, keeping the SUV hidden from highway view. The driver pointed at the undulating gray ribbon that extended beyond the parking lot. "Sam's place is above the basin, little more than a mile from here." He slapped his thighs and said, "Okay, team. How do you wanna attack this?"

Moon Deer opened a GPS app on her iPhone and tapped to launch the satellite view. After a minute of waiting for the page to load, she asked, "Is this it, a quaint hilltop hideaway sporting a green metal roof and a nice yard surrounded by mature trees?"

Sommers craned his neck to examine the small screen. "Yep, that's it."

Moon Deer sustained her sarcastic tone by waving a peace sign with her fingers held over her head. "So, she's got a cottage on Victoria Lane. You've got a log home on Victoria Lake. Isn't that sweet? Kinda like matching goddamn sweaters."

Sommers was about to respond when O'Leary snapped his fingers. The detective rolled his eyes and shook his head. "Let's focus here. We know there's no driving to the front door because we're suspecting foul play. My concern is there's a couple rough ol' boys, armed to the hilt, waiting atop that hill."

O'Leary focused his attention on Moon Deer's phone. "If we walk the parkway, we're looking at twenty minutes, but we lose the element of surprise. There's also the chance a neighbor mistakes us for a paramilitary terrorist group and calls the cops." O'Leary scrutinized the terrain map for another minute, then pointed at the screen. "This trail looks simple enough for the first half-mile, but after that, the ridge off the back of the property looks rough. Pretty steep, am I right?"

Sommers adjusted his baseball hat, then nodded. "You've got a good read on it. There's sixteen hundred feet of elevation change between here and the top of Diablo Ridge. Drops nine hundred feet off the backside. Then there's a six-hundred-foot rise to the backyard." He pointed at the screen. "See how this hill sits in a basin? The views in all directions are pretty spectacular, but it'll make for a challenging hike."

O'Leary zoomed in on the map, then backed off when the image pixelated. "So, we're looking at about sixty minutes of rigorous hiking. Won't the bad guys spot us when we pop up outta that canyon?"

"I don't think so," Sommers said, turning to point at a distant ridge. "The trees are thick from that dogleg up to the property line."

O'Leary stepped from the car with his binoculars. Sommers and Moon Deer climbed out while the detective surveyed the winding trail and assessed the lofty ridge that blocked his view of Victoria Lane. Then the former Army Ranger tilted his face skyward and closed his eyes, running some silent calculations.

Sommers watched as O'Leary's lips quivered in time, performing secret mathematics. Then O'Leary turned and gawked at Moon

Deer, looking her up and down, gauging her prowess and fitness level. Sommers shook his head, anticipating the tirade that was sure to come.

Moon Deer slammed the car door and marched over, shaking her fist in O'Leary's face. "Screw you, soldier boy! I can take whatever this trail dishes out, and then some. Don't think for one minute I can't whip your ass. I've dropped plenty of guys, bigger and tougher than you. So don't underestimate me, cowboy."

O'Leary grinned to the point of almost laughing, but Sommers grabbed him, telling him to let it go. Sommers could tell the detective felt amused, maybe even smitten, by Joy's boisterous charisma.

O'Leary jacked a fresh magazine into his handgun, then studied the western sky. "There's always a bigger bear, darling," he said, locking eyes with her. "We've got just over an hour of daylight left. We'll have to hoof it unless you're banking on a night fight—not the best idea when you're tracking from an inferior position." O'Leary turned to scrutinize the exhausted pilot. "And what about you, gramps? Ya up for a hike?"

Sommers, accepting O'Leary's challenge, showed uncharacteristic boldness as he snapped to life. "After eight days of fighting wildfires in the Rockies, this'll be a walk in the park." He stretched his achy muscles and watched with curiosity as Moon Deer and O'Leary geared up for their raid. So much for being alike, their preparations couldn't be more different.

First, Moon Deer looped a holstered Glock 17 onto her belt. Then she pulled a twelve-gauge shotgun and tactical-grade rifle from the back of the SUV. The eager deputy lifted herself onto the tailgate and strapped a Ruger .22 onto one ankle and a serrated hunting knife to the other.

Moon Deer caught the two men watching her operation. "Shit, I know that look. You pervs are getting hard watching a hussy play with guns. Fuckin' pigs," she said with a wink and a wry grin. With a growl in her voice, she jacked a shell into the shotgun. "If I go down, it sure as hell won't be from a lack of fuckin' firepower."

The two men nodded their approval and resumed their preparations.

Moon Deer hopped down and watched O'Leary zip a Kevlar vest over his sleeveless compression shirt. He checked the safety on his SIG Sauer P226, then secured it in a Velcro pocket under his left arm. She nodded with an appreciative grin stretching across her face.

O'Leary cocked an eyebrow and asked, "You wearing a vest, sweetheart?" She rolled her eyes, then started stuffing her daypack with extra ammunition. O'Leary sneered his disapproval, then locked eyes with Sommers and shook his head.

The detective unpacked a second vest for Sommers from the back of the Tahoe. "I'm not sure this one's big enough for you, but it'll have to do." Sommers dabbed his sweating forehead with the back of his hand. He peered across the canyon at the sweltering sun, then shot O'Leary an incredulous look.

O'Leary tossed the vest over the big man's shoulders. "You have a son, right? God forbid, I have to be the one to tell the boy his dead father refused to wear life-saving protection because it was too damn hot." Sommers nodded, hoping that Moon Deer heard the detective's insistent rant. O'Leary squatted and tightened the laces on his cross-trainers. Then he stood and slapped himself all over his arms and legs like a wrestler about to scuffle. "Okay, let's do this."

Moon Deer huffed as she slammed the tailgate shut. "That's it. One measly SIG in a sticky holster?"

O'Leary, wearing his game face, lifted the binoculars back to his eyes. "I travel light—one part agile, two parts hostile." He looked over at Sommers and winked. "One shot's all I'll need." The confident detective watched as the muscular lumberjack cinched a timeworn leather tool belt around his waist. "What the hell is that?"

Sommers, also looking serious, tapped his hip and winked. "Two of my favorite axes, but one throw is all I'll need."

Moon Deer strutted over and patted O'Leary's back, shaking her head. "Don't push it. He's a deadeye, trust me."

O'Leary looked on with skepticism as Sommers locked the car and adjusted his baseball cap. Then, like Dorothy and her misfit friends promenading into the Haunted Forest, the small team of trackers set off down the trail with Sommers in the lead, stepping double-time.

It took less than ten minutes for the ambitious trio to reach the base of Diablo Ridge. They gulped from their water bottles, then tightened their straps and laces. Sommers examined the rugged slope, then looked over his shoulder at his restless crew. "As you can see, it gets tougher from here. Watch for falling rock and loose footholds. Grabbing onto the scrub, that's hit or miss. Everything's parched and brittle. I'll be waiting for you greenhorns up top." Then, using his hands and feet like diggers, the big lumberjack scrambled up the sheer side of the rocky, tree-lined hogback.

Before long, Sommers began putting some serious distance between himself and his younger partners. O'Leary dodged a falling chunk of sandstone, clutching a low tree limb to steady himself. "Okay," he said, catching his breath. "I can admit when I'm wrong. I underestimated the big guy. He's a goddamn machine."

Moon Deer stopped alongside O'Leary, hanging onto his shoulder for balance. She kicked her boots into the rocky crust, creating a firmer footing for herself. After a few seconds of recovering her wind, she said, "Sommers has the determination of ten men. His size intimidates most people. But that's a pittance compared to his resolve. I've known him a long time and let me tell ya, he's fuckin' relentless. Just be glad he's on our side. It's one thing to mess with him. You mess with his people, and he turns into a goddamn grizzly."

O'Leary wiped his brow with the back of his arm, then turned his baseball cap around backward. "Good to know." Then he changed the subject. "Nice that there's a breeze up here." O'Leary pulled himself up two more steps, reaching back for Moon Deer's hand. "What's the story with you two? I mean, it seems like something's there, but maybe I'm misreading the vibe."

She latched onto O'Leary's hand and pulled herself up to rest against a large boulder. "Sommers and I are best friends—at least, I thought we were. At one time, I thought it could've been something more, but now...." She glanced up the hill, watching her friend approach the summit. "He's made his fuckin' bed. Now he's gotta sleep in it."

Moon Deer trudged a few steps ahead of her climbing partner, then slipped on loose rocks and began sliding down the slope. O'Leary grabbed her around the waist to keep her from toppling to the bottom. She grumbled as she steadied herself, then brushed the oatmeal-colored flecks of dust from her face. "Shit, man. No need to get all handsy with me. I got this."

O'Leary held his free palm to the sky. "Hey, just trying to help here. You've got three Cabela's stores strapped to your ass. For cryin' out loud, I've seen entire squadrons pack less."

Moon Deer, instead of biting his head off, looked into the man's eyes. Their dreamy moment suggested more than a walk in the park. A passionate kiss seemed storybook imminent, but both wanton hikers just sputtered and laughed.

Thirty minutes later, the frazzled couple joined Sommers on the peak. They found him in the shade of a basswood tree, leaning against the trunk and studying the solitary house atop the next hill. He leered at the pair, trying to determine what was so funny. He shook his head and chugged from his water bottle, then wiped his sweaty forehead with his shirtsleeve. The dogged leader pointed across the rocky gorge. "No movement over there. Looks too quiet, way too quiet." On cue, a gust of wind sailed through the cedars, whistling a foreboding tune.

O'Leary slipped the binoculars from Moon Deer's pack and steadied himself against a tree trunk. He scanned the hilltop across the canyon, then cleared his throat and said, "I can see the back end of a four-by-four behind the garage. Red Jeep ring a bell?" O'Leary handed the field glasses over to Sommers.

The big man adjusted the focus. "Okay, I see it. That's Bud Wolcott's ride. He's supposed to be in Cabo, fishing with his buddies. I asked him to check on the place three days ago, but he never reported back." Sommers slapped at a fly on the back of his neck, then fidgeted with his tool belt. He turned, saw the concern on Moon Deer's face and tried to explain it away. "He just needed a place to park, alright?"

She finished her water and shook her head. "I've had a shitty feeling about this from the very beginning," she said, clearing her throat with a cough. "I mean, what the hell are we standing around for? Let's get our asses over there."

Another thirty minutes of traipsing through thorny brambles and across the dusty scrabble put the sweat-soaked trio at the edge of Samantha's backyard. They watched and listened for several minutes, trying to feel the vibrations of an occupied home. O'Leary raised his finger to his lips, thinking he heard music, maybe a ringtone.

Sommers pulled out his phone and dialed Bud's number, but once again, the call went straight to his voicemail. Moon Deer stooped to pick pine needles and cockleburs from the tops of her socks. Looking up at Sommers, she said, "Your baby momma's lucky. That's some fuckin' cottage. Got you whipped pretty bad, huh?"

Sommers didn't care for her tone. He stammered before changing the subject. "It's a rental. Landlord's a businessman in Fargo. Besides, Sam's done very well for herself. Offering her money would be disrespectful to her."

O'Leary held his palm up, silencing their squabbling. "Doesn't Bill Wenner own this place?" Sommers nodded, and O'Leary shook his head. "Now there's a blast from the past. That gigantic son of a bitch was an enormous pain in my ass. Ever met him?"

Sommers crouched in silence, focusing on the house, missing the detective's question. O'Leary tapped his partners on the back, pointing in different directions, coordinating a stealthy approach with his hand signals.

A reddish sun sagged beyond the basin's western rim as Moon Deer trekked north towards the front of the house, using the trees for cover. O'Leary did the same, but circled south. After five minutes, Sommers' patience evaporated. He stood and walked straight through the shadowy yard towards the garage.

With only dim twilight remaining, Sommers pressed the four-digit code on the door's control panel. Nothing. He repeated the sequence, and again, and got the same result. Moon Deer and O'Leary caught up with him as he turned the key, opening a service door with deliberate caution. Sommers turned to see their annoyed faces. "No alarm, power's out," he said, whispering and pointing. "That's her car. Follow me."

As they felt their way through the darkness, O'Leary asked, "Where's the electrical panel?"

Sommers waved, then held a finger in the air. "It's off the kitchen. We're almost there." Two seconds later, Sommers tripped the master circuit breaker. Without warning, the kitchen lights came on. Moon Deer and O'Leary recoiled into shooting positions—guns drawn and locked out front, squatting in the middle of a chef's kitchen. The edgy trio heard Gutfeld's mocking laughter playing on a television in the next room.

Moon Deer snapped at Sommers. "How 'bout a fuckin' warning next time, 'eh?"

Sommers ignored her bluster, leaning in close while pointing up the stairs. "Lilly's room, the boy's room, and a bathroom—only access is this stairway." Moon Deer rolled her eyes, then slinked away with her gun drawn. Sommers leaned towards O'Leary and pointed in the opposite direction. "Family room and three-season room—exits to the yard. I'm gonna check the back bedroom."

O'Leary flashed a thumbs up and treaded towards the back of the house. Sommers opened the flashlight app on his phone. Two steps into the dim hallway, he spotted dried blood spattered across the pale hardwood floor. Two steps further, his beam of light caught a pair of reddish-brown smears sweeping along the wall.

Sommers switched the phone to his left hand and unsheathed his ax with his right. He caught the whiff of something putrid as he crept through the bedroom towards the bath. He stopped short before opening the door. His sense of smell, his years of experience, and his intuition affirmed the gruesome face of death lurked beyond the bathroom door.

Sommers shook his head, noting this wasn't the unconventional life he signed up for. He feared stumbling into a dead body, worried about the safety of his friends. He thought about Noah and the fate of his boy's mother. His mind raced, trying to keep pace with his pounding heart, narrowing his perception of time into a series of slow motion snapshots.

Once again, apprehension and curiosity bested his patience. He twisted the knob and reached in to flip the light switch. Sommers recoiled his hand, covering his nose and mouth. After catching a terrifying glimpse, he looked away, feeling queasy and light-headed. The nauseating, unmistakable stench of necrosis washed over him, and the grisly scene burned an image into his mind he'd never forget. A muffled dribble slipped past his lips. "Oh my God."

Bud Wolcott's lanky body lay in a contorted, blood-soaked jumble at the bottom of Sam's Jacuzzi tub. Sommers winced while his eyes scanned the room. He placed his ax and phone on the vanity, then covered his nose and mouth as he leaned closer to examine the gruesome scene. Bud's ashen face conveyed torture, his mouth and eyes were wide open, showing the terror of his last seconds. Dark streaks of dried blood covered his head like horrific face paint.

The killers carved a bloody S into Wolcott's forehead, and his neck, slashed from earlobe to earlobe. Sommers surmised Wolcott had died from drowning in his own blood. The fingers on his left hand pointed in different directions, broken like frail sticks courtesy of his cruel assailant. The attackers belted Wolcott's bruised wrists and ankles with plastic restraints. It was clear the man fought his attackers until the very end. Sommers couldn't stomach this brutality, but he couldn't look away, and he stood paralyzed by the unthinkable.

Sommers turned to listen as the TV went silent, his partners' footsteps tiptoeing down the hall. O'Leary called out. "Hey Sommers, the house is clear. Find anything?"

Sommers thought he hollered, "*Help! Back here.*" Then soon realized no sound escaped his mouth. In the next moment, the two officers filled the open doorway, squinting their eyes and pinching their noses.

A wide-eyed Moon Deer surveyed the room. Blood-spatters and ghastly smears defiled every inch of the white ceramic tile. "What the fuck happened here?" She asked, her eyes watery from the putrid odor. She stepped forward and peered into the tub. "Holy shit! Who the hell is that?"

Sommers removed his hat and spoke through a moistened hand towel. "That's Bud Wolcott. He's supposed to be fishing the Pacific. I asked him to check on things here. I should've stayed with him." Sommers dropped his face and shook his head. "This is my fault."

O'Leary holstered his gun and stepped into the room to take in the scene. He crouched near the bathtub, his eyes assessing the crime with icy precision. Then, without a fuss, as if he'd seen this kind of carnage a thousand times, he said, "That's bullshit. You had nothing to do with this."

He stood and placed his hand on Sommers' shoulder. "You

remember Miles Potter? I found him in a motel bathtub, sliced in half, just like your friend here. You realize this changes things. Don't you? A clandestine witch-hunt? Not anymore. Someone's sending a message. If you want to protect your family, we need big-time reinforcements, and we need 'em now." O'Leary pointed at the big man's cell phone. "Make the call."

Moon Deer, always the antagonist, pointed at the top of Bud's severed head. "Any chance Sam and Bud had a falling out? Shit, for all we know, she could be the one sending the message. I mean, who the hell abandons their kid?" Sommers' face flamed with outrage. He glared at Moon Deer, unable to tolerate her insolence.

Before Sommers could respond, a loud clap exploded behind the house. A window shattered, and the three hunters flinched, then ducked. They heard running footfalls, two or three pairs crossing the backyard. Moon Deer launched into full-speed pursuit, dashing from the room after they heard a second gunshot in the yard. O'Leary looked at Sommers and said, "She's not wearing a vest." He pulled his gun and turned for the door.

The big lumberjack grabbed O'Leary's arm, stopping him in the doorway, almost lifting him off the ground. "I'll make the call," Sommers said, locking eyes with O'Leary. The detective returned the big man's hard stare. Sommers relaxed his grip and took a deep breath. "Joy is ruthless. Best tracker you'll ever see. But she'll shoot to kill without batting an eye. Don't let her do it. We need information, not more blood. Hurry, go get our girl."

O'Leary scrambled out the back door and Sommers took another deep breath to calm his nerves. He dialed 9-1-1 and waited for an answer. "Yes, ma'am. Dale Sommers. Bud Wolcott is dead. Yes, murdered. We're at the end of Victoria Lane. Yes, ma'am, 1074. A lot of blood. Gunshots fired out back." Sommers crouched and peered out the back window, listening and catching breath. "One ambulance, at least. Yes, I can hold on."

Sommers tuned out the dispatcher's voice while he hung on the line. He heard shouts and more gunfire off in the distance—three, maybe four guns firing in sporadic, rapid succession from the depths of Devils Bathtub. Sommers turned and glanced at the bloodied bathroom, then spun away. He paced the floor beside Sam's bed, listening to the gun battle and conflicted about what he should do next.

The shouts and the gunshots grew more distant, then fell silent. A chill ran through his body, and Sommers shuddered as he fought to compose himself. Time passed in slow agony as he sat on the edge of the bed, covering his face and trying to mask his despair. He'd seen death in many forms before, but this was different. This unearthed his worst deep-seated pain.

Sommers recalled Moon Deer saying things would get ugly. He had to admit she was right. What worried the distraught lumberjack most was the savagery and bloodshed were just beginning. A grim awareness swirled around Sommers like a ruddy whirlpool. Everyone and everything he loved was now in danger.

Four hundred miles northeast of Spearfish Canyon, Ted Lindstrom snapped pictures of a fresh, interpretive carving on the southwest face of a mature oak tree in the middle of Grahams Island. Unmistakable markings, engraved with precision into the blackened, lightning-scarred wood. The woodcut measured two feet wide and twelve inches tall, and stood four feet from the ground. The carving featured a pair of feathery wings stretched out wide with a circle drawn between them. In the middle of the ring, a canoe carrying two paddlers.

Lindstrom could only speculate at its meaning. Even-spaced

below the decorative wings were five large Ss. Two of the letters had Xs painted over the top of them with blood-red nail polish. Lindstrom attached his pictures to a series of text messages for Sommers. He felt the edges of the mysterious epitaph with his fingertips, trying to absorb its essence, then clicked send on his cell phone.

Two hundred fifty miles south of Grahams Island, Stewart Barnes had settled in, soaking in his nightly ritual. He'd sip aged whiskey, smoke a Cuban cigar, and admire a violet sunset while lounging in a steaming hot tub until his skin wrinkled like a prune. This evening wasn't much different from the others, except the Chief of the Lake Traverse DSS lay naked, face down in bubbling hot water, garroted with a string of patio lights wrapped around his puckered neck.

Chapter 14
Don't Look Back

"Don't look back, a new day is breakin'."

The damp pavement of US Highway 75 shimmered and steamed as a saffron sunshine emerged from the retreating clouds. The sun's warmth swept away the stubborn remnants of the Alberta Clipper as it rolled southeast towards the Twin Cities. Mounds of dirty snow shriveled in the ditches, lingering evidence of the rare August snowstorm.

More often than not, missing person cases offer a frustrating logistical crapshoot; research-intensive, emotional, and exhausting. Julie Hughes found her three-hour drive to Kittson County to be a welcome respite, not a grind. She savored her time behind the steering wheel as an opportunity to explore country back roads and taste a bite of freedom. Most importantly, it gave her a chance to ponder the circumstances of Tommy Fulgham's disappearance.

Julie rolled the driver's side window down, letting the afternoon freshness muss her blonde curls. She waxed grateful, feeling fortunate to be alive. The investigator enjoyed good health, a loving man, and an interesting job. Her future brimming with hope, Julie

Hughes, for the first time in her life, felt something close to pure contentment.

State highways 58 and 68 traveled so straight, Julie could've set her cruise control, locked the steering wheel, and taken a catnap. She scrolled through Spotify playlists on her car's infotainment screen, trying to find the perfect songs to fend off her drowsiness.

Just another band out of Boston kept her spirits aloft and her toes tapping while cruising along a tree-lined stretch of secluded two-lane. Julie sang to the forests and meadows, her heart overflowing, understanding that after years of ridicule and disappointment, her life had taken a turn for the better.

After turning left off Route 57, Julie spotted a farmer mowing along the top of a soggy ditch that separated corn stalks from the tar-n-chip road. The person steering the riding mower in straight lines appeared to be a middle-aged man—burly, wearing work boots, canvas overalls sagged to the waist, and a dingy red baseball cap pulled down low over his eyes. Not breaking many stereotypes, the farmer had a foot-long piece of yellow straw hanging from the corner of his mouth and a pair of blue headphones covering his ears.

Julie turned her Jeep into the long gravel driveway. She parked near a hand-painted sign, with the words *"fresh sweet corn, 12 for $5"* scrawled in yellow paint on a graying, warped sheet of half-inch plywood. She had, for the moment, eluded the farmer's detection.

Julie soon learned that he was a she. The sweaty farmer cut the corner of her last row, wheeling the mower in a tight U-turn, then spotted the visitor leaning against the front fender of her Jeep. The farm woman chugged over and cut the engine. She swung her leg over the seat and stepped off the mower like an agile wrangler climbs from his trusty steed.

The thick, manly-looking woman smiled, plucked the headphones from her ears, and reached out to shake Julie's hand. "Phew, it's a steamy, hot mudder this afternoon. Hope you haven't been waiting long. Peg McFarland, welcome to our humble slice of heaven." Peg swatted at a horsefly, then waved her arm, pointing out the endless string of crop rows. "You like corn? It's been a good year for corn."

Julie's hand felt small and wimpy within McFarland's rough and powerful grip. She guessed the farmer was between forty-five and fifty, with a broad, cheery smile and bright, enthusiastic eyes. At two-hundred fifty pounds, the Lord built Peg McFarland more like a defensive tackle than a corn farmer. The curious investigator lowered her sunglasses. "Julie Hughes. Yes, I have a long-standing appreciation of corn. Looks like you'll be harvesting soon."

McFarland surveyed her western field, pride beaming across her face. "Yep. That snow made the greens pop like crazy. We'll harvest most of the sweet corn next week, the ethanol corn, maybe two weeks after that. We'll see what the weather and the market bring." Peg tossed her straw in the ditch, then looked Hughes up and down as she wiped her brow with a plaid handkerchief. "What brings a pretty little thing like you out to the country?"

Julie, sensing she was being profiled, hooked her glasses on the pocket of her sweat-dampened blouse, then pulled out her phone and made a few swipes with her fingers. "I'm looking for Tommy Fulgham." She rotated the phone so McFarland could see the picture of the young DNR officer. "He's missing."

McFarland rolled her eyes and tucked the rag into her back pocket, re-examining Hughes from head to toe. "You a cop?"

Julie shook her head no.

McFarland exhaled, then smiled and waved her hat like a fan. "Follow me up to the house. We can grab a seat in the shade. I just brewed a batch of tea, lemon wedges to boot. Got a few sticky buns left over from breakfast." Julie, banking on a quick answer, tried to steer clear of the farmer's offer. However, McFarland had already started her mower and kicked up crushed gravel as she sped towards the farmhouse.

A minute later, Julie rocked on a porch swing, sipping sun tea from a chilled canning jar. She explained her responsibilities as a private investigator and how her preliminary research led her to McFarland Farms. Julie gazed out at the endless expanse of tall leafy rows. "You run all this yourself?"

McFarland huffed, then wiped her brow. "It feels that way sometimes. Hard to get any help these days. No one wants to break a sweat—nobody wants to work for a living. Tell me, how the hell are people gonna eat if nobody's willing to bust their hump?" She sipped from her glass, then fluttered her meaty hand above her head. "Oh, we've got a few seasonal workers, Mexicans and Somalis—they'll work for cash, but they're so damn hard to keep around. Seems all they care to do is fuck and fight." Peg let out a ghoulish cackle as she brushed grass clippings from her overalls.

She took another drink from her jar, then said, "My husband ran to Hallock to pick up some chicken tenders and slaw from Chester's. They've got a cheap chicken special today—might be roadkill, but it's still finger-licking good." McFarland fluttered her plump fingers and unveiled a silly grin. "Gus has a coupon for free fries—should be back soon. Why don't you join us for supper? We don't get many visitors 'round here."

Julie, with civility, tried to excuse herself from the invitation by stating she was meeting her husband for a pizza at Johnny Bravo's in Drayton. She placed her sweaty glass on a windowsill, pulled a small notebook from her pocket, then got down to business. "Mrs. McFarland. Tommy Fulgham was last seen a week ago, moving between Kittson and Pembina County. His GPS data says he spent about an hour here before heading west. What can you tell me about that?"

"For Pete's sake, call me Peg." McFarland said, motioning to see Tommy's picture on Julie's phone again. She puckered her lips and shook her head. "His poor parents, so hard to understand why bad things happen to good people. It's been quite a deal up here, all over the evening news." She paused for a few seconds, her eyes tracking towards the western horizon. "Yep, Tommy stopped by last week. He asked me if he could take water samples from along our shores." Peg motioned with her hands. "Our property comes to a point down where Two Rivers meet—water flows west from there. There's a small fishing pier and a rickety gazebo at the end of this trail."

Julie nodded, then jotted a note. "Did you let him?" She asked.

A pulsing breeze pushed a lock of brown hair across Peg's cheek. She pushed it aside and studied the skepticism on Julie's face. "Take the samples? Sure, no harm in that, right? Why would I refuse?"

Julie studied McFarland's eyes because her responses sounded cagey, yielding more questions than answers. The investigator slipped a newspaper clipping from her notebook. "This article is from five years ago. It says McFarland Farms paid a hefty fine levied by the EPA. The article also mentions corruption and water pollution. What's that about?"

McFarland scratched at the back of her neck, then stood and paced around the porch, her heavy work boots thumping and creaking the weathered planks with each step. "That had nothing to do with us," she said. "The county water commissioner, Colin Stroud, took bribes and looked the other way while our neighbors let their greywater drain into the river. Me and Gus wouldn't play ball—paid the price for it, too. Stroud got some sweet kickbacks from all those state and federal agencies. Now he's a bigshot in St. Paul. Dude's got a corner office overlooking the river." Peg gulped her tea and shook her finger. "Anyway, we don't do dairy anymore, just grain these days."

Hughes closed her notebook and tucked it back into her bag. "Interesting, but they didn't send Tommy Fulgham all the way out here for no reason. Do you mind if we walk down to the river? I'm trying to retrace his steps as best I can."

McFarland was about to respond when her cell phone rang. "It's Gus. I gotta take this." Peg stepped away from Hughes into the yard. Soon, her gestures and movements made it apparent the couple wasn't seeing eye to eye. After another two minutes of heated phone conversation, the sturdy farm woman stepped back to the porch. "You wanna see the river? It's 'bout a mile from here—we'll take my Sidekick. Only seats two, but fast as hell. C'mon, let's roll."

The late afternoon sun burned hot as Julie and Peg bumped along a rugged dirt path towards the junction of Two Rivers. McFarland shook her head. "Gus got held up at the hardware store," she said. "That's his way of saying he ran into a couple of buddies at the bar. Anyway, the chicken's gonna be another hour or two. I told him you'd be joining us—hope you're hungry. I told him to get extra tenders."

Julie tried to respond, but Peg shut her down, and said, "Now, now. Fair warning. I'm not good at taking no for an answer. It's just chicken fingers, for heaven's sake. Besides, I figure you owe me some proper company after dropping that EPA bomb on me."

Julie shrugged and nodded as the pair made a sweeping turn into a rolling valley. "Kinda off the beaten path, aren't we? Has anyone else searched this area? DNR, BCA, anybody?"

McFarland shook her head and cranked the steering wheel, sliding to a stop near a long strip of limestone riprap. "Not unless Gus brought somebody down here. But he don't care much for outsiders—would've told me. Lil' Gussie don't say boo without my say so."

Peg scanned the area and pointed at the shoreline. "Snow switched to rain overnight, the water's up, and flowing fast. It's pointless to come down here. Any footprints or clues you're looking for would've washed away. Look around. This is the only place where Tommy could've gotten to the water's edge without some serious trouble."

Julie examined the weed-covered, isolated shoreline. She nodded, showing McFarland's assessment was accurate. "Could Tommy have fallen in?" She asked, lifting her chin at the rolling brown current. "Could he have drowned?"

McFarland looked at Julie with a bit of surprise. "No, he didn't drown. He was a strapping young man. After he collected his samples, I asked him to stay for lunch." Peg smacked her lips and shook her head, looking down in the mouth. "The boy said he had a sandwich in his truck. I think he was just shy, that's all."

Julie walked in a circle, writing a note about Peg's comment. She paused and surveyed the setting in all directions. "Did he mention where he was going after Two Rivers?"

McFarland dabbed her sweating forehead with her rumpled handkerchief. "He didn't say. Like you said before, he drove west outta our place."

Julie pivoted and stared at the crimson sun, sagging low along the western horizon. "How long would it take me to get to the Red River?"

"If you take Highway 16 south to Route 175, about fifteen minutes." McFarland winked and pointed. "This dirt track will get us there in less than five. Collar those titties, girlfriend. Here we go."

Just as the eager chauffeur said, five minutes later, Peg and Julie stood in the shade of a concrete overpass watching the brown water ooze past. Julie took a sniff and winced. "Stinks something awful down here."

"Sure does," McFarland said. "Smells like carp guts mixed with coon shit."

The two women walked the area searching for clues, swatting at biting flies and pesky mosquitoes as they trudged along.

Julie huffed her displeasure as she scraped gobs of thick sludge from her shoes. "This sucks! No breeze, and everything's covered in muck." As she turned to leave, she pointed at a pair of dark shadows in the cloudy water along the shore. "See 'em?" She asked. Peg shook her head no as Julie peeled off her shoes and socks, then tip-toed into the muddy water.

A short time later, a thin red line provided the only light seeping from a cloudless western sky. The two women raced back towards the farm with two waterlogged toolboxes bouncing in the back of Peg's RTV. The water samples confirmed McFarland's story. Tommy Fulgham made it at least as far as the soggy banks of the Red River.

Julie's cell phone vibrated as she picked the sticky mud from between her toes. McFarland cupped her chest with her manly hands and flashed a wry grin. "Good thing I'm wearing my sports bra," she said with a cackle. "You best scrub them dogs when we get back, else you'll get a nasty rash. Surprised you get a signal way out here. Who's your provider?"

Julie smiled before she said, "It's my husband. I should take this." McFarland blew a saucy kiss and gave Hughes a thumbs up. Julie couldn't hear him over the noise of the Sidekick's engine. She put him on speakerphone and shifted in her seat. "Hey Jack, how's it going?" Julie was about to launch into an eager explanation about the boxes she pulled from the river, but he cut her off.

"Livin' the dream, but sorry, hon—change of plans. I'm on my way to the airport. I need to get out to Spearfish right away." McFarland pouted after seeing the disappointment on Julie's face. She pulled the four-wheeler to the side and killed the engine.

Julie rolled her eyes and shook her head. "Spearfish? I thought we agreed…"

Again, Jack interrupted her. "I know, I know," he said. "There's been a shooting. Details are sketchy. O'Leary's being airlifted to a trauma center in Rapid City. He's hanging in there, that's all I know. They're questioning Sommers. Moon Deer told me it's a complete shitshow out there. Sorry, Jules, they need me. Gotta go. Love ya, babe."

McFarland leaned closer, looking into Julie's worried eyes.

"Shooting? I tell ya, this country's goin' to hell in a handcart." She tapped Julie on the thigh and said, "Don't worry your pretty little head. We have extra room. Stay as long as you like. Gus better be settin' our table with that chicken, else I'll beat his skinny little ass." Peg fired up the RTV and mashed her foot to the floor. In a flash, they fishtailed along the rutted trail, racing for home.

One-hundred fifty miles south of Hallock, Cesar Flores, a scruffy car porter at Wenner Motors, sloshed his mop bucket around the showroom floor. Wearing a pair of white earbuds and a sleeveless Dos Equis t-shirt, Flores spent most of his time texting and fielding calls on his cellphone. Without warning, Big Bill Wenner stomped from his office with the nub of a cigar dangling from the corner of his mouth. He waved his stubby arms like a frantic, red-faced dinosaur.

Wenner flicked a lump of ash on the ground near Cesar's feet. With a snarl in his voice, he said, "That son of a bitch! He missed the goddamn drop in Grand Forks. There's no sign of him up north. That asshole's gotta be headed this way. Any sign of that fuckin' truck?"

Flores shrugged his shoulders and shook his head—either not understanding or not hearing Wenner's rant. The hefty man stomped around the showroom floor, watching an occasional car roll past the front windows. Flores rolled his bucket into a corner, then flashed his thumbs across his phone. He grabbed a key from behind the service desk, stepped to the windows, then waved the key in front of Wenner's saggy jowls. "Gotta cook the Mustang," he said. "Auction man's comin' today."

Wenner rocked back and forth like an agitated walrus, dismissing the servile Latino. "Yea, yea, whatever. It's about goddamn time you did some actual work 'round here."

Flores rolled his eyes, then slinked his way towards the used car lot. He paused in the doorway and pointed. "Hey boss, is that the truck you're looking for?" Wenner slogged to the front window for a closer look, and Flores spun away, slipping out the back.

Moments later, a noisy Ford pickup appeared, black with tinted windows. Obnoxious rap music thumped its subwoofers, and the truck cut a reckless smoke-filled U-turn before skidding to a stop in front of Wenner Motors. Big Bill puffed his cigar and postured in the front window, waving his arms. "Goddamn it, Rivers! Get that infernal piece of shit outta here!"

Quick as lightning, two masked gunmen waving black assault rifles stood in the truck's bed. They showered the dealership's front windows with bullets, and shards of shattered glass exploded in every direction. Panicked bystanders shrieked and scrambled for safety, hiding under and between the rows of cars.

The gunmen aimed their rifles at Wenner, and the furious giant froze. "Don't shoot! Whatever's up your ass, we can work it out." Squealing tires broke the momentary silence as a white Mustang jumped the curb and flew west on Highway 52. Wenner puffed his cigar and shook his head. "Goddamn punk."

The first gunman shouted, rage seething through his mask. "On your knees, fat ass. Now!"

The second gunman motioned to the gapers hiding along the sidewalk. "Get the fuck outta here!" Two teens scrambled to their feet, then dashed away. A third teen still crouched behind a car, held his phone over his head, recording the stunning attack.

The first gunman sprayed the car with bullets, shooting the windows out and perforating the hapless Taurus with two dozen holes. The senseless teen tossed his phone aside and dashed away, yelling for his companions to wait up. Sirens blared in the distance as the two gunmen tracked their weapons back to the sweaty, rotund car salesman.

Wenner plopped to his knees, assuming an awkward, pleading posture. With a glint in his eye, he muttered under his breath. "Well, shit. I've had a good run." He reached behind his back, jerking a shiny pistol into view. "Burn in hell, you goddamn…" Wenner squeezed off one wild shot before a burst of ferocity rang out. A stream of bullets tore into his flabby chest, and Big Bill's smoldering cigar tumbled to the floor.

The gigantic man teetered and shuddered before flopping into a molten thud. Wenner's bullet-riddled body lay face down, placid across a bed of sparkling red glass. The sirens grew louder as the assailants sped for the cover of Interstate 94. Onlookers crawled from their hiding places with their mouths agape, disbelieving the gangland-styled carnage they'd just witnessed.

Five minutes east of Wenner Motors, Dean Rivers pulled to the shoulder to allow a parade of emergency vehicles to pass. He muttered to himself. "What the hell's goin' on?" Then his phone chimed with a text message. Rivers tapped to read the screen. *"Wenner's dead. Meet me at the zoo."*

Rivers tucked a pinch of tobacco into his lower lip as a noisy helicopter hovered overhead. He sat motionless, staring through the windshield, wringing his hands on the steering wheel. Rivers spit a sloppy brown splash into the street, then pulled away from the curb. He wiped his mouth and shook his head. "What the hell—it's a nice day. Say, I wonder what's happening at the zoo."

Chapter 15
Less Conversation

"A little less conversation, a little more action, please."

The bleary-eyed pilot, chewing on a cappuccino stir stick, peeked over his shoulder and saw Jack Hughes lost in a daydream. The lone passenger stared at his reflection in the side window of the private jet he'd chartered to the Black Hills. Four thousand feet above the soggy scrub of North Dakota, Hughes connected his phone to the USB charging port hidden inside his armrest. He skimmed through a harried thread of text messages from Dale Sommers. The lawyer's thumbs tapped with a flurry, sending one last reminder to his friend. *"Don't say another word. I'll be there soon."*

Seconds later, Hughes felt his phone vibrate with an incoming call. Ted Lindstrom, affirmed by Jack's caller ID. The pilot closed the cockpit door, so Hughes put Lindstrom on speaker phone. "Talk to me, sheriff. What's going on?"

"Hey Jack," Lindstrom said. "Sorry about the background noise. I'm crossing the causeway and the wind's howling like crazy. Listen, I know my instructions were to meet Sommers in Spearfish, but there's some wacky shit goin' down in Fargo. I gotta get back there, like pronto." Lindstrom fired off his questions while he had a consistent connection. "I heard about the shooting at Sam's place. Any updates on O'Leary? What about Moon Deer? I can't get anyone on the horn. Say, where are you, anyway?"

Hughes summarized what little he'd heard about the shootout above Devils Bathtub. He told Lindstrom a butcher slashed Wolcott to ribbons. Sam was running, and authorities were looking at Sommers through skeptical eyes. O'Leary rested in Rapid City hospital bed with two holes in his side, fortunate to be alive. The lawyer mentioned his next call was to pry some details outta Moon Deer.

Lindstrom spent the next few minutes describing the hieroglyphics he discovered on Grahams Island. He said, "I think the etchings are some sort of scorecard left by Sam—tallying her targets. There are other symbols that need deciphering by someone smarter than me. It's like you said. She's on the hunt, eliminating her threats one by one."

"Don't sell yourself short, sheriff. You're smarter than you look." The lawyer chuckled as he stared out his window, looking down through some wispy clouds. "I think we're over Jamestown, wheels down in Rapid City in about two hours. Send me the pictures you shared with Sommers, would ya? And hey, what's so damn important in Fargo?" Hughes heard Lindstrom exhale and thought the old sheriff sounded tired and cramped.

Lindstrom coughed to clear his throat. "Trouble caught up with Big Bill Wenner. And I guess I didn't know him like I thought. You know he was Sam's landlord, right? Small world, huh?"

"Sure is. I'd love to know how those two hooked up. They couldn't be more different. That colossal bastard's operation is bigger than we realized. Word on the street is Wenner and the DSS have been fighting a turf war for years. Hey, since you're heading back that way. Why don't you shake him down? See if he knows anything about her disappearance."

After a soppy moment of silence, Lindstrom, with concern resonating in his voice, said, "Too late, Jack. Story's blowing up all over social media. Two gunmen with assault rifles mowed him down, execution style, about an hour ago. Downtown Fargo is crawling with first responders. Check your newsfeed. Just don't expect to hear the whole story. There's live video coming from a drone over Highway 52. The DSS is claiming responsibility—calling it Wenner's Last Stand."

"Well, shit," Hughes said, sitting in stunned silence, tapping his pen against the armrest. "This changes things. Doesn't it? Better put your detective's hat on and haul ass. See if you can dig up a motive. Gotta be witnesses, maybe camera footage. Use those Spidey senses of yours. Somebody has gotta know something."

"I'm letting these horses run wild as we speak." Ted held his phone up to capture the sound of squealing tires and the roar of the Dodge's supercharged engine. "I'll make better time once I hit the highway. You're covering my speeding tickets, right? Oh, and Jack, one more thing. You think the Snakes are sending a message, trying to flush Sam out into the open?"

"Great minds, Theodore. Hopefully, we can get to her before the DSS does. Text me when you get to Fargo." A sudden burst of turbulence jostled the plane as Hughes clicked off his call. He gripped the center armrest with one hand while jotting notes into his legal pad with the other.

Before long, the jounces subsided and Hughes skimmed through the Wenner story on his news app. He shook his head and returned to drawing boxes and arrows on his yellow paper. Nothing obvious bubbled from his chicken scratch, so he left a section of the page blank. After two minutes of staring down at the capital of North Dakota, he dialed Moon Deer's number. "Joy. It's Jack. How the hell are you? This a good time to talk? I'm a few thousand feet above Bismarck, so I may lose you."

"Jack. Good to hear your voice. Greg's in surgery. Lost a lot of blood—got a hairline fracture in his wrist. The EMTs say he's in great shape—should be back on his feet in no time." After a moment of bleak silence, Moon Deer said, "I was too fuckin' aggressive, should've stayed on higher ground. Story of my life, huh?"

Hughes heard the regret in her voice. "Don't worry, deputy. O'Leary's a fighter, tough as one of Rosie's ribeyes."

Joy let out a half-hearted laugh. Then, after another awkward pause, Hughes said, "Sommers is being interrogated by a half-dozen dicks wearing gym shoes and polyester suits. I told the big guy to take the fifth until I got out there. Word's gotten out, he's honest to a fault. The feds are trying to take advantage of his paper-thin filter. Has anyone taken your statement yet?"

Moon Deer said no, then mentioned she'd seen a couple of plainclothes cops hanging around the hospital cafeteria. She added it was only a matter of time before they cornered her. Hughes said, "Hold them off if you can. Let's keep 'em guessing. Tell me what happened at the lodge. Go slow, I'm taking notes."

Moon Deer spent the next few minutes describing the team's hike around Devils Bathtub, discovering Bud Wolcott's ravaged body, and chasing bad guys into the canyon. She said, "Greg was examining the bloody mess in the bathtub when we heard shots fired in the yard. I wasn't wearing my vest. He gave me shit about it before we hit the trail. You'd think I'd fuckin' know better, right?"

Moon Deer's question hung in the air for a second, then she said, "I sensed the danger on our approach, but full disclosure, I wanted all that smoke." Again, she hesitated, her self-blame hanging in the quiet. "Once the shooting started, I pulled my Glock and ran out the back. It was pitch black at that point, so I had my ears trained down the slope. Then bam! A goddamn bullet caromed off a tree just inches from my face."

"Jeez. You okay?"

"Medics plucked a couple splinters the size of matchsticks from the side of my neck—stitched me up during our flight. Tiny fuckin' potatoes, all things considered."

"Still, close call." Hughes said, before flipping the page. "What happened after your near miss?"

"I crawled to the edge of the woods and squeezed off a few blind shots, hoping to create a stir down in the ravine—hit nothing but rocks and trees."

"Where were Sommers and O'Leary while you were shooting?"

Moon Deer moved the phone to her other ear, muffling the speaker for a few seconds. Soon, she shifted her attention back to the call. "The nurse just mentioned the surgery's taking longer than expected, some scuttlebutt about clotting. Anyway, Sommers told us he'd hang back to call 9-1-1, wait for the first responders. I heard O'Leary chasing after me, but we lost each other in the dark. He must've seen a muzzle flash, because he got off one shot. I'm pretty sure he hit one of those assholes, 'cause I heard screams, then splashing down in the creek."

"Considering the darkness and your cover, I don't understand how O'Leary got shot."

"I've been running the scene through my head. There must have been a second shooter. I heard a rifle's crack, very distinct, and from a different direction, but I'm not one hundred percent sure. A lot of echoes and ricochets out there. Anyway, Greg tackled me like a football player. The fuckin' slug bit him waist high, right side, through and through. He fell on top of me after he got hit. If not for the gunfire and the blood, it would've been very erotic. The man's blessed below the equator, if you know what I mean."

Hughes clicked his pen while blurting a nervous snicker. "I'm drawing a graphic picture in my notes. I'll send you a copy for posterity. So, you think there were three gunmen?"

"Two guys with rifles down range from the house. I believe the third guy was their rabbit—had a handgun. Thinking through it again—sure seemed like a professional operation. They had night gear, and they knew what they were doing. Three feels right, maybe four. I gotta tell ya, Jack. I lost my fuckin' cool out there. We could've been killed."

Moon Deer paused, catching her breath. "And you're right about O'Leary—tougher than boot leather. But he's gonna be outta commission for a while. We can't count on him for any more snake wrangling. No doubt about it. That sexy sonofabitch saved my life."

Hughes wanted to learn more about Wolcott's death, then realized he'd lost his signal. Jack stared at his notes for a moment, clicking his pen close to his ear. He scribbled the word *informant* in the middle of the sheet and circled it, adding a question mark. After another minute of peering out the side window, he tossed his legal pad into an adjacent seat, then reclined his seat and shut his eyes.

From the porch swing at Sam's place, Sommers dialed his mother's number, hoping to speak with his son. His phone pushed one flickering bar of signal strength, confirming another spotty connection. He heard jostling and fumbling at the other end of the line. His uncle, Grumpy, answered after coughing and belching. "Yeah, the hell you want?"

"Hey Grumps," Sommers said, shaking his head. "How's things on the lake? Noah there?"

"Phelps and the boy are splashing around between the fuckin' docks. Little guy keeps searching the sky while zooming around the yard. Got his arms stretched out like a goddamn loon. Sure as shit, if that rug rat gets any faster, he'll go whizzing off over the lake. Gracie's pokin' around her garden. Everyone wants to know when ya gettin' back?"

"Not sure. Another day, maybe two."

"Heard that one before. Say, I'm teaching the little ankle biter to play cards. He's not as good as Phelps, but already better than you."

"Huh, you don't say." Sommers pursed his lips, then cut to the chase. "Grumps, I'm calling in a favor. Can you mobilize the Petersons and put Sheriff Williams on speed dial? There's trouble brewing out here and I don't want the Lake Victoria crew to suffer for it."

Grumpy snorted as he said, "Way ahead of you, kiddo. Al and Bob have armed themselves to the gills—taking turns on watch. You know those amped up crackerjacks are fuckin' nocturnal, right? Things are good here. Jus' take care of your shit. Any asshole comin' for the boy has gotta get past us first—good fuckin' luck. The slobbering beast never lets the kid out of his sight, and Gracie's got your dad's old Winchester settin' on the porch. Sleep easy, kid. We're loaded for bear."

Sommers was glad he called. He appreciated Grumpy's preparedness, if not his colorful vernacular. He said, "Okay, then—gotta go. Thank the twins for me. Tell everyone I said, hey."

Grumpy unleashed another flurry of expletives when Sommers' phone dropped the call. The big man cocked his eyebrow at the small screen, then nodded as he mumbled something about divine intervention.

In the shade of his machine shop at Norman Farms, Jerry Reynolds' t-shirt soaked in sweat. He scrubbed at the toasted smears of bug guts, polishing his '66 Chevy to a high-gloss shine. Resting in the corner, his console radio played only two kinds of music, oldies or classic country. He bobbed his head in time, glad nobody fiddled with the station while he was away. As Reynolds buffed the last strip of pasty film from the Impala's turquoise hood, he hummed along with Elvis Presley.

Satisfied with the results, Reynolds gulped a cold Dr. Pepper and shifted his attention to a crippled garden tiller. The rusty little beast wouldn't fire, and Susan Norman said she wanted to plant a row of evergreens along the fence line.

First, Reynolds drained the gas tank and changed the oil. Then he replaced the fuel filter, air filter, and the spark plug. He looked up and spotted Ed Norman's old pickup chugging up the drive just as he yanked the starter rope. On the second pull, Susan's tiller belched a puff of blue smoke, then shuddered to life.

The methodical mechanic opened the choke, slid the throttle to fifty percent, then leaned against his workbench, sipping his soda pop and listening to the small engine chug its way towards a smooth idle. Reynolds nodded and flashed a satisfied grin, wiping his rough hands on an oil-stained shop rag.

Reynolds assembled a make-shift ramp to load the tiller onto a small flatbed utility truck. Soon, he bumped along the gravel driveway towards Susan Norman's clapboard farmhouse. Edward's filthy pickup sat in the turnaround, blocking the front porch. Jerry parked a suitable distance from the door, then shuffled towards the wrap-around deck.

Reynolds listened to the couple arguing. Edward's hollering flooded the yard with abusive obscenities. The old man pivoted towards his truck, choosing once again to keep his distance. Then he heard breaking glass and the desperate cries of a cornered woman. Susan's screams matched Edward's shouts decibel for decibel. Reynolds slipped a crowbar from the truck's bed box, then strode back and sat on the front steps.

Angered and appalled, Susan learned Edward had cut a deal with the DSS, promising to give them the Ford F150 purchased from Big Bill Wenner. The crux of their disagreement was that the exchange was a bribe, guaranteeing the Snakes a controlling interest in a Pembina-based destination resort. Edward completed the deal without consulting with Susan, who had arranged a similar, but more lucrative, deal with Wenner.

Edward bellowed like an angry bear, tossing chairs aside and flipping the kitchen table on its top. "That truck's none of your goddamn business—got nothin' to do with you. Pull your head outta your ass for one minute and listen. My deal's our ticket to a better life."

Susan smashed dinner plates in the kitchen sink, then slung a third plate, almost decapitating her fuming husband. "What better life? No kids, no future. I'm wallowing in this fucking pig-stye with a worthless, pathetic excuse for a husband. Because of your goddamn addictions, we've got a handful of nothing. Listen good, dumbass. I get real-time notifications from the bank and my fuckin' phone buzzes every thirty seconds. How much do you owe 'em, two-hundred, three hundred thousand? I mean, what the hell, Ed? You've pissed it all away."

Susan shrieked as Edward heaved a kitchen chair through the front window. With venom in his voice, he said, "Doesn't matter what I owe 'em. They want that fuckin' truck, and they'll pay the moon to get it. It would have squared things for me. You need to step way the fuck off. I know what I'm doin'."

Susan stood with her arms crossed in front of her chest, fighting back the tears welling in her eyes. "Know what you're doing. Now that's funny. If that damn truck's so goddamn priceless, then why'd you send those two yokels to get it?"

Edward looked down, kicking at the floor with his boot. "Long story—don't matter, anyway. The Snakes fucked things up and your hillbilly boyfriend went rogue on us. To make matters worse, Wenner's dead and that truck's nowhere to be found."

Edward ducked and stumbled as Susan fired two more plates at his head. "That's fuckin' great! You are without a doubt the stupidest man I've ever met." Susan, her face beet-red, made a thrusting motion with her hips. Then shook her finger within an inch of her husband's nose. "Every guy in this county wants to get in my pants, but you're too strung out to even get it up. Ugly, dumb, and impotent, I mean, c'mon man. What fuckin' good are ya?"

Jerry Reynolds, still seated on the porch, could almost hear the veins popping in Edward's face and neck. He peeked through the open doorway to see his boss swallowing pills by the handful. The furious cowboy whipped the empty bottle aside, then snapped a wooden leg from the overturned table. Edward gripped the heavy stick with both hands, swinging it like a crazy ape and smashing a ceiling fan to bits.

Susan screamed and fired a coffee mug at his head. Edward ducked, sidestepping the ceramic missile. Spittle shot from his mouth as he shouted. "You worthless, two-timing bitch! I've got witnesses. By my calculations, you've fucked every cowboy in the county. Rednecks, Indians, wet-backs, makes no difference to you, right? No babies? It's your own goddamn fault. But hey, it's not like you haven't been tryin'. Let's not forget how I bailed you outta KC—regretting it every day. This numbers bullshit of yours ends right fuckin' now."

Reynolds had heard enough. He stomped his boots up the porch stairs, cleared his throat, and shouted through the screen door. "Mrs. Norman, I fixed the old tiller like you asked. Wanna ride out to the fence line? You can show me where you want those shrubs planted."

Moments later, Susan stepped from her kitchen, shaken and wiping the damage from her cheeks. After surveying the rolling sunlit pastures, she said, "Thank you, JR. Give me a second, won't you?"

Edward shouted obscenities from behind the tattered drapes. "Where's the goddamn truck, old man? Susan, get your ass back in here! We ain't done with this."

The troubled woman fought to compose herself, stepping into

the yard while tapping a message into her phone. She glanced up at the sky. "I've always appreciated your timing, Jerry. Let's go. It's a delightful afternoon for a ride."

Reynolds nodded as he slid behind the steering wheel, twisting the key. They left the furious cowboy staggering around on the porch, cursing and waving his table leg like a caveman's gnarled club.

For the next few minutes, they rode together in silence. Susan alternated between tapping on her phone and glancing up towards Highway 5. Reynolds distracted himself by inspecting the fencing, looking for rotten posts and breaks in the barbed wire. Susan signaled for the driver to pull over, and they parked in the shade of a large, weather-beaten cottonwood tree. From a dry creek bed almost a half mile from the house, they watched Edward leaning against his truck, kicking at the ground and puffing on his cigarette.

A warm breeze rustled the leaves and Susan stepped from the truck to stretch her legs. Reynolds climbed out and tugged on the tie-downs, making sure the tiller was secure. He looked up in time to see a large, white SUV turn from the highway onto Valley Road. The Escalade, stirring up a cloud of road dust, had fancy wheels and tinted windows. Reynolds noted the personalized Missouri license plates. "Looks like we've got company," he said, shading his eyes. "Friends of yours?"

Susan cocked her eyebrows, then pointed her chin towards the house. "They're here to see my pitiful husband about a horse."

They watched the SUV drive up to the house and park near Edward's dusty pickup. Four of the largest men Reynolds had ever seen climbed out and surrounded his boss. Reynolds leaned towards Susan. "They look like offensive linemen. Wildcats?"

Susan shook her head and turned away. "Not exactly."

Reynolds watched as the men engaged in a heated debate. Then the largest man snatched the table leg from Edward and, with an effortless flick, sent it flipping into the weeds. Edward threw a hard right-cross, but the muscled-up driver caught the punch with his hand and squeezed, causing Edward to cower and crumple to the ground. The three other behemoths took their turns punching and kicking the hapless cowboy, bashing him into an unresponsive, suffering lump. Their vicious beating took its toll in less than a minute.

Soon, showing the same confidence as when they arrived, the four beasts climbed back into their Escalade and drove away. Reynolds, his legs trembling, slid back behind the steering wheel, shaking his head. He watched Susan tap on her phone from the corner of his eye. He pointed with his thumb and asked, "You're the one they call Numbers, right?"

Susan didn't respond. She stood and watched the big car roll away, a plume of dust billowing in its wake. The old man stared across the field and winced at the decaying house, the shattered windows, and the lifeless body slumped in the front yard. Susan continued to ignore him, tapping her thumbs on her small LED screen.

Reynolds licked his chapped lips and wrung his hands on the steering wheel. His fatigued eyes scanned the surrounding pastures before stopping at the manicured yard where his stately Chevrolet sparkled in the late afternoon sunshine. He saw no sign of the migrants, and Susan's handy grunt, Manny Rodriguez, was nowhere to be found.

After another minute, Reynolds turned and scrutinized a wisp of gray smoke as it twisted skyward above the seedy, smoldering pile that used to be the old Holstein barn. Another breeze, slight and almost reassuring, lifted the rattle of cicadas buzzing in the trees that surrounded his hollow.

Reynolds sighed, dropping his chin to his chest. He reached for the key, but Susan nudged his elbow, stopping him. She pocketed her phone and slid into the passenger seat while locking onto the old man's tired, defeated face. "Don't play coy with me, JR. I mastered the ruse years ago. My friends in the Escalade will be back soon," she said, shading her eyes behind a pair of dark sunglasses. "Plain to see, they're in no mood to talk. Drop me at the highway and head on home. I don't want you anywhere near this shit. Tomorrow, we'll plant a few shrubs and you can tell me all about your trip to Fargo."

Reynolds dabbed sweat from his forehead, then pursed his lips and nodded as he twisted the key.

Chapter 16
Lucky Penny

"Jokers turn kings and diamonds to dust."

A gloomy morning sky draped a misty gray shroud over the Black Hills, matching Dale Sommers' somber mood. He sat on Samantha's back porch sipping bottled water, waiting for his obstinate lawyer to arrive. Lengths of yellow crime scene tape surrounded the growing number of officials gobbling doughnuts and gulping coffee in the backyard.

Meanwhile, their grumbling deputies scoured the rugged slope leaning into Devils Bathtub. Sommers learned a team of FBI agents out of Denver would soon join the state and local officials. Like the others, they'd trudge through the house, poke around the backyard, and tramp along the rocky, tree-lined hillside without finding answers.

A young female investigator, a field agent with the South Dakota State Police selected for this encounter, stepped into the screened porch and asked to take a seat. Sommers motioned towards an empty Adirondack chair. "Be my guest."

She scooched the seat closer to Sommers, then reached out to shake his hand. "Jo Douglass, SDSP. Nice place. Quite a view from up here." Douglass was of average height, average weight, fit and attractive. This despite no make-up, jewelry, or other frilly feminine adornments. Native American, she had smooth skin, alluring dark eyes and shiny, shoulder-length black hair braided in the back.

Douglass started with the same line of questioning Sommers had already answered four times. After enduring several hours of scrutiny, he'd become skilled at filtering out the accusations and the gibberish. What the big lumberjack wanted most was to settle into his captain's seat and fly home to Minnesota.

Sommers slipped his government ID, issued by the U.S. Department of Agriculture, from his shirt pocket and handed it to the officer. "Name's Sommers. That piece of plastic will address ninety percent of the questions I'm permitted to answer."

Douglass grasped the ID card and cocked a skeptical eyebrow. She scribbled notes into a small pad, recording the big man's information. Sommers sipped his water and watched the bustle of activity in the backyard. He glanced at his watch and wondered what was taking Jack Hughes so long. "Jo?" He asked, twisting the cap back onto his water bottle.

"Short for Joanna," she said as she returned his identification card. "Lac Clair Minnesota? Sounds exotic. What brings you out to the Black Hills, Mr. Sommers?"

He shifted in his chair so he could face the pretty officer. "I was in the neighborhood." He pointed at a beverage cooler and offered Douglass a chilled bottle. "I stopped by to check on things for a friend."

Douglass declined the drink with a wave, then studied her notes for effect. "Samantha Stevens. Is she a friend of yours? She rents this place from Big Bill Wenner. Am I right?"

Sommers rolled his eyes and leaned forward in his seat. He pointed his water bottle at Douglass' notepad. "I'll bet the answers to those questions are already on that paper. What is it you really want to know?"

"There's no need to be difficult, Mr. Sommers. We're just making small talk, getting to know each other."

"My friends don't take notes and raise their eyebrows when we talk about the weather, Ms. Douglass. Like most people, I get sorta cranky when I don't get enough sleep. For the past six hours, I've been answering the same pointless questions. Meanwhile, a sadistic killer roams these hills. It's already been a long day and I just want to go home."

"Soon enough, Mr. Sommers." Douglass licked her finger, then turned the page of her pint-sized notebook. "Is that your Tahoe parked down at the trailhead?" Then, before Sommers could answer, two gentlemen wearing tailored navy-blue suits stepped into the backyard. Athletic builds, hardened faces, and hundred-dollar haircuts—the federal agents from Denver had arrived. A senior officer from the local authorities greeted them. The sheriff nodded towards the porch, where Sommers and Douglass engaged in pleasantries. Then he whistled and waved to Douglass, asking her to join the meeting in the backyard.

After shifting his chair, Sommers watched the foursome exchange handshakes outside of his earshot. The sheriff showed cordial leadership and pointed in three different directions, setting the stage and sharing his impressions. He cocked his head to Jo Douglass, and she flipped through several pages, summarizing her research. Their conversation lasted another five minutes before the two feds turned and approached the house.

Former football players maybe, ex-military for sure, these guys were the no nonsense types sent in to bust kneecaps and extract answers. Sommers stood, anticipating their introductions, but the agents stepped in and walked past him without breaking stride. They avoided his eye-contact as they marched towards the back bedroom.

A short time later, the federal agents returned to the yard, joined by a third agent, another Native American. He was a short, muscular man, wearing khaki pants and a dark blue vest. A white patch showed his affiliation to the Bureau of Indian Affairs. The B.I.A. agent flailed his hands and pointed at Sommers, accusing him of something.

Following their debate, the sheriff stepped away while the others checked their cellphones. Sommers heard shouts echoing from down in the basin, and he watched Douglass fumble for her cell phone, answering a call. She propped her phone under her chin and scribbled another note before disconnecting. Then she reunited with Sommers in his screened-in holding pen.

Douglass remained standing, exuding an air of dominance as she tucked her phone and notepad into pockets. She adjusted her shirt and gun holster. "The game's changed, Mr. Sommers. Better tell the folks back in Minnesota you won't be home for dinner."

He shrugged his shoulders and turned his palms to the ceiling. "That was the South Dakota CSI team calling," Douglass said, motioning towards the rocky slope. "They found another body down in the creek."

Sommers stood and asked, "Body?" He could feel his face flushing and a cold sweat saturated his undershirt. "Who?"

"Don't know. Female, long, dark hair, Native." Douglass pursed her lips and rocked on the balls of her feet. "Gunshot wounds, one to the leg, one to the head. That's all I'm at liberty to say."

Sommers adjusted his baseball cap, then slumped back into his chair and folded his arms across his chest. Douglass said, "Agents Colletti and Wagner want to ask you a few questions. They're disgruntled long-timers who got passed over for cushy high-paying promotions. Meaning, they're a couple of rough ol' boys who don't take crap from anyone. A bit of free advice, because I like you. Dispense with the attitude and give 'em straight answers. Will you do that for me?"

Moments later, as if they'd rehearsed the routine a thousand times, Agents Joe Colletti and Donald Wagner stepped onto the porch. They nodded and directed Douglass to rejoin the other officers in the yard. Sommers stood to shake their hands, but the two agents spent the next few seconds sizing him up, offering no cordial introductions. The dark-haired agent, the one Sommers assumed was Colletti, pointed at him. "Have a seat. You're not going anywhere."

"I prefer to stand. Thank you." Sommers locked eyes with the pair, not intimidated by their harsh scrutiny. He'd dealt with their kind many times before. "You guys know we play for the same team, right?"

Colletti remained deadpan and focused, not amused. "Special Agent Douglass says you traveled five-hundred miles to check on this place for a friend. We're having a hard time believing that—must be some special friend."

"What's so hard to understand?" Sommers asked, locking eyes with Colletti. "Where I come from, that's what friends do."

Wagner rolled his eyes as he paced the floor. "Body armor, a rented Tahoe with an arsenal stuffed in the back." He motioned with his hand. "That hillside's littered with shell casings. I mean, shit. It looks like the fuckin' OK Corral down there."

Sommers shrugged his shoulders, following Jack's advice and not verbalizing anything of consequence.

"What about Bud Wolcott?" Wagner asked, leaning into Sommers' face. "Was he your friend?"

Sommers considered lashing out, but restrained himself, knowing the more he resisted, the longer it would take him to get home. With clenched fists and fiery eyes, he said, "Yes, Bud was a friend. He was a good man."

The two agents glanced at each other, then Colletti asked, "Who's Lilly LeBlanc?" Sommers stared at the agent, giving his best poker face. He wanted to avoid the question, and his insides burned.

He knew these hard-asses were putting the squeeze on him because they had nothing else cooking. Colletti turned and pointed east past the ridge Sommers and his partners hiked the previous day. "I'm surprised Douglass didn't mention it. State police found LeBlanc's pickup at the bottom of Squaw Creek. They can't determine the exact time of her death, but they say it's been at least a day, maybe two."

Wagner chimed in, scratching at his chin. "Strange thing is, they found an empty booster seat in the back. They're checking into birth records. Somebody mentioned she provided daycare. A mountain biker stumbled upon the spot where she flipped her car. There's a second set of tire impressions that look damn close to the treads on that Jeep parked in the driveway. See where this is going? Every officer in that yard has you in their crosshairs."

Sommers glared at the gloomy sky, choking back his anger and remorse. He dug his fingers into his pockets and shook his head without saying a word.

Colletti turned to watch the police activity in the yard. "We're ninety-five percent certain another vehicle rammed LeBlanc's truck over the edge." The agent pivoted to face Sommers nose to nose. "Assuming we're right, then we're talking about another murder. What amazing, unfortunate timing. Three dead bodies surface while you're out here checking on your special friends. How do you explain that strange coincidence? C'mon man, what are the chances?"

Wagner unfurled a devilish grin, showing his insolence. "Coincidence, my ass. Let's cut the bullshit, shall we? Where the fuck is she?"

Sommers stepped to the window, crossed his arms, and exhaled a deep sigh. "I'm not sure who you're talking about. Maybe you flatfoots should check the ravine."

Colletti pointed at him and said, "You're skating on thin ice here, Sommers. Your lack of cooperation tells us you're hiding something, harboring a criminal at the least. I snap my fingers, and the state of South Dakota will charge you with obstruction. Trouble is, Mr. Sommers, the DSS doesn't play nice. And right now, they're two steps ahead of us." Colletti folded a piece of chewing gum into his mouth. "For your own protection and the safety of the people in this community, we're taking you back to Denver for a custodial interrogation."

Wagner turned to the backyard and whistled. "Douglass. Get in here and read the suspect his rights."

Sommers was about to explode when his slowpoke lawyer leaned in from the doorway. "I can speak from first-hand experience," he said, clutching a box of doughnuts he purchased from a local bakery. "Dale Sommers doesn't need your protection. In fact, I'm kinda surprised he hasn't stuffed you bozos into a burn barrel by now." Hughes surveyed the brouhaha in the backyard and shook his head. The brash lawyer handed the pastry box to Wagner, then slipped a business card from his back pocket. "Jack Hughes. Which one of you clowns is the bad cop?" Hughes turned and flashed a wink at Sommers, then patted his shoulder. "Don't say another word. I'll take it from here."

In the trauma wing at McKennan Hospital in Rapid City, Doctor Cody Parsons cracked the door open and peeked out from room 110. He looked left, where two agents paced the floor at the end of the hall. Then he looked right and spotted Joy Moon Deer sitting near the waiting area, charging her cellphone in an office cubicle. Parsons tip-toed to her side and tapped her shoulder. She jerked to readiness, balling her fists as she looked up at him.

After raising his hands and making his introduction, Parsons said, "Mr. O'Leary will awaken soon. The procedure went as expected, pretty smooth. His physical therapy will be lengthy and uncomfortable." Parsons motioned to his beltline. "He'll have a pair of nasty looking scars on his side." Then the bookish doctor pointed at his wrist. "We screwed a small titanium plate to his scaphoid. He'll need to shoot left-handed for a while. Are you with those gentlemen hovering around the coffee machine?"

Moon Deer leaned back to peek around a divider. Two men, natives, one tall and one short, sipped coffee. They scrolled through pages on their phones while leaning against the snack machines. "Nah. They're cops. BIA, I'm guessing," she said, shaking her head. "Cold-blooded assholes, if you want the truth."

Parsons nodded. "Yep, kinda thought so. That's why I'm ducking, giving you the first crack at Mr. O'Leary."

Minutes later, Parsons convinced the two agents to hike around the corner to Perkins for breakfast. He emphasized it would be several hours before the detective regained consciousness. In room 110, Moon Deer slid a chair beside Greg O'Leary's hospital bed. She settled in, holding his hand while he slept. Moon Deer studied the detective's sallow face, then watched his chest rise and fall with each breath. She stopped counting the myriad of medical tubes and wires attached to him when she got to eight.

He'd been through a lot over the past twenty-four hours. They all had. Moon Deer could never be mistaken for a sentimental soul, but O'Leary risked his life to save hers, and for this, she pledged to be forever grateful. As O'Leary stirred towards consciousness, Joy recognized something had changed. The axis of her world tilted and her life was now dangerously and wonderfully different.

Even with Moon Deer's encouragement, it took O'Leary a full half-hour to overcome his confusion and come to grips with his condition. The fading anesthesia allowed a flood of soreness and nausea to wash over him. Two frazzled nurses scurried in to run a battery of tests, then administer antibiotics and painkillers. Moon Deer sat on the edge of his bed as they finished their assignments and closed the door behind them.

She searched her hero's groggy, bloodshot eyes. "First off, thank you," she said, leaning close to him. "We got you into this fuckin' mess. Shit, what am I saying? You saved my life. Don't know if I'll ever find the right words." O'Leary squeezed her hand and nodded. His chapped lips didn't move, but his sleepy eyes shared something she interpreted as sweet. Moon Deer shared her gratitude by planting a tender kiss on his forehead.

She settled back into her chair and pointed towards the end of the hall. "Two cops are hanging around the hospital. BIA or FBI, and they'll find their way here to hassle you. Jack recommends taking the fifth until your head clears and we have a better idea of what the fuck we're dealing with."

O'Leary nodded and motioned to a plastic mug with a bendy straw. Moon Deer brought it to his mouth, and he sipped before swallowing with a wince. The detective took a deep breath and marshaled his thoughts. "They question you? Tell me straight. What happened up there?"

Moon Deer scrolled through messages on her phone. "Jack sent me a text. CSI found a body in the creek below the house, a young female, Native American. Someone from the BIA was at the scene. Might be the dude banging on the coffee machine. Jack says they read the big man his Miranda Rights—'bout a dozen agencies are fighting over who has jurisdiction. Anyway, a state cop interviewed me during our flight, and by the time we landed, their advance team confirmed my gunshots hit nothing but trees. Those assholes confiscated my Glock."

O'Leary grimaced as he shifted in his bed. "Fired one shot, accounted for the decline, aimed low. Darker than shit. Hit the runner below the waist, I'm certain of it." He laid there hushed, motionless. Then a morbid notion slumped his cheeks. "Maybe it was Sam."

"Funny," she said, rubbing his shoulder. "That very thought occurred to me as I was skimming through Jack's texts. Listen, no matter what. It was self-defense. Maybe she was trying to outflank us, thinking we were intruders. Or maybe she was just trying to help. Maybe she thought we were the fuckin' Snakes?"

"That doesn't explain the other shooters and their strategic positioning. They baited us into a chase. Sam used to be DSS royalty. There's no way in hell they'd burn her before getting what they want. Besides, from what I've heard, it'd take more than one shot to bring that filly down."

Moon Deer stood and paced around the room. "There's more," she said, tucking her phone into her back pocket. "Jack said the state police recovered Lilly LeBlanc's body from the wreckage they found in Squaw Creek. Shit, that's gotta be two hundred feet below the highway." O'Leary flashed a confused expression on his face, and Moon Deer shrugged. "LeBlanc was the boy's nanny. She was returning from Minnesota when she got rammed off the fuckin' road. Jack told me the FBI's convinced she was murdered."

O'Leary shook his head. "Three killings, forty-eight hours, all linked to Sommers. The hell are we gonna do?" Moon Deer and O'Leary sat sullen for a few minutes before she disrupted their uneasy silence by turning on the TV.

Fox News broke away from election coverage to update viewers about the massacre in Fargo. O'Leary sat up and stared at the TV as witnesses described the gangland execution of Big Bill Wenner. He sipped his water, swallowed hard, and turned to Moon Deer. "Did I say three? Better make it four. This shit's gotten outta hand."

Moon Deer exhaled a deep sigh and muted the TV. She sat staring into O'Leary's face, watching him drift off to sleep. Then she slid back in the chair with her arms folded across her chest. She closed her eyes and grinned, letting the warmth and the fatigue take her down.

Troubled Water

Six hundred fifty miles northeast of Rapid City, Julie Hughes, an early riser, stirred in the predawn darkness of McFarland's tiny guest house. She heard Peg's voice somewhere in the yard. Julie was certain her husband was sleeping off his hangover in the main house. She opened her eyes and recalled the McFarlands spent the previous night eating too much chicken, drinking too much beer, and talking too much smack.

Gus McFarland was nothing like Julie expected—a twitchy little black man resembling Sherman Hemsley from The Jeffersons. His wife outweighed him by a hundred pounds, and it became clear why Peg called the shots at McFarland Farms.

The grizzled farmer's real name was Gus Johnson. He took his wife's last name because, in his words, there were already too many Johnsons in Minnesota. Julie wasn't sure what it was, but she got the feeling Peg and Gus were hiding something. Her plans for the day included driving to Pembina County to find out why Tommy Fulgham's work truck spent the night there more than a week ago.

The sleepy investigator stepped onto the chilly linoleum floor and felt her way in the darkness to a kitchen window on the musty house's west side. She pulled the curtain back far enough to peek into the yard. Hughes watched four Somali laborers unload plastic sheeting and stacks of storage totes from the back of a plain white delivery truck.

They trudged away while Peg supervised four other workers, seedy Latinos, packing heavy bins back into the truck's cargo hold. McFarland barked orders in basic Spanish while checking boxes on a page affixed to her clipboard. Her assistant slid the full bins onto a digital scale, then slapped labels on the containers after they passed the farmer's inspection.

Julie tip-toed back to her room to grab her cell phone from the nightstand. She disabled the flash and crept back to the kitchen window. Selecting video mode, Julie recorded the last few totes being loaded onto the delivery truck. With sunrise only minutes away, Peg's assistant closed the liftgate, then two of the Latino entourage climbed in and drove away. The other two dissolved into a nearby cornfield carrying stacks of empty bins.

McFarland, standing under a yellow yard light, spent two minutes flipping through her checklist. She turned and leered at the guest house before making her approach. Julie scooted back to her bedroom and slipped under the covers.

Peg's heavy footfalls echoed from the kitchen, and soon the smell of coffee wafted down the hall. Julie heard singing birds and chirping crickets, signaling the dawn's promise of a new day. The investigator remained curled and covered, facing away from the shadowy hall. As daylight seeped between the drapes, Peg McFarland stepped into the open doorway, sipping hot coffee and watching her mysterious guest snooze through the sunrise.

Chapter 17
It Don't Come Easy

"Got to pay your dues if you wanna sing the blues."

Parked near a pair of empty summer camp vans, the racy white Mustang GT was easy for Dean Rivers to spot in the north lot of the Red River Zoo. Cesar Flores stood in the hazy sunshine with his arms crossed and a smoldering cigarette hanging from the corner of his mouth. He leaned against the front fender, wearing dark sunglasses and a smug grin across his face. Rivers backed his pickup into the shade of a red maple tree two parking spots away and climbed out, leaving the engine running and the driver's door open.

Flores tapped a lump of ash from his smoke, then lifted his chin. "You Rivers?"

Rivers nodded.

"Anyone following you?" Flores asked.

The wary farmhand looked around and shook his head.

Flores cocked his head towards the street. "Hear 'bout Wenner?"

Rivers nodded again to affirm he'd heard the news of the Main Street Massacre. Flores peeked over the top of his black Ray-Bans. "Don't say much, do ya?"

To Rivers, Cesar Flores appeared to be in his mid-twenties. But the young man carried himself with a confidence and toughness beyond his years. Rivers flashed two fingers in front of his mouth, bumming a cigarette from the tattooed, muscled-up Mexican. Flores sparked his lighter, and Rivers savored a full drag. He tilted his head back and exhaled smoke from his flared nostrils. The two men sneered at each other, neither card player showing their hand. Impatience, at last, bested the prickly farmhand. "Well. You called this meeting. The hell you want?"

"You had business with the fat man," Flores said as he stepped away from his car and tilted his head towards the black pickup. "Nice truck. But bad news, am I right?" Then he dug a blue key fob from his pocket and twirled it on his finger, much like Wenner did the previous day. "Wanna make it go away? Cesar's your hombre, holmes."

"How?" Rivers asked, side-eyeing an old lady walking a long-haired dachshund past Norman's black truck.

After a long final drag, Flores let swirls of smoke seep from his nose, then flicked the butt into the brush that framed the parking lot. He opened his car door and settled into the driver's seat, then revved the throaty V-8 engine. "Follow me, bro."

Rivers trailed Cesar's Mustang north on 42nd Street for five minutes. They zig-zagged under I-94 before continuing north on 36th Street. The downtown area remained thick with first responders and news choppers. Considering their questionable intentions, Rivers thought they drove far too close to the Fargo police station, only one block from their sinuous route.

Minutes later, Flores and Rivers weaved through a secluded, dismal industrial park, then doubled-back towards 7th Avenue. After circling another block, the pair parked in an alley across from Valley Auto Body. The crumbling garage braced heaps of gnarled, rusting car parts piled high against its graffiti-stained walls.

Flores slid from the Mustang and jogged back to Rivers' window.

He pointed his thumb at the sleazy two-story building. "Truck's blocking the door. Hang here a minute."

Rivers dug out his cell phone and dialed Jerry Reynolds. He left a voicemail message requesting, with some reluctance, a lift back to the farm. Then he sat and watched as two sweaty Latinos unloaded blue storage totes, one after another, from the back of a filthy white cube truck. A third Latino remained seated behind the steering wheel, watching videos on his cellphone. A fourth animated worker emerged from the garage carrying a clipboard. He pointed with his pen and barked obscenity-laced orders at his grunts.

Flores lit another cigarette, then lifted his chin towards the peculiar mid-day activity. "Pull into the shop after the truck's gone. Wait for my signal."

Rivers cocked his eyebrows, then glanced at his phone, checking for messages from Pembina County.

Ten long minutes passed until the greasy Latinos piled into the delivery truck and pulled away from the garage. The driver locked his angry eyes onto Rivers as the truck rolled past. It belched a gassy exhaust cloud, then turned and rumbled west towards the Interstate. Flores inched his car forward and honked the horn. Soon the shop's overhead door opened, releasing pungent vapors punctuated by the sounds of Latin rap music.

Flores leaned out his window and gave Rivers a whistle, then motioned for him to pull in. Seconds later, Rivers heard tires squeal, and he turned to watch the Mustang speed away. The garage door lowered behind him, so he cut the ignition and climbed down from the driver's seat. The rumpled farmhand scanned the gloomy garage, then stood and stared at his reflection in the shiny black fender, skeptical of this entire shady arrangement.

Pungent odors from welding torches and paint fumes filled the dingy workshop. A funky cannabis haze clung to the cobweb-covered ceiling rafters. Buried under layers of dust and gray primer, a

1960s Chevy Nova sat sullen in a mottled spray booth. Nearby, a late model Corvette rested on jack stands, the interior and wheels stripped from its glossy yellow shell. Looking out of place, four dozen blue totes lined the side wall near a service door dimpled with bullet holes. Rivers grabbed his duffel from the back seat, then whistled and called out. "Hey! Anyone home?"

Soon, the music stopped, and a voice echoed from above. "Up here, dumbass." Duane Rivers wobbled in the shadow of a landing at the top of the stairs, wearing the same grubby clothes from two days earlier. He'd wrapped his broken right hand in a makeshift collection of cloth bandages. The skinny, blackened fingers of his left hand clutched a vapory joint. "The hell you doin' here?" He asked, slurring his words with a dulled edginess to his voice. "Ya bring me a fuckin' phone?"

Dean Rivers shook off his initial surprise and stood silent for a moment, pondering his son's questions and considering the grim reality of this encounter. Deep down, he realized there wasn't enough room in North Dakota for two angry Rivers. "Phones are stuck in China, back-ordered. Your boy led me here to dump this truck." Rivers pointed at his son's ragged mitt. "I gave you a fist full of cash to get your hand fixed. What gives?"

Duane hiked up his sagging pants and scratched under his arm like a scrubby, strung-out monkey. "Ten grand don't even cover the x-rays. The hell you thinkin'?" Then the petulant teen plodded down the stairs, drawing another toke from his roach. He exhaled his smoke and leaned against the railing, scowling at his rumpled father.

Dean Rivers shook his head, not hiding his disgust, worried the wasted teen's joint was going to spark a catastrophic explosion. "Maybe I was thinking the same thing you were thinking when you and your buddies tried to carjack a cop." The irritated father held out his hand. "Gimme the ten K. I'll be damned if you're gonna spend my winnings on meth and weed." Then he leaned closer and pointed his thumb towards the door. "I'll get way gone, and you'll never see me again. Ever."

Duane snickered, then belched a sloppy, nasty cough. "Shit, dude. The money's gone." He waved at the plastic bins stacked along the wall. "Even if I had the cash, no way in hell you're getting it back. You fuckin' owe me, man."

Duane's lethargic defiance and the shop's foggy ambience led Rivers to an understanding. The cube truck's payload wasn't tubs of Bondo or sleeves of sandpaper, and Valley Auto Body wasn't just a seedy chop-shop. VAB was a distribution center for black-market pot, serving the entire Upper Midwest. His ten thousand dollars was mere chicken feed for this fetid operation. "Really?" Rivers asked, chewing his lower lip as he nodded. "You're a goddamn junkie. Explain how I owe you anything but a slap upside your filthy head."

Duane rocked on his heels ten feet from his despised father. He snuffed his joint out on a rusty quarter-panel, then slipped a small handgun from the pocket of his hoodie. "For killing Ma and leaving me with shit."

Rivers dropped his bag and raised his hands, preparing to plead his case. Duane flipped and fumbled the gun in his left hand like a bungling wild west clown.

Without warning, a pair of deafening pops shattered the lull. Duane's first shot ricocheted off the gray Nova's rusty bumper. The second shot fired from the twenty-two-caliber pistol punctured his father's throat just above his shirt collar. Soon, a pulsing stream of blood drenched the man's t-shirt. Dean Rivers crumpled to his knees, then flopped face-first onto the dusty concrete floor. Close-range and lethal, the bullet burrowed through the man's neck, then spit from his back. The shot nicked his spine, and all but guaranteed Dirty Dean's demise.

Jose Guyton and Ozzy Rodriguez, hearing the gunshots, scrambled from an adjoining break room with a billowing cloud of smoke hot on their heels. Jose said, "What the... Dude! Cuz told us to grab the goddamn truck, not shoot the fuckin' driver." He clasped the sides of his head and tugged at his hair. "Who is this asshole, anyway? Ya fuckin' killed him, didn't you, Duane?"

Ozzy used the toe of his workbook to roll the hapless hayseed onto his back. Dean Rivers lay in a pool of blood and grime, his breathing ragged, clinging to his crappy life. He gazed into Ozzy's inquisitive face. Then Dean's eyes widened with recognition as he recalled the sinister faces that danced in the blaze at Norman Farms. His visions and their unsettling context became clear. Ozzy Rodriguez was an uncanny, haunting resemblance to his older brother, Manny.

Duane Rivers tossed the gun aside and stood in a daze, looking down at his expiring father. "It was an accident, man. Got nothing to do with that stupid truck. This asshole beat my mom to death with a croquet mallet. Tried to hang it on me. The abusive motherfucker's gettin' what he deserves."

Jose Guyton, still showing the cuts and bruises from the beating he took from Greg O'Leary, said, "Dude, you're stoned out of your fuckin' mind. I told you that twenty-two was a jumpy piece of shit. Now we gotta clean up another one of your fuckin' messes. The cartel knows you fuckin' bailed on us at Casey's." Jose stomped around in a circle, waving his hands. "You know what I think? I think we're done taking the fall for your crazy bullshit."

Dean Rivers lay dismayed and unmoving in his widening puddle of slick red ooze. Jose and Ozzy huddled off to the side, whispering in Spanish. Then, in a split second, Ozzy leaped and snatched a twenty-nine-inch breaker bar from a rolling tool cart. He swung the tool at Duane's head. The unsuspecting stoner never saw the hardened steel club streaking towards his ear. Ozzy smashed the side of Duane's head with a sickening and fatal crack. The teen's quivering legs gave way and his body crumpled to the floor beside his father.

Jose shouted as he fluttered his hands over his head. "Holy shit! The fuck you do that for?"

Ozzy wiped a sticky string of spittle from his chin with the back of his hand. "The river's shallow and muddy this time of year. But we can sink two bodies, jus' the same as one." The elder Rivers, fading, but hanging on, crooked his eyes to gaze upon the ravaged husk that used to be his son. He recognized Duane's ghastly profile from the menacing Pembina flames. The boy's beaten, angular face rounded out Dean's haunting trilogy.

Jose leaned closer to see if either of the two Rivers was still alive. "Damn, bro." He poked at Dean's chest with a wooden paint stick. "Hey, cowboy. What's the deal with this truck?" Dean Rivers, unable to move, barely able to speak, blinked his eyes and twitched his head, trying to communicate his ignorance.

Ozzy shuffled over and picked up Duane's twenty-two. After several seconds of examining the dying pair, he connected the blood-soaked hick to Norman Farms. Ozzy stood over the older man with the small handgun pointed at the farmer's pallid face. "Aye, vaquero, dónde está mi hermano?"

Rivers shifted his eyes between the two gangbangers, and then his dead son. He smirked, lamenting the fact that his last resting place was on a cold, hard floor instead of between Angie McCormick's bouncy, warm breasts. With a feeble, sputtering stammer, he said, "Manny smelled like shit, rotten to the core. Killed the Fulgham kid in cold blood and now he burns in hell. You fucking wetbacks will burn with him. Soon."

Ozzy Rodriguez displayed a quizzical, almost pitying expression on his face before he aimed the muzzle and pulled the trigger.

Ten seconds too late, Jerry Reynolds stepped from the shadows of the tool cage, waving a sawed-off shotgun. "Drop the gun. Show's over."

Rodriguez laughed before slapping Jose on the back. "Shit, man. Get a load of Elmer Fudd?"

"Who the hell's Elmer Fudd?" Jose asked.

His eyes ablaze, Reynolds pumped cartridges into both barrels of his twelve gauge. Rodriguez hesitated, cursed in Spanish, then tossed the pistol into a pile of boxes and packing paper. The old timer reached over and pressed a green button on the wall, lifting the garage door. Ted Lindstrom stood silhouetted in the brilliant opening. He looked every bit the modern-day gunfighter with a shiny revolver cocked in each hand.

While Reynolds trained his shotgun on the two gangbangers, Lindstrom lashed their wrists and ankles with nylon cord. He plastered their mouths with strips of duct tape, then dragged their squirming bodies into a grubby single-stall bathroom. Reynolds studied Duane and shook his head, then crouched beside Dean Rivers, feeling for a pulse. "He's gone," he said, looking up at the retired sheriff.

Lindstrom scrutinized the bloody heaps, then shook his head. "Shit, I knew the boy was nothin' but trouble," he said. "But Dirty Dean was just a good ol' boy. What the hell did he get himself into?"

Reynolds stood and peered out the door. "Caught in a numbers game," he said, brushing Bondo dust from his pants. "But now's not the time for shootin' the bull."

"Agreed," Lindstrom said. "Well shit, we've got three vehicles and only two drivers. Can't leave anything traceable behind. How do we make this work?"

Jerry adjusted his baseball cap and pointed his shotgun at the pickup truck. "This Ford's got a hitch. I spotted a car trailer behind the shop—seems to be in decent shape. If you help me hook 'er up, I'll tow my Chevy back to the farm."

Lindstrom scanned the ceiling and walls for security cameras. Surprised and satisfied there weren't any, he said, "No problem, but we've gotta hustle. The cartel will be back to check on their boys." He used his phone to snap pictures of the bodies and the stack of storage totes. "Say, for yuks and grins, I think I'll follow you back."

Reynolds glanced back at the two dead bodies on the floor. "Appreciate the company."

———•———

Twenty minutes and three miles later, Ted Lindstrom followed Jerry Reynolds into the right lane of northbound I-29. Heat vapors, shimmering in the sweltering August sun, rose from the pavement like phantoms. Jerry's snail-paced forty-five miles per hour tested Lindstrom's patience. Ted's Charger SRT, and Jerry's '66 Impala, formed a small hot rod procession that stuck out like a bandaged thumb.

Lindstrom shifted his eyes between the sparse southbound traffic and his rearview mirrors. He searched for any aggressive, suspicious movements. Five miles north of Fargo, Lindstrom's rearview mirror filled with a rising, mushroom cloud of black smoke. Soon, his phone chimed, flooded with notifications, and he switched his radio from classic rock to news-talk.

Lindstrom listened as an on-sight reporter described the massive blasts that shook an industrial complex on the northern fringe of Fargo. He said lootings have broken out across the city. The breaking news confirmed Ted's hunch about the deadly explosion. Despite his anonymous 911 call, the drug cartel arrived at Valley Auto Body before the cops did.

Expelling a heavy sigh and calming his nerves, Lindstrom tapped his infotainment screen. He dialed Jack Hughes' phone number. "Jack. It's Ted. How's our boy doing?"

Hughes said, "The big guy's fit to be tied, but holding it together better than most. We're here another day, maybe two—waiting for CSI to finish in the basin and watching the weather. The feebs backed off on pressing charges once I convinced them Sommers never touches a gun, and his fishing buddies include the Secretary of the Interior and the 8th district's highest ranking federal judge. What's going on with you? Anything helpful from Wenner's?"

"I got sidetracked on my way to the Ford dealer. Turn on the news and you'll see why. Me and my pal Jerry Reynolds were allegedly at Valley Auto Body, but we didn't do any shooting and we had nothing to do with the explosion, I swear. Poor guy's pretty shook, but I think he knows more than he's sayin'. Bodies are piling up, and we've still got more questions than answers."

Lindstrom folded a piece of chewing gum into his mouth, then adjusted his rearview mirror. "Say, tell Sommers we've got our mitts on the infamous black pickup truck. We found the registration papers in the glove box, and the last signature on the title belongs to someone named Hunter, dated three years ago. Anyway, we're on our way to Pembina County, keeping our heads down. I'm trying to reach O'Leary, but I keep getting his voicemail. Any word?"

"Try Moon Deer's phone. She's sitting bedside, stuck to his hip like crazy glue. Poor guy's got two holes in his side, and now he's got a big pain in the ass, too." Jack chuckled, caught his breath, then said, "The surgeon said O'Leary's gonna be fine. Moon Deer's gonna hang out in Spearfish while he recovers—gonna stay here at the lodge and keep her eyes peeled for Samantha and her so-called friends."

"Makes sense, I guess. But that puts us down two guns, and shit's breaking loose from here to Sunday. Wish we could lean into Sam's DSS expertise right about now."

"I know, right? But there's not much we can do about it. Say, I'm calling in a favor. Can you jog over to Kittson County? Julie's investigating a missing person's case. She may have stumbled into a hornet's nest—political corruption and drug trafficking. McFarland Farms, it's off the beaten path, nestled between Two Rivers. I'll text you the GPS coordinates."

Hughes fumbled with his phone, catching his breath before he continued. "Lock and load, buddy. Sommers is gonna get Schmitty up there with a drone, but I'd like another pair of boots on the ground ASAP. Once Jules smells blood in the water, there's no telling her to back off."

Lindstrom mulled over the fluky ties of Two Rivers, then agreed to provide ground support in Minnesota. "I'll check on your girl—make sure she's safe, but Tommy Fulgham's not missing. He's dead." For several minutes, Lindstrom shared what he'd learned at the body shop. Then he clicked off and dialed Moon Deer's number. "Joy Moon Deer. It's your Uncle Ted. How's my crazed little sex kitten?"

Moon Deer huffed, then said, "You're kinda creeping me out, ya itchy old pervert."

Lindstrom laughed, continuing to scout both the oncoming and passing traffic on Interstate 29. "Thanks a hell of a lot. I'll deal with you later. I called to harass O'Leary. How's Rambo doing?"

"Once the nurse takes his catheter out, he'll be doing great." Moon Deer smacked her lips. "I'm gonna give him a fuckin' sponge bath he'll never forget—check his blood pressure, if you know what I mean."

"I feel ya, sis. But go easy scrubbing the boys, ya hear?" Lindstrom overhead laughter and the sounds of the cell phone getting passed across the hospital room.

O'Leary cleared his throat and said, "So, Dr. Lindstrom, I presume. How's it goin', partner?"

Lindstrom checked the odometer and made a mental note of the highway mile markers. "Slow goin'. Got eight hundred horsepower and I'm using 'bout two of 'em right now. I swear to God, we're gonna be in deep shit if my man can't find his gas pedal."

O'Leary said, "Take my word for it, ya ugly ape. Speed isn't your biggest problem. Tell me what happened in Fargo. Oh, let me guess. It was the Rivers kid and a couple of Mexican punks. Am I right? Anyone else?"

"Feeling better, 'eh. Returning to your offensive old self." Lindstrom laughed, then said, "We didn't see anyone else, but you nailed it. Both Dean and Duane Rivers were belly up before we hightailed it outta there. From the looks of him, you've already met Jose Guyton. His cousin, Cesar, tipped off the hit at Wenner's, then took off from Valley Auto Body before the shit hit the fan. Coincidence? I don't think so."

Lindstrom cleared his throat, then checked himself in the rearview mirror. "By the way, many women say I'm not only smart, but mature and handsome, to boot. When's the last time anyone complimented the cut of your jib?"

O'Leary sputtered a crude noise, then said, "Looks are very overrated. Women don't want my jibs trimmed. They want someone who can make 'em laugh." He fumbled with the phone as he shifted in his hospital bed. "I'm still working my way out of a fog here. Who was the other gangbanger? Any plausible connection to Sam?"

"Ozzy Rodriguez. Heard of him? Reynolds believes he had a brother, a convicted felon, working as a two-bit laborer at Norman Farms. The farmhand went missing about ten days ago. And get this, Dean Rivers admitted to killing Manny Rodriguez before he kicked."

"Fulgham's dead, isn't he?" O'Leary asked.

Lindstrom paused, then said, "Just between us. Reynolds believes Manny Rodriguez shot and killed the Fulgham kid. Then Rivers killed Rodriguez to protect Susan Norman."

"Susan Norman?" O'Leary's voice cracked a bit as he asked. "Protect her from what?"

"Reynolds thinks she put a spell on him, but that sounds crazy, right? Anyway, we're driving up to Pembina County. At the rate we're going, we should arrive in hmm… About two to three days. I'm assuming we'll stumble into some answers up there."

Lindstrom was about to share his theory with O'Leary when

he spotted a black Ford F-250 almost identical to the rig Reynolds was driving. From across two lanes and a grassy median, Lindstrom could see a dark-skinned passenger pointing out Jerry's truck to the dark-skinned driver.

The pair craned their necks as they passed, speeding south on I-29. A second later, Lindstrom checked his rearview mirror and caught the black truck bounding across the littered median, churning an illegal U-turn about a mile back. O'Leary was in the middle of an obscene joke, but Lindstrom interrupted him and said, "We've got company. I gotta go."

Lindstrom downshifted and stomped on the gas pedal, breaking his rear tires loose as he swerved into the left lane. He pulled alongside Reynolds and motioned for him to roll his window down. Ted pointed with his thumb and yelled over the noisy road gusts. "Company. Two Indians in a black truck. We've got to get you off the Interstate. Like, right now!"

Lindstrom swiped to Google Maps on his infotainment screen, studied the checkerboard pattern of roads, then pointed ahead. "Next exit is Buxton Road, 'bout two miles. Take Highway 21 east into Minnesota. Stay on the back roads. Meet me at the farm in two hours. I'll try to hold 'em off, but get the goddamn refrigerator off your back. I'm serious. Step on it, man!"

Reynolds adjusted his baseball cap, then flashed a grin and a thumbs up before disappearing behind the tinted window.

The detective backed off the throttle and watched Jerry Reynolds roll north towards Buxton Road. Lindstrom slowed until the black pick up filled his mirrors, then sped up again, inviting a chase. A few tense minutes passed, and he watched Reynolds exit below a rise. The sly old timer parked under the highway overpass, waiting for the pursuers to zoom past his hiding place.

Once north of Buxton Road, Lindstrom laughed, then shouted, "Okay, bitches, suck on this." He buried the gas pedal, and the dual exhaust thundered its delight. Soon, the muscular Dodge rushed along at an easy one-hundred miles per hour. It streaked past crooked billboards and expansive amber fields. The persistent hunters tried to keep up, but their black truck grew smaller and smaller within Lindstrom's rearview mirrors.

Ted glanced at his tachometer and smiled, seeing he had another two thousand RPMs to play with before hitting the redline. He laughed out loud, shifted into overdrive, then eased off the gas pedal. He cranked up the stereo and bobbed his head with the thumping subwoofer. Lindstrom's lighthearted grin affirmed rural North Dakota looked pretty damn good streaking past his window at one-hundred twenty miles per hour.

Chapter 18
Simply Irresistible

"How can it be permissible?"

The BIA investigators and the South Dakota CSI team, after two full days and dozens of unanswered questions in their pockets, continued their inspections in the lower reaches of Devils Bathtub. Indoors, on their hands and knees, Jack Hughes and Joy Moon Deer scrubbed the frigid bathroom tiles, cleansing the bloodstains, but not the abhorrence of murder. Dale Sommers, fresh from an excruciating phone conversation with Bud Wolcott's mother, worked at the back of the house. Earlier, he fixed a busted window frame, but now he squeezed wood putty into a spray of bullet holes. He hummed his favorite songs and felt the warmth of the sun as it climbed above the eastern hogbacks.

Moon Deer puffed a lock of hair from her eyes, then wiped her brow with the back of her gloved hand. She grimaced and pointed her scrub brush at Hughes. "I've got a shitty taste in my mouth."

Hughes glanced at his cell phone, then sagged back on his haunches. He shook his head after checking his reticent phone for a second, then a third time. "I know, right? These fumes are burning my nostrils. Let's keep at it. We're almost finished."

"No, not that," she said. "I'm talking about sleeping in Sam's bed, squatting on her toilet, and driving her goddamn car back and forth to Rapid City. It just don't feel right."

Sommers, displaying his usual sharp timing, stepped into the open doorway with a steaming cup of coffee in each hand. A weary gloom shone in his eyes, and a forced smile creased his face. "Looking better, 'eh?" He passed the mugs and waited for his friends to finish their sips. Then his smile disappeared, and he locked into Moon Deer's eyes. "We all agreed, remember? Those DSS thugs have unfinished business. And apparently, Sam does too."

He caught himself and gazed through the repaired bedroom window. Then, following a moment of stiff silence, Sommers leaned closer into Moon Deer's face. "Your Irish suitor has requested your presence. He'll be out of the hospital soon, and rehabbing under your careful watch. So quit your bellyaching. By the way, he insisted I leave a pair of tactical vests on the bed. His and hers."

Moon Deer slurped her coffee, expelled a loud belch, then huffed as she returned to her scrubbing. "Ya big lug, jus' cuz you're twice my size—that bluster don't mean shit to me." Then she turned away and winked at Hughes with a mischievous grin curling her lips.

Three hours later, Dale Sommers and Jack Hughes sailed thirty-five hundred feet above the Cheyenne River Reservation. The pilot pointed the spinning propeller northeast, and favorable tailwinds rushed the pair towards home. The previous thirty minutes, their conversation exhausted the usual topics of fishing, sports, and the weather. After a pregnant pause, Hughes said, "Your mechanic's a piece of work. What did he mean by no hard landings?"

Sommers shifted in his captain's seat. "Otto's something, isn't he?" Then he looked over his shoulder. "He's ordering a few suspension parts. He was telling me to take it easy on the front wheel until he can swap 'em out."

Hughes rolled his eyes and shook his head, peering through ribbons of wispy clouds floating past his window. "Julie's not answering her phone. Hope she's okay."

Sommers adjusted his baseball cap and nodded. "C'mon Jack, everyone knows she's a fighter. Besides, you told me Lindstrom's on the road to Kittson County." The pilot, seeing the concern plastered across his confidant's face, changed the subject. "I've been thinking about Tommy Fulgham's parents. Want me to call our BCA guy?"

"You'd better let me call the BCA. How 'bout you call your peeps at the DNR? I've been trying for two days straight. But they're not giving me the time of day."

Sommers nodded again and Hughes plucked a flip phone from his carry-on bag. He requested quiet by holding his index finger to his lips, then tapped a series of numbers on the keypad and put the call on speaker mode.

After several rings, the call connected. Hughes said, "Hey buddy, guess who?"

The officer from the Minnesota Bureau of Criminal Apprehension cleared his throat and cursed under his breath. "Shit, Jack. Every time you call, life gets pretty damn complicated. Tell me you're on a burner or I'm hanging up right now."

Hughes laughed before he said, "What's the matter, honey? Too much coffee this morning? Don't get your balls in a twist, I'm on a nineteen-dollar Walmart special—surprised it even gets a signal up here."

The agent, spouting his irritation, said, "I'm trolling above a hungry school of smallies. Make it quick, man."

"Tommy Fulgham's not missing. He's dead, gunned down by a loony Mexican with a deer rifle—killer's dead, too."

After a quiet, contemplative moment, the BCA agent said, "Not surprised. Where are the bodies?"

"I don't know for sure. But I have it on good authority…"

"Jack, you know I can't do shit without a body. What *do* you know?"

Hughes flipped through a few pages on his yellow pad, skimming his notes. "What I can tell you is when North Dakota CSI gets to sifting through the rubble at Valley Auto Body, they'll find the bodies of Ozzy Rodriguez and Dirty Dean Rivers. Their charred digits will point you towards Tommy Fulgham."

The agent said, "From what I heard, the blast rattled buildings for miles around. Burnt fingers and toes scattered across the valley—not that fucking helpful."

"I get your point. But that doesn't change the fact that you and your boys will have to coordinate with the ND BCI to close the Fulgham case. I'm tryin' to save you some time and a mountain of paperwork."

"So help me, Jack. If you're screwin' with me." Hughes heard splashing noises in the background, then the agent whooped and said, "Shit, fish on. And it's a whopper. Call me later, man. Gotta go." Hughes listened to the agent's phone tumble into the hull of the boat just before their call disconnected.

Hughes ejected the tiny sim card, then tossed his burner phone into a garbage hopper. He leaned forward, facing the pilot, and saw the tired skepticism in his eyes. He patted Sommers on the shoulder. "Well, at least someone's enjoying these last days of summer."

The pilot straightened the yoke, then slid his phone from his shirt pocket, squinting as he swiped through his contacts list. Hughes asked, "Who are you calling?"

"An old friend," he said. "Well, not a friend, exactly. Someone I share a professional history with." He tapped the screen, dialing the Department of Natural Resources headquarters in St. Paul. A pleasant receptionist picked up after three rings. Sommers said, "Colin Stroud, please."

Hughes closed his notepad and leaned his head into the cockpit. "The head of the DNR?" Sommers waved him off and nodded to confirm.

The switchboard transferred Sommers' call twice before Stroud's secretary said the commissioner wasn't available. "What is the nature of your inquiry?" She asked. "Care to leave a message?"

Sommers glared at the screen and shook his head. "The nature of my call is urgency. I need to speak with Mr. Stroud."

The assistant put Sommers on hold for several more minutes before returning to the line. "I'm sorry Mr. Sommers. The commissioner isn't available to speak with you. I'll transfer you to his voicemail."

Sommers waited for the generic greeting to finish. "Stroud, since you're a smart man, I'm assuming you know who this is and why I'm calling. You can bet your last dollar that my next call will be to the EPA. Soon after that, I'm calling the DEA and Fox News. You know how this will go down. I'm giving you until noon tomorrow to get back to me." Sommers disconnected, checked the time, then slipped the phone back into his pocket.

Hughes tapped his fingers together, performing a mocking little clap. "Well done, big man. Next, you'll be threatening the governor, and we'll have the feds crawling up our asses again."

Sommers considered that as he dialed the overhead speakers to some sixties music. Hughes reclined his seat back, pouting while muttering to himself with his eyes closed.

Julie Hughes stepped onto the front porch and into the golden morning sunshine. She stretched her arms behind her back and shook out each of her legs. Wearing a pair of trail joggers, baggy shorts, and an oversized hoodie, she slipped into her earbuds and selected an upbeat playlist on her phone. Next, she tightened her hairband and skipped into an effortless trot, following the perimeter of the cornfield. Two minutes later, she looked over her shoulder and saw Peg McFarland, a half-mile away, sitting high atop her tractor, chugging along in the opposite direction.

Feeling sluggish from two sticky buns and a large coffee, Julie inhaled a unique mix of country aromas; river algae, liquid fertilizer, and a distant skunk. The morning breeze also carried a whiff of something else, something that didn't fit the morning blend.

The rosy jogger came upon a dirt trail that ran east and west along the north branch of Two Rivers, twisted dense scrub on her left, and tall rows of corn to her right. Five minutes into her run, Julie's phone grabbed a weak cell signal and chimed with threads of text messages. Most were from her husband, Jack.

Julie slowed to a walk and turned the volume down to focus on skimming through her texts. First, she learned Ted Lindstrom was on his way to Pembina County. Second, she was relieved to learn that O'Leary, although denying his considerable pain, would heal and survive. Jack's next message mentioned his hatred of flying, but also said he trusted Sommers enough to get him back to Minnesota in one piece.

Then Julie's feet came to a sudden stop as she read Jack's last message over and again. "Call in the dogs. Tommy Fulgham's dead." She dropped her arms to her sides and kicked at some loose dirt with the toe of her shoe. Squawking crows shook Hughes from her momentary daze and she tilted her head skyward, letting the eastern glow bathe her face.

After multiple failed attempts to call her husband, Julie sent a brief text message confirming she'd received his messages. She said she missed him and attached a heart emoji. Then Hughes tapped the play button on her music app and resumed her jogging.

A few strides later, she stepped into a narrow clearing where the grasses and the gravel bore a unique gradient and color. She traced a puzzling pathway running from the river to the middle of McFarland's corn field.

Julie followed the yellowish trail north between some flood-damaged trees to a muddy riverbank. She discovered a submerged four-inch pipe hidden beneath fallen leaves and black netting. She snapped a picture with her phone, then reversed her track and followed the faint line across the path and into the crop rows.

One half mile into the dense acreage, Julie stumbled upon a gas-powered pump surrounded by sedge. Just beyond the wiry thicket sat a low-slung greenhouse the size of a football field. A canopy of green mesh covered the enormous potting shed. The mysterious odor revealed, Hughes aimed her phone and began snapping pictures of the hidden nursery, filled with leafy marijuana plants, as far as her eyes could see.

Julie jumped with a start as the pump fired and water misted from the greenhouse's tubular frame. She caught her breath and stepped back from the spray, switching her camera to video mode. Then, without warning, Julie heard rustling among the cornstalks. She wheeled in time to see two farmhands, Latinos, each carrying a long-handled spade. Neither looked imposing, but they approached her with contempt in their walk and malice in their eyes.

The younger of the two men said, "Hey, chica. Private property. You're not allowed here." The sweaty workers stood ten feet away, licking their lips. They inspected Julie up and down with lustful smirks on their grimy faces. Whispering in Spanish, they snickered and slapped at each other like a pair of stoned circus clowns.

Julie snapped their picture, then slipped her phone into the front pocket of her hoodie. "My bad," she said. "I was out for a run—guess

I got turned around." She pointed past the way they came. "I'm staying with the McFarlands."

The two workers exchanged sideways glances, then the older of the pair held out his hand. "No pictures, princesa. Telefono, por favor."

"Por que?" Julie asked.

"Negecio secreto." The younger man said.

Julie covered her pocket with her hands and scanned the surrounding rows of corn. She cocked an eyebrow and shook her head. "Sorry muchachos, not today."

The gardeners inched closer. Close enough that she could smell their filthy clothes and their vapory breaths. Without warning, the burnouts attacked with clumsy lunges. Julie expected their charge and kicked the younger Latino in the groin, doubling him over. She kicked him a second time, crunching his nose. The suffering farmhand rolled on the ground, one hand between his legs, and the other covering his bloody face.

The older worker leaped and grabbed Julie in a bear hug, using the spade's handle to trap her arms. She strained and wriggled, wrapping her fingers around the wooden handle. Next, she lurched her upper body forward, launching the aggressor high over her back and slamming him to the ground. She kicked him twice in his midsection. Then, using a two-handed baseball swing, she clunked the shaken man upside his head with the back of the shovel's crusty blade.

The investigator dropped the shovel and took off between the crop rows. She made a bee-line for the farmhouses, leaving the two wounded farmhands writhing on the ground. A short time later, Julie bounded into the guest house, grabbed her duffel and keys, then dashed out the door. Her Jeep peppered the small clapboard house with a spray of dirt and gravel. Julie cut a raucous, whirling U-turn, then bolted down the driveway towards Route 16.

Soon, she slammed on the brakes and slid to a stop. "Shit. Too late." Thirty feet away, Peg McFarland sat atop her tractor with a devilish smirk on her face. Her woeful husband, Gus, leaned against the rear wheel with his scrawny fingers clutching the barrel of a rifle. Four Latinos in a rusty old pickup slid to a stop a few yards behind Julie's 4x4.

Two men in the cab, then the two battered stoners in the bed, stumbled into the driveway. One of the injured workers had a bandana tied over his blood-streaked scalp, the other had dirty rags stuffed into his nostrils. Both shuffled behind the first pair, looking timid and sore. All four workers stopped and stood with their arms folded across their chests.

Peg raised her manly hands, palms up, into the air. "What's the matter, sugar? Can't stay for supper?"

Julie stuck her head out the window. "Not today. Gotta see a man about a truck." After peeking into her rearview mirror, she leaned into the passenger seat and popped the glove box open. Julie felt around with her hand, but came up empty.

"Looking for this?" Peg asked. Julie sat up and watched the beefy farm woman slip Jack's .38 from the pocket of her overalls. The Latinos stepped closer while Julie and Peg glared into each other's eyes. An unexpected buzzing noise, like angry hornets carrying tiny chainsaws, broke the stalemate. Julie watched everyone's eyes track upward, scrutinizing the unidentified object hovering in the sky.

Gus lifted the rifle to his shoulder and closed one eye. "Goddamn gooks. This farm ain't for sale. You commie assholes better get the fuck outta here!" The humming drone floated over the cornfield, then dropped in low over the gathering in the driveway. Julie stepped from her Jeep to get a better look.

Then, with impressive timing, Ted Lindstrom emerged from the cornstalks as Gus was about to squeeze off a shot. Lindstrom slipped a pistol from his shoulder holster and took aim at Gus McFarland.

"That drone's U.S. government issue—not a Chinese chip anywhere. Drop the rifle, McFarland. Hands on your head." Gus glanced at Peg, then scowled as he placed the gun on the ground near his feet. Lindstrom then trained his pistol towards Peg. "You too, lady. Party's over."

Peg spit, then tossed the pistol aside. Julie scampered down the driveway, kicked Gus's rifle away, then retrieved Jack's .38. She pivoted towards the heated Latinos as Peg hollered, "Sick 'em, boys! Whip their asses!"

Lindstrom adjusted his aim and pointed skyward. "Uh, uh. Not a good idea, hombres." He fished his phone from his pocket and held the screen high towards their puzzled faces. "There's a mighty expensive camera strapped to that bird. Say cheese, jackasses. You're on YouTube Live." Lindstrom turned back and let out a laugh. "Smile pretty, Peg. You and your gang will be the lead story on The Five tonight."

Lindstrom waved as the baffled workers slinked back into their truck and backed away. He holstered his gun and climbed into the Jeep's passenger seat. Julie flashed a thumbs up, then watched the noisy drone soar higher above McFarland Farms before drifting away.

She said, "Don't you fret, Peg. We'll be back for more of that sweet corn. Tell you what. We'll bring a few friends. How's that sound, sugar?" The large woman spit at the ground, then flashed her middle fingers at the Jeep as they sped away.

Julie and Lindstrom dabbed their eyes, trying to catch their breaths after a fit of hysterical laughter. She fluffed her hair, then patted the steering wheel. "Where to, cowboy?"

"My Charger's parked under a billboard around the corner. You can drop me there."

"Then what?" She asked, adjusting her mirrors.

"Follow me into Hallock. Schmitty's gonna meet us there. We'll clutch coffees and make a few phone calls." Lindstrom pointed towards his car and shifted in his seat. "My buddy's got a resort near Lake Bronson. It's deserted, but it's a good place to pull everyone together and plan our next moves. If nothing else, we can drink beer and do a little fishing."

Julie pulled over and put her Jeep in park. She lifted her chin and said, "Nice ride, screams of mid-life crisis." Then she grabbed Lindstrom's arm as he opened the door. "We've stepped in something big and stinky, haven't we?"

Lindstrom grinned as he climbed out and shut the door. "Euripides said, danger gleams like sunshine to a brave man's eyes."

Julie winked as she wagged her finger. "Or a woman's."

A short time later, speeding east on Highway 175, she rolled down her window and let the wind fluff her curly blond hair. With the sun glinting off the muscle car roaring ahead of her, she laughed out loud and cranked up her music.

Chapter 19
Gimme Some Water

"Mama never understood what it's like for a losing man."

With a light touch, Dale Sommers drew his paddle through the water, stirring small ripples. A blushing red sun descended over the western shore of Lake Victoria, and the inland sea relaxed, letting the canoe float along with ease. A pair of loons proclaiming their love, yodeled in the distance. The clear shallows of Sandy Point invited lighthearted exchanges and whimsical exploration. Noah, wearing a small, orange life vest and cut-off jeans, knelt upon the bow seat. The little boatswain leaned over the gunwale, pointing out sunfish, painted turtles, and an occasional sea monster disguised as a weed bed.

Captain Sommers stretched his back, then rested the paddle across his thighs. He gestured towards a tree-lined slope where Grumpy and Phelps moseyed through a clearing, then dissolved into the family's north woods cemetery. Noah's attention lingered on the tiny waves trailing along the canoe's polished wooden hull.

Across the lake, Jack Hughes sat on the DeRoxe Club's cozy patio, studying his notes and unwinding with a platter of jerk chicken nachos and a frothy mug of beer. Further up the road, Grandma Gracie curled up on her sofa with a quilted throw and a large bowl of popcorn. With her remote control in hand, she grinned and sighed as she tuned the television away from kiddie cartoons.

Victory Bluff, a wellspring of horror and inspiration for the Sommers family, bloomed with salmon-colored hues. The cracked escarpment stretched one hundred feet above the rocky eastern shore. Noah craned his head skyward, studying the boulders and trees perched high along the lofty rim. The water under the boat grew dark and intimidating as the pair drifted closer to the bluff's furrowed face.

Sommers turned and waved at an older couple, a man and woman, puttering along in their aluminum fishing boat. The sunburned anglers returned his greeting as they motored towards their south shore cottage, calling it a day. Noah waved and shouted hello to the neighbors as they cruised past. Soon, the boy's focus shifted back to the mystical cliff. After a minute of hushed contemplation, he turned to face his father. "Momma?"

Sommers peered up at the top of the haunting ledge and adjusted his baseball hat. "I'm sorry, son," he said, shrugging his shoulders. "I don't know what to say." Then the tongue-tied captain glanced over his shoulder and surveyed the north woods. He exhaled a heavy sigh as he turned back to face his perplexed helmsman. "The most important thing is you're safe here."

Noah fiddled with the straps on his life jacket, his lips quivering, tears welling in his eyes.

Sommers tugged his paddle through the water with more urgency, gaining some distance from The Watcher atop the parted crag. He looked over the side into the water. "Can you see any more sea monsters down there?"

Noah scanned the onyx depths of Townsend Drop-off, shrugged his shoulders and shook his head.

Sommers alternated sides with his paddling, then nodded. "That's good. How 'bout we fetch Grumpy and Phelps, drive over to Gary's Place for ice cream?"

Noah rubbed the tears from his eyes with his balled-up fists, then sat taller in the bow. With flushed cheeks and a meager smile, he said, "Okay."

A short time later, Noah showed more interest in live bait than frozen desserts. Sommers plopped a dog biscuit into his son's bowl of melting ice cream, then placed the dish on the floor for Phelps. Gary Johnson blitzed the checkout lane, then the kitchen counter, preparing to close his diner for the evening.

He returned to the table with a warm cinnamon roll for Jack Hughes and a hot fudge sundae for Sommers. Johnson powered off his neon sign, then peeked out the drive-thru window, watching a small RV pull away from the gas pumps. He twisted the top off a bottle of water, sputtered through his lips, then slid into the window booth beside his friends.

In the back corner of the convenience store, Grumpy held Noah in his arms, hoisting the toddler high enough to see into the bubbling bait tanks. Noah worked a small net by its wooden handle, trying to corral the darting minnows and threadfin shad. When fruitful, the playful angler examined each catch before plopping the squirmy fish back into its tub. Sommers watched Phelps finish his treat, then lope to the back. The curious dog wagged his tail, drawn to the boy's enthusiastic splashing.

Johnson tapped Sommers on the arm, then pointed down the first aisle. "Kid's a natural born fisherman, caught more in five minutes than you have in five years."

Sommers looked over his shoulder and grinned. "Just imagine the damage he'd do with a bigger net."

Hughes pointed with his fork, cream cheese frosting dribbling from the corner of his mouth. "A few years from now, their roles will be reversed, and Grumpy will be the one up to his elbows in the tank."

Johnson nodded, wiping the table with a dish towel. "So, what are you boys up to?"

Sommers glanced over at Hughes, then slid his wary eyes back to Johnson. "You remember Vernon Plummer?"

Johnson scratched at his chin. "You betcha. Hell of a banjo player. Died 'bout five or six years back. Ran a joint called Vern's Last Resort, west of the state park. Nice place back in the day. Good fishing. Why do you ask?"

The big lumberjack licked chocolate sauce from his spoon, then pointed his thumb at Hughes. "Jack's wife and Ted Lindstrom are hiding out at Vern's. Other than a nettlesome herd of varmints, they say it's abandoned. We're flying to Hallock sunup tomorrow, gonna do some two-state recon with them."

Hughes, speaking with his mouth full, said, "Lindstrom unearthed a murder in North Dakota, says a crazed Mexican killed Tommy Fulgham. Julie's part bloodhound. Everyone knows that. Anyway, she stumbled upon some drug dealers posing as corn farmers. She thinks there's something bigger going on up there, something that's polluting the water. The DNR and the hayseeds on both sides of the river are being tight-lipped, acting strange."

Johnson scrunched his forehead and looked past Sommers towards an aisle lined with boating supplies and fishing gear. "You told me your crew went searching for Noah's mother. I'm failing to see the connection here. What am I missing?"

The attorney glanced across the table at Sommers, then shrugged his shoulders while scraping the remaining frosting from the plate with his fork. Hughes said, "It's a bit of a stretch, but Big Bill Wenner was Samantha's landlord. A plausible connection seems to be a black Ford pickup delivered to a dairy farm in Pembina County. It's on a salvage title last signed by C.J. Hunter." Hughes licked his lips, then wiped his mouth with a paper napkin. "Anyway, the truck belonged to a deranged DSS operative before that. You remember that big kerfuffle with Andie Hansen? Hammerin' Hank was Sam's flunky when she ran with the Snakes."

Sommers tapped his spoon on the dish and lifted his chin at Johnson, who sipped his water, looking puzzled. "You remember the big biker dude who came in and bought candy and smokes with a hundred-dollar bill?"

Johnson scratched at the back of his neck and shook his head.

Sommers shrugged and said, "Julie's learned Tommy Fulgham's DNR truck spent several hours at the same dairy farm the night he went missing."

The shopkeeper pursed his lips and dried his fingers with the dish towel. "Shootings, missing persons, and illegal drugs, maybe you best leave this to the authorities."

Sommers stared out the front window, shaking his head. "There's a half-dozen three-lettered agencies pounding the pavement from here to Wyoming. Right now, none of 'em could find their backsides in the dark using both hands. Still, there's no guarantee waiting for Samantha when she surfaces."

Hughes licked the frosting from his fork, then pointed the tines at Johnson. "Say, does the name Jerry Reynolds mean anything to you?"

"Now there's a blast from the past," Johnson said with a nod and a grin. "J.R. rebuilt the cylinder heads on my big-block Chevy. Must've been about eight years ago. Gearheads told me that old timer could fix just about anything, and they were right. I remember he drove a sweet '66 Impala, turquoise two-door, faster than shit. I can't imagine he's still alive."

Sommers said, "Well, he is. And your fix-it man might be our only shot at finding Sam."

Johnson folded his arms across his chest, then pointed his chin towards Grumpy and Noah. "Takin' the boy with you?"

Sommers shook his head. "Nah, too dangerous."

Johnson stood and scowled, gathering the dirty dishes from their table. "Dangerous, huh? I realize it's not my place, but being a father isn't a part-time gig. You, of all people, should know that."

Sommers adjusted his baseball hat, then rapped his knuckles on the table. "Yea, how many kids you got, Gary?" The two men glared at each other until Hughes leaned across the table, placing his hand on Sommers' steeled shoulder.

Just then, Noah scampered back to the table with his net full of flipping minnows. "Feeeshies!"

Hot on his trail, Grumpy hobbled over, shaking the cramps from his arms. "Say, ya goddamn goofballs. What do you call a fish with no fuckin' eyes?" He leaned against the booth, coughed, then made a sound like a leaky air hose. "Fshhhhh."

Johnson rolled his eyes and stomped away. "I gotta finish closing. Grumps, your roll is on the counter. Don't let the door crack your ass on the way out."

The next morning, Julie Hughes parked her Jeep in the shade of a cottonwood tree at a wayside off County 57. The secluded turnaround sat two miles east of the Highway 175 overpass where Tommy Fulgham parked his work truck for the last time.

Sommers climbed out and pointed at a blue Mini-Cooper with an empty roof rack parked near a gnarled picnic table. "Heard this is a popular drop-off point for kayakers." Julie nodded, and the two hikers checked their packs. They cinched their laces, silenced their phones, and started down a dirt trail towards Two Rivers.

Julie dabbed sweat from her forehead, already feeling the intensity of the mid-morning sunshine. She took the lead as the path narrowed between tall weeds and willow saplings. She swatted at flies and whispered over her shoulder. "I still can't believe those jackasses took Tommy's water samples. Why would they do that?"

Sommers said, "Marijuana plants get mighty thirsty. You

mentioned the siphoning equipment. I'm sure we'll find a leach field near the greenhouse, and a discharge pipe further downstream. Fulgham's samples could expose serious water violations, making the McFarlands repeat offenders. That would bring a lot of unwanted attention to their drug operation." Sommers swatted at a deer fly with his baseball cap. "Did the DNR ever return your calls?"

"Hell no," Julie said, shaking her head.

"I'll rattle a few cages after we reconvene with Ted and Jack. There's no tellin' what those two are gonna find in North Dakota."

Julie and Sommers stepped at a brisk pace across a crusted flood plain. They hiked another quarter mile, then followed the shaded riverbank onto a large eastward facing oxbow. They climbed to the top of a rise that overlooked the caramel-colored river, and beyond that, endless rows of emerald-green corn. Sommers slipped a pair of binoculars from his pack and crouched underneath the boughs of a jack pine.

Perched a half-mile away, he had a clear view of two farmhouses, a few decaying tool sheds, and a giant, shiny new pole barn. Hughes tapped her phone, checking for messages, then opened her notes app. Within the shade of the pines, they slid onto their stomachs, preparing for a lengthy stay.

The pair sipped water as the minutes passed heavy in the stifling heat. Thirty minutes later, a solitary white SUV turned into McFarlands' driveway. Julie nudged Sommers with her elbow. "Get your goggles on. We've got visitors."

Sommers leaned forward onto his elbows and adjusted the focus with his index finger. "A large human wearing coveralls just stepped onto the porch. He or she is tapping on their phone."

"That's Peg McFarland. Quite the looker, eh?" Julie, a master at short-hand, began taking notes on her phone. "Who's in the car? Can you read the tags?"

Sommers turned his baseball cap backwards, then fiddled with the zoom setting on his field glasses. "Cadillac Escalade, tinted windows, too dark to see who's inside. Missouri plates, I think. M, no wait. N-U-M-B-3-R-2. Numb ears? That makes no sense."

"Numbers," Hughes said after slapping the big man's shoulder. "Maybe they're accountants."

Sommers rolled his eyes and sputtered through his lips. "Four people are getting out of the car. The driver's a big, muscled-up dude, shaved head, aviator glasses. Passenger's a short blond woman. The cupcake's wearing cowboy boots, shorts, and dark sunglasses. Two men wearing suits just climbed from the back." Sommers shifted on his elbows and readjusted the focus. "I can't see the face of suit number one. The second is… My old pal Colin Stroud."

"Stroud. Where've I heard that name before?" Julie asked.

"Commissioner, Minnesota Department of Natural Resources." Julie nudged Sommers' shoulder. "Gimme those."

The agitated investigator fiddled with the binoculars. "Dude, these things are about a hundred years old. I mean, c'mon man." She followed the gathering in the front yard, reciting the details to Sommers.

Julie watched Peg McFarland and the blond-haired cupcake greet each other with handshakes. The driver leaned against the front fender of the SUV, sucking on a toothpick and surveying the area as McFarland got into a heated conversation with the suits. Peg made a brief call on her phone, and a few minutes later, her husband, Gus, emerged from the barn carrying Fulgham's two black boxes. Four grimy farmhands also appeared, trudging along as they brought up the rear.

Julie pounded the ground with her fist. "Sonofabitch. They're handing over my boxes." She passed the binoculars back to Sommers and swiped on her phone, trying to take pictures, but the digital zoom pixelated the view. "Tell me what's going on. Who's got those samples?" Sommers shifted forward, then reported the action to Julie.

The big lumberjack said Gus looked angry as he passed the boxes over to the golden-haired cowgirl. McFarland, a wiry man, started flailing his arms and mouthing off to the suits. The giant driver put the boxes in the back of the Escalade, then walked over and smacked Gus with a back-handed slap to the face. Gus shook off the blow, then charged, but the driver caught him in a fireman's carry, lifting Gus high overhead and slamming him to the ground at Peg's feet.

Peg's laborers moved in to fight, but she waved them off, directing them toward the hidden greenhouse. The boot-wearing cupcake stepped over Gus's writhing body, then climbed back into the Escalade. Her suits exited next, after sharing some parting words with the woeful farmers. McFarland's crew disappeared into the cornfield. Then the burly driver turned and scanned the length of the river from the highway to the western fork, scrutinizing the elevated oxbow.

Sommers lowered his voice. "Don't move. He may have spotted us."

"Crap. What do we do now?" Julie asked.

"Hold still. Let's see what they've got in mind."

A rear window of the SUV rolled down, where the driver had a quick conversation with suit number one. Then he opened the back of the Cadillac and pulled a rifle from a leather carrying case. He braced the barrel on the driver's side mirror, then searched the rise through his scope. After a couple of passes, the shooter locked on to Sommers' antique binoculars. Sommers said, "Stay low and scooch back into the trees. The big guy has got his rifle pointed right at us."

"C'mon Sommers. We're more than a half mile away—eight hundred yards, maybe more. Ain't no way…"

In a flash, the pair heard the rifle's register, followed by tree bark exploding just above their heads. They scrambled behind the pines and down the backside of the hill before hearing another gunshot ring out behind their position. Sommers and Julie made a mad dash for the wayside, bypassing the loopy hiking trail. "I hope those were just warnings," he said. "That first shot would've impressed the heck out of our boy, O'Leary."

The pair hid behind the Mini-Cooper, catching their breaths. Seconds later, they watched the white Escalade race past the wayside before breaking hard to make a left turn onto Highway 16. "Assholes," Julie said, dabbing sweat from her forehead. "Let's go get 'em."

Sommers searched through his pack, then lifted his chin at Julie's Jeep. "All the way to Missouri?" He asked, shaking his head. "Easy there G.I. Jane. We don't have the horsepower, the firepower, or the manpower for an over-the-road hunting expedition."

Julie pulled Jack's .38 from her pack, puckering her mouth while nodding her head. "How about a sit-down with Peg McFarland instead?"

After resting another minute, they climbed into the Jeep and drove east on County 57. As they approached the McFarlands' farm road, Sommers pointed out a billowing cloud of black smoke rising from the corn. Before long, the sound of sirens jarred the quiet countryside.

Julie slowed the Jeep down and stuck her nose out the window, taking in a big sniff. "Damn shame, and such a waste." She pulled a lock of hair away from her face and grinned. "You want me to turn in so we can catch a buzz?"

Sommers shook his head and waved for her to drive on. "Let's head back to the resort. I'm calling another meeting."

Julie huffed as she rolled her eyes. "Some resort. Vern's place makes Grumpy's cabin look like Mar-a-Lago. What a dump."

Sommers shrugged his shoulders and changed the subject. "Sounds corny, I know. But thanks to you, McFarlands' drug operation has gone up in smoke." The big man rolled his window down, watching the fields and forests pass by. "Jules, you're good at math. How 'bout we do a little digging into a numbers racket?"

Julie sipped from her water bottle after dabbing sweating from her face. "I like your thinking, big guy." Then she winked at him. "First things first, boss. My husband's gotta check me for ticks."

"Lucky you," Sommers said, grinning as he turned his hat back around. "Jack strikes me as a very thorough man."

Chapter 20
Trouble

"I really should be saying goodnight."

While Dale Sommers and Julie Hughes were ducking and dodging bullets, Ted Lindstrom and Jack Hughes pulled to the shoulder and parked southeast of the Highway 175 overpass. They sat in the exact location Tommy Fulgham had two weeks before. Birds and bugs celebrated with song and a saffron sunshine pushed the morning heat and humidity. Jack stepped out and peered over the guardrail, scrutinizing the caramel-colored, slow-moving river. He rubbed his eyes and wrinkled his nose. "Stinks like the pit under Grumpy's outhouse down there. Fulgham deserved hazard pay."

Lindstrom shook his head as he slipped a pair of binoculars from the glove box. "The boy deserved better than he got, that's for sure." He lifted the field glasses to his eyes and surveyed the horizon in all directions, then pointed northwest beyond a pair of looping oxbows. "Pembina County, home to Norman Farms. Susan Norman and Jerry Reynolds may not realize it, but they're up to their keesters in trouble. They better have their welcome mats out, 'cause we need to have a sit down with them."

A minute later, Lindstrom waited for a thundering eighteen-wheeled grain hauler to pass into North Dakota, and waved the rolling dust cloud from his face. He pivoted and pointed east towards a patchwork quilt of farm fields; soybeans, corn, and alfalfa. "Kittson County, home of the notorious Peg McFarland and her felonious troop of noxious lowlifes."

"So, are you saying we're wading into the beast's belly?" Jack asked, swatting at a horsefly. After getting the silent treatment from his partner, he puckered his lips and nodded. "I'm already regretting this suggestion, but let's hold our breath and hike our asses down there. Julie found Tommy's water samples in that muck. Maybe we'll find something too."

Lindstrom rummaged through his backpack. "Where the hell is my bug spray?" He dropped the canvas bag at his feet and stood tall on his toes, sniffing the air. "You smell that?"

"C'mon man, my eyes are watering like Niagara Falls. We're downwind of some foul nastiness that'll never wash outta my hair."

"No, Mr. Fancy-pants. Not that." Lindstrom spun Jack around and pointed out a dismal black cloud billowing from the middle of a cornfield two miles away. "That," he said, lifting the binoculars to his eyes and taking another big sniff. "Smells just like Jimmy Buffett and the Coral Reefer Band, Chicago, summer of '86."

Jack sputtered as he rolled his eyes. "Dude, you're old."

"Maybe so, but I have good taste and my memory's as sharp as a filet knife. Many women have told me my prominent nose enhances my sexy vibe. Watch your mouth, son. Old or not, I can still kick your preppy ass from here to Sunday."

Jack slapped himself on the knee, dramatizing his fit of sarcastic laughter. He slid back into the passenger seat and began tapping and swiping on his phone. "Yo, Chuck Norris, let's ride. Jules and Sommers have front-row seats to the bonfire."

After a howling, smoke-filled U-turn, Lindstrom's Charger raced east along the rural two-lane. Jack tapped the notifications icon on his phone, studied a transcribed voicemail message, then tapped to open Google Maps. "Julie got my text. She says they're fine—parked at a wayside off County 57. She said a muscled-up mercenary took a few potshots, and almost nailed 'em. McFarland's hidden hothouse is a reeking inferno—looks like arson. She also says first responders from Hallock and Lancaster are swooping in like seagulls to a clambake." He jerked his head, then pointed his thumb. "Whoa there, Bandit. That was our turn."

Lindstrom whirled another smokey, sliding U-turn, then powered onto Highway 16. He almost side-swiped a white panel truck, its cab filled with four bug-eyed Latinos. The driver said, "There go Peg's minions with another haul. Wanna mess with 'em, then pass 'em off to the BCA?"

Jack braced himself with one hand on the dashboard and one hand on the door handle. "Got bigger fish to fry. Besides, the state will just cut 'em loose. No such thing as consequences, no such thing as accountability these days. A month from now, they'll be TikTok legends, dancing to a stupid jingle about drug dealing and stickin' it to the man. Here's 57, turn right." Lindstrom's tires howled and road grit shot in all directions. Jack shifted in his seat and pointed out the windshield. "There's her Jeep, up on the left. See it?"

A short time later, the foursome leaned against their car fenders, watching the hubbub while sipping from their water bottles. The flashing lights and the wailing sirens of emergency vehicles interrupted the posse's good-natured barbs and jabs.

Sommers took a break from his laughter, texting Schmitty to request a fly-over with one of his drones. Soon, an ambulance whirled its emergency flashers as it turned from McFarland's farm road, then rolled east towards Hallock. Julie and Jack faced each other, pursing their lips and furrowing their eyebrows. Julie snapped her fingers. "Gus," she said, tossing the key to her husband. "Counselor, I know you've still got ambulance-chasing in your blood. I call shotgun—let's go."

Lindstrom and Sommers paced the dusty wayside, using every shred of rural bandwidth with their cell phones. They watched Hughes and Hughes chase Gus McFarland's ambulance towards the county hospital. Sommers dialed Colin Stroud's number and received nothing but platitudes and resistance from the commissioner's staff. Next, he called Joy Moon Deer's number, leaving a voicemail message after six rings. Then, after several tries, he got Greg O'Leary on the line. Sommers asked, "Hey partner, how's rehab going? Are you growing fond of those Black Hills?"

"Feeling fine," O'Leary said with a half-hearted chuckle. "Therapy's a pain in the ass—sucks having to do everything left-handed. But ya know what? I kinda like it out here. It's pretty damn quiet though—cabin fever's crushing my groove. How's it going with you guys? Any leads on Sam's whereabouts?"

"Things are shaking loose on both sides of the valley. But one minute, it seems like we're gaining traction, the next, we're sliding back. Our battles might have nothing to do with Sam and her history. Who the heck knows?" Then, following a contemplative pause, Sommers said, "Hey, since you're still connected to your MIC friends, can you run a Missouri plate and pull a background check on Susan B. Norman?"

"Sure, I can do that. Welcome the work, to be honest. Besides, I could use a goddamn break. Joy's been clinging to me like a wet towel. She's a fuckin' sex machine. You should've warned me about her."

"Hey, I wasn't the one with my nose buried in her cleavage. Where's she at, anyway? I keep getting her voicemail."

"She just got back from her morning run. She's parked at the end of the driveway, talking with that cute state cop."

"Jo Douglass?" Sommers asked. "What do you suppose that's about?"

"I don't know for sure. They've had more than a few roadside chats. Joy claims it's just small talk between Indian law dogs. Yesterday, she said they discussed sports bras and shoulder holsters. But from my vantage point, Douglass is running out of pages in her notepad."

"Hmm, Joy's gotta be more careful—shouldn't be running off on her own. Have her call me, wouldja? I appreciate you guys hanging back and holding the fort down. I'll text you the plate number in a few minutes—need to choke the details out of Ted. Keep your eyes peeled and your ears to the ground."

O'Leary signed off. "Aye, aye, captain. Oh, and go easy on the ol' sheriff. He's Bogarted a few joints in his day. Ted talks a good game, but he's got only two or three marbles still rolling around upstairs. Know what I mean?"

Soon, Lindstrom and Sommers ventured west on Highway 5, rolling into the amber expanses of North Dakota, where the terrain became more wind-swept and brittle. The pair fell silent after comparing their notes and debating the motives for the recent crime spree. Lindstrom, after smacking his lips, said, "You know, I've connected with a park ranger at Devils Lake. My contact's stationed at Grahams Island, and she's been tracking the oak tree engravings, sending me pictures."

"Why do I get the sense you're about to hit me over the head with some troubling news?"

"Because you're a modern-day Renaissance man who's in touch with his feminine side."

Sommers nodded and primped his hair with a mocking gesture. "On that point, we agree."

Lindstrom adjusted his mirrors and silenced the radio. "Sam, assuming it's her, has crossed out four of the five marks on her etching. My interpretation, she's eliminated four snakes, leaving just one cold-blooded target. Who that is remains to be seen, but I'm confident his days are numbered."

Sommers shifted in his seat and adjusted his baseball hat. "Or hers," he said. "Why aren't we hearing more about this? You'd think a trail of dead mob bosses would be newsworthy."

"In my experience, what happens on the rez stays on the rez. Besides, have you watched the news of late? Unless it's a migrant tranny getting pistol whipped by a white cop, you're not gonna hear about it."

Lindstrom slid his sunglasses to the top of head and glanced across at his passenger. "I'll bet this Hellcat there's an army of ambitious amateurs scheming to take her out. Even in the slim chance we find her, Sam is still a calculating executioner. She'll be on everyone's most-wanted list, and an A1 target for the Native mob."

Sommers rolled his eyes and shook his head. "Many have killed in the line of duty, killed to protect others. Doesn't make 'em bad people—heroic, when you really think about it."

Lindstrom nodded his head. "I get it, and I'm sure she's got her reasons. But you'll always be looking over your shoulder, wondering when the fangs of revenge will bite, wondering when the feds will come knockin' on your door. Mark my word, friend. Child Services will steal your kid away. I've seen 'em do it for less."

Sommers thought the words rolled from Lindstrom's lips like sixteen-pound bowling balls. "You're sounding a lot like Moon Deer," he said, shaking his head and pinching the bridge of his nose. He turned and stared out the passenger window, watching the scrub and the trees pass by. A mile past the familiar oxbows, his phone vibrated against his sweaty, shaky palm. He tapped the screen and waited before studying the map. "County access road's up on the left, 'bout half a mile."

Soon, Lindstrom pulled into the circle drive and parked near the front porch of a faded yellow two-story farmhouse. Aside from the buzzing cicadas and chirping finches, Norman Farms basked in a quiet, clammy sprawl. "Place looks deserted," the sheriff said. "And stinks like a roadkill gopher, 'eh?"

Sommers tilted his head back and drew a sniff. "This was a profitable dairy farm back in the day. But for the second time today, I agree with you. Death's rancid breath smells nasty, unmistakable."

Lindstrom stepped from the car, then leaned in through the open window. "Better wait here. You stomping up the front steps is like Frankenstein's monster trudging through the village—suggests a confrontation. Know what I mean?"

Sommers scowled, sitting like an overgrown child with his arms folded across his chest. Lindstrom rapped his knuckles on the roof of the car, then pivoted towards the house. After his third step, he froze and watched the largest man he'd ever seen squeeze himself out the front door. The behemoth stomped onto the porch, crunching and cracking the deck boards with his heavy footfalls. He sported a shaved head, a single, bushy eyebrow, and no neck. His muscular upper body stretched a Gold's Gym t-shirt to its threadbare limits.

After taking a gulp, Lindstrom peeked over his shoulder and saw Sommers still seated in the passenger seat, with a knowing grin stretching across his face. The sheriff turned back and blurted a nervous laugh. "Damn, boy. You're 'bout as big as a mountain."

The unibrow monster stepped down into the yard and folded his thick arms across his massive chest. "Cuckoo's Nest," he said with a voice that resonated like a tuba. "Very unoriginal, man." He glanced over at Lindstrom's Charger, then shifted his glare back to the investigator. "The fuck you want?"

"Looking for Susan Norman. She home?"

The monster shook his head and asked. "You a cop?"

Lindstrom scratched at the back of his neck, then swatted at a fly and said, "Retired. Investigating a missing persons case. Kinda stinks 'round here, 'eh? Will Mrs. Noman be back soon?"

The monster shrugged his massive shoulders. "Look, man," he said, furrowing his monumental eyebrow. "There's nobody here. I think you should..."

Just then, the screen door snapped open and a second monster, almost identical to the first, lumbered onto the porch. Monster number two possessed two distinct eyebrows and a jagged scar trailing down his dimpled chin. His muscular arms featured dark sleeves of tattoos winding towards his broad shoulders.

Sommers twisted the bill of his baseball cap to the back, popped open the door, then climbed out from Lindstrom's Charger. The two monsters exchanged sideways glances, then nodded with silly grins creasing their faces.

Lindstrom raised a palm towards Sommers, signaling for him to hang back. Then he lifted his chin at the unibrow monster. "What about Jerry Reynolds? Old-timer—drives a blue-green Chevy. Seen him around?"

The tattoo monster scratched at his crotch and snorted. "Ain't nobody here, pops. How 'bout you and your date be like trees and get the fuck outta here?"

Sommers stepped closer. "Ha, good one." He swatted at a cloud of gnats, then flashed a quick wink at Lindstrom before squaring up in front of the tattooed monster. "Ed Norman's place, right? I hear he's pretty easygoing—don't think he'd mind if we looked around a bit. You gorillas gonna try to stop us?"

Again, the two monsters grinned at one another. But before either could make their move, a third monster, shirtless and bigger than the first two, came crashing through the front door. The giant pounded his chest and growled like a bear as he bounded into the yard towards Lindstrom. Sommers leaped and caught the beast in mid-air, driving him to the ground. The big lumberjack heard the titan's collarbone snap under their weight after putting all of his aggression into the textbook open-field tackle.

The shirtless monster squirmed across the ground, howling and cursing. A split-second later, the unibrow monster lunged at Lindstrom, spouting obscenities through his manic grimace. The investigator side-stepped the attacker, elbowing him hard behind the ear. At the same instant, he stuck his boot out, tripping the top-heavy beast. Lindstrom's fancy footwork sent the angry giant crashing to the ground beside his injured sidekick.

The tattooed monster, seeing his friends in a pickle, jumped on Sommers's back and gripped the big lumberjack with a choke hold. The pair stumbled into the weeds and flopped around like a pair of catfish, each wrestler struggling to gain the upper hand.

Sommers ducked a vicious cross-face, then landed a series of punches to the beast's midsection, doubling him over and snatching his breath. From the gravel turnaround, Lindstrom pulled his .38 from a sticky holster hidden beneath his t-shirt. "That's enough," he said, shouting over the din. "Simon says freeze."

The loud crack of a rifle report echoed from somewhere behind Lindstrom's car. The noise brought the skirmish to a halt. Sommers and Lindstrom scrambled and crawled to a patch of burnt grass beneath the Charger's front bumper. Sommers, peeking under the oil pan, watched two pairs of boots step from a white SUV. A booming voice disrupted the momentary calm. "I can hit a flea in the ass at fifty yards. I can see your fuckin' foot's a helluva lot bigger than a flea. Better toss that pistol, mister."

Lindstrom curled his feet underneath his legs, then looked over at his sweating, panting partner. Sommers, wearing a haggard look of resignation, pursed his lips, then nodded. Lindstrom shook his head, then flipped his chrome-plated Smith and Wesson into the weeds. "Dammit," he said in a whisper. "Had 'em right where we wanted 'em."

Monsters one and two grabbed the two snoops by the ankles and dragged them out into the open. The burly combatants hefted them up like five-pound sacks of potatoes. Then, despite encountering some stubborn resistance, the beasts pinned the unwelcome visitors' arms behind their backs.

The racy woman Sommers recognized from McFarland's barnyard strutted over and stooped to pick up Lindstrom's handgun. She handled it with confidence, pointing it at Lindstrom's chest, then at Sommers. Her sun-glass shaded eyes tracked him up and down, then lingered on the lumberjack's sweaty, chiseled face. With an easy, confident drawl, she said, "Let 'em go, boys. This ain't no way to treat our guests." She pulled a golden lock of hair past her ear, then handed the .38 back to Lindstrom.

Sommers shook his arms out, then locked eyes with monster number four, the driver who fired shots at him hours earlier. Lindstrom holstered his gun and studied the sultry woman wearing a lacy sleeveless blouse, short-shorts, and snakeskin boots. Then he crossed his arms and nodded as she removed her sunglasses, exposing a pair of bright blue eyes above her beaming, fearless grin.

With recognition lighting his face, Lindstrom nodded and said, "Well, I'll be damned. Looks like our number's up."

Chapter 21
Solitary Man

"Melinda was mine 'til the time that I found her."

Dressed more like day hikers than lawyers, Jack and Julie Hughes marched along a lengthy corridor, sanitized tile glowing beneath the lugged soles of their boots. Near the midpoint, a woman wearing green medical scrubs slammed her clipboard down. She hung her head and leaned on her elbows, bracing herself on the counter in front of the nurse's station. "I've had it," she said, rocking on her heels and shaking her head. "I'm gonna wring his skinny little neck. Somebody better call Walter, see if he's got an open locker at the morgue."

The Hughes couple glanced at each other, then tip-toed to the counter. Julie held her husband back and cleared her throat. "Excuse me. We're looking for a patient, Gus McFarland. The receptionist told us ER transferred him to this wing."

The shift nurse pounded her fists on the counter, grabbed her clipboard, then stomped off towards the cafeteria. She flitted her hand as she shouted over her shoulder. "Somebody take these tree huggers to see the blasted chicken man."

A second nurse, wearing blue scrubs, peered at a computer screen, then pointed towards the end of the hallway. "Mr. McFarland's in room one-twelve. I'll walk you down." After only a few steps, the nurse stretched her arms out wide, stopping the couple in their tracks. "I gotta warn you, his room is full of cops. At least I think they're cops. The chicken man is in rare form this afternoon." The smiling, portly nurse peeked over the top of her glasses and introduced herself as Betsy Robbins. Pleasant and grandmother-like, Robbins smelled like lavender-scented soap, and her white gym shoes squeaked when she walked.

Robbins said, "We heard one of his cornfields caught fire." She pursed her lips and paused as she stared at a yellow sunshine beaming through the tall vestibule windows. Then she shifted her eyes back to the visitors, studying them with her eyebrows furrowed and her face scrunched. She tilted her head and tapped her chin with her pen. "You guys don't look like cops. It's obvious you're not blood relatives. Friends of the family?"

"I'm Jack Hughes, Mr. McFarland's attorney. This is my wife and lead investigator, Julie Hughes." The three shook hands and continued walking towards the shouts erupting near the end of the hall. "Sounds like Mr. McFarland's had a rough morning. What's with all this chicken man stuff?"

"You two aren't from around here, eh?" Robbins asked, looking around to see if anyone was listening. "We've got a diner down the street called Chester's. They make the best chicken tenders ever. Even with this crazy inflation, you can still get three biguns for five bucks. Anyway, Gus sits in a corner booth and chows down on fried chicken almost every day. The guy weighs a hundred and five pounds soaking wet, hard to believe he holds Chester's all-time tender-eatin' record. Folks say he can put away two dozen of 'em without breakin' a sweat. That includes a crock of Chet's sauce and a basket of double-dipped cheddar fries."

Julie cocked her eyebrows and nodded as they approached the

clamorous room. "Does the chicken man come here often? What's he in for this time, if you don't mind me asking?"

Robbins fiddled with her name badge, then leaned closer to Julie. "Gus visits us about once a week. He's got a bad habit of shooting his mouth off until someone shuts it for him. This time, the beating's worse. We heard some muscled-up gangster threatened his wife. Rumor has it Gus got whipsawed trying to stick up for her."

Betsy fired a little snort from her nose as she giggled. "Peg rolls like an angry cement mixer. Everyone 'round here knows she's tough as a pan steak. Anyway, the chicken man's got a bump the size of a melon on his noggin and a few cracked ribs. Hopefully, he's only staying the night—you know, just for precaution. Ya think he's goin' to jail?"

Jack rolled his eyes and asked, "For what? Eating fried chicken and getting his ass kicked?" He made a sputtering sound, then leaned over and whispered something into his wife's ear. Julie turned and strode away with a shrewd grin stretching across her face. Robbins adjusted her glasses, then tugged at her earlobe.

After watching his wife sashay off, Jack thanked Robbins for the intel, then pushed his way into the crowded room. He fanned a stack of business cards in his hand, making them available to McFarland's unwelcome visitors. "Okay, show's over, everybody out. McFarland, don't say another word. We've got to establish some ground rules, like pronto."

Gus grimaced as he leaned forward from his pillows. "Who the fuck are you?"

"Mr. McFarland, I'm your attorney, Jack Hughes. Your wife called me in a panic. Judging from that bump on your head, I can see why you wouldn't remember me."

McFarland flipped him the bird, then farted loud enough for everyone to turn away and smirk. One agent quipped, "Smartest thing he's said all day."

Hughes stepped towards McFarland's hospital bed and lifted his chin at the battered patient. "Ah well, doesn't make much difference. The state's gonna banish you to Stillwater. You'll be eating nothing but roadkill rabbit and Idaho Spuds with your redneck cellmate for the next ten years. Best shut that vile trap of yours, unless that's the future you fancy."

One by one, representatives from three-letter agencies huffed their displeasure and filed from the small stuffy room. Hughes nodded at agents from the DEA, the AFT, and the DNR. Hughes' fishing buddy from the BCA flashed anger in his eyes, then turned and stopped in the open doorway. "Text me when you're done with him. We need to talk." The officer folded a piece of chewing gum into his mouth, checking his cell phone as he trudged away.

Hughes closed the door and dragged a heavy vinyl-upholstered chair closer to McFarland's bed. Then he slipped a yellow pad from under his vest. "Lordy, this room reeks of hair gel and foot powder." The lawyer clicked his pen and plopped himself into the squishy orange chair. "Okay, Gus, time to cut the bullshit. Let's see if we can help each other out here."

McFarland cracked his knuckles and stared up at The Weather Channel playing on a small ceiling-mounted television. After several seconds, he said, "Look bro, I don't know you. My wife don't know you. I ain't tellin' you jack shit."

"Good one," Hughes said without looking up from his notes. "Well, then I guess we'll just sit here in this stench and learn more about tsunamis." A lengthy advertisement for lawn tractors took over the screen, so Hughes used the break to swipe through a series of text messages on his phone. He glanced over at the insolent patient. "Say Gus, did you know growing marijuana with intent to distribute is a felony in this state?" McFarland remained still, but peeked at Hughes from the corner of his eye.

Just passing time, Hughes scribbled a few notes on the yellow paper, then tapped on his chin with his ballpoint pen. "You're looking at ten years in prison and a hundred thousand dollar fine. And guess what? This morning, we spotted your drug mules driving into North Dakota. Sounds a lot like interstate drug trafficking, doncha think? There's no telling what those feds have in store for you." Hughes leaned closer to McFarland's bed. "Let's get real here. Maybe I'm looking in the wrong places, but you're the only black guy I've seen in this county. Good luck trying to catch a break from a jury. Your trial will be a curious shitshow for all to see. So cut the crap Gus, 'cause I'm the only gig in town."

McFarland squirmed in his bed, blocking Hughes with a pillow while biting his tongue. A squabble broke out in the hallway and Julie Hughes skipped through the doorway, carrying a cardboard box filled with chicken dinners from Chester's. "Sorry about the commotion, guys. I gave each of the feds a three-piece chicken box and the jerks started squabbling over biscuits and coleslaw." She handed a steaming Styrofoam tray and a stack of paper napkins to her husband.

"Thanks, Hon. Mmm, smells good," he said, licking his lips. "I'm starving."

"You're welcome, sweetie. I cheated and munched on a tender in the car. Betsy knows her chicken—pretty damn good. I gave her a plate because she's sweet. I also gave one to that raging nurse in the green scrubs. Greenie-meanie almost cracked a smile."

Julie set the big box on a small round table opposite McFarland's bed, then sat and began salting her food. Moments later, she looked up and mumbled through the fried potatoes filling her mouth. "Sorry, Gus. We haven't eaten at all today. You mind?"

McFarland twiddled his fingers, then pointed at her. "You were snooping around with Peg yesterday. Our boys should've taken you out when they had the chance. Filthy fuckin' beaners—useless as teats on a bull." He sat up taller in his bed, scrunching his face and smacking his lips. "You motherfuckers know each other?"

"I'm sorry," Jack said, wiping a dab of sauce from the corner of his mouth. "Gus McFarland. Meet Julie Hughes. The hottest investigator north of the Rio Grande."

Julie wolfed a bite of chicken and nodded. "Friends with benefits. Right, Gus?" She dabbed her mouth and pointed her thumb. "Jack's my boss, but not for long if he doesn't start paying me better." She turned and winked at her husband, then cocked her head towards the box on the table. "Hey Jack, there's two more dinners in there. You want 'em or should I let the guys down the hall fight over 'em?"

Gus wiped his slobbery mouth and cleared his throat. "What the hell, lady? How 'bout repaying my hospitality with some of your tender white meat?"

Julie rolled her eyes and shook her head before turning back to the bruised patient fussing in the folding bed. "You're a dirty old man, Gus. But maybe we got off on the wrong foot. You promise to watch your mouth and answer our questions, sparing the shenanigans?"

Gus nodded as he crossed his heart, so Julie rolled the tray table from across the room. "I'll answer your questions," he said with a scowl scrunching his face. "But his, not a chance."

Jack looked up at Julie and flashed a thumbs up, then sat back and prepared to take notes.

Like a ravenous animal, Gus started dipping and chewing while Julie wiped her fingers on a napkin. Betsy Robbins stuck her head into the room, but Jack shook his head and waved her out. He activated the voice recorder app on his iPhone and gave his wife a nod.

Julie sipped from her water bottle before launching into her questions. "Mr. McFarland, we know all about your covert marijuana farm. Tell us more about the operation. Can you expound on the distribution channels and any big-name clients? How much are you shipping these days?"

"No fuckin' idea," Gus said, shaking his head before stuffing an entire chicken tender into his mouth. "That's Peg's department."

"Funny," Julie said. "Just yesterday, she told me you run the show."

"That crooked bitch. I got nothin' to do with the weed. I keep the machinery running and the goddamn workers in line. That's it."

"Okay then. How about you explain the water pump and the four-inch pipe leading to the river?"

Gus licked his fingers, then wiped them on his bedsheet. He let out a belch that reverberated around the small room, then raised his palms towards the ceiling. "Don't know what the fuck you're talkin' about."

Julie frowned and tapped on her phone. She turned the screen towards Gus, showing him the pictures she took the previous day. He rolled his eyes and started picking through his second box of chicken.

After interjecting with a chuckle, Jack pointed his pen at Gus. "Siphoning water without a permit is a crime. You're looking at another year in jail and a thousand dollar fine. Safe to assume you don't have a permit, am I right?"

Gus made a hissing sound and flipped him off, extending both of his greasy middle fingers above his head.

Julie interrupted their bickering. "Okay guys, that's enough. Let's shift gears here, shall we?" She stood and paced the room. "There was a gathering in your yard this morning, white Escalade, four occupants. Who were they?" Gus licked his thumbs and shrugged his shoulders. Julie pointed at him and said, "The boxes you gave them are evidence in an ongoing murder investigation. Tampering with evidence is a serious offense, Gus. So is obstruction."

Jack shook his head while clicking his pen. "Ooh, now we're up to a life sentence and another hundred thousand dollars. Ya see where this is going, Gus? Soak up those tenders, chicken man. They could be the last ones you dip. I'm talking years here."

Julie waved him off and said, "My husband is an excellent attorney, one of the best in the country. If you give us something we can share with the authorities, he can negotiate a plea deal, get your sentence reduced, maybe even suspended with supervision."

Jack said, "Your call, McFarland. Play your cards right. You could walk after paying a small fine."

McFarland tilted his head back, staring at the ceiling while smacking his puffy lips. "What about Peg?"

Jack said, "Different deal. Like my wife said, she's trying to toss your ass under a double-decker bus right now."

After several seconds of clumsy silence, Julie began filling the box with trash from their meals. "C'mon Jack, let's go. Apparently, the chicken man isn't a card player."

McFarland reached out, snatching Julie's arm at her wrist. Crumbs of chicken breading spewed from his mouth as he spoke. "They'll fuckin' kill me. They'll torture my nigga ass and then they'll fuckin' kill me."

Julie twisted her arm free, placed the box of garbage on the floor near the door, then set the lock. "Who?"

"Take your pick, the fuckin' cartel, the greedy politicians, them crooked Indians. They all got a stake." Gus dropped his head and began scratching at a mosquito bite on his elbow. "My fuckin' wife slaps the shit outta me regular, and that's when she's in a good mood. If she finds out I flipped on her, she'll beat me to death with a goddamn garden hose."

"I'll talk to my guy," Jack said. "We'll get you some protection."

McFarland looked out the window and huffed. "Yea, whatever man."

Julie said, "C'mon Gus, stop being so pigheaded." She moved the tray table aside and leaned on the edge of his bed. "Say, how'd you like to sue the guy that put you in this room? Give us those names so we can get to work on your case. Let's start with that blond-haired woman. Who's she?"

Gus grimaced as he shifted in his bed. He closed his eyes and muttered under his breath. "The big asshole with the wrestling moves—don't know him. But he's one of her goddamn bouncers."

Julie nodded and said, "That ogre pulled a rifle and took a couple of shots at me. I'd like to nail his ass. Tell us about the woman. Does she run the show?"

"Hell yea. That's Suzy Norman. She's married to a racist prick. Peg says she's good with a calculator—runs numbers for the KC syndicate. They pull the usual shit: prostitution, drugs, money laundering. Been at it for years. Cops must be getting their cut, 'cause they won't fuckin' touch 'er."

Julie said, "I saw you give the DNR boxes to a tall guy wearing a gray suit. Tell me about him."

McFarland shrugged. "Don't know him. Peg said he's a big shot with a corner office in St. Paul. That candy-ass said he'd shut us down if we didn't torch the weed and hand over the boy's water samples."

"What about the other fancy pants?" Julie asked. "The Asian guy."

"Never seen him before. Got a nasty growth on his face. Thing looks like a fuckin' leech with three hairs growin' out of it. He didn't say shit. Norman called him Mr. Sway."

Jack nodded and Julie slid a three-page document onto Gus's tray table, then turned to fetch Robbins from the hall. Jack said, "Mr. McFarland, you need to sign this form. It's not a bill, just an agreement that I'm your attorney of record. I'll handle all of your legal matters, including your estate, should something unforeseen happen to you." He placed his pen on the table in front of Gus and patted him on the shoulder.

McFarland crossed his arms and looked away. "Unforeseen? You goddamn grifters. I ain't signing shit."

Jack leaned over McFarland's hospital bed. "I hate to break it to you, Gus. The dealer dealt this hand from the bottom of the deck and you're not holding any aces. If you don't sign, your farm's gonna end up in the hands of the guys who kicked your ass. Now, does that seem fair to you?"

Julie reappeared with Robbins, and a janitor named Morris in tow. Jack stuck the pen in McFarland's hand and pointed to blank lines near the bottom of each page. Gus looked around the room at his four visitors and took a deep breath, then scrawled his name on one of the bottom lines. Morris and Robbins added their signatures, then exited into the hall. After Julie applied her notary stamp, she signed and dated the document. Jack nodded, then slipped the completed forms between the pages of his legal pad.

Gus folded his arms across his face, shading his eyes. "Listen up, assholes. I feel like crap. Goddamn room's spinning and my head's pounding like a fuckin' bass drum."

Jack slid one of his business cards onto the tray table. "Thanks, buddy. Got what we need for now. I'll fetch the nurse for you." Julie patted Gus on the shoulder, then turned for the door.

Gus gave a small wave as he shouted from his bed. "Later, white meat. Remember, name's Johnson, Gus Johnson. And hey, send the fuckin' bill to my future ex-wife. Kill the lights, wouldja?"

Across the river, Susan Norman lowered her sunglasses, then mashed her foot on the accelerator. She whirled the ATV's steering wheel and whipped up a plume of dust. The bumpy trail provided direct access to Highway 5 from the river. Sommers sat in the passenger seat, clutching the grab handle and surveying the rolling fields of Pembina County. Ted Lindstrom sat in the back, rocking in time with the cart's jounces and swerves.

They rode in silence along a narrow two-track path leading

towards a clearing overlooking the river and surrounded by trees on three sides. Susan's right-hand placement alternated between the gear selector and Sommers' denim covered thigh. After several minutes, she pointed out a steel-sided building, barn-red with white trim. "That's Jerry's place. Edward's father spotted him a few acres when he got back from Vietnam. The property's landlocked, but it's a sweet spot; mature trees, decent views, easy access to the river and the highway. Beats the heck outta the travel trailer he used to live in. I haven't seen the old guy since he got back from Fargo. But if he's around, his flag is a flyin'."

"We saw this place on our drive out," Sommers said, pointing with his thumb. "I remember seeing an American flag flapping in the breeze. You're right, nice spot he's got down here. Good to know the leftist radicals haven't purged all the patriotism from this fair land."

From the back, Lindstrom said, "Hear, hear, brother." Then he tapped Norman on the shoulder. "Been a while, but I've got a buddy that works as a farmhand up here somewhere. Name's Rivers, Dean Rivers. You know him?"

Susan turned after glancing at a dark mound about a half-mile away, then she shrugged and shook her head. "Rivers, you say? Never heard of him." Seconds later, she hit the brakes, bringing her four-wheeler to a skidding halt. She sipped from a fancy aluminum water bottle, then pointed. "That's his flag pole. Like I said, no flag, no JR."

Before Norman could drive off, Lindstrom said, "I found Jerry in a bit of a pickle down in Fargo. He doesn't strike me as someone who locks his doors. Mind if we look around?"

Norman bit her bottom lip as she looked over at Sommers. He cocked his eyebrows and nodded, so she grinned and said, "Why the hell not? I mean, what could it hurt?"

On their walk down the driveway, Sommers explained that a Morton Building is a pole barn constructed with metal panels. Reynolds crafted his building with a small residence attached to its southern wall, giving him views of both the northern pastures and the winding river. The trio stepped through a large overhead door into the shade of Jerry's cavernous machine shop.

The sweet aroma of diesel fuel mixed with bearing grease hung in the air. Workbenches, power tools, and air compressors lined the two longer walls. An open garage door at the opposite end allowed the afternoon sunlight and a fusty river breeze to waft into the building.

Norman leaned against the door frame, swiping through messages on her cell phone, while Sommers and Lindstrom snooped around. Lindstrom tip-toed across the garage, past an old fishing boat on an aluminum trailer. Farther back, he lifted the elastic corner of a woven car cover, unveiling a shiny chrome bumper. "Just as I thought," he said. "Jerry's Impala. It's loaded just the way we primed it. Well, at least we know he made it this far."

"Didn't stick around long, did he?" Sommers asked. "Took his flag with him?" The big man turned in a circle, stepping in place. "I can't get over the size of this shop. You can tell he loves this place. It's spotless, organized with painstaking care."

Lindstrom crouched down and pointed to a pair of tire tracks leading out the back door. "Just enough dust to show us which way he went." The retired sheriff called out for Jerry, knocked on the door to his residence, then twisted the knob. He cracked the door open before turning back towards Susan. "His door is unlocked. We're gonna check inside."

Norman looked up from her phone and flipped her hand. "Be my guest. But I'm telling you. He's not here." She glanced up at a clock hanging above the door. "Make it quick, would ya? Gotta get cleaned up. The Mavericks are playing on the main stage at the fair tonight."

It didn't take long for the men to search the house since it comprised four rooms; a small bedroom with an attached bathroom, an eat-in kitchen, and a cozy sitting room featuring a sofa and a flat-screen TV. Like the oversized barn, Jerry's house offered rural simplicity and cleanliness.

Lindstrom pointed at an end table next to a leather easy chair. On the table sat a half-filled coffee cup, a pair of binoculars, and a dog-eared assembly manual for a 2020 Ford F-150. Lindstrom stuck his finger in the brew. "Still warm. He's gotta be close. C'mon, let's go."

On their way out, Sommers stepped to a corner shelving unit shaped like a rowboat. The shelves contained an assortment of knick-knacks, including several die-cast toy cars and a few framed photographs. Sommers lifted a black-and-white photo of a man holding a rifle and wearing Army fatigues. He turned the picture towards his partner. "This Reynolds?"

Lindstrom leaned closer for a better look and nodded. Sommers said, "Handsome guy, means business—got grit in his eyes. I thought you said he was a mechanic?" Lindstrom shrugged his shoulders as he searched the kitchen cabinets, then pivoted for the door.

Sommers eyes tracked to another black-and-white photograph, a five by seven, old and faded. He picked up the picture and felt the heft of its wooden frame in his hands. He walked it over to a window and scrutinized the subjects in brighter light.

After several seconds, Sommers shifted his gaze out the window to a nearby pasture full of dry weeds, bent grasses, and a blackened pile of rubble. He closed his eyes and heard the sounds of workingmen, the banging of their hammers and the scratching of their saws. He squinted through his eyelids, trying to see the obscured details.

Lindstrom nudged Sommers from his daydream. "C'mon, big man. Time to shove off."

Sommers opened his eyes and lowered his sights back to the sun-faded photograph. Soon, a spark of recognition warmed his chest. Pictured within the sturdy frame, a group of four men stood next to a woodpile in front of a large, unpainted barn. A metal sign above the door read Barn #2 in block letters. Parked in the background, a rusty GMC pickup truck had S & E Lumber hand-scrawled on its door with white paint. The men wore overalls and work boots, and each worker clutched a tool in his gloved hands. One man, wearing a leather tool belt and a camouflage painter's hat, appeared to be Jerry Reynolds.

Off to one side, a big dog sat at the feet of another worker, looking up at his master's sour face. A young boy, age five or six, sat atop the stack of hand-hewn logs. Sommers' finger tracked over the picture, stopping at a muscular man leaning against the barn with a look of accomplishment on his face. His clothes stained from sweat, the man had his arm draped over the shoulders of another boy, aged eight or nine. The boy wore a backwards baseball hat, baggy overalls, and a satisfied grin. Both of the boy's hands gripped the wooden handle of a hatchet, its steel blade glinting in the sunlight.

Sommers adjusted his baseball hat, then closed his eyes as he pinched the bridge of his nose. "Ted, wait up a minute. I think I found something."

A short time after Sommers tucked the old picture under his shirt, Norman parked her ATV in front of her faded yellow farmhouse. She ran her fingers through the hair on the back of Sommers' head. "You look like you could use some arm candy. How 'bout taking me to the fair?"

Sommers shook his head as he climbed out. "Not tonight. I'm going hunting." He adjusted his baseball hat and tapped his fingers on the roof of her cart. "What about your husband? He got a sweet tooth?"

Norman rolled her eyes and shook her head, pouting as she flipped her hands like two jittery butterflies. "Ed's not into me, never has been. Partying with some burnouts on the rez, I'd guess." She swiped a wisp of hair away from her eyes. "Don't you go fretting over him. He won't be back anytime soon."

Sommers shrugged and turned to find the unibrow monster sitting on the front steps, chewing on a piece of straw. The two men lifted their chins as they exchanged frosty stares.

Lindstrom shot Sommers a look of concern as he slid from the back seat. He fished a key fob from his pocket and looked up to see the sniper monster leaning against his Dodge Charger. Lindstrom bit his lower lip and clenched his fists. "You mind peeling your sweaty ass off that fender? Bank still owns that wildcat."

Susan Norman climbed out and strutted towards her front door. "You boys play nice, ya hear?" Then she flipped her hair opposite a warm, stinky gust of wind. "Oh, and Sommers, if you change your mind, I've got a VIP pass with your name on it. Could be fun." Then she disappeared behind the mangled screen door, letting it clap against the jamb.

Sommers and Lindstrom approached their car as the sniper monster stood tall, with his sculpted arms folded across his chest. "You fucking clowns are gettin' off easy," he said. "If you're smart, you won't show your ugly faces 'round here. Ever."

Lindstrom reached behind his back for his gun, but Sommers shook his head and pulsed his hands, palms down. He stepped towards the muscled-up mercenary, lifting his chin at him. "Or else what?"

The sniper monster cocked his head towards a nearby waste retention pond and inhaled a big sniff. "Deep shit, my friends. You fuck around with us, you're gonna find out."

Lindstrom and Sommers shrugged their shoulders, then shared a laugh as they climbed into the car. Lindstrom goosed the engine, then leaned out the window. "Step aside, friend." Then he cranked the steering wheel and powered the car into a dusty, drifting U-turn.

Sommers tipped his hat at the two monsters standing in the yard with grimy scowls on their faces. "We'll be seeing ya," he said as they rolled towards the highway.

Sommers slipped the old picture from under his shirt. He held it up and studied the scene, then trained his eyes back to the pile of charred rubble bulging from the northern cow pasture. "That smoldering mound used to be a magnificent barn," he said. "Solid maple framing, cedar-sided, mortise and tenon joinery. Pop's crew built it to withstand anything. Why the heck did they just burn it to the ground?"

Lindstrom shrugged as he turned left onto Highway 5, speeding east towards the twisting muddy river. "There's an old soldier hunkered down somewhere 'round here. I'll bet he knows."

The big lumberjack thought about the solitary man and his secluded, modest home. Sommers considered the man's tools, polished and sorted with thoughtful precision. He also appreciated the old man's values, grounded in virtue and tradition. Then, after a few minutes of quiet contemplation, he nodded at his driver. With a tight jaw, Sommers tapped the dashboard and pointed at the familiar bridge leading back to the land of ten thousand lakes. "C'mon sheriff, let these horses run."

Lindstrom grinned as he downshifted and floored the gas pedal. "Now you're talkin', partner."

Chapter 22
Rock'n Me

"Well, I've been lookin' real hard and I'm tryin' to find a job."

A Minnesota sunrise, glowing red from Canadian wildfires, seeped into the shadows below the stately ash trees lining the shore of a deep, mile-long finger jutting west from Lake Bronson. Vern's Last Resort stretched across five acres of forest, straddling a large cove adjoining the serene western shore.

Julie Hughes, wearing an oversized flannel, stood near the end of a timeworn dock, flipping a spinner bait into the shallows near an outcrop of limestone riprap. Her husband, Jack, sat on the rotting porch of a dilapidated cabin. He had his phone crooked below his ear, listening to his hospital recordings, and updating some notes scribbled inside his legal pad.

After returning from Hallock, Ted Lindstrom stepped from his car and called out to the team. "Breakfast is served." He placed two cake-sized boxes and a grocery sack on a picnic table covered with an assortment of pink sticky notes. "There's a quaint little bakery on the edge of town," he said, before biting into a doughnut. "Got us a dozen bagels. The cake doughnuts looked too good to pass up, so I grabbed a dozen, chocolate frosted."

Jack looked up from his yellow pad. "You get coffee? God help us if Jules doesn't get her morning cup of Joe."

"In the white box." Lindstrom nodded as he surveyed the shoreline. "Beautiful morning at the lake. She catchin' anything?"

"Hooked a small pike a few minutes ago. I'd keep my distance if I were you. She's pissed about the lack of hot water around here."

"Got two full gas cans in the trunk. I'll get the generator going after breakfast. I grabbed a chocolate milk for Sommers. Where'd he wander off to?"

Hughes tilted his head towards a grove of paper birch and jack pine. "Back in the woods, taking his frustrations out on a pair of rotting tree trunks."

"Tossing those axes again, huh?" Lindstrom asked, before sipping his coffee.

"I gave up watching after five minutes. Dude was dead center on every throw." Jack pulled a pair of steaming coffees from the box, popped the tops and poured a dash of creamer into each cup. "He's had enough of this boy scout stuff, homesick as hell—misses his kid."

"I get it," Lindstrom said, gnawing on a plain bagel and repositioning two of the sticky notes. He cocked his eyebrows and waved his hand above the weathered table. "Where are the Gus McFarland notes?"

"My BCA guy called just after you left for town. McFarland's dead. Brain aneurysm. We're kicking ourselves for not asking him why Norman's suits wanted those water samples so bad. Peg, as you would guess, flipped everything on Gus. Now she's dug in, pleading the fifth." The lawyer shook his head as he grabbed the two steaming cups and strode towards the dock.

Lindstrom plopped into a rickety lawn chair and brushed pastry crumbs from his thick mustache. "Well, shit."

A minute later, Sommers appeared from the trees carrying a

dozen pieces of splintered firewood. With his t-shirt and baseball hat soaked with sweat, the big lumberjack sported a tight jaw and a spark of determination in his eyes. He stacked the wood on the porch, then tapped Lindstrom's shoulder. "Did I hear someone say breakfast?"

Lindstrom pointed his thumb at the table. "In the bag, big buy. Have you heard about McFarland?"

Sommers nodded, then began chugging his chocolate milk. Lindstrom stood and waved a doughnut over the rows of sticky notes. "Aneurysm, my ass. Gus got whacked."

Sommers wiped his mouth with the back of his hand, shook his head, then lifted his chin at the dock. "They catching anything?"

Focused on the notes, Lindstrom munched on his doughnut, but didn't answer. Sommers rapped his knuckles on the table, then peeled a sticky note from a middle column. "Where the heck is Jerry Reynolds?" He asked, looking out across the lake. "And who is he hiding from?"

Lindstrom sipped his coffee, then shrugged. "Don't know. Lots of questions on that table, not many answers. Has O'Leary checked in with you this morning?"

"Not yet," Sommers said, shaking his head before chomping into a chocolate chip bagel. He motioned towards a hazy western sky. "Big storms are churning out west. NWS says we're gonna get slammed, damaging winds and hail. They're saying a hundred-year rain event is a real possibility." Then he peeked at the time displaying on his phone. "Twenty-four hours," he said, motioning to the table. "If we haven't cleared this table of paper by then, I'm flying home. All this trouble is more than we can handle."

Lindstrom patted Sommers on the shoulder and turned for the dock. "Let me fetch the others. Clock's ticking and we've got a load of crap to sift through."

The foursome spent the next thirty minutes chewing and

speculating, making no significant progress. Then, without warning, Sommers' phone chimed with a message and he tapped the screen to read his text. "It's O'Leary. He wants me to call, says it's urgent." Sommers glanced up at the others, then tapped his phone. "Talk to me, buddy. Whatcha got?"

O'Leary, battling a spotty signal, said, "You better sit your ass down for this one."

Fearing the worst, Sommers removed his hat and wiped his forehead. "For cripes sake, please don't tell me the snakes got Moon Deer."

"Shit, no. She's in the shower." Then, following a few seconds of static, O'Leary laughed and said, "I asked for her hand, and she said yes."

"The connection's awful here," Sommers said, shifting the phone to his other ear. "Did you just say you proposed to Joy?"

Julie blurted out a laugh and punched her husband's arm. "I told you!"

Sommers said, "We're sitting around our make-do conference table in the woods. Let me put you on speaker. Okay, go ahead."

O'Leary said, "Mornin', friends. You too, Ted. As I was sayin', we went into town last night, had dinner, and may have gotten overserved. Well, one thing led to another, and I popped the question. At first, she thought I was drunk, just pulling her leg. Then, after a few more beers, she said, 'What the hell.'"

Julie chimed in. "Close enough to a yes for me. Safe to assume there was some premature consummating happening last night?"

"Does Popeye eat canned spinach? We did a little more consummating this morning, just to make sure." Laughter and congratulations erupted around the table. O'Leary joined in the laughter, then shifted the topic to the business at hand. "Jack, grab your legal pad. I've got a helluva story for you."

Jack said, "Way ahead of you, Rambo. Fire away."

"Since Joy's in the shower, allow me to skip to the South Dakota subplot."

Jack flipped through his notes to a previous page filled with boxes and arrows.

O'Leary said, "Joy told me Jo Douglass has a line on Samantha's whereabouts. Douglass has been tracking two DSS operatives posing as BIA agents. They've been criss-crossing the Dakotas, trying to foil Sam's next move."

Lindstrom interrupted. "Let me guess. Two Native American dudes that look like bikers, one tall and one short, driving a black F-250."

The phone crackled, then O'Leary said, "You got it, buddy. Just for kicks, I compared the tread pattern on Wolcott's Rubicon with the F-250 XLT. Both roll on P 275/70-R18s. The Ford came with Michelins, the Jeep rolls on Goodrich's. I noticed Wolcott had custom wheels and tires installed, and guess what?"

Sommers said, "They're Michelin 18s." He adjusted his baseball hat, then leaned onto the table with both fists. "Solid, but still circumstantial. We're already ninety percent sure the snakes killed Lilly and Bud. But why?"

Jack tapped his pen on his chin and said, "All in the name of flushing Samantha into the open." He lifted his chin at Sommers. "Remember Wagner and Colletti? They were more interested in her than the evidence right in front of their eyes."

O'Leary said, "Douglass says the DSS is pulling out all the stops, trying to throw a net over Sam before the feds do."

Lindstrom, after swallowing his coffee, said, "With only one Chief left, they gotta be closing in. How do you think Big Bill Wenner factors into this mess?"

O'Leary waited for the cell signal to clear, then said, "Just getting to that. Looked like a cartel hit, right? But the Latinos never took credit for it. We all know they go hard for style points. Anyway, I've got an old Army buddy who went Deep State without telling me. He spends most of his time crunching data and building AI simulations for the DHS. Anyway, he dug into some classified files and it turns out Wenner and Numbers were long-time business associates in Kansas City. Word on the street is she still cooks the books for Wenner Enterprises. Small world, 'eh?"

Jack flipped to a different page on his yellow pad. "Just to confirm, this is Susan Norman you're talking about, correct?"

O'Leary said, "That's right. After Wenner moved his operation to Fargo, the IRS started putting the squeeze on him, but the FBI called off the dogs. They hauled Wenner in and made him cough up what he knew about the DSS and their burgeoning war chest. Seems like he omitted details about his links to Susan Norman and Patti Hawkins."

Jack looked up from his notes, shifting his eyes to Sommers. "That seals it. Big Bill knew all about you and Sam."

Julie asked, "So the snakes whacked Big Bill and tried to pin it on the cartel. That doesn't make any sense. A turf war in Podunk, North Dakota?"

"I know, right?" O'Leary said. "But here's the twist. The Wenner file is three years old. The FBI buried Big Bill's testimony, holding out for a bigger score. My DOJ buddy said a whistleblower came forward requesting protection in exchange for incriminating information."

O'Leary coughed and cleared his throat before continuing. "The informant said Ed Norman cut a deal with the DSS, guaranteeing himself a partial stake in a casino resort. Meanwhile, his wife went behind his back and worked out a separate deal with Wenner. There's another complication. My contact says the EPA's been sniffing around the Norman property for years, but the FBI's been throwing up roadblocks and sitting on their hands while the fighting escalates. I'll give y'all one guess who the whistleblower is."

Sommers studied the notes stuck to the table, then picked up his phone. "Jerry Reynolds."

"Bingo!" O'Leary said, fumbling with his cellphone. "Listen guys, Joy just stepped out of the bathroom wearing nothing but her tattoos. I'll shoot you an email with a PDF attachment. It's got everything you want to know about Numbers Norman, and then some. Gotta go."

Sommers tried to catch O'Leary before he signed off, but heard only a click, followed by cellular white noise. He scanned Jack's assortment of sticky notes, then looked around the table, locking eyes with each of his three remaining teammates. "I'll put a call into the EPA. It appears we've got no shot finding Sam until we get our hands on Jerry Reynolds."

Jack closed his notes and tossed a second bagel to Sommers. "I think Samantha's ship has sailed. But maybe there's more we can learn from Susan Norman."

Julie tapped her husband on the shoulder. "Forget her. We need to have a heart-to-heart with Peg McFarland."

Lindstrom stood and began peeling the notes from the table. "There's an old man hiding out somewhere 'round here. We have questions, he has answers." He lifted his chin at Sommers. "Reynolds needs our help. Let's go get him."

Sommers said, "How about you gas up that generator first? I need to talk to Jack for a minute, learn more about his meeting with Gus McFarland."

Thirty minutes later, Jack and Julie waved as Sommers and Lindstrom drove off towards North Dakota. Julie silenced her radio and turned into the long gravel driveway leading to Peg McFarland's farmhouse. She parked behind Peg's riding lawn mower and the couple stepped into the yard. They found the large woman seated on her porch swing with a straw tucked into the corner of her mouth and Gus's shotgun resting across her thighs. Julie whispered to her husband. "Are you packing your thirty-eight?"

He gave her a wink and a nod as they slinked towards the front steps.

Peg stood and pointed the gun's barrel at the couple, the straw bobbing in front of her lips as she spoke. "That's far enough. I should blast both you numskulls to kingdom come. Best turn your asses around and head back the way you came."

Julie raised her palms skyward. "We don't want any trouble, Peg. We heard about Gus and thought we could help."

McFarland stepped down into the yard with the shotgun still in harm's way. "Yea, well, you've been nothing but trouble since the moment we met. Gussie would still be alive if it wasn't for you and your meddling friends."

Jack grinned as he motioned to Peg's yard sign. "We'd like to buy some of your sweetcorn before we go. Five bucks a dozen, right? Sounds like a good deal to me."

McFarland let out the smallest snort of a laugh and lowered her gun as the lawyer reached for his wallet. Instead, he jerked his pistol from the small of his back and stepped into a shooter's position with the muzzle pointed at Peg's chest. "Doesn't have to be like this, Mrs. McFarland. Just answer a few questions, sell us some corn, then we'll be on our way."

Julie said, "Put the gun down, Peg. We just want to talk." The three rivals eyed each other for several seconds until at last McFarland lowered the shotgun to her side.

She waved her arm towards the house. "C'mon kids, let's sit in the shade. I've got sweat trickling down my ass crack."

Julie and Jack smirked as they took a seat on the porch stairs. Peg stepped inside to fetch a jug of sun tea and three mason jars filled with ice. A minute later, she tossed a burlap bag filled with sweetcorn on the step near Jack's feet. "Five bucks. But since you're a highfalutin lawyer and all, let's make it ten."

Jack stood and fished a ten-dollar bill from his wallet. "Worth every penny, I'm sure."

McFarland laughed before slapping his shoulder. "I'm just shittin' ya, Jack. Corn is on the house." After a few minutes of small talk about the weather, she pointed at Julie. "Okay, Barbie-doll, hit me with those questions of yours."

Jack nodded at his wife and he slipped a small notepad from his back pocket.

Julie sipped from her glass, then held it in front of her face. "Mmm, good tea," she said, licking her lips. "There was a white Escalade parked here yesterday. We recognized Colin Stroud, and Susan Norman. Who was the Asian man wearing the blue suit?"

McFarland closed her eyes and pursed her lips. She rocked a few times on the swing, then opened her eyes. "Shui, Ro Lin Shui. I think he's a bigshot in Pembina County. Might be a lawyer like your hubby here. Wouldn't surprise me if he's CCP—has that air about him. Got a disgusting growth on his face. Looks like a fuckin' leech."

Julie smiled and shook her head. "That's what Gus said—word for word."

The burly farmer hung her head and nodded as she continued rocking on her swing, its support chains groaning from her weight. Julie patted the farmer's foot. "I'm sorry, Peg."

The sound of chirping crickets and rustling cornstalks rose above the murmur of a somber breeze, and the smell of burnt leaves hung in a noontide haze. "Mrs. McFarland," Jack said, stepping into the yard. "I'm sure you've heard that Tommy Fulgham's dead. Why would Stroud and Shui risk their political futures over those stupid water samples?"

A look of confusion washed over McFarland's face. "That's the damndest thing. I don't know."

Julie stood on the steps and asked, "What did they promise you in exchange for those boxes we pulled from the mud?"

McFarland stopped swinging and turned to face the wisps of smoke rising from the long rows of green and gold. "They said we could keep our farm."

Jack climbed the steps and handed a contract and a pen to McFarland. He said, "In no time at all, if it hasn't started already, there'll be an endless line of sharks circling you with confusing questions, maybe even outrageous threats."

Julie stepped closer and handed the farmer one of her business cards. "Sign the form, Peg. You can deflect all of those snoops to us. We'll take care of you."

McFarland sat up and shook her head. "Like you took care of Gussie?" Then she scanned her fields and exhaled a deep, melancholy sigh. She pursed her lips and dabbed her weepy eyes. "I've got nobody. I've got nothing. Just these burned fields. Can either of you tell me why the world keeps shitting all over me?"

Julie put her hand on McFarland's shoulder. "We're sorry we couldn't help Gus. But now we're here, trying to help you." She waved her arm towards the rows of corn. "How's the story gonna end, Peg?"

McFarland tossed the pen back to Jack, then stepped into the yard with her arms folded across her chest, staring at her emerald-colored crop. With her back to them, she wiped tears and beads of sweat from her face with a plaid handkerchief. "If you guys drive me to Hallock, I'll sign those goddamn papers. As a bonus, I'll tell you a story that'll knock both of you on your asses."

Jack and Julie looked at each other with raised eyebrows, then nodded their approval. Jack asked, "Mind if we stop by Chester's for a bite?"

McFarland looked skyward and laughed. "We'll park our butts

in Gussie's booth and chow down. Sounds fun. Let's hit the bank first."

A minute later, she climbed into the Jeep's passenger seat, then leaned towards Julie and pointed at a long, swooping scar on the inside of her muscular arm. "We've got one hell of a storm coming. I can feel it deep inside. How 'bout you?"

Chapter 23
No Time

"No time left for you, on my way to better things."

Sommers sat tall in the passenger seat, steadfast and deep in thought, while Lindstrom's Charger raced back into North Dakota at eighty-five miles per hour. South of Norman Farms, the driver parked behind a collapsed billboard sign advertising Frostfire Ski Resort. A copse of willows and cottonwoods surrounded the splintered heap, creating a shady, secluded hiding spot for Ted's car. As the noontime temperatures soared, the two men gulped bottled water, preparing for their mile-long hike to Reynolds' garage.

Lindstrom opened the door to step out, but Sommers grabbed his shoulder, pulling him back against the leather seat. "Whoa Ted, hold up a minute. I've been thinking about O'Leary's report. Let's rehash what he said—make sure we're not missing anything."

Sommers adjusted his baseball hat, then started counting on his fingers. "Susan Norman had some sort of deal with Wenner. Now he's dead. Ed Norman had a casino agreement with the DSS, and now he's nowhere to be found. Jerry Reynolds, for some unknown reason, has taken off for God knows where. Somewhere in the middle of all this is Samantha and a snakebit pickup truck. So tell me, what's Susan's next move? She has access to Wenner's financial records. Why hasn't the DSS or the feds come after her?"

Lindstrom scratched at the back of his neck. "Now that you mention it, we haven't seen a single cow." Then he took a big sniff. "And yet, it smells awful 'round here. Swarms of flies everywhere."

Sommers rolled his eyes and shook his head. "You're not paying attention to what I said. What's Susan's endgame? Do you think she's courting another investor?"

"This place is a ghost town and Susan Norman rolls like South Beach, the pieces don't fit at all. Ya got someone in mind?"

Sommers nodded but didn't answer. He buckled his seat belt and pointed his thumb towards Susan's farmhouse. "Change of plan. Drop me at her front door."

Lindstrom shook his head. "I don't understand. You wanna butt heads with her defensive line again?"

Sommers grinned and said, "I've been tackled by worse. Just drop me at her porch, then go do your investigation thing at Jerry's. And hey, don't overlook his floors. I got a feeling."

Lindstrom scratched his head, then folded his arms across his chest. "First, tell me what you're up to."

"Susan wants to take me to the fair," Sommers said, scrunching his face into a pout and shrugging his shoulders. "Sausage, sweetcorn, and carnival rides. Doesn't sound all that bad to me."

Lindstrom backed his car from the shade. "She just wants to get you on The Zipper ride, partner. I don't like it, but you're the boss." He spun a dusty U-turn and wheeled back towards Highway 5. "Just remember, she has a history with Wenner. If Jack's right, she knows all about you and Sam. And Noah."

Before Sommers could respond, his phone vibrated in his pants pocket. "Pull over. It's Julie, with an update from McFarland's. I'll put her on speaker." Sommers held his phone towards Lindstrom. "Go ahead, Jules. You're on speakerphone."

She said, "Hey guys. Peg McFarland had Gus's shotgun across her lap, and we had to talk her out of blasting us to the moon. Once we talked her down, she gave us a bag of sweetcorn and the name of the Asian guy palling around with Norman and Stroud."

From somewhere in the background, Jack chimed in. "We drove her to Valley Bank in Hallock," he said. "She signed some legal documents, and we gave her some assurances. I'll need to file some paperwork with the county clerk within the next day or two. Sommers, I'll explain the details later, but we'll need your signature on a few things ASAP. Julie will notarize them. Ted, if you can still spell your name, will need you to sign as a witness."

"Good one, tough guy," Lindstrom said. "Come talk to me when you figure out how to shoot that gun of yours."

"Where's McFarland now?" Sommers asked, interrupting their childish jabs. "Any sign of her lackeys?"

Julie chimed in from the background. "She just ran inside the funeral home to get some information. It was only her at the farm, and she didn't have much to say. I think she's coming to grips with the fact that she's alone." The two phones went silent for a long, sober moment. "Anyway, we're driving out to Cavalier after lunch. We want a few minutes with the county water commissioner, Ro Lin Shui. Peg thinks he's a Chinese Nationalist, so I skimmed through some of his TikTok videos. Let me tell ya, he's something else—not anything close to the traditional midwestern mold."

Jack said, "I think that's gonna put a wrap on Kittson County, at least for now. What are you guys up to?"

"Against my wishes," Lindstrom said. "Sommers is taking Susan Norman to the county fair. I'm gonna run a fine-toothed comb through Jerry's place. How about if we rendezvous at the Corner Diner for early-bird supper? They've got a homemade meatloaf that's outta this world."

"Real food and indoor plumbing?" Julie asked with a sarcastic huff. "Sounds like heaven to me. Sommers, watch your back, man. By all accounts, that woman is the queen of manipulation, nothing but trouble. Here comes Peg. We gotta go."

A short time later, Lindstrom watched Norman and Sommers drive off in her Mustang with the top down. He stepped from the window and began moving furniture and looking under the rugs. Within five minutes, the investigator discovered Reynolds' floor safe hidden beneath a TV stand in the family room. He gave up on the combination lock after several failed attempts, shifting his attention to the veteran's closets and drawers.

The sounds of voices and slamming car doors interrupted his search. Lindstrom peeked out the kitchen window to see the four monsters, one wearing a sling around his elbow, climbing into their SUV. The quartet kicked up a rolling cloud of dust as they sped away. Lindstrom stepped into the garage and sent a text message to Sommers. "Heads up, partner. Four KC linemen chasing after you."

Cicadas buzzed in the cedars as Lindstrom stepped into the yard and surveyed the neighboring pastures. He hiked the half-mile trek to the charred rubble piled between Norman's house and Jerry's shop. Along the way, he picked up a long stick and soon stood boot-deep in gray ashes, wiping sweat from his eyes and swatting flies away from his face. His poking and stirring uncovered bolts, hinges, and other assorted pieces of blackened hardware.

Lindstrom swept aside an assortment of burnt beer cans and mason jars. He squatted near a pile of melted scrap, discovering a blackened western-style belt buckle. After wiping and scrubbing the trinket, he lifted it high, inspecting it in the daylight. He pocketed his find, then stumbled as he pivoted for the cool shadows of Reynolds' homestead. He cursed after his boot thumped hard against something hollow and haunting. The retired sheriff looked down to find the sooty, sunken eye sockets of a human skull glaring up at him.

Sommers and Norman sat on opposite sides of a picnic table in the shade of a large oak tree. Susan gulped beer from a sweating aluminum can, her arm around the waist of a giant stuffed teddy bear seated at her side. She set her can down and leaned her chest over the table. "Where'd you learn to throw like that?" She asked, licking beer foam from her lips.

Sommers shrugged, then sipped lemonade from a plastic souvenir cup with a bendy straw.

Susan ran her fingernails along the big man's muscular arm. "Cat got your tongue?"

Sommers set his drink on the table and swatted a bee away from his straw. "I was just thinking about Jerry Reynolds. Any idea where he might've gone?"

Susan pulled her hair to the side, then held the cold beer can against her neck. "Phew, hot one today." Her eyes tracked a line of kids riding dreary ponies along a chalky path that encircled the fairgrounds. "J.R. wanders off the grid from time to time. Where he goes is his business."

Sommers took another sip and cocked his head towards a rutted hay field used as a parking lot during the fair. "What do you know about that truck he's driving? Doesn't seem to suit his old-world proclivities. Besides, everyone knows he's a Chevy man."

Susan puckered her lips as she carved her initials into the tabletop, using the pull tab from her beer can. "Edward promised the Ford to some Indian friends of his, but I guess the deal fell through. Maybe he told Jerry he could drive it until he gets back."

"Folks are saying Bill Wenner sat on that truck for almost three years. I wonder who gunned the big guy down—could be any number of people, I presume."

Susan kept carving without looking up or responding.

Sommers checked the time on his phone. "Ya know, things seem pretty dead back at your farm. When's the last time you talked to Edward? Are you expecting him anytime soon?"

Susan stood from the table, snatching her small leather handbag from the bench. "I'm thirsty—gonna fetch me a bucket of beer. Want another lemonade?" Sommers shook his head, then watched her sashay away.

Surrounding the beer tent, lustful men and envious women gawked at Susan's blond hair, tanned legs, and buxom chest. At some point, their wandering eyes would shift to the picnic table in the shade, trying to place the stranger she'd left behind to watch her bear.

Sommers felt his phone vibrate on the table. He tapped the screen to check his message, then looked up to see Susan handing two bottles of beer to each of her bouncers. Monster number four turned and locked eyes with Sommers. He lifted one of his bottles in a toast, then downed his beer in a single sloppy gulp. Sommers countered by raising his plastic cup, then slurping through his yellow bendy straw.

Before long, Susan strolled back to the table carrying a sweating silver pail. She had a silly grin stretching her lips. Sommers said, "You must be a VIP with all that muscle looking after you."

Susan flitted her free hand. "A girl can't be too careful these days. Just say the word and I'll send them away. Then you can have me all to yourself."

Sommers scanned the fairgrounds, ignoring her suggestive comment. "As I was saying, what do you and Edward have planned for the farm? It's no secret the dairy business has soured. People say you're good with numbers, and you keep hinting that your marriage is on the rocks. Don't tell me you haven't discussed business with him?"

"You a cop? Why all these silly questions? Edward this, Edward that." Susan twisted off a bottle cap, then flicked it into the weeds. "I bought him out years ago. The farm's mine. He blew all his money on booze and drugs." She took a gulp, then pointed the bottle at the lumberjack's nose. "Don't go fretting over spilt milk, big guy. I'm doin' alright—better than alright."

"Okay, that's interesting," Sommers said, slipping the bottle from her hand and placing it on the table in front of the giant pink bear. "If you're planning to sell the farm, I'd like to make you an offer."

Norman looked him up and down, then sputtered through her lips before laughing out loud. She grabbed his drink and sniffed the end of the straw. "What the hell did they put in this cup?" After rolling her eyes and shaking her head, she looked past Sommers and pointed. "Get a load of those idiots."

Sommers turned and watched three of the four monsters taking turns swinging a huge wooden mallet, trying in vain to ring the bell atop the High Striker game. Sommers blurted a muffled chuckle, then said, "So much for steroids and bulging deltoids. I suppose I shouldn't laugh. They say the carnies rig a lot of these games."

"Think you can do better?" Susan grabbed her bear, then grabbed Sommers' arm and dragged both from their seats. "C'mon, big talker, grab them beers. Let's see what you got." After a few strides, she spanked him on his backside. "There's a cover band playing at Hudson's tonight. How 'bout I tuck you in after a night of dancing?" Sommers slurped his lemonade, sidestepping Susan's blunt proposition.

On their way through the courtyard, Sommers's phone chimed. He tapped Norman's shoulder and said, "Go on ahead, I'll catch up. Gotta take this."

"Your investment banker?" She asked, before hitting him with another eye roll and a mocking laugh. Then she pranced over to join the crowd gathered around her flunkies, all hovering around the strongman game.

Sommers held the phone to his ear. "Go ahead, buddy. I had to break away from the crowd for a minute."

"Get my message about Norman's bodyguards?" Lindstrom asked.

"Yep. I'm watching 'em right now—making fools of themselves in the arcade."

Lindstrom repositioned his phone, sounding short-winded. "I stumbled into an acquaintance of yours. He's over in that pile of slag that used to be the Holstein barn."

"Who?" Sommers asked. "What are you talking about?"

"I found bones and teeth. Human, for sure. Probably males, based on the other pieces of evidence I found in that pile. The ND Crime Lab's on their way. I'm gonna show 'em around. They're gonna take my statement, then I'm coming to pick you up. Think you can stay outta trouble for another hour or two?"

"Wait, you're saying there's more than one?"

"I'm assuming one is Tommy Fulgham. The other could be Ed Norman or Manuel Rodriguez, maybe both. The flies and the stench tipped me off. It sure looks like a mass cremation site to me."

"Any sign of Reynolds?" Sommers asked.

"Nope. But you were right to check his floors. There's a safe tucked under the entertainment center—got a combination lock. I couldn't crack it."

"Well, I don't know what to say, but I'm not surprised. Know what I mean?" Sommers removed his hat and scratched at the back of his head. "Call O'Leary and Moon Deer. See if they can dig up some history on Reynolds. Then call Jack and let him know what's going on. Tell him I want to make an offer on the Norman place."

"That's creepy, man. Why don't you let things settle for a few weeks? You could get it for back taxes and fees. Say, try to keep Susan's party together and don't let on. I wanna be there when Numbers Norman and her henchmen get their asses hauled in for questioning. I'll text you when I'm on my way."

Sommers pocketed his phone, fitted his hat, then tried to erase the stunned look from his face. He soon joined the crowd that stood watching Norman's monsters take their cuts with the big hammer. "You alright?" Susan asked. "Looks like you've seen a ghost."

Sommers waved her off. "Has anyone banged that bell yet?"

"Ha, not even close." Then she chugged the rest of her beer.

Monster number four turned towards Sommers then wrapped his meaty paws around the wooden handle. "Came back to find out, didn't you? Big fuckin' mistake, pal." The sweaty behemoth roared as he took his mighty swing, but the black puck traveled only eight feet up the sixteen-foot pole. The crowd groaned in collective disappointment.

Sommers puckered his lips and shook his head. The monster with the sling elbowed him hard in the ribs. "You're next, old man."

Monster number four, panting and scowling, extended the hammer towards Sommers. The big lumberjack winked and said, "Pay attention, boy—you just might learn something. Here, hold my drink."

The restless crowd laughed, picking up on the fervent rivalry. Sommers spit into his palms and rubbed them together. Then he cinched his grip around the handle, studying the glistening bell ten feet above his head.

Susan aped, shaking the big bear in Sommers's face. "You're not having second thoughts, are ya?" She danced around and said, "C'mon, big guy, do it for me. Do it for that biker chick of yours. Better yet, do it for the boy."

Sommers glared at her with a clenched jaw and a furrowed brow. He leaned into her face and said, "Pick a hand."

Susan giggled as she rolled her eyes, then pointed at his hardened right biceps. The murmuring crowd inched closer and held a shared breath. Sommers set his feet, braced his left arm behind his back, then raised the heavy mallet high above his head.

Troubled Water

With the speed of lightning and the force of thunder, Sommers dropped into a squat and dropped the head of the hammer with an earth-shattering blow. The black puck rocketed skyward before blasting into the bell, sending the shiny dish sailing into the air. A ringing note echoed across the fairgrounds, stopping people in their tracks.

The sun-drenched crowd looked up with their jaws agape, watching the silver disc sail like a frisbee before it fell, landing with a hollow thud, fifty feet away. The throng erupted with applause, and Susan jumped into Sommers' arms. She wrapped her legs around his waist and her arms around his neck. She planted a firm, moist kiss on his lips, then slid back to her feet. "That was amazing," she said, beaming like a prowling cat. "And that thing you did with the hammer wasn't half-bad either."

Sommers dropped the bruised mallet at the feet of monster number four. He wagged his finger and said, "Sometimes you're the hammer, and sometimes you're the nail."

Norman's sweaty bouncer squared up to the big lumberjack, cracking his knuckles and puffing his chest.

Sommers nodded and said, "Your move, boy." Then he held up two fingers. "Hospital or jail. Either way, it'll be bad for you. Wanna find out?"

The monster glared at the big man for a long, bitter moment, then kicked at the hammer and stomped away, joining his grumbling sidekicks. Sommers fished Jack's business card from his pocket and handed it to Norman as the couple stepped away from the cheering crowd.

"What's this?" She asked as the distant wail of sirens grew louder.

"My representation. Mention me, would ya? It gets me a discount." Sommers adjusted his baseball cap, shading his eyes with the bill. The big lumberjack looked up and noticed dark clouds gathering along the western horizon. "All things considered. I had a pretty good time. Thank you, Susan." He tipped his hat to his date, then turned and walked away.

Numbers Norman dumped her prize and pouted, standing speechless and alone in the dusty lane. Near her grubby sandaled feet, a mottled teddy bear and a dented bell baked in the orange afternoon sun.

Chapter 24
Here Comes the Rain

"Your love's a heartache that's torn me apart."

Ted Lindstrom shoveled meatloaf and mashed potatoes into his mouth like he hadn't eaten in weeks. Jack Hughes gnawed on a pulled-pork sandwich while his wife, Julie, munched on a grilled chicken salad. Sommers' untouched dinner grew cold because, one by one, star-struck patrons stopped at the table to congratulate the humble lumberjack on his theatrics at the fair.

An old timer sporting a wiry gray beard that framed his dark, wrinkled face stepped forward and cleared his throat. He tipped his frayed cowboy hat and leaned into the foursome's booth. After patting Sommers on the back, he cleared his throat and said, "I saw you leave Numbers Norman stewing in the midway. Good for you, good for The Nation." Then he stuck a toothpick into the corner of his mouth and smacked his lips. "Better watch your back and look after your friends. That witch clamps onto grudges like a rusty bear trap."

Sommers tapped the bill of his baseball hat with his fork. "Thanks, mister. I'll keep that in mind. Say, do you know Jerry Reynolds? Seen him around?"

The brittle Native scratched at the back of his neck. "Well shoot, everyone knows the fix-it man—only warrior older than me from these parts. Haven't seen him 'round much." The stranger wobbled as he tipped his hat to Julie. "Name's Branch." Then he hiccoughed and hobbled away. Sommers' troupe turned their heads and watched the old timer shuffle his way through the door and into the crowded street.

Lindstrom wiped a dribble of brown gravy from the corner of his mouth, then tapped his fork on Julie's salad bowl. "So, tell us about this Chop Suey guy. What did you find out?"

Julie finished chewing, then sipped her iced tea as she plucked a small notebook from Jack's shirt pocket. After flipping past a few pages, she said, "Ro Lin Shui, county water commissioner, forty-three years old. He wasn't available, but his administrative assistant was more than willing to spill her guts for us."

Jack pointed a french fry at Lindstrom. "It seems Shui can't keep his hands off the apprentices, male or female. Besides his CCP allegiance, he's a grade-A creeper and a poster child for the alphabet mafia."

Julie scowled and nodded her head. "Shui is also a board member for a covert LLC called Oasis Financial. Their mission includes acquiring agricultural properties near U.S. military installations. The governor just signed legislation restricting the purchasing power of Chinese investors. Oasis provides Shui with some convenient anonymity."

Lindstrom cocked his head to the side. "Grand Forks Air Force Base is sixty miles south of here." Then he leaned over the table and pointed his fork at Sommers. "Seems to me Chop Suey's playing a numbers game."

Sommers cut into his meat loaf and nodded. "You're right. So, now we know the object of Susan Norman's financial attraction."

Jack pointed his bottle at Sommers after sipping from his beer. "You mentioned making an offer on the Norman place. The going rate is two thousand dollars an acre. You're looking at five million, give or take. Shui's secretary says Oasis is prepared to pay way more than market value."

Julie poked Sommers's hand with her fork. "And that got me thinking about land valuations and Fulgham's water samples. What would obliterate the appraised value of twenty-five hundred acres, zoned agricultural, in Pembina County?"

Jack interrupted by grabbing his notepad and wagging his finger in the air. "Hint. O'Leary mentioned the EPA's been snooping around Norman's farm for years."

Sommers swallowed a bite of room-temperature mashed potatoes, then adjusted his baseball hat. "Hold on a minute," he said. "Let's assume Fulgham's samples show contaminants from Norman Farms. That information would drive the valuation down. But Norman let Stroud and Shui swoop in to take those boxes. What's her angle?"

Again, Jack wagged his finger as if he was stirring the air above the table. "What would the EPA do if those samples revealed something toxic, something deadly and irreversible? What if the Canadians got wind of the situation and forced additional testing?"

Sommers stared into his half-empty water glass while scratching at the coarse, graying stubble on his chin. "The EPA would condemn the property and leverage The Clean Water Act to purchase it for pennies on the dollar. The acquisition would be legitimized through a writ of eminent domain."

Jack nodded, showing his approval. "Well stated, counselor. Right now, there are dozens of open eminent domain lawsuits across the Dakotas. Corporations have been sanctioned by the government to pilfer strategic properties. Under the guise of common good, the projects range from gas pipelines and carbon capture, to wind farms, and flood control measures. Eminent domain assumes fair compensation to the owner, but we know what happens when politicians get involved in business matters. So, you're right. If her farm's polluting the watershed, Susan could take a colossal hit."

Julie said, "She could challenge the writ in federal court, but that could take years to settle."

Lindstrom said, "And it would cost her a fortune. Wanna bet Stroud is on the Oasis board alongside Shui? Norman's gonna make sure they get their cut for suppressing the damning evidence."

After sipping her tea, Julie tapped the table with her finger. "They're trying to pin everything on the McFarlands, but Peg's drug business brought unwanted attention to the valley."

Jack picked at the label on his beer bottle. "That, and they couldn't trust Gus to keep his mouth shut. The Numbers Gang knew he wouldn't play ball, and they killed him for it." He pointed his bottle at Sommers. "We had quite the visit at Valley Bank in Hallock. I'll explain later—too many eyes and ears around here."

Sommers shook his head and counted on his fingers. "Okay, but we're still no closer to answering a few key questions; what did Wenner tell the feds, and what does Reynolds know?" He swirled the splash of water remaining in his tumbler, then swallowed the last gulp. He banged his empty glass on the table and exhaled a heavy sigh. "And we're not one inch closer to finding Sam."

A friendly, top heavy server with pink highlights in her hair strolled over and offered something from the dessert menu. After the crew declined, she slid the tab across the table. Sommers reached for his wallet, and a woman he didn't recognize stepped around the server and plucked the check from his fingers. She said, "It'd be my pleasure to take care of this." Before Sommers could respond, the attractive woman offered her business card, then winked with a grin before turning away.

Lindstrom cocked his eyebrows, then nodded with his lips puckered. "What did I tell you? The scenery is very underrated around here. Who the heck was that?"

Sommers shrugged as he watched her stroll towards the register. "Don't know." He regretted feeling, amidst all his troubles, the tug of her beauty and the allure of her self-confidence. Average height, with a fit curvy figure, the striking woman wore a plaid sleeveless blouse, form-fitting jeans, and black western boots. Her strawberry blonde hair had a professional, shoulder-length cut, and her green eyes drove a chilly spike into his chest. If he was honest with himself about this encounter, she was the most enchanting woman he'd ever seen. He turned back and lifted his chin at Lindstrom. "She's too young for you."

Lindstrom brushed his mustache with his fingers and shrugged. "Ya think?" Then he scooped a heaping mound of potatoes from Sommers's plate, wincing as he swallowed the chilled bite. He wiped his mouth and fluttered his eyelids. "She sure batted eyelashes at you, big fella."

Sommers sputtered through his lips, then shook his head. "Like a hole in the head, mister." He stood from the table and passed the woman's card to Jack without reading it. The big lumberjack left a twenty on the table and furrowed his brow. "Lord knows how, but the bad guys know about my son. I gotta get back to the lake."

Julie looked up and asked, "When?"

"As soon as Ted finishes chewing, he can drop me at the airport."

Jack studied the woman's business card and cocked an eyebrow. "Hmph, EPA," he said, clipping it to a page inside his notepad.

A sudden clap of thunder shook the Corner Diner. Outside, huge raindrops and pea-sized hail pummeled sightseers scurrying for cover. Gusts of wind howled, rattling the doors and windows, sending dismal warnings of more to come. Sommers adjusted his baseball hat and peered up through a skylight, seeing its clouded glass peppered with water and ice.

Lindstrom opened the weather app on his phone, then swiped

to the radar view. "Welp. It's gonna be a soggy night at the Last Resort."

Julie rolled her eyes and shook her head, then gave her forehead a loud slap.

Jack nodded, then leaned in and whispered to Sommers. "Looks like you're grounded again. Just as well. We've got business to discuss. Papers to sign."

Sommers stood and stepped to the front windows. He looked every bit like a fabled giant as he crossed his arms and watched the torrents turn the quaint summer festival into a saturated catastrophe.

A shriveling purple sunset lost ground to the approaching storm clouds. Peg McFarland sat in her ATV, parked in the shadows below the Highway 175 overpass. It was the same sticky riverbank where Manny Rodriguez fired a bullet into Tommy Fulgham's chest.

Gus's shotgun rested across her lap as she watched an occasional eighteen-wheeler rumble into Minnesota. She drew a long drag from her joint, holding the smoke while lifting her face to the sky. Thunder boomed in the distance, and Peg peeked over her shoulder, watching sinister clouds streaked with lightning creeping towards the valley. She nodded her head and let the smoke seep from her parted lips.

This was her new routine, hiding in the brush, smoking weed, and watching the spotty traffic roll towards Two Rivers. Peg's phone vibrated, and she tapped the screen to read her tip from Hamilton. She swiped to her weather app, studied the red blobs on the radar map, then sucked another vapory hit from her joint.

Long minutes passed without a single car. Then, a racy Dodge Charger she recognized rolled towards the bridge, slowing with its headlights on and its wipers sweeping the windshield. McFarland snuffed out her smoke and stepped from her four-wheeler, pressing the recoil pad of the shotgun against her shoulder. She took a deep breath, then took aim at a Jeep's windshield. The four-by-four approached the overpass, trailing the Charger by twenty seconds.

A driver and a passenger, the shooter saw their faces through the windshield, illuminated by the milky glow of the Jeep's dashboard lights. She tapped the trigger with her index finger, squeezed the pump with her left hand, then ground her boots into the clay, bracing herself for the explosion.

Then, from out of nowhere, a bullfrog croaked near her feet. McFarland exhaled and lowered the barrel of the gun. She lifted her chin at the passing four-by-four. "Don't worry. I'm not gonna waste my ammo on you, Barbie-Doll. Shit, we coulda been friends, right? Mr. Froggie here agrees, says I should let you pass." Again, the bullfrog croaked and Peg watched the Jeep's taillights fade into the night.

Five minutes later, a third pair of headlights appeared, the familiar white Cadillac with Missouri plates. Like the Charger, the speeding SUV slowed as it approached the narrow bridge. The heavy thumping of music matched the volume of the approaching storm.

McFarland glanced down at the frog and raised her eyebrows. She paused for Froggie's reaction, then nodded and took aim. "This is for you, Gussie." She squeezed the trigger, and the gun kicked like a mule, blasting away at the SUV's grill and front fender. Tires howled on the damp pavement and the big car jerked to the right, plowing through the aluminum guardrail.

McFarland shielded her face as the Cadillac flipped into the air with yellow flames bursting from under the engine. Lightning flashed, and the wreck plunged twenty-five feet, flopping into the Red River with a bone-jarring splash. The hapless Escalade landed on its roof, then bubbled and hissed like a dying animal as it bobbed, then sank into the murky water.

Before long, the churning stopped, and all that remained were three steaming tires poking above the swells. McFarland heaved Gus's shotgun into the river, then brushed her palms together three times. She climbed back into her ATV and turned towards the dark loneliness awaiting her at home.

Bumping along the valley trail, McFarland sparked another joint. She surveyed the swaying fields, then turned north towards the old fishing pier. The thunderstorm's fury loomed over her shoulder, turning the sky to a haunting shade of yellow-green. Fierce winds kicked up, bending and whipping the overhanging willows.

Soon, she stepped out and straggled to the far reaches of the weathered planks. Just a few feet away, she discovered a blue heron pecking at the bones of a dead catfish. McFarland savored her smoke and nodded at the long-legged bird. "Sorry to interrupt your dinner. How 'bout this crazy weather, 'eh?"

The heron raised up, looked around, then went back to nibbling on the carcass. McFarland turned to gaze upon her farm. The lightning flashes illuminating a massive blackened hole in the middle of her magnificent field of greens. Large raindrops began pelting the leaves, and she drew one last hit from her roach. She flipped the smoldering butt into the surging river and looked back at the lanky bird. "I've always regretted never learning how to swim. Until tonight."

The heron squawked, and with three flaps of its powerful wings, it sailed away. Peg pursed her lips and nodded her head. "Okay, then. I guess that settles it." Lightning sizzled and thunder exploded as the skies opened overhead. She stretched her arms out wide, letting them float weightless on the advancing cyclone.

Margaret McFarland lifted her face to the cloudburst cascading from the heavens. Then the lonesome farmer leaped as far as she could into the gale, following the blue-gray bird into the gloom.

The torrential rains were just beginning in the Red River Valley, but six hundred miles southwest, the skies remained fair over Spearfish Canyon. Greg O'Leary and Joy Moon Deer sat in the backyard, warming their feet beside a crackling bonfire. Perched high above Devils Bathtub, they listened to the rapids slosh in the creek below.

The couple held hands and sipped their beers, watching a rosy sunset wither beyond the western peaks of the Black Hills. Angry thunderheads tracked miles to the south, rumbling and flashing as they rampaged across the great plains.

O'Leary poked at the glowing clinkers with a stick, then leaned over and kissed Moon Deer on her forehead. "You're pretty quiet tonight. Something on your mind?"

Joy swirled the last of her beer in its bottle, then downed the frothy remains. She wiped her mouth on her sleeve and blurted her muted belch. "Jo was supposed to meet me for a run after breakfast. She blew me off."

"Considering she's a cop," he said, waving his hand. "I wouldn't take it all personal."

Moon Deer stood and tossed a narrow log onto the fire. She watched a plume of orange embers float skyward, then settled back into her Adirondack chair. "Nah, that's not it. She acted strange when I pressed her for an explanation—told me to take care of you and stay in my fuckin' lane."

O'Leary puckered his lips and shook his head. "Were those her exact words?"

"She sounded very conflicted this morning. She asked me if I knew what a shapeshifter was. Then she asked me if I'd met Samantha Stevens before Sommers did."

"What the hell's that about?" O'Leary nudged a smoldering chunk of bark into the flames with the toe of his boot. "Maybe she thinks of you as a medicine woman."

"The correct term is midewiwin." Moon Deer cocked her eyebrows after tossing her empty bottle into a nearby paint bucket. "She believes Sam has mystical powers and can change herself into a bird. I laughed at her and she got pissed. She kept insisting our ancestry bonds the three of us into a sacred sisterhood.'"

"What a load of crap." O'Leary made an obnoxious sputtering sound, then caught himself and bit his lip. "You don't believe her, do you?"

Moon Deer waved smoke away from her face, then hung her head, glaring at the dancing flames.

Swallowed in a heavy moment of silence, the couple sat and watched nature's light show dancing across the pink southern sky. O'Leary reached for Joy's hand, and he said, "I see I struck a nerve. Chalk it up to cultural ignorance. I'm sorry, hon."

Moon Deer nodded while squeezing her fiancé's fingers.

O'Leary yawned and stretched his arms out wide before changing the subject. "My DHS contact says the feds are shifting resources to North Dakota—digging deeper into Wenner's operation. What do you suppose that means?"

"If you're talking about Colletti and Wagner, then good riddance. They're a couple of fuckin' bozos." Soon, claps of thunder boomed beyond the jagged hogbacks, growing louder, prowling closer. Moon Deer crossed her arms and shifted in her chair. "I think we're wasting our time out here. Don't get me wrong, this vacation vibe feels like a honeymoon—I've never been happier. But if the real action's north of Fargo, then that's where our asses should be."

O'Leary nodded. "You're right. I'm feeling kinda stir crazy. We're lovers and we're fighters. There's no denying that. Let's call Sommers in the morning—get back in the goddamn game."

Moon Deer stood from her chair and extended her hand towards O'Leary. "You better let the doctors decide if you're game ready," she said with a wink. "I'm fuckin' pooped. Ya comin' to bed?"

O'Leary poked his stick at the fire, then turned to watch a bolt of lightning streak across the threatening horizon. Moon Deer leaned over and kissed him on his ear and he looked up at her. "Like you, this fire's burning hot. But I'm gonna fuss with this log for a few minutes. I'll be along soon enough."

He watched her step into the house, waited another minute, then pulled his Glock-19 from under his chair. O'Leary squeezed the grip in each of his hands, feeling the gun's contours and balancing its weight. He reacquainted his fingers with the mechanics while focusing each of his eyes over the sight, training his left to match the right.

As the fire's glow faded, O'Leary shifted his chair so he could scan the tree line at the back of the yard. His eyes tracked east to west, then back again. Over and over, the detective peered into the shadows, inspecting each leaf and scrutinizing every blade of grass. He lifted his face and sniffed the night air as it grew darker and more humid with each passing minute. Before long, the wind kicked up, and he waved a tuft of smoke from his face.

A skilled sentry with a license to kill, Greg O'Leary, stood and holstered his gun. Then he turned and squinted at the trees swaying high above Spearfish Creek. With a voice little more than a whisper, he asked, "Why won't you show yourself, my feathered friend?"

A ringing crack of thunder echoed in the canyon and O'Leary backed his way towards the lodge. As the first few drops of rain fell, he nodded and tapped at the pistol's handle with his fluttering fingers. "Soon enough, Hawk. Soon enough."

Chapter 25
Goodbye Yellow Brick Road

"When are you gonna come down?"

Sommers awakened with a start from his disturbing nightmare. Confused by the unfamiliar darkness, he sat up from his cramped twin-sized bed and rubbed his eyes, trying to recall where he was. Flashes of opaque light illuminated the rafters and the knotty-pine corners of the tiny bedroom. Dismal winds moaned through every crevice, rattling the rickety old cabin.

He heard Ted Lindstrom snoring on the sofa in the next room, and his memory became clear. The lingering thunderstorms were among the worst rains Sommers had ever seen. He never imagined he'd be able to sleep through mother nature's latest tantrum. But at long last, exhaustion bested the big lumberjack.

His dream began pleasant enough. On a fresh, sunny afternoon, he held Noah's small hand as they hiked to the top of Victory Bluff. He wanted his son to see the inspirational bird's-eye view of the special lake they called home. Phelps trailed off Noah's hip, his tail wagging while his nose sniffed at every aroma the north woods offered. At the rim, one hundred feet above the indigo depths of Townsend Drop-off, the trio looked skyward to see a red-tailed hawk circling above the treetops.

Noah pointed at the majestic bird and mimicked its high-pitched screech. Then he stretched his arms out wide, testing his wings. The spirited boy dashed in circles, picking up speed with each orbit. Phelps barked and chased as the anxious father tried to corral his son from launching himself off the cliff. The hawk let out another shrill cry and a gust of wind lifted the toddler into the air, sending him soaring high above the water.

Sommers stood frozen at the brink, watching his son laughing with his arms outstretched, rising on a thermal, flying like an eagle. Noah swerved and darted between the trees, then streaked across the shimmering lake. He waved to his grandma Gracie, standing in the yard, then he turned back and swooped in low to tease his barking companion.

Sommers leaped with every bit of his strength, trying to snag one of his son's legs and pull him back to solid ground. He missed. Inertia and gravity sent the woeful man tumbling over the side and speeding towards the water. He didn't fear the deadly impact. Instead, he dreaded the abyssal emptiness that would darken his son's heart. That's when he opened his eyes.

The rumble of distant thunder served as his wake-up call. Sommers reached for his cell phone to check the time, but found his phone's battery was dead. He kicked his cover off, then turned and sunk his feet into two inches of chilly water. After shaking off his initial surprise, he stood and sloshed his wary feet through the musty cabin, feeling his way in the dark, past the kitchen to the front door.

Sommers tiptoed outside to find Jack Hughes seated on top of a picnic table, barefoot, with his pant legs rolled up to his knees. Jack sipped from his beer, then raised the bottle towards Sommers. "Come on out, the water's fine." Sommers sniffed the air as he leaned against the door frame, peeling off his wet socks and hiking up his pant legs. He trudged through the black, foot-deep water and joined his friend atop the table.

Hughes inhaled a hit from his joint and offered the smoke to his friend. The big man raised his eyebrows and shook his head. "No thanks," he said. "I didn't think you partook in the ganja. Where'd you get that?"

Hughes exhaled his smoke into the balmy breeze. "Peg McFarland put a few samples in the bag with our sweet corn. Not bad for home grown." He snuffed out his butt on the wooden table and reached for his beer. "Julie has helped me conquer most of my vices," he said. "But you know me. I'm no choir boy. Nights like this, I need a little something to take the edge off. You throw axes at trees and cast faux frogs into the rushes. Me, I drink a little drink and smoke a little smoke."

Sommers rocked on his backside and watched lightning flashes spark across the eastern sky. Then he nodded his head, thinking everyone he knew walked a fine line bolstered by psychological crutches. "What time is it?" He asked.

Hughes pointed at a multi-band transistor radio parked at his side. "My phone's dead, but would you believe this damn thing works? Got a police band and everything—only picks up two AM stations way out here. NPR says it's three thirty, but I'd take that with a grain of salt."

"So. How bad is it?" Sommers said, rubbing his eyes. The big lumberjack stood on the table and surveyed the darkness, feeling like a sailor trying to spot dry land. "We're not getting outta here, are we?"

Jack snorted and said, "I turned the volume down because that crazy weather alarm squawked at me every thirty seconds. Ten inches of rain, at least a half-dozen tornados. They're calling it the storm of the century. The Red River's already above flood stage, and all the main roads in the valley are under water." Jack waved his arm towards the yard. "And good luck finding Vern's driveway."

"The closest weather station's out at the airport," Sommers said. "Any reports from Kittson?"

"Eighty mile per hour winds tore the roof off the hangar and the runway's washed out—hope your plane's insured." Hughes chugged the rest of his beer, then belched before tossing his empty onto a pile of rubbish soaking on the porch. "Good news. No rain for the next few hours. The bad news is the tail of this storm is gonna come through and whip our asses sometime tomorrow afternoon."

"So, what are we gonna do?"

"You swim?" Hughes asked before blurting a laugh. Then he pointed at a decrepit shed sagging into the lake. "Lindstrom said there's an aluminum fishing boat buried under a blanket of cobwebs—says it's got a fifteen horse Evinrude at the stern. Who knows if it's seaworthy? But we've got five gallons of gas and judging from this yard, there's nothing but water between here and Hallock. We could dry out at a hotel, maybe rent a monster truck."

"Are you serious?" Sommers asked. "That is why you shouldn't do drugs." He folded his arms across his chest and shook his head. "Sheesh! We're eight miles from town, maybe twice that far if we follow the river."

Hughes slapped his hands on the table. "Our cars are sitting in a foot of water. We've got no power. All the cell towers are down, and this lake is rising by the minute. If you've got a better suggestion, I'd love to hear it." Hughes shook his head, cleared his throat, then cracked open another beer. "Worst of all, Jules is fit to be tied. After she kills me, she's gonna kick Ted's bony ass for bringing us to this resort from hell."

Sommers turned away and surveyed the yard, trying to memorize it during the lightning flashes. "Where is she?"

"Sleeping in the Jeep—got her AirPods in," he said. "Ever since that dustup on Blackhawk Road, she's had a thing about storms, especially at night."

Sommers put his meaty hand on Jack's shoulder and exhaled a heavy sigh. "Everything's gonna be alright." Then he sat and swirled his toes in the cool, dark water. "Is it too early for a business meeting?" He asked. "Tell me more about your conversation with Peg McFarland."

"Well, let's see," Jack said, rubbing his hands together. "Where do I begin?" The lawyer rocked on his haunches and motioned with his hand. "Peg has got nothing but a lot of bad luck and a lot of land. As you might guess, the cartel has robbed her blind. At some point, the taxes and insurance are gonna pull her under. Stroud keeps promising her a green energy deal, but never follows through. Until this week, he accepted her kickbacks while turning a blind eye to her drug operation."

Jack sipped his beer, then continued after muting a belch. "I've learned there are three or four sketchy iterations of her property map. Apparently, there's more there than meets the eye. One thing's for certain, McFarland's got more land than Susan Norman. And with water along two sides, it's got far greater potential."

"Greater risk, too," Sommers said, motioning to the water beneath their feet. "I'm assuming you're getting to the point now. You know, the part that has something to do with me?"

"Keep your pants on, big man—just getting to the good stuff." Hughes exhaled a sloppy sputter, then flipped his bottle cap onto the garbage pile. "I circled back with Betsy Robbins. She's kinda out there, but she seems to know a little something about everything. She claims there's a parade of buyers looking to purchase McFarland's farm, including our friends at Oasis Financial. Then she said something strange. Robbins asked me if I believed in ghosts and buried treasure."

Sommers rolled his eyes. "Oh no. You didn't."

Hughes cleared his throat and patted Sommers' leg. "I'm handling McFarland's legal and financial affairs. I need you to sign a lease. You're purchasing the mineral rights to Peg's twenty-six hundred acres. She can continue farming if she chooses, but the contract will include a provision claiming anything historical."

Sommers raised his eyebrows. "How much is that gonna cost me?"

Hughes counted on his fingers. "About a mil-dough."

"English, please."

"One point one million dollars," Hughes said. "Seems like a fair price to stick it to Stroud and Shui. Look at it this way. You're throwing Peg a lifeline for twenty percent of what we offered Norman—planting our flag for a potential windfall."

"Potential?" Sommers sputtered, then slapped his forehead. "What's in it for you?"

Hughes chuckled and fluttered his toes in the water. "My usual cut of whatever we find buried in the muck out there."

"Okay, I'll bite," Sommers said. "What do you think's out there?"

Hughes shrugged his shoulders. "Don't know for sure. But my sources seem convinced there's a ghost town buried out near the point. They say the site was a flourishing trading post in its day—had a hotel, a post office and a bank. If we get outta here alive, Julie and I are gonna sift through the county records, bone up on fur trading."

The prominent lawyer sipped from his beer, then wiped his mouth on his sleeve. "I'm also gonna call the attorney general's office—open a conspiracy investigation. We're gonna put those Oasis commies outta business." Jack grinned as he leaned into Sommers. "Say, we could use a good landman. Got any recommendations?"

Distant thunder continued to rumble as an encouraging sunrise brightened the eastern sky. Sommers ignored Jack's innuendo about his old flame, Andie Hansen. Again, he stood on the table and turned in a complete circle, scanning the horizon in every direction. He saw nothing but trees poking up from an eerie, endless sea. Then he gave his friend a lighthearted shove. "Ever dream you could fly?"

Soon after first light, the feisty Evinrude coughed a cloud of blue smoke, then sputtered to life. It took some time, but Dale Sommers learned to put his faith in Jack Hughes, despite the lawyer's brazen demeanor and unconventional methods.

On this day, Sommers had to hand it to Hughes. He was right about using Vern's old fishing boat to escape the rising tide at The Last Resort. Following a brisk forty-minute ride, the quartet drifted into the sleepy town of Hallock.

A salmon-colored sunrise burned through the clouds and fog, and the morning air, once again, hung thick with bugs and humidity. Lindstrom pointed the bow west and idled the outboard motor. The rumpled troupe floated between the center field wall of Hallock Field and the rusty gates of Greenwood Cemetery.

Over the starboard side, only the largest of the grave markers broke the boundless expanse of Two Rivers. Port side, flooded dugouts acted as bookends for a woeful chain-link backstop. Only the cheap seats, the top few rows of the bleachers, remained visible above the surging water.

With sunrise warming their backs, the curious boaters rode in silence as Lindstrom zig-zagged through a quiet residential area of modest ranch houses. A few early risers awakened to find their trees damaged, their cars dimpled from hail, and their gardens submerged beneath an unwelcome sea.

A yellow dog sat beside his master on the front porch of a beige house with white trim. The old timer puffed his pipe and flicked his fishing rod, casting a rubber worm into the flooded street. Julie cupped her mouth and asked, "Catching anything?"

The dog stood and let out a single woof, and the angler tipped his hat. He pointed the bit of his pipe across the street and with a voice like eighty-grit sandpaper, he said, "Just wanton looks from the neighbor lady. Don't stare, Nixie will rush off to throw her robe on. Show over."

The quartet chuckled, then Lindstrom goosed the motor twice. "Tight lines, right mister?"

The old man puffed his pipe. "You know it, brother. Gotta keep my tip up." Sommers reached into his pocket and tossed a biscuit to the anxious pooch. "Nice catch, Willie," the fisherman said with a laugh.

Sommers leaned his elbows on the bow, pleased to see his sturdy Midwestern neighbors hadn't lost their sense of humor in the face of brutal adversity. Chester's Chicken advertised a catch of the day special on their marquis sign: fried catfish.

A few community members taped makeshift cardboard signs to their houses. One read, no migrant buses today. Others, less political, read: boats must yield to swimmers, fish snagging prohibited, and no wake boarding on Sundays.

Sommers' posse sailed past the county courthouse. Jack scribbled a primitive map in his notepad. Julie pointed past a flooded intersection where the traffic lights stood tall and dark on their yellow posts. "The hospital's around the corner," she said, pointing her thumb. "There should be a little motel down that street."

Before long, as boat traffic picked up in the downtown area, Lindstrom cut the motor and Sommers tied the bowline to a porch pillar at the Gateway Motel. From the street, the homespun place looked to be a cross between an old-time gas station and an antique store. Timeworn license plates from all fifty states paneled the outer walls. The foursome sloshed up the front steps, then crowded into a small sticky office.

A sleepy, middle-age man with a prosthetic hook at the end of his left arm greeted the bedraggled group with leery eyes. He wore a plaid sleeveless shirt, canvas pants, and work boots. He cut his graying hair very short, and military tattoos decorated his muscular upper arms. From behind the counter, he said, "Tellin' y'all up front. We got no electricity, no phone, and no internet—goddamn carpeting's soaked to the bone. Hector is on his way with a pump and a generator."

Julie asked, "Got running water, maybe a hot shower?"

The grizzled desk clerk scratched at the whiskers on his chin, then pointed his thumb over his shoulder. "Got a small pool out back. Don't know if it's above water, but it was warm before the rains came."

Julie tugged at her damp shirt and shorts. "What about attire—dress code for the pool?"

The man squinted his eyes, scrutinizing the travelers, skepticism showing on his weathered face. "Y'all not part of some crazy woke outfit, are ya? We had some punk-ass kids come through here last week. Dressed like cartoon animals, pissin' and shittin' everywhere. Called themselves furries, I think." The one-armed man rolled his eyes and shook his head. "What a fuckin' mess. I tell ya, this country's heading straight to hell in a handcart. And I mean in a hurry."

Jack interrupted the man's rant, extending his right hand. "Name's Hughes, this is my wife, Julie. Our boring friends, Sommers and Lindstrom. We're the reddest Minnesotans you're gonna find outside a reservation." Jack pulled his hand back and reached into his wallet, then he slid a pair of hundred-dollar bills across the counter. "I think we'll skip the pool. Can we get two rooms for the night?"

The man looked over each of the four again, then shook Jack's hand and grinned. "Name's Wes Duncan. Welcome to the Gateway Motel and Emporium. Anything not nailed down is for sale." Duncan stuffed the money into his front pocket, then grabbed two keys from a rack behind the counter. "You can leave your boat tied off out front. How 'bout rooms seven and eight? More highway noise back there, but who's drivin', right? Best chance at stayin' dry—close to the pool if you change your minds. Right this way."

In short order, Sommers and Lindstrom were back in their boat motoring west, aiming for Reynolds' garage. Earlier, they discussed their frantic search for the missing veteran with Wes Duncan. The desk clerk recalled Reynolds and his old Chevy, but hadn't seen him in quite some time. Duncan mentioned that the state police called his brother, a big rig tow-truck driver, requesting his help with an emergency at the Highway 175 overpass.

Before shoving them off, Duncan topped off their gas can and charged their cell phones from his generator. He filled a Styrofoam cooler with ice, bottled water, and snacks from his vending machines. Duncan wiped his sweating forehead with the back of his right hand. "Under different circumstances, I'd grab my gun and ride along. But there's a hell of a mess to clean up here—more rough weather on the way."

With the water still rising, Jack and Julie Hughes stayed behind to freshen up. Later, they'd hitch a ride to the courthouse in Hector's jacked-up four-by-four. Julie notarized the signatures on the McFarland contract, then Jack sealed the documents and his notes in a two-gallon Ziploc bag. He pulled the drapes aside and looked out at a ghoulish red sun. Turning from the window, he ran his fingers through his wife's wet hair. "More trouble's coming," he said, shaking his head. "We've only got a few hours."

Six hundred miles southwest, a bright sunrise melted the shadows clinging to Spearfish Canyon. Highway A14 remained shiny and damp, and the mountain air smelled fresh from overnight rains. Sweat beads formed on Joy Moon Deer's face and neck. Her heart pounded, and she controlled her breathing, inhaling through her nose, exhaling out her mouth. Before she left, she told O'Leary this was her least favorite 5K loop. She jogged south along the shoulder of the winding parkway, pacing herself for the grueling uphill jaunt back to the lodge.

As she approached her turnaround at the Iron Creek Trailhead, Moon Deer discovered her friend, Jo Douglass. The stranded officer, wearing mirrored sunglasses and a campaign hat, leaned against the door of her police cruiser with her arms folded across her chest.

The squad car's raised hood glinted in the bright sunshine. Moon Deer squinted and surveyed the area as she slowed to a walk. She gave Douglass a quick shoulder hug, then dabbed at the sweat running down her face. "Morning, Sarg," Moon Deer said, catching her breath. "This is the kinda shit that happens when you speak of the dead. What seems to be the problem?" Moon Deer shielded her eyes and once again, scanned the highway in both directions. "I'd give you a lift, but it's uphill the whole way back and your ass is way bigger than mine."

Douglass gushed a sarcastic laugh, then waved Moon Deer over to look into the engine compartment. "Morning, skanky-pants. You're too kind," she said with a scowl on her face. "Fischer's on call—truck's on the way." The officer removed her hat and fanned her face. "Dash light is on. I think it's a worn serpentine belt. You know cars better than me. Care to take a look?"

Moon Deer hesitated before surveying the secluded wayside. Then she turned and leaned over the front fender. "Shit, this belt looks brand new to me. Maybe your alternator's fucked up."

The rapids of Iron Creek splashed behind her while Spearfish Creek sloshed below the ribbon of shimmering asphalt. Joy Moon Deer never moved—she never had the chance. Two men, one tall and one short, wearing camo-colored hoodies and N-95 masks, pounced on her from the shadow that concealed the rocky trailhead.

Chapter 26
Run to You

"She says her love for me could never die."

The two explorers sat upright between the gunwales and Vern's old fishing boat skipped along with the big lumberjack operating the tiller. A crimson sun appeared overhead and the noonday temperature surged past ninety degrees. Sommers sniffed under his arms and wondered which smelled worse, the fetid flood waters or his sweat-stained t-shirt. Lindstrom caught the gesture and waved his hand in front of his nose. "Give it up, captain. Your deodorant failed you days ago."

Sommers opened the throttle, pushing to keep Lindstrom upwind from his embarrassing stench. Their little fifteen-horse outboard, following several hiccups and backfires, buzzed like a June bug dancing on a hot skillet. Lindstrom leaned forward over the bow, keeping an eye out for rocks and stumps, anything resembling a devious iceberg. He lifted his chin and hollered as he pointed far beyond the starboard side. "McFarland's farm. Maybe we should check it out, see if she needs help."

Sommers examined the broken rows of golden tassels poking above the black water. Wind and hail left most of the greens drooping and tattered, sinking any hope of Peg cashing in on this year's corn crop. He shook his head, reversed his baseball hat, then opened the throttle. He shouted over the wind and the propulsion. "We can hit 'er place on the way back. Let's focus on Reynolds and staying ahead of the next storm." Lindstrom shrugged, then nodded in agreement while he examined McFarland's inundated field.

Minutes later, a noisy National Guard helicopter pulsed over their heads, winging for the Red River. Sommers adjusted to port, tracking its tail rotor. After chugging along for another half-mile, Lindstrom waved, then motioned his palm downward. "Slow down, Skip. We're coming up on Highway 175—there's quite a hubbub below the bridge."

The smell of diesel exhaust hung in the air and a magnificent Peterbilt wrecker sat gleaming in a shallow pool southeast of the overpass. Fire-engine red, the imposing rig sparkled with hundreds of chrome adornments. The doors advertised Duncan's Towing in bold black script. Its driver, a large serious-looking man, wore camo-colored hip waders, leather work gloves, and a beige Stetson hat. Sweat glistened on his skin as he hurried around, pulling levers, adjusting cables, and anchoring heavy straps with his hard, tattooed arms.

Sommers killed the motor, then inched their boat closer by pulling a warped canoe paddle through the water. The clamorous chopper hovered high overhead, its rotors stirring tiny ripples across the flooded river. Police cruisers and ambulances from either side of the border turned away any stray vehicles that dodged the roadblocks, and a police boat from St. Vincent bobbed in the water north of the bridge.

The last of the rescue divers climbed aboard the boat and stripped off his snorkeling mask and muddy gloves. He shook his head and signaled with three fingers to a waiting paramedic, then flashed a perfunctory thumbs up to the tow truck driver.

Duncan splashed around to the driver's side of his truck, adjusted his cowboy hat, then lifted a lever that revved the husky diesel engine. He raised a second lever, activating an overhead winch. The massive rig leaned several inches as the cables tightened and the motor strained. The truck's winch completed three full turns before a mammoth glob of sludge and weeds crept up the riverbank. Brown water gushed from the wreck's gaping wounds.

Duncan's rig reeled in another fifty feet of thick cable before the driver lowered all the levers. He pulled a shop rag from his back pocket and sloshed towards the gnarled, overturned SUV. Sommers and Lindstrom watched Duncan hold his nose while he wiped mud from the Cadillac's grill emblem. Then he pulled a twisted mass of weeds from the front license plate. Duncan looked up and shouted to the first responders watching from atop the bridge. "Show-me state."

Vile, cloudy water trickled from the hapless lump. Then, without warning, a bald head, pale blue with dark red streaks and one bushy eyebrow, flopped with a syrupy thud against the cracked windshield. Lindstrom winced and looked back at Sommers. "And you thought you were having a bad day."

The big man slid the crooked paddle under the aluminum seats and shook his head. "I've seen enough." Then he yanked the starter cord and pointed the bow towards the slim opening under the bridge. "Better duck," he said. "You're liable to lose your head." Sommers tipped his hat to the onlookers upon the bridge and bumped the throttle, guiding the boat into the shadow beneath the overpass.

Fifteen minutes later, Sommers released the throttle. He pulled the motor forward, raising the lower unit from the water, allowing the boat to drift into Reynolds' flooded garage. Lindstrom hopped out and looped the bowline around a cast-iron bench vise. "Three inches of water, but still no sign of Jerry," he said.

"No sign of his old Chevy, either. What's that tell ya? Let's have a look inside."

After removing their boots, the two men rummaged through the same barren drawers and cabinets, not finding anything bigger than a breadcrumb. Sommers wandered around the small family room, scratching at his chin. He stopped to marvel at Jerry's collection of classic Matchbox cars parked inside a decorative display case. "Hey, Ted. Where'd you say that safe was?"

Lindstrom rubbed his palms together before shoving a small entertainment center away from the wall. He stood with a proud look on his face, pointing at the floor.

Sommers crouched for a closer look, studying the keypad before he tapped a few random combinations. After several failed attempts, he looked up at Lindstrom and asked, "What year is Jerry's Impala?"

"1967. No wait, '66."

Sommers rolled his eyes, then punched numbers as he spoke. "One, nine, six, six." The latch released with a metallic click, and he opened the heavy door. Inside, he found a single scrap of yellow paper. Sommers stood and unfolded the note. He read the handwritten message to himself and nodded.

Lindstrom threw his hands in the air. "Well. What's it say?" Sommers handed him the slip and Lindstrom read it aloud. "You're two late." He flipped the paper over, searching for more writing. Then he squatted and ran his fingers around the opening in the floor. "That's it?"

"That's it," Sommers said. "What do you think, Sherlock? Is T-W-O a mistake, or a clue?"

"Who the hell knows?" Lindstrom scratched at the back of his head. "Let's see if Susan's around."

Soon, the retired sheriff took his turn at the tiller, guiding the boat around the mound of charred remains he discovered the previous day. All but the very top of the pile lay concealed below the clouded water, and the yellow crime scene tape was almost invisible below their hull.

The pair approached Norman's battered farmhouse as a faint rumble of thunder echoed beyond the distant hills. Sommers lifted his eyes to the sky, seeing dark cumulonimbus clouds swelling over Manitoba. "Welp," he said, adjusting his baseball cap. "Here we go again."

Soon, the curious shipmates discovered the burgeoning river flowed straight through Norman's filthy waste retention pond. Lindstrom held his nose and steered the boat through the putrid, flooded pasture. The same forces that destroyed McFarland's cornfields landed a roundhouse punch to Norman's house.

Lindstrom pulled right to the front porch, where noxious waves lapped against what remained of the dog-eared planks. They discovered the roof torn off, and the windows blown out. Sommers called out for Susan, but Norman Farms sounded the same as it looked, abused and discarded.

A second clap of thunder shook the northern plains, and the sun withered behind a bank of towering thunderheads. As the sky turned yellow and the wind picked up, Sommers settled back into the bow. "Let's get outta here. Step on it, man."

Lindstrom checked the fuel gauge, shook his head, then jerked the starter cord. After six empty tries, Lindstrom slapped the side of the engine case and cursed at the reticent Evinrude. He spit into his palms, rubbed them together, then gave the rope a ferocious tug.

Sommers looked back at an ominous western sky and the little outboard puffed a cloud of smoke before sputtering to life.

Minutes later, the pair squirted from beneath the overpass, buzzing towards Hallock. The disgusting wreck was gone, and the emergency team had left the scene wrapped in yellow tape. Farther east, Peg McFarland was nowhere to be found. Sommers pointed at something moving on top of a solitary garden shed soaking in an expanse of water interrupted by a few bare and broken trees.

Lindstrom banked the boat starboard, making a beeline for the lonely storage building. He shouted over the motor. "Is that a dog?"

Sommers shaded his eyes and nodded, then scanned the desolation, wondering how the sullied pooch ended up huddled atop a decaying storage shed.

The sable shepherd mix whimpered and twitched her tail as Lindstrom steered the boat along the puckered clapboard siding. Sommers searched his pockets for a dog biscuit, but pulled only a shred of lint, recalling Willie caught his last cookie back in Hallock.

Next, he tried coaxing the wary pup to drop into his arms. When that appeared fruitless, he cut a length of nylon rope from the anchor with his pocket knife. Sommers fashioned the line into a makeshift harness and tossed the coil over his shoulder. Then he motioned to Lindstrom. "Give me a boost, would ya?"

Their boat rocked and Lindstrom grabbed a door frame with one arm while pressing his shoulder under Sommers' backside. He grunted and strained. "Damn, ya big lug. How 'bout you toss my ass up there?"

Sommers shook his head. "Seriously? You think you can pull yourself over the edge? C'mon, wimpy. Put your back into it."

But after several seconds of straining and grunting, Lindstrom lost his grip, and the boat shifted and tipped, sending Sommers belly-flopping into the drink. The dog stood and barked, circling with a noticeable limp. Sommers surfaced and shook water from his face, standing neck deep in the brisk water.

He threw his soggy hat at Lindstrom, then tossed the rope onto the roof, snagging an air vent. He grabbed a door frame, braced his legs, then clambered his way to the eave. The edge was slippery, but after some struggle, Sommers found his grip, lifting himself high enough to throw his leg up and over the side. He continued pushing and shifting his weight, then pulled himself to a seated position on the mossy shingles. Lindstrom pumped his fist, and the dog hobbled over to lick the climber's soggy face.

Sommers surveyed the area for any sign of humans, then

examined the skinny, shivering pup for injuries, noting no collar or tags. "You're in rough shape, girl. No worries, we'll take good care of you." He looped the harness around each of the dog's four legs. Next, he fashioned the remaining rope into a handle with a length of leader and lowered the whimpering dog over the edge to Lindstrom's waiting arms.

A cluster of large raindrops pelted the roof, and a crackling bolt of lightning fractured the western sky. Three seconds later, thunder boomed across the sodden countryside, and the dog squeezed into a crevice under the boat's middle seat. Sommers tried repelling down the side of the shed, but the rope unraveled under his weight, and he plunged head-first back into the water.

Lindstrom enjoyed a fit of laughter before helping his waterlogged friend flop into the boat. Sommers wiped his face and caught his breath. "Thanks buddy," he said as he reached out to untie the dog's harness. He covered the weary pooch with a dry burlap sack and ruffled her ears. "Today's your lucky day." The pup followed her burly hero to the bow, dragging the makeshift cover and curling up at the big man's feet.

Lindstrom said, "Doggone Lucky's a good name for her, 'eh?" Then he examined the threatening sky. "Let's hope some of that rubs off on us."

Sommers glanced back at Lindstrom, giving him a wink and a nod. "Okay, Cappy. Take us to where the fair winds blow."

Greg O'Leary, seldom a patient man, had waited long enough. His right foot tapped against the chair leg while he checked his watch, then he swiped through messages on his cellphone. Moon Deer's morning workouts lasted an hour. Two hours had passed, and she wasn't responding to his calls and texts. He logged into his laptop and pinged her iPhone. It was offline, but showed its last location at the Iron Creek Trailhead. He jacked a fresh mag into his handgun, grabbed the key to Samantha's Blazer, and soon rolled into the lingering shadows of Spearfish Canyon.

At the first sweeping curve south of Victoria, O'Leary pulled onto the narrow shoulder, allowing a northbound ambulance to pass. He looked ahead, checked his rearview mirror, then wrung his hands on the steering wheel before driving on. Around the next bend, from high ground, he saw a half-dozen blue and red flashing lights. He slowed and watched aspen leaves and long ribbons of yellow crime-scene tape flutter in the morning breeze.

O'Leary slammed on the brakes, bringing the SUV to a skidding stop. He backed up and parked in a secluded spot above the Long Valley Picnic Area. The detective climbed out and tucked the gun behind his back, then sprinted a quarter mile to the next hairpin curve. A young service officer, a large man with long hair and broad shoulders, stepped into the lane and threw his hand up, halting the gasping jogger. "Investigation in progress," he said. "No one's allowed down there. Road's closed."

"Investigating what?" O'Leary asked, catching his breath and flashing his veteran's identification card. "Who was in the ambulance?"

The cop puffed his chest out and looked O'Leary up and down. "Not at liberty to say—officer down. Don't give a damn 'bout your card. Like I said, you can't go down there."

"The hell I can't—try stopping me." The young officer put one hand on his radio and the other on the jogger's chest. O'Leary, lightning quick, snatched the officer's wrist, then twisted while turning and ducking. He flipped the man over his hip, slamming him flat on his back, knocking the wind out of the man. O'Leary pressed the heel of his boot into the cop's chest, holding the man's arm in a painful, disabling lock. "Now there's two officers down. Never, ever put your hands on a meat eater."

O'Leary scanned the scene below, making sure nobody noticed their little dustup. Then he pulled his gun from behind his back and pointed it at the trembling man's face. "Not everyone's who they seem," he said. "I'd watch my back if I were you." O'Leary glanced up and down the road, then helped the officer to his feet while reading his name tag. "Okay, Preston. Last chance. What happened down there?"

Tears welled in Preston's eyes as he shook his head. "Don't know. I was finishing my AM route when I got the 108 call. They're not sharing the ID."

O'Leary studied the boy's trembling face, then peeked over his shoulder, squinting at the rocky ridges above the trailhead. "I'm going hunting." He flashed his pistol in Preston's face. "You never saw me. Got it?" O'Leary relaxed his grip after Preston nodded.

The service officer rubbed his shoulder, trying to massage the pain from his arm. "What did you mean by meat eater?" He asked.

"Special forces," O'Leary said, scanning the parkway in both directions. "First in, last out. Blood on our hands." The detective lifted his chin at Preston. "Remember what I said. Watch your back, boy." Then the former Ranger backed into the woods with his gun still trained on the shaken officer.

Before long, O'Leary sidestepped into a ravine, then climbed to the top of a rocky ledge overlooking the police activity. He stretched out on his stomach and used his phone to zoom in on the details while snapping pictures. He watched crime scene investigators examine an abandoned police cruiser.

One technician measured red spatter on the front fender, while another waved a metal detector over tracks in the gravel lot. A third officer reached behind the front wheel with a long grabber, pulling a bloodied trooper's hat into view. O'Leary exhaled a weighty sigh, then rested his forehead on the frigid slab.

Below, a county sheriff spoke to three state troopers, waving his hands and pounding his fist. The sheriff pointed at the trailhead, then turned and pointed at the ledge where the peeping hunter held his breath. O'Leary ducked and slid back into the pines, then checked his phone before tracking between the trees and rocks that lined the bubbling creek.

North of the parking lot, two massive boulders marked the trailhead. O'Leary found convincing markings along the well-worn path. Foot prints, two pairs of lugged soles, and a pair of intermittent swirls led him north towards Iron Creek Lake.

Farther along he found bent grasses, scattered gravel, and drops of blood. The trail curved along the creek, where O'Leary paused beside an outcropping of granite boulders. A few steps farther, he discovered a jagged rock, shaped like an arrowhead, at his feet. He stopped and tracked his eyes higher.

On the smooth, dark face of the rock, he found a fresh etching carved out in pale lines. The rudimentary illustration showed a river. On one side of the river stood a four-legged animal below a crescent moon and an enormous bird. On the other side of the river, two stick figures, one tall and one short.

O'Leary snapped a picture of the drawing, then scanned the trail ahead and behind, finding it empty. He jogged another mile and a half, crossed an earthen dam, then trekked north along the shore of a small lake dotted with fishermen in kayaks. He crossed a dirt road and approached a wooden sign. It was a map showing hiking trails, a campground, and a boat launch. O'Leary leaned against a picnic table, catching his breath while he surveyed his rugged surroundings.

Beyond the lake, camp site number two sat shaded and vacant, nearest the main entry road. O'Leary crouched and examined the footprints and fresh tire tracks embedded in the moist gravel. He compared the tread pattern with the pictures he'd saved on his phone. The detective nodded and snapped a photo of the new patterns, then stood and turned for the campground store.

Inside the gloomy shop, a large Native man wearing a sleeveless flannel shirt and a dark handlebar mustache sat behind a counter sipping coffee and hovering over the pages of a girly magazine. In the far corner, a delivery man with a small disfigured hand stocked a rusty refrigerator with tubs of nightcrawlers and wax worms.

O'Leary stepped across the creaky wooden floor and cleared his throat. "Hmm, nice place you got here," he said with a smirk creasing his face. "I'm looking for a couple of friends of mine, fishing buddies. Driving a black pickup. Seen 'em?" The long-haired clerk looked over the top of his rag, glanced out a side window, then shrugged and shook his head.

The delivery man closed the fridge with his elbow and leaned on his handcart. "Friends of yours, ya say?"

O'Leary said, "Yea, well. You know how it is."

The delivery man rolled his eyes and made a sputtering sound, then wheeled his cart for the door. "Your fishing buddies wrangled a drunken squaw into their back seat 'bout twenty minutes ago. Drove outta here like nothing happened. Classy friends you got there. Real classy." He shoved the front door open with his hip and shielded his eyes as he stepped into the light. "See you next week, Stan. I'm heading out west. Gonna hike the Absarokas for a few days."

The big Indian waved without looking up, then unfurled a lewd centerfold and turned it sideways in the light.

O'Leary caught the driver near his panel van after chasing him across the gravel parking lot. "Wait up, mister. You heading to Spearfish?" He asked.

The driver opened the rear doors with his good hand. "Not directly."

"Here. Let me help you with that," O'Leary said, lifting the two-wheeled dolly into the back. "I need to get to Victoria ASAP. Do you mind giving me a lift?"

"I've seen the trash you call friends. Why would I do that?"

O'Leary looked around, then said, "That woman you saw wasn't drunk. She's a deputy sheriff from Minnesota."

The driver slammed the rear doors. "No shit. And how do you know that?"

"She's my fiance," O'Leary said. "Those two men aren't friends. They're operatives with the Dakota Sioux Syndicate, Snakes. They grabbed her while she was out jogging—beat her senseless, I'm guessing."

"That sucks, man. Why don't you call the cops?"

O'Leary shook his head and kicked at the dirt. "Long story, man."

The driver folded a piece of chewing gum into his mouth, then offered a stick to O'Leary. "Name's Porter—folks call me Lefty. Get in."

The pair drove for several minutes, engaging in small talk about politics and the weather. At last, O'Leary said, "I thought Spearfish was north. We've been driving south for quite a while."

"Not from 'round here, are ya?" Lefty shifted in the driver's seat. "Victoria's a two-mile hike along the creek. This southern route covers sixteen miles, and the northern loop's twenty-four. That's mountain life for ya." The passenger checked the time on his phone and shook his head. Lefty motioned with his little hand and said, "Not sure how fast you walk, but Tinton Road's gonna save you 'bout twenty minutes."

O'Leary nodded, tapping his fingers on the armrest. "I gotta tell ya, this canyon's got me feeling trapped this morning. Ya ever feel that way?"

Lefty surveyed the rocky peaks, and the scattered stands of poplar and pine, then sighed. "Shit, I had somebody once," he said before shaking his head. "But now I'm a simple man—live a simple life.

Don't know your situation. Honest to goodness, I don't know what I'd do."

O'Leary watched the driver peek into his rearview mirror every few seconds. Porter glanced across and said, "If you don't mind me saying. Indian women and children go missing 'round here every day, hundreds each year. Most of 'em go unreported and none of 'em ever get found. You really think you'll get her back?"

O'Leary furrowed his brow and counted on his fingers. "First, those assholes are gonna call any minute demanding a ransom. Second, my girl's a grizzly. They relax for one second—she'll rip their fuckin' heads off." O'Leary gazed out the window, watching the rocks and the gray guardrails pass. At last, he broke the long, heavy silence. "They don't know who they're dealing with."

Lefty nodded after glancing into his rearview mirror. "Seems to me they messed with the wrong guy."

O'Leary cracked his knuckles and shifted in his seat. "Damn straight, brother."

Following two sweeping uphill curves, Lefty slowed before the 14A roadblock. He lifted his chin at the crime scene, then turned to face his passenger. "Anything I should know?"

"It's best you don't," O'Leary said. "I can get out here. You're a good man, Porter. I owe you one."

Lefty reached across and shook his passenger's hand. "Godspeed, mister."

O'Leary climbed out and stepped from the road into the woods, where he watched Lefty make a u-turn and drive away. He hid among the trees, outflanking the sheriff and his team of investigators. Before long, he arrived back at the picnic area above the whitewater of Spearfish Creek. He scanned the area before making his way back to Samantha's Blazer. He watched an older couple in the shade of a shelter spread peanut butter on slices of bread while two youngsters splashed in a shallow pool below a small waterfall.

After checking his phone for messages, O'Leary started the car and turned for the exit. All at once, two squad cars screeched to a stop, blocking his path. Then a third car appeared, blocking him from backing up. O'Leary found himself surrounded by cops with their shotguns drawn, all aimed at him. He locked his pistol and cell phone in the Blazer's console, then stepped out with his hands clasped behind his head.

Following their commands, O'Leary sprawled face down on the pavement while a state cop handcuffed his wrists. The harsh officer jerked O'Leary to his feet and patted him down with rough hands. Standing nearby, Officer Preston couldn't contain his delight as he read Miranda Rights to his fuming captive.

O'Leary said, "Get this asshole outta my face. Someone gonna tell me what the hell this is all about?"

The sheriff said, "You're under arrest for the murder of Officer Jo Douglass."

O'Leary sputtered and snorted his disbelief. "Yea, whatever."

Preston elbowed him in the ribs, then laughed as he waved his gun in O'Leary's face. "You were right about one thing, dipshit. Not everyone's who they seem. I can't wait to see you get the needle. You sonofabitch."

"Roger that," O'Leary said. "We'll see who laughs last." Then he lifted his nose and sniffed the air while another state cop escorted him to an unmarked sedan. He shouted over his shoulder. "Say, Preston. You need to change your fuckin' pants, man. Stinks like baby shit up here."

Chapter 27
Hold Back the Rain

*"Yes, we're miles away from nowhere
and the wind doesn't have a name."*

Sommers, steeled in northern Minnesota for over five decades, experienced more than his share of rough weather. He'd survived blinding blizzards, skin-piercing ice storms, and raging tornados. Late winter ice dams and spring flooding of the river valleys were a yearly expectation, but these Labor Day torrents were unlike anything the big lumberjack had ever seen.

Sommers, Lindstrom, and Lucky Dog huddled while holding on for dear life inside Vern's leaky fishing boat. They buzzed and bobbed their way back to Hallock with another downpour snapping at their heels. Lindstrom navigated with no clear sightline, and he complained that his visibility was less than fifty feet. Meanwhile, Sommers split time, peering beyond the bow and bailing water from the hull with a dented coffee can.

From behind their frothy wake, Sommers heard a freight train of destruction barrelling down on their tiny craft. He turned to face this menace just as a baseball sized hailstone ricocheted between the aluminum seats, followed by another, and three more bombs soon after that. Lucky Dog scurried and squeezed herself under the big man's legs as Sommers tossed his small pail aside and draped a rumpled burlap sack over his head. "Cover your noggin and get the lead out," he said while flipping a second bag to Lindstrom. "Pummeled by ice," Sommers shouted. "Be a helluva way to go, wouldn't ya say?"

Lindstrom hollered above the din as he fumbled with his pathetic shield. "I've had the throttle wide open for fifteen minutes—we can't be far."

Sommers leaned across the gunwale, shielding his eyes and shouting over the wind and rain. "You're assuming we're going the right way." Seconds later, he waved and pointed beyond the port side. "Fairgrounds. There's a shelter. Stay left." Then, somewhere within the clamor of the squall, Sommers heard what sounded like Gallagher giving a watermelon a solid whack.

He waved and shouted, but the ragged boat continued banking hard to the right. He looked over his shoulder and saw Lindstrom slumped on his side with crimson lines trickling down his face. Sommers felt a chill race up his spine, recalling Bud Wolcott and the grisly scene above Devils Bathtub. "What the…"

With Lindstrom collapsed against the tiller, their boat continued to spin in tight circles. Sommers tried standing in the bow, but stumbled and fell between the seats. Lucky Dog barked at the bedlam and the tousled bosun's mate scrambled towards the stern on all fours. At last, Sommers steadied the boat, and despite his poor visibility, scanned in all directions, trying to find his bearings. He closed his eyes and focused on the noise, then aimed the boat opposite the storm's clamorous front.

Next, he tended to Lindstrom, stretching the unconscious man across a seat, slipping padding under his head and feeling for a pulse. "Hang in there, buddy," he said as he split a sleeve from his flannel, then pressed the damp cloth against his partner's bleeding crown. "We're almost there."

Lucky Dog shivered at Sommers' feet and he recalled the hospital sitting kitty-corner from their hotel. Before long, he exhaled a sigh, spotting a reddish glow from the emergency entrance sign. He reversed his hat, furrowed his brow, then guided the boat along a swollen creek and under a narrow railroad trestle. The sodden trio made a beeline through the flooded fairgrounds, dodging hailstones as they bumped along.

Sommers, bombarded and bruised, shielded his haggard friends from the falling ice stones, some the size of acorns, some bigger. An overflowing ditch provided passage across Highway 75 into downtown Hallock. After rounding a corner, he killed the sputtering motor, tilted the powerhead forward, and coasted under the canopy of the hospital's entrance.

Lindstrom squirmed and groaned as Sommers heaved the wounded man over his shoulder in a fireman's carry. Lucky Dog, waterlogged and whimpering, sat trembling in the bow. Sommers turned and hollered over his shoulder while propping the door open with his boot. "Don't fret, girl. You're next."

Soon, the smells of antiseptic spray and lemon-scented floor polish wafted around the waiting area where Sommers and Lucky Dog settled into a corner sofa. The harried hospital staff dropped what they were doing and tended to Lindstrom's injury.

In a nearby room, they stitched his scalp, then whisked the concussed man away for x-rays and a CT scan. A kind-hearted nurse brought peanut butter sandwiches and bottled water, then wrapped Lucky's sprained leg with a compression bandage. As the minutes became hours, Sommers iced his bruises and dozed off with his hairy companion nestled into his side.

Later, after watching nurses tuck a bandaged, snoring Lindstrom into his hospital bed, Sommers lifted Lucky Dog over the gunwale of Vern's dimpled boat, setting her atop the middle seat. He pulled the starter rope several times before snapping his baseball hat against the motor in frustration. The anxious pooch provided supervision with a tilted head, showing her skepticism. Sommers puckered his lips and stepped into the frigid, knee-deep water, snatching the severed bowline from under the seat. Then he trudged along Birch Street towards the Gateway Hotel with Lucky Dog in tow.

Remnants of the storm dispersed and drifted southeast, leaving clear evening skies and a humid summer breeze in their track. Sommers studied the horizon, inhaling a deep breath. Then he turned left on 7th Avenue and spotted one-handed Wes Duncan on the roof of his hotel, swinging a mallet. Sommers sang out, waving his hat. "If I had a hammer, I'd hammer in the morning…"

Duncan stopped pounding at the corrugated metal and pivoted to rest on his seat. "Nice timing, brother. Jus' finished tackin' this last patch."

"Artisan's work, Wes. There's no doubt. You're moving up in the world," Sommers said with a wink and a grin. "Everybody okay?"

Duncan nodded. "Seen worse." Then he pointed his hammer at the boat. "Found yourself a friend, 'eh?"

"This is Lucky." Sommers reached back and ruffled the dog's ears. "I traded Lindstrom and a bushel of corn for her after he toasted the motor."

"Got the best of that deal, fer sure. Where is that skinny flatfoot?"

"Kittson Memorial—sleeping off a headache. Hailstone the size of a melon plunked him good."

Duncan chuckled and shook his head. "The hell ya say." Then he shrugged. "Who knows? Might've knocked some sense into him."

Sommers nodded, then cocked his head towards the back. "Mind if we bag out here tonight?"

"Room's paid for. Got a pair of generators pumpin' out twenty amps each." Duncan spit a roofing nail into a can, then slipped the hammer into his tool belt. "Tie your line and hold my ladder, wouldja?"

Sommers sloshed over the side and grabbed the front rails. "Julie and Jack around?"

"Hector drove 'em up to Pembina County." Duncan stepped down and gave the good-natured dog some vigorous petting. "They filed some papers at the courthouse—dropped something in your room before they took off."

"Hmm." Sommers said, adjusting his hat and rubbing his sore shoulder. "They say when they'll be back?"

"Nope. But getting 'round is pretty damn hard right now. I'd think they'd wanna be back before dark." Duncan set his nail can on an empty planter box and motioned for the office. "They mentioned you have a thing about phones. Maybe you should check your messages once in a while."

Sommers lifted Lucky from the boat, then slipped his cracked, waterlogged phone from his pocket. Duncan shook his head and opened the office door with his hook. "C'mon in. You look like you could use a drink. We'll put your phone in a baggie of rice and charge it up—see what happens." Then he motioned with his good arm. "Storm knocked the cell towers out. Landlines are down, too. We can get my brother on the radio if there's an emergency. C'mon Lucky, you too."

Duncan tossed his work belt in a corner and cracked open a bottle of beer, offering one to his guest. Sommers shook his head and pointed his thumb at a dormant Coca-Cola machine. A moment later, the two men clinked their bottles and sat at the counter sipping their drinks. Lucky Dog curled up on a rug at her guardian's feet and let out a sigh.

Sommers flipped his bottle cap into a nearby garbage can. Then he turned and gazed out the window, watching the copper-colored flood waters shimmer beneath the hazy late afternoon sunshine. Following a thick moment of silence, he said, "Come hell or high water, I need to get home." Then he looked down at Lucky Dog, shifting her eyes and perking her ears. "*We* need to get home."

Duncan nodded, then tapped the countertop with his hook. "Well, your heart's not in Hallock. Any fool could see that." He sipped his beer, then lifted his chin towards the window. "Jack said trouble follows you 'round like a shadow."

Deep in thought, Sommers nodded without looking back. "I don't go looking for rough water, but that hasn't stopped the whitecaps from breaking against me." He swirled the soda at the bottom of his bottle and stared at an apricot sky through the glinting rain-streaked windows. "I guess Jack's right. Best keep your guns handy."

Duncan slid his empty bottle aside and twisted the top off a second beer. He drew a large gulp, then muffled a belch. "Wyatt told me he pulled a Caddy from the river. Missouri plates, three dead. Trouble?"

A welcome breeze puffed through the screen door, and Sommers drummed his fingers on the counter and nodded. "Plenty more where they came from."

With the sun sagging lower against a pink western sky, Duncan listened to Sommers describe his situation, his friends, and their clandestine mission. Lucky Dog sat close, munching on vending machine cheese crackers and lapping water from a mixing bowl. Another long moment of silence washed over the two men, and they watched a BNSF freight ramble towards Canada.

Duncan caught Sommers staring at his prosthetic hook. He tapped on the metallic appendage with his beer bottle, making a ringing clink. "Lost it in Helmand Province a few years back—Humvee hit a mine." Then he shook his head and pointed his bottle at a fading photograph tacked to a shelf behind the register. "Lost plenty more back here, to be honest with you."

Sommers leaned closer, studying the picture of a smiling woman seated atop a chestnut-colored horse with a white snout. Looking like a calendar girl, she wore a western hat, riding boots, and not much else. Highlighting the background, a green valley with a bubbling stream lined with trees. "Beautiful. And the woman's not half bad either. Who's she?"

Duncan smirked. "That's my girl, Annie." He gulped his bottle dry, then wiped the foam from his mouth with his shirt. "Was." He shook his head and slid his bottle aside, stacking it alongside the other empties. "When I turned stateside, I hated everyone and everything under the sun. Hated myself, most of all."

The crusty veteran cracked open another bottle and sipped. "Ahh, she ain't no dummy," he said. "Annie wanted no part in tending to a broken man." Duncan waved his hook towards the windows. "Married an actor and moved to Montana. I hear she's got two or three kids and a bunch of horses." Then he lifted his bottle in a toast. "Good for her."

Sommers nodded and raised his pop bottle high above the counter. "There's an ocean of pain out there—drown us all if we let it." Then he watched the flashing red light on the last rail car roll past the outskirts of town. He turned back to face Wes. "How 'bout now? Got your mainsail set?"

"Mmm, buddy." Duncan shrugged and let out a sigh. "Treading water and gettin' by. You know how it is." Sommers closed his eyes and nodded because he'd felt Duncan's heartache more than once or twice.

The men sat and listened to a distant train whistle sing a lonely, somber tune. Sommers downed the rest of his Coke and tossed the empty into an overflowing trash bin. He gave his host a pat on the shoulder. "You're a good man, Wes. Thank you for your kind hospitality." Then he stood and stretched his arms wide before crouching and ruffling Lucky Dog's ears. "C'mon, girl. Let's grab some shuteye."

Duncan used his key to let the bedraggled pair into room seven, then turned and staggered towards the pool. Sommers explored the dank, musty room, finding a spare blanket on a shelf. He knelt and fluffed the fuzzy quilt into a nest for Lucky, but she just sat staring at him with her head tilted and her ears drooped. Sommers shook his head and said, "Well, alright then." He picked her up and placed her on the sagging double bed. "Ashamed to say, I've bedded worse."

Sommers sat on the foot of the bed, unlacing his soggy boots as Lucky curled into a ball at his side. The big man stripped off his wet socks, then sat up with a sigh and stretched his back. He spotted a long white cylinder propped in a corner chair.

Sommers stared at the cardboard tube, trying to dissect its mysterious contents, page by page. He felt certain Jack and Julie had left something noteworthy, but he'd grown weary of the complications steering him away from the simple things that mattered most. He pulled the damp, creased postcard from his pocket, studied the faded picture, then gave it a sniff. The alluring scent he craved was gone.

Sommers, alone with a ragamuffin dog on his hip, tossed the tattered card aside, then leaned back and closed his eyes. The pillows smelled like cigarette smoke and beer sweats, but exhaustion soon overwhelmed the big man's concerns.

Six hundred miles southwest of where Sommers slept through breakfast, the municipal building in Deadwood, South Dakota, bustled with activity. Two heavy-handed bailiffs escorted Greg O'Leary, wearing leg shackles and handcuffs, to the defense table near the front of Courtroom 110. O'Leary, donning an orange DOC jumpsuit, sat and surveyed the cavernous room before dropping his eyes to his twiddling thumbs.

A tall ceiling, clad in planks of white pine and supported by heavy cedar trusses, amplified even the faintest of whispers and reflected the power and finality of the arena. Walls paneled with wood displayed colorized portraits of judges past, but no windows. The judge's rostrum stretched across the front of the room, resting atop columns of green marble. A small group of lawyers huddled in the back corner, swiping through their cell phones and cracking sexist jokes.

The puffy-chested bailiffs remained standing at the defense table, hovering over O'Leary. He jangled the chain between his wrists. "You boys wanna take it down a notch. For cryin' out loud, you're suckin' all the air outta this place. Any chance you pansies are twins?" In unison, the pair shot him a hard stare before putting their index fingers to their lips.

O'Leary said, "Listen here, Neanderthals. Chains or no, I could tap dance on your skulls and walk right outta here without breaking a sweat. Ain't nothin' you or your friends could do about it. Just think of the embarrassment." The two giants stood like statues, facing forward, pursing their lips and shaking their heads.

The suits milled around for a few more minutes before assuming their positions in the courtroom. Then, with a booming voice, one bailiff called the room to order, and the other introduced Judge Clayton Stearns.

O'Leary stood from his chair as a middle-aged man wearing a black robe wobbled in from behind the stage. He had a spotted bald head, and wire-rimmed glasses framed his round face. The judge scanned the room before cocking his bushy white eyebrows and stroking his thick handlebar mustache. Stearns, resembling Walter Brimley, banged his gavel three times and, with a raspy voice, made a few perfunctory remarks.

The judge motioned for the gallery to sit, then he sat and flipped through some pages fixed within a three-ring binder. He said, "The case of the People versus Mr. Gregory J. O'Leary." Stearns pointed at the defendant's table with the gavel's handle. "Mr. O'Leary, we are here today for your initial appearance. The state has charged you with the first-degree murder of Officer Joanna Douglass. Do you understand the gravity of this grievous accusation?"

O'Leary glanced across the aisle, studying the litigators seated at the prosecutor's table. The dapper foursome tapped on their legal pads with golden pens, smirking and licking their chops. Then the manacled veteran turned back to the judge's bench and shrugged. "Yes, your Honor."

Stearns glimpsed at his watch like he had somewhere else to be, then leaned forward in his seat. "Very well. The State alleges that you, Mr. O'Leary, unlawfully and with malice aforethought, killed Officer Joanna Douglass while she was in the line of duty. The state will be seeking the maximum penalty: death by lethal injection. How do you plead?"

O'Leary examined the chain between his wrists, then looked up, staring into the judge's face with defiance in his eyes. "I'm not required to enter a plea, your Honor."

A ringing murmur rose from the gallery, and Stearns struck his block twice. "Alright, that's enough. Order in the courtroom." He looked down at O'Leary, matching the accused's contempt. "Very well, Mr. O'Leary." Stearns raised his chin at the defendant. "You have the right to remain silent. Anything you say can and will be used against you in a court of law. You also have the right to have an attorney present during questioning. If you cannot afford an attorney, the state will appoint one to you. Do you understand these rights?"

O'Leary nodded. "Yes, your Honor."

Judge Stearns flipped a page, folded his hands upon the bench, then said, "The court notes your acknowledgment. Mr. O'Leary, are you represented by counsel?"

O'Leary took a long moment scanning the courtroom, then shook his head. "I'm in between jobs. I…"

A prosecutor stood from the next table, waving a newspaper above his head. "The Fargo Police Department forced Mr. O'Leary to resign following a litany of excessive force charges. His checkered past is strewn with brutality and indiscretion."

Stearns turned and pointed his gavel at the prosecutor's table. "Silence, Mr. Becks. You'll get your turn." He shook his head and turned to the stenographer. "Reporter, strike the prosecution's remark." Then he pointed at the prosecutor. "Now Mr. Becks, do I have to drag you into chambers and review basic courtroom procedure with you?"

Becks sank into his seat and shook his head. "No, your Honor."

Stearns tugged at his mustache, then smoothed a wrinkle from the sleeve of his robe. "Very well. Mr. O'Leary, the court appoints Ms. Paula Capri, Public Defender, to represent you." The judge lifted his chin towards the back of the courtroom and motioned to her with a curling index finger. "Ms. Capri, you have a few minutes to confer with your client. Keep it brief."

Capri, a young shapely brunette, just over five feet tall, elbowed her way past the bailiffs, shoving them aside. Then she sat and huddled with O'Leary, tapping notes into her smartphone with a thin stylus. The judge looked up from his binder and watched the spunky public defender shake her head and wave her arms. O'Leary leaned back in his chair, folding his arms and staring at the high ceiling. Across the aisle, the district attorney joined the group seated around the prosecution's table. After several minutes, Judge Stearns tapped his gavel on the bench. "When you're ready, Ms. Capri, we'll proceed."

Capri stood from the defense table and tugged at the bottom of her suit coat. "Your Honor, Mr. O'Leary understands the charges against him, but he wishes to enter no plea at this time."

Stearns said, "Mr. O'Leary, do you understand that entering no plea means you are not admitting or denying guilt?"

O'Leary glanced at Capri, then looked at Stearns and nodded. "Yes, your Honor."

Stearns flipped to a different page in his binder, then stroked his mustache again. "Very well. The state will present its case at a preliminary hearing within 14 days. This court will formally enter your plea at that time. I'm setting your bond at one million dollars. Until then, you are remanded to the custody of Lawrence County. Bailiffs, escort the defendant."

The district attorney, Travis Thorne, stood and cleared his throat. "For the record, your Honor, the State requests the court deny bond because of the heinous nature of the crime and the flight risk posed by the defendant. For crying out loud, this savage slashed Ms. Douglass' throat from ear to ear."

Capri stood and marched to the front of the defendant's table. Objection, your Honor. My client has no prior criminal record. He is a decorated veteran and a respected member of the law enforcement community. Mr. Thorne's accusations are out of line and denying bond to this man is excessive.

Judge Stearns said, "Mr. O'Leary, are you seeking employment? Do you have ties to this area that would incentivize you to remain and face trial?"

Capri leaned over the table and whispered in her client's ear. Then O'Leary shifted his attention to the judge. "I have friends and business opportunities in Spearfish. I've long considered spending my retirement years here."

Stearns pivoted to the prosecution's table. "Mr. Thorne, do you have any evidence of Mr. O'Leary attempting to flee this jurisdiction?"

Thorne wore an expensive pinstripe suit, and his dark hair lay slicked back on his head. "Mr. O'Leary is unemployed. He's a divorced man without children. His so-called friends occupy an area where three recent homicides remain unsolved." He furrowed his brow and pointed at the defendant. "If you asked me to describe the ideal candidate for flight risk, it would be that man right there."

Stearns studied the gavel as he spun it between his fingers.

He exhaled a sigh and shifted his eyes to the defense table. "Mr. O'Leary, understand that the court must consider the safety of the community along with your flight risk. I am inclined to deny bond at this time, but I will allow your attorney to file a formal motion for reconsideration."

O'Leary spent a lengthy moment staring at the cuffs around his wrists, then he leaned over and whispered something to Capri. She tapped a note into her phone, then nodded to her client. O'Leary stood and scanned the room. At last, he exhaled and said, "Your Honor. The only thing I'm guilty of is being in the wrong place at the wrong time. I'm an investigator, and a damn good one. While we waste time running unfounded accusations up a flagpole, a pair of cold-blooded killers roam these hills." He shook the chain between his cuffs. "Behind bars, I'm of no help to you or anyone else."

Once again, Judge Stearns flipped the page in his binder, then looked up and glared at O'Leary while tapping his fingers on the bench. "Very well. Mr. O'Leary," he said. "I'm setting your bond at $100,000. You will be subject to electronic monitoring and must remain in this tri-county region until your trial. Any violation of these conditions will result in immediate re-arrest. Do you understand?"

O'Leary smirked, then nodded. "Yes, your Honor."

Thorne threw his hands in the air as the judge gave the block a single whack with his gavel. Stearns said, "This court is adjourned. We will reconvene one week from today for a preliminary hearing. Mr. O'Leary, Mr. Thorne, I urge you both to use the time wisely."

The beefy bailiffs nudged O'Leary, directing him from the courtroom. The relieved defendant glanced back at Capri, who gave him a wink and a smile. As the others filed out, Travis Thorne approached the bench. He lifted his chin at the judge, who was packing away his papers. Thorne said, "Your Honor, I think we just made a terrible mistake."

Stearns paused before turning to leave. "Perhaps. But sometimes

I have to go with my gut, and my gut tells me that O'Leary is an honorable man. Frankly, we could use more like him around here." Then the judge wobbled away, leaving Thorne and Capri standing in the courtroom exchanging flinty stares.

An hour later, O'Leary stepped into the bright sunshine that warmed the sidewalks along Water Street. Clutching a plastic shopping bag containing his meager collection of belongings, he shaded his eyes and looked north, then south. A police cruiser rolled up and slowed along the curb. Officer Preston shouted as he leaned from the open window with his middle fingers extended. "Go suck a grenade, you fuckin' butcher!" Then the black and white car sped away, rounding the next corner with its tires squealing.

O'Leary shrugged, then turned and waved at a surveillance camera mounted above the courthouse entrance. He pulled his camouflage baseball hat from the sack, snugged it atop his head, then he pivoted and ambled north along Water Street.

After a few strides towards Pine Street, a crumbling delivery van pulled to the curb. Lefty Porter leaned over and shoved the creaky passenger door open. "Get in," he said with a wave and a grin. O'Leary, without moving, surveyed the buzzing streets of downtown Deadwood. Porter honked the sickly horn. "Today, man. I know where the snakes took your girl."

O'Leary climbed into the mottled passenger seat and Porter wheeled away, his rusty van leaving puffs of black smoke in its wake. O'Leary settled in and fumbled with his bag. "Are you the one who posted my bail?"

Porter smirked, turning the steering wheel with his good hand. "What's that old saying? You shouldn't judge a book by its cover."

O'Leary shook his head and said, "Okay, then. Seems I'm indebted to you." He rifled through the bag, finding his dead cell phone. He held it towards the driver, showing him the dark screen. "Can you do anything about this?"

Porter took a peek and shook his head, then turned north onto Highway 85.

They rode in silence for several minutes while O'Leary stared at Porter's deformed right hand. "Is she still alive?" O'Leary asked. "Where'd they take her?"

Porter shrugged, then glanced over at O'Leary. "Don't know about her condition, but my friend Stan's got some explaining to do."

O'Leary creased his brow and cracked his knuckles. "Ya got weapons?"

Porter cocked his head towards the back, then winked and nodded. "Does Barbie have plastic titties?"

O'Leary smirked and stared out his side window. "Yep, I guess she does." Then he adjusted his cap and massaged his bruised wrists. "Okay then, time to rattle some cages." O'Leary turned and looked at the driver. "We're gonna get bloody."

Porter nodded again, then glanced down at the black band around his passenger's left ankle. "I'm counting on it."

Chapter 28
Across the River

"Then she moved back around here thirty-five weeks ago today."

Julie Hughes pounded on the paint-peeled door to room seven. "Sommers, wake up. Get your colossal ass outta that bed!" Her shouts triggered Lucky Dog into a fit of snarls and woofs. "Ya sleeping with hounds again?" She asked in a huff. "Sheesh, some guys never learn." Again, Julie rapped her knuckles on the rough particle board. "C'mon man. We gotta roll—trouble's afoot."

Sommers sat up with a start, searching the darkness, trying to remember where he was and wondering why an agitated mutt bounced between the fusty pillows. The big man ran his fingers through his tousled hair, rubbed his drowsy face, then massaged the dog's hairy neck.

"Hold your horses. Gimme a second, wouldja?" He stumbled around in the dingy shadows, feeling his way. "There's gotta be an escape hatch around here somewhere." After stubbing his little toe against a bedpost, he grumbled and limped to the door, unhooking its puny chain and cracking it open. Then he squinted and shielded his eyes from the fierce morning sunshine, standing in the same dank clothing he'd worn the previous three days. Lucky bounded from the bed, joining him at his side with her tail wagging.

"Who's your date?" Julie asked, squatting to greet the curious pooch. "Kinda skinny, ain't she?"

Sommers fitted his Stihl baseball hat onto his rumpled head, then looked down and smirked. "According to Lindstrom, she's Doggone Lucky." Then he looked past Julie and surveyed the parking lot, noticing the flood waters had retreated very little overnight. He watched Hector cinch a rope around his truck's trailer hitch.

The ambitious Mexican climbed in and dragged Vern's crumpled fishing boat off the 7th Street curb with a screeching metallic scrape. Sommers cringed and ruffled Lucky's ears, then turned back to Julie. "Unlike the other females in my life, she clings to me like a cocklebur." He stepped back from the doorway and cocked his head. "C'mon in. Where's Jack?"

"Over at the hospital. Duncan told us what happened to Ted," Julie said, stepping in and scrunching her nose. "Stinks like ass in here. What the hell?"

Sommers sniffed under his arm and winced, then lifted his chin at his hairy scapegoat. "Cheese crackers." He turned and pointed at the glossy white cylinder propped in the corner. "What's in the tube?"

Julie leapt across the dreary room and snatched the container. "No time for that now." She grabbed Sommers' arm and dragged him towards the door. "Hell has broken loose in the Black Hills." She looked up at Sommers with watery eyes, then shook her head. "Jack's gonna have to explain. C'mon Lucky, let's boogie-boogie."

Before their hike to the hospital, the trio stopped by the hotel office, where Sommers grabbed two cake doughnuts and his mutilated cell phone from Wes Duncan's crumbling counter. Duncan scratched at his crotch, then lifted his prosthetic hook, pointing at the clamor outside. "Prop's bent and the transom's split. Hector wants to know what you've got planned for that old relic."

Sommers shook his head, then ripped a doughnut in two, feeding half to his slobbering sidekick and stuffing the other half into his mouth. He offered the other doughnut to Julie, who raised her hand and shook her head. "I'm good."

Sommers felt a tug at his arm and he motioned to Duncan. "Sell it for scrap. We gotta run." Then, after several brisk steps, Sommers pivoted back to their host and raised the second pastry above his head. "Thanks for breakfast. If anyone comes looking for us, we've taken off. Montana."

Duncan rolled his eyes and shrugged, then whistled and waved for Hector. The manager with the open fly started humming a tune as he retreated into the office, letting the screen door spring shut with a resounding clap.

Ten minutes later, Julie and Sommers stepped into a crowded hospital room to find Ted Lindstrom wearing a bandage across his head, haggling with a pair of nurses and demanding to leave. Jack Hughes sat in a corner, hovering over an open newspaper, listening to his phone messages and scribbling notes across his yellow pad.

Meanwhile, an Asian custodian wearing green medical scrubs and a pair of white earbuds rapped along with his music as he wheeled his cleaning cart past the horde towards the bathroom. Lucky Dog tip-toed in and leaned against Lindstrom's bed, wagging her tail and gazing up at a serving tray of neglected breakfast.

Sommers stood with his arms crossed, filling the doorway like a hulking tree braced against a frosty wind. Betsy Robbins, wearing her blue nurse's smock, shuffled from across the hall with a clipboard crooked under her arm. She used the plank to smack the big man's shoulder. "Well, looky what the cat dragged in." Then she shifted her eyes to Lindstrom. "Your buddy's out to lunch. Poor guy doesn't know what day it is."

Sommers scratched at the back of his neck and shook his head, watching Julie hand-feed room-temperature eggs to the hungry, orphaned pooch. He looked down at Robbins and tapped his finger on her clipboard. "What's the official prognosis?"

Robbins pointed at her notes with a gnarled ballpoint pen disguised as a flower. "Got a knot the size of a kumquat on the back of his head, eyes dilated like pie plates. Vitals appear stable. Can't blame him for being sour as vinegar, coulda been a lot worse. Doc doesn't know when he'll get his memory back. It kinda comes and goes. He should be okay after a few days' rest—not going anywhere today, that's for sure."

Sommers nodded while staring down at his boots. Then he looked up to find Jack Hughes waving him into the room. Sommers whispered as he leaned into Robbins. "Would you mind breaking up this party? We've got some private business to discuss." Robbins creased her forehead and pursed her lips before nodding at him with a wink. Then she snapped her fingers and began escorting the hospital staffers out.

Jack signaled for Sommers to lock the door, then motioned for him to come sit at a small corner table. The lawyer ruffled his newspaper and pointed at a headline that Sommers read to himself. Jack said, "Snakes grabbed our girl and slashed Jo Douglass' throat. Local cops arrested O'Leary. They're trying to pin everything on him. Travis Thorne's the DA out there. I've heard he's got some history with Big Bill Wenner. Anyway, Thorne asked for the death penalty, but the judge cut our boy loose. Go figure, huh?" Jack rolled the paper and slapped the table, making Lucky cower and curl at Sommers' feet. "This shit has gotten way outta hand. We're down three guns, waging a war on three fronts."

At the crack of the newspaper, Lindstrom sat up in his bed and searched the room with a blank stare. Soon, a spark of recognition brightened his face. He grinned and said, "We'll if it isn't Doggone Lucky and her lumbering white knight." Then he leaned back into his pillows, closed his eyes and began muttering the lyrics to *Wichita Lineman.*

Sommers, feeling the weight of the world upon his chest, adjusted his orange baseball hat and shifted his gaze to Julie, watching her pace the floor, blowing her nose into a tissue and dabbing her eyes. She glanced at her smartphone and said, "It's been over forty-eight hours. She's dead. Those evil bastards tortured her, then cut her to ribbons, just like Bud Wolcott."

Lindstrom licked his lips, then cleared his throat. "Moon Deer's one-hundred percent badass. She's alive." He shook his head and cracked his eyelids open. "She has value, else the goddamn snakes would've left her bleeding with the chief. Judge Stearns used to roll with Bud Wolcott, got a full-dress Harley. He ain't no dummy. He's counting on Rambo to clean up the mess out there."

Jack rolled his eyes and said, "Shit, man. I hope you're right."

Sommers stood and leaned over the bed with his arms taut behind his back. "Betsy Robbins says you can't remember what day it is. What makes you so sure about Moon Deer and the judge's mess?"

Lindstrom sipped some water through a bendy straw, then chuckled as he spied the four faces around his bed. "It's Tuesday. Who the hell's Betsy Robbins?" He fluffed his pillow and settled back, closing his eyes and smacking his lips. "The hell am I doin' here, anyway?" He fluttered his eyelids and pointed at Jack. "And who the hell are you?"

Jack made a sputtering sound and shook his head. Sommers sank into his chair and clasped his hands behind his head. Then he leaned back and stared at a gaping hole in the watermarked ceiling.

Julie fed Lucky a slice of whole-grain toast, then pushed the tray table aside. She sat on the edge of Lindstrom's bed, her weepy eyes tracking to the others before settling on Sommers. "Well. What are we gonna do now?"

Sixty minutes later, Hector dropped Julie Hughes and Wes Duncan in the fetid muck that swallowed Vern's Last Resort. The pair slogged through the yard, arguing about who should drive Lindstrom's Hellcat back to Hallock. Julie won the argument, claiming she could drive a stick better than most men, especially a one-armed hick with a burning case of jock itch. Duncan flipped her the bird, then pouted as he spun away in Julie's Jeep, spraying wet sand and mud in every direction.

Next, following a bumpy drive between miles of water-logged ditches, Hector parked outside the service hangar at Kittson Airspray. A cursing mechanic on a creeper wheeled from beneath Sommers' plane. He wiped his hands on an oil-stained shop rag, then stood to greet the men with his greasy handshakes.

"Pardon my French," the lanky man said, looking his three visitors up and down. "Name's Beech. This your bird?"

Sommers wiped his hand on his pant leg, then stepped forward and nodded. "That's right. This here's Jack Hughes, and that's Lucky Dog."

Beech looked the trio over and shook his head, then tossed his rag aside. "What's the big hurry?" He asked, motioning to the airfield. "Runway is still under a foot of water—you'd get farther in a goddamn Jon boat."

Jack rolled his eyes and elbowed Sommers in the ribs. Lucky sniffed around and squatted over a cluster of gangly weeds, then ambled over and sat at Sommers' feet with her tongue hanging out the side of her mouth.

Sommers ruffled her ears, then adjusted his baseball hat and said, "If it wasn't important, we wouldn't risk it." He pointed his thumb over his shoulder. "Man on the phone said we could use the highway. It's been done before."

Beech huffed, then shook his head. "Highway 22? Yea, right." He pointed past Hector's truck. "Tower's got an obstructed view in both directions." Then he motioned with his arm. "Got railroad tracks at one end and potholes big enough to sink a school bus at the other.

Every single day, the knuckleheads in their goddamn tuner cars race along here pushin' ninety and blowin' every stop sign in the county."

No sooner had the words left his mouth, a noisy Toyota rocketed past, leaving a swirl of road dust and blue exhaust smoke in its wake. "See what I mean?" Beech shook his head and shrugged. "Damn kids." Lucky stood and tucked her tail, pressing her weight against Sommers' leg.

Jack leaned forward with his finger in the air, but Sommers held him back. The big man said, "Seen worse. Now, are you gonna help us get outta here or not?" Beech furrowed his eyebrows and rocked on the balls of his feet with his arms folded across his chest. Sommers broke their stare-down, thrusting his index finger towards the highway. "Wyatt Duncan's gonna use his wrecker to block traffic coming from Highway 75, and Hector here will stop everything coming from Emerson Road."

Beech scratched at the back of his head, then turned his filthy palms up. "Hey, your dime, your dance floor." He motioned back to the airplane and kept whining. "Some flood water seeped into the fuel tanks. We did our best to clear things out, but..." Then he kicked his creeper aside and squatted under the prop, pointing at the front landing gear. "Your struts are shot, and the nose wheel is hanging by a thread."

Hector tapped a message into his phone, then motioned to the highway and gave a thumbs up. Jack nudged Sommers, rolling his eyes and shaking his head. Sommers waved him off, then nodded as he poked Beech in the chest. "Parts are on back-order. Got no choice here—we're goin' up."

Beech stepped back with a scowl stretched across his gaunt face. "Okay cowboys, load 'er up." He pointed at a small rusty tractor parked near the hangar's concrete apron. "I'll even tow this death trap out to the road for ya." He laughed as he fetched a stack of orange traffic cones for Hector, then motioned at the sky. "If you're headed west, better check the weather. NWS says you're gonna encounter some headwinds. Max range today, maybe six-hundred miles. For you, maybe six-hundred feet. If the F.A.A. comes a callin', you never talked to me."

Beech crawled like a monkey on all fours, snickering as he clipped a tow strap to the Cessna's undercarriage. He stood and arched his back, then moseyed over to his tractor and started fiddling with the controls. Hector cursed in Spanish, then took off with Beech's traffic cones. Jack grumbled as he packed three gear bags and the enigmatic white cylinder into the plane's cabin. Beech's tractor chugged to life after a backfire, followed by a puff of noxious exhaust. Jack turned to Sommers. "You think his first name is Some?"

Sommers shook off his lawyer's joke and smirked. "I think it's Sandy. No joke." Then he used Jack's phone to call home, leaving a voicemail message with Grumpy, hoping everyone was okay and mentioning they'd be back in two days, three days, tops. He left another message with O'Leary, telling him to hang tight—calvary's on the way, six hours out. Lucky yipped and circled at Sommers' feet after Beech's tractor backfired a second time. The pilot stroked her bristled hair, then carried her up the stairs and got her settled inside the cabin.

Jack slid into seat one and cinched the seatbelt across his lap. Lucky jumped into seat two and pressed her nose against the window, watching her master feel his way around the plane's fuselage. Sommers looked up and examined the orange windsock fluttering above the hangar, then flashed a half-hearted thumbs up to the restless mechanic, who sat upon his sputtering tractor spitting and swearing up a storm.

After a moment of heavy contemplation, Sommers wheeled and planted his right foot on the airstair's bottom step while leaning against the handrail and scrutinizing the nose wheel. He lifted his face in time to see a gray pickup truck wheel past the corner of the building and skid to a stop in the gravel turnaround.

Sommers stepped down, admiring the driver as her sensuality flowed from the shiny Silverado. She waved and shouted above the noise of Beech's tractor. "Sommers, wait up! Got a minute?" She wore western boots, faded blue jeans, and a black leather vest over a plaid sleeveless blouse. She glided towards the big man with a mellow breeze fanning her shiny hair. He stood mesmerized as she plucked a pair of dark sunglasses from her face, then stretched a few golden strands away from her dramatic green eyes.

The driver stepped forward and examined the Cessna, running her fingers along the wing before blocking the stairs. "Nice plane," she said, hooking her glasses on the pocket of her vest and tucking her thumbs into her front pockets. "Mr. Sommers. I'll cut to the quick. We need to have a candid discussion about the Norman property." She extended her firm right hand. "D.T. Hardesty. EPA, region eight director." She peeked over her shoulder at the flooded runway. "Got time for a cup?"

Sommers looked up to see Jack and Lucky studying the pair through the open hatch. He nodded at them and held his index finger up to signal a momentary delay. "Sommers, US Forest Service," he said, shaking Hardesty's hand while appreciating her athletic, suntanned arm. "Not much of a coffee drinker—chocolate milk's more my speed."

"Then chocolate milk it is. Shall we?" Hardesty cocked her head towards her waiting pickup truck.

Sommers nodded, then caught himself and turned away, lifting his chin towards Highway 22. "We're kinda in a hurry. Raincheck?"

Hardesty puckered her lips and tugged on her earlobe. "Hmm, that could work. When?"

"Not sure when we'll be back this way," Sommers said as he sank into her unrelenting eyes. "How's this supposed to go?"

Hardesty pulled an iPhone from her vest pocket. "Got your phone handy? I'll text you my contact card."

Sommers adjusted his hat and unveiled a frown. "Phone's

busted." Then he glanced up at Jack, who flicked one of his business cards, sending it fluttering down the stairs.

Jack shouted through the open doorway. "Good to see you again, Ms. Hardesty. Say, what does DT stand for? I'm dying to know."

Hardesty scraped the heel of her boot across the damp gravel and shook her head in silence.

"Oh c'mon," cried Jack. "For real?"

Hardesty slipped her vest open, exposing a sticky holster tucked under her left arm. She winked and said, "Oh, I could tell you. But then I'd have to shoot you."

Jack sputtered through his lips and rolled his eyes. "Yea, whatever. All things considered. You'd be doing me a favor."

Sommers adjusted his hat again and shook his head. "Don't mind him. He's afraid of flying." Then he motioned to Beech, who sat revving his tractor's engine. "We need to get going."

Hardesty bent over and picked up Jack's business card, huffing after giving it a quick look. "Huh, I've got one of these in my bag." Then she turned and locked eyes with Sommers. "Susan Norman gave me one just like it a couple of days ago." She raised up on her toes and whispered into the big man's ear. "Can you keep a secret?"

Sommers nodded, absorbed in her balmy aroma.

Hardesty, her voice cool and breathy, said, "Back in the day, I showed up during an Iowa tornado. Bad timing seems to be my calling card. Never met my mother, but my father was the smartest person I've ever met. Anyway, he used to call me Double Trouble. My friends just call me DT." Then she winked before slipping her sunglasses down over her eyes. "I'll call ya."

Sommers gave a small wave and watched her drive away. As he climbed the airstairs, he felt the speed of the earth's rotation and the tilt of its axis. An intriguing breeze whistled around his ears, singing a prophetic tune. He stopped mid-step and did a double-take, noticing the windsock above his head had reversed directions.

Beech's tractor stalled twice, and it took him ten minutes to drag Sommers' airplane a quarter mile to the soggy shoulder of Highway 22. The cranky mechanic scrambled around and unfastened the tow straps, then signaled by winding his arm and pointing at the hazy western sky.

Sommers fired the engine and let the revs build during the last of his pre-flight checks. Jack used his phone to confirm both Duncan and Hector were in position. Then the pilot steered the plane onto the empty stretch of pockmarked two-lane. That's where the engine stalled.

Beech shook his head and shouted, raising his palms to the sky. "Not too late to back out. Tomorrow's another fuckin' day, know what I mean?"

Sommers waved him off and restarted the engine. As a freight train rumbled through the crossing behind the tail, the pilot checked his clearance on the port and starboard sides before pushing the throttle forward. In just seconds, the small plane shook and rattled as it bounced along the yellow centerline, gaining speed. Sommers reached down to reassure Lucky Dog, trembling against his ankles.

The pilot felt a slap on his shoulder and he turned to see his wide-eyed lawyer pointing with desperation towards the windshield. Jack gasped, laboring to get his words out. "Heads up, man! The fuck is that?" Then he leaned forward for a closer look. "Ahh, shit!"

Sommers jerked his head around in time to see a northbound pumper truck turn right from Coon Creek Road onto eastbound Highway 22. The stainless-steel tanker from Anderson Sewer and Septic rumbled straight for Sommers' spinner, closing fast. The pilot shook his head and said, "Right you are, Jack."

Jack slapped his forehead and shielded his eyes. "We're gonna eat shit then kiss our asses goodbye."

Sommers growled and shook his finger at seat number one. "Not today! Now sit back, and strap in. More importantly, shut your mouth. We got this!" Lucky Dog whimpered, circling the cockpit twice before wedging herself under the pilot's seat. Sommers' mind raced through a series of calculations, recalling evasive maneuvers that his mentor, Jim Thompson, with some hesitation, demonstrated—procedures that no flight instructor or training manual would dare endorse.

Chattering along at forty knots, Sommers knew there was no time to stop. He'd snap off the nose wheel by slamming on the brakes, giving the insufferable Sandy Beech long-term bragging rights. Pivoting side to side, he looked out each window to see stands of wind-damaged trees lining the mucky roadsides. "No place to ditch this bird," he muttered to himself. "Last resort, indeed."

Jack peeked through his fingers and bawled as the pumper truck gobbled up the distance to impact. "For God's sake, man. Do something!"

Sommers remembered his dream about little Noah gaining speed before launching himself over the edge of Victory Bluff—soaring and circling high above the water. The pilot shouted as he pressed the throttle forward to full. "Hang on to your hat. Here goes nothing." Sommers checked his gauges and applied back pressure to the yoke. At sixty knots, he lifted the nose to eight, nine, ten degrees, then retracted the flaps to reduce the drag. "Gonna be close!"

The pumper truck swerved to a sudden stop in a cloud of tire smoke. Sommers pulled and twisted the yoke opposite the truck, then slid the throttle back to avoid stalling. The small plane lifted and arched from the makeshift runway, mere inches from disaster. Jack looked out his window and shouted a whoop, then sat back and exhaled a heavy sigh. "Shit, man. That *was* close."

Sommers nodded and steered his airplane in a tight circle, rising above the remote airfield. Beech stood atop his tractor seat, fists on his hips, shaking his head. Duncan flashed his emergency lights and blasted the wrecker's noisy air horns. After climbing and leveling at eight hundred feet, Sommers adjusted his airspeed and looked down to see the driver of the pumper truck standing in the middle of the road, thrusting both of his middle fingers towards the heavens. Farther ahead, Hector jumped up and down in the intersection at Emerson Road, pumping his fists and waving a triumphant goodbye.

The pilot adjusted his baseball hat, then reached down to ruffle Lucky's ears as he scanned the skies ahead. He exhaled a full cleansing sigh and glanced to the north, spotting a familiar Chevy pickup parked in a wayside south of Highway 1. A pretty cowgirl leaned against the front fender, one hand on her hip, and the other holding her phone overhead. Sommers pulsed the wings to let Hardesty know he caught her sign.

After a few minutes, Jack loosened his seatbelt and leaned forward. "Have I ever mentioned how much I hate flying?"

Sommers sipped from his water bottle, then smirked. "Only about a thousand times." Lucky climbed into seat number two, pressed her feet in circles around the padded cushion, then curled into a ball and leaned her head against the armrest.

Jack nodded, then turned somber, staring out his window. "Sommers, why are we doing this? I hate to be a Debbie Downer, but Sam, Hawk, or whoever the hell she is these days, she's never coming back. Joy's gotta be dead by now, and O'Leary's marching into a buzz saw."

Sommers nodded, then looked down and studied the charred, flooded hole in the middle of Peg McFarland's farm. A moment later, they bumped through some low clouds above the brown, swollen banks of the Red River. Sommers could see the mud slick where Wyatt Duncan's wrecker pulled Susan Norman's demolished Cadillac from the muck.

Breaking the thick silence, the pilot leaned back and peeked over his shoulder. "Abraham Lincoln said, 'To ease another's heartache is to forget one's own.'" Then he drummed his thumbs on the yoke.

"Trouble," Sommers said. "I've dragged my best friends into a river of trouble—up to me to get 'em out."

Jack said, "That's pretty deep, man. Deep and kinda dark." Then he folded a piece of chewing gum into his mouth and changed the subject. "Hardesty's something else, huh? What do you s'pose she wants?"

"God only knows," Sommers said, trying his best to hide his guilty smirk. "I'm sure we'll find out soon enough." A few seconds later, Lucky lifted her head to Jack's blaring rock 'n' roll ringtone.

Six hundred miles west, a white mustang convertible sped south on South Dakota Highway 22. Susan Norman wore short-shorts and had her NDSU t-shirt knotted high above her midriff. She had painted her fingernails red, and she wore her blonde hair tied back in a ponytail.

After fidgeting in her seat, she tuned the radio to some classic rock, then pressed the clutch and shifted into overdrive. The speedometer leveled at eighty-five, and the behemoth reclining in the passenger seat scrunched his nose and rubbed his eyes. "Holy shit, it stinks like I'm back at your farm—hate that fuckin' place."

"Well shit, Beef," Norman said, shaking her head. "There's nothing there for you, nothing but trouble. And for that matter, anything worth a damn is beaten or dead."

Beef watched Schmidt's Cemetery streak by on his right, and thirty seconds later, they passed Johnston's Cemetery on the left. "That's for damn sure," he said, furrowing his brow. "You promised me that black truck. Now three of my bros are gone and I ain't got shit to show for it."

Norman turned the radio down and wagged a finger at her ornery passenger. "Listen, you whiny bitch. I told you yesterday. That truck's long gone. Thorne's gonna take care of us—got the keys to Wenner's safe. Soon as I get intel on the boy, you can take both our shares and hitchhike your ass back to KC."

"Why the hell you get in bed with them fuckin' crooks? Wenner could never be trusted, everybody knows that." Beef cracked his knuckles, then ran his hands over his shaved scalp. "And don't get me started on them fuckin' snakes."

The giant passenger picked at his teeth in the rearview mirror and said, "I don't care if you've got the hots for him. I see that fuckin' lumberjack I'm gonna bust him to pieces." Then the giant turned and glared at Norman. "Believe it or not, I have limits. Don't count on me for your half-assed kidnapping scheme. I ain't no pedo—that shit's messed up, man."

Norman cranked the steering wheel and slammed on the brakes. The tires howled, and the Mustang slid to a jittery stop on the washboard shoulder. She tapped and swiped her phone, launching a video and holding it to her passenger's face. "Remember this?" she asked, her red lipstick twisted into a wry grin. "I'm sure they've found Edward's body by now. Ooh, and who's that kicking his brains across the yard?"

Norman puckered her lips and nodded. "This video's a handy insurance policy, wouldn't you say?" The driver turned and poked her finger into the big man's chest. "Don't push me, Beef. I'll put your balls in a bench vice, and I'll savor every turn of the screw."

Beef shook his head, then reclined the seat and folded his arms across his chest. "Just drive," he said, motioning with his fingers. "Let's get this over with. I'm fuckin' hungry."

Chapter 29
One Tree Hill

"We turn away to face the cold, enduring chill."

Lefty Porter's battered delivery van wobbled as it groaned, railing against the snug curves of Spearfish Canyon Parkway. After passing through the ghostly mist of Bridal Veil Falls, Porter pulsed his wipers, stretching a gooey smear of bug guts and bird crap across his cracked windshield. He cursed under his breath and glanced over at his undaunted passenger.

Greg O'Leary hunched forward in his seat and pointed through one of the few clear spots remaining in the glass. "Wayside is on the left," he said, shifting to his side and fishing for the key in his pocket. "Blazer's parked behind the trees above the trailhead. Pull in here. I'll grab my gun."

Porter huffed as he gripped the glossy suicide knob with his good hand, spinning the oversized steering wheel and squealing his bald tires. "Okay, but you won't need it. We're gonna find your cutie, cut a deal—get 'er back in one piece. Cop flashin' a heater's gonna cause some serious shit."

O'Leary turned and glared at Porter. "Got loads of experience with hostage negotiations, do ya?"

After circling the lot and parking the van, Porter shook his head and motioned with his tiny, disfigured hand. "Look. Not a goddamn car anywhere."

O'Leary stepped out and turned in four compass directions, shielding his eyes from the biting afternoon rays. "Well, shit," he said, as Spearfish Creek's petulant waters churned far below the canyon's craggy walls. He waved a deer fly away from his face and leaned into the open doorway, surveying the contents of Porter's broken-down ride. He scrunched his nose and pointed with his thumb. "What's with all the blood stains back there?"

Porter twisted in his seat, craning his neck. "What blood?" He asked, scratching at the back of his head. "Oh, that," he said, hitting the detective with a sideways look. "Nabbed a wounded deer after droppin' you off the other day. DNR frowns upon it, but the rez dogs pay me fifty bucks a head."

O'Leary rolled his eyes, then nodded before shutting the door and turning away. Porter backed from his parking spot and rolled alongside, his head sticking out the window. "Hey, man. What gives? I thought we's a team."

"Yea, well. I was wrong about you," O'Leary said, waving as he strode towards the highway. "Thanks for the lift—think you better sit this one out."

Porter rolled forward and said, "Hey amigo, you're forgetting a thing or two." He waved his good hand in a circle above his head. "There's a million acres of forest 'round here, prob'ly two hundred miles of hidden caves." He stabbed the brakes and cracked a devilish grin. "I know where the goddamn snakes hole up, and I know where they've got your girl. And you don't," he said, wagging his small finger. "Now get in."

O'Leary rubbed his eyes, shook his head, and settled back into the passenger seat before slamming the creaky door. "I'm bunkin' at a place at the top of the hill. You can drop me there. I need to check on things, grab some gear."

Porter snickered and waited for a truck to pass before turning onto the winding parkway. "Wenner's place—know all 'bout it."

O'Leary, following two minutes of leaden silence, pointed and said, "There, on the left, park near the garage, wouldja?" He climbed out and cracked his knuckles. "Wait here. I'll just be a minute or two."

Porter puckered his lips and sputtered as O'Leary stomped past the dimpled hood to the open driver's side window.

"Ya know, Porter. You're forgetting something too," he said, gripping the sill hard enough to turn his knuckles pale. "Handicapped or not, I'll beat you within an inch of your life to get what I want. By the time I finish tanning your hide, you'll be eating your meals through a straw and wiping your ass with your feet." O'Leary cocked his head towards the gruesome mess in the back of the van. "So help me God, she'd better be alive."

Porter returned O'Leary's dogged scowl and poked his mutated finger at the detective's chest. "You owe me ten grand, tough guy." Then he lifted his chin towards the house. "Like I said, no fuckin' guns."

At the service door, O'Leary entered the security code and stepped into the garage. He flicked a light switch, back-locked the door, and let his eyes adjust to the gloom. He discovered Samantha's Blazer parked in the first bay. Shards from the driver's window glinted across the seats, and the center console lay on its side in a mangled heap. His cellphone and his service revolver, long gone. He finished inspecting the car's interior, then turned and peeked through the garage window, observing Porter leaning against his dented fender, smoking a joint and staring off into the hills.

O'Leary pivoted for the house and lurched, stopping to study a large map tacked to the wall behind a makeshift collection of fishing gear. Above the rods and reels, colored push pins marked some of Big Bill Wenner's favorite fishing spots. A few pins anchored faded photographs of the blubbery man posing with his fishing buddies, showing off their prized catches.

The detective reached up and plucked a red thumbtack from the center of Iron Creek Lake. It was the marker closest to Wenner's mountaintop retreat. He twisted the pin from the snapshot and puffed air across it, blowing the dust and cobwebs away. O'Leary flipped the card, checked the back, then turned it over and held the picture to the light.

The photograph showed Wenner wearing a pair of blue Ford coveralls, standing with his work boot on the front step of a campground store. The stub of a cigar jutted from the side of his chubby face, and a stringer of yellow perch dangled from his meaty hand. Near his right hip stood a tall man sporting a pair of Ray-Ban sunglasses and a leather jacket. The dapper man, looking fresh and out of place, wore a heavy gold chain, and combed his dark hair slicked-back on his head. "Well, I'll be," O'Leary said under his breath. "It's the great outdoorsman, Travis Thorne."

The detective shifted his focus to a third man in the picture, seated on a cooler with a rolled cigarette poking from his boorish mouth. In one hand, he gripped a glinting filet knife, brandishing it like a sword. Looped around his diminutive hand was a bloodstained, braided line tied to the lip of a plump rainbow trout.

O'Leary shook his head and slid the photograph into his pocket. He traced his fingers along the trails that curled across the map. Then he glanced over his shoulder and peeked through the window before tiptoeing into the house. The detective stopped in the kitchen and cupped his ears while holding his breath. He sniffed the stagnant air before stooping to inspect the dust patterns on the counters and floors.

After listening for movement, he stepped onto the screened porch. He dropped to a knee and pried up three of the cedar floorboards. O'Leary felt around with his hands before lifting Moon

Deer's bulky haversack from the hole and taking inventory of its contents. "Maybe I should start packing like a woman," he said to himself, while his eyes probed the trees bordering the backyard.

Sandwiched between two boxes of ammunition, O'Leary discovered two banded sleeves of one-hundred-dollar bills. Like shuffling a deck of playing cards, he fluttered the ends of the new bills, exposing a sticky note tucked inside one of the bands. He sniffed the scented paper, unfolded the note, and read the message. "Some cats are just snakes in disguise."

The detective furrowed his brow, returning one strap of bills into the pack while slipping the other into the front pocket of his gray hoodie. O'Leary jammed a nine-round magazine into Moon Deer's Glock, then slipped her gun into a Velcro holster fastened high around his chest and hidden beneath his baggy sweatshirt. "No guns, my ass," he said in a snit. Then he slipped the canvas bag back into the hole and replaced the planks before searching the rest of the silent house.

A feeble blare from a car horn echoed along the hillside, and O'Leary hurried back to the garage to take a last look at Wenner's fishing map. Eighteen miles of winding road led to the park entrance on the opposite side of the canyon, but only two miles of hiking trail separated him from Stan's campground store. He closed his eyes and wiggled his calculating fingers, then stepped out in time to smell the pungent smoke swirling from Porter's open window. O'Leary cocked an eyebrow and waved the cloud from his face. "Medicinal, right?"

Porter looked him over and smirked, flicking the smoldering butt into the weeds. He grumbled over the sound of the van's idling engine. "C'mon man, we ain't got all day."

O'Leary turned and gazed at a reddish sun sagging over the western hogbacks. "How long of a drive we got?" He asked.

"Thirty minutes, give or take."

O'Leary nodded, then flipped a strap of hundreds into the driver's grimy lap. "We're even," he said, pointing his thumb towards the house. "Gimme another minute—forgot to lock 'er up."

Porter let out a groan as he leaned over and tossed the cash into his cluttered glove box. O'Leary caught the glint of a large hunting knife nestled within a jumble of traffic tickets and rolling wrappers. He puckered his lips and cocked an eyebrow, then turned and jogged back to the cottage.

A moment later, the detective slipped out the back door and dashed through the yard. He clambered between the trees, then side-shuffled the rugged slope towards Spearfish Creek. At the bottom, he heard the sickly trumpet of Porter's horn as he crawled through a highway viaduct that ran wet with trickling water.

Crouching and panting in a wash of damp sand and pebbles, he looked up and watched Porter's rusty delivery van rattle across the narrow overpass. O'Leary cinched his shoelaces and repositioned his holster, then dabbed sweat from his forehead with his sleeve before scrambling up the embankment to the Iron Creek Trail.

Fifteen minutes later, after jogging past the first mile marker, O'Leary slowed to a walk and stepped into the shade of a limestone rock outcropping to catch his breath. He wiped beads of sweat away from his eyes and surveyed the trail stretching beyond the canyon walls.

Before long, he resumed his jog, taking another ten minutes to reach the second mile marker above Pettigrew Gulch. With the glistening cyan water of Iron Creek Lake now in sight, the winded detective climbed halfway to the top of a rock formation to get an unobstructed view of the emerald valley.

Wedged between two pillars of dark granite slag, O'Leary studied the lake and its neighboring campground. A low sun warmed his face, and he shielded his eyes as he watched a pair of aging fly fishermen untangling their lines, packing to leave. From across the basin, a slight breeze lifted the smoke of a campfire, its woody scent mixing with something tangy and familiar. O'Leary slipped the handwritten note from his pocket and studied the cryptic message about cats and snakes. He sniffed the paper and nodded before returning it to his back pocket.

As the anglers rolled from sight, O'Leary surveyed the now deserted campground and picnic areas. Seconds later, he reversed his search and caught sight of a white convertible parked behind a cabin hidden in the shade of a poplar grove.

O'Leary took a breath and shifted his weight, preparing to climb from his hiding spot. He jerked to a halt and nudged himself back into the crevice. That's where he watched the largest man he'd ever seen duck his head and step onto the cabin's front porch. The bald, shirtless behemoth leaned against a post, talking into a cell phone. After a few seconds, the man pocketed his phone and snatched a pair of binoculars from a window ledge. The giant began examining the rocky ridge abutting Pettigrew Gulch. He made two slow passes with his field glasses, stopping each time to focus in O'Leary's direction.

O'Leary twisted sideways and buried himself deeper between the monoliths, holding his breath, remaining still. From the corner of his eye, he watched the brawny monster step back into the cabin, only to return seconds later, clutching the handle of a leather gun case. He placed the padded bag on the porch railing, ran a long zipper down the side, and extracted a combat-ready rifle fitted with a long-range scope.

The muscled-up sniper stepped into the yard and stretched out in the grass, propping the gun's barrel across the top of a sawed-off tree stump. It was then that Lefty Porter's ramshackle van came tottering along the lake road, towing a putrid cloud of dust and smoke. O'Leary watched Porter stumble from the van, shouting and waving his hands, then squatting behind the sniper, pointing towards the dark chasm that defended the sweating detective.

Without warning, from somewhere behind O'Leary's perch, a gunshot rang out, its report echoing across the basin. The bullet splintered the monster's tree stump, sending the giant scrambling to the cover of the cabin. Porter hit the ground and crawled beneath his delivery van. O'Leary heard the cocking of a rifle maybe twenty-five feet above his head. Another loud crack and the second shot ripped through the front tire on Porter's van.

Again, the clicking sounds of a reload as Stan emerged from the campground store, wearing a sleeveless flannel vest and swinging the barrels of a shotgun in front of his face. A third shot from the ridge shattered a log post inches from Stan's face, sending him sprawling to the porch and slinking back into the store. Following a few seconds of distant shouting, a bullet whistled past O'Leary's ear, snapping through the tree branches hanging above his head.

O'Leary didn't flinch as a second shot rocketed from the cabin's direction, the bullet ricocheting off a nearby boulder. After adjusting his position, the sniper fired a third shot over O'Leary's shoulder, striking with a thud something hidden in the rocks behind his view. Above the momentary quiet, he heard Porter's muffled shouts. "You get 'im?"

Norman's monster nodded and motioned with his rifle. "You gotta spare in the back?" Porter crawled from his hiding spot, brushed himself off, and flashed a thumbs up signal. The giant backed into the woods, shouting as he made his way towards the campground store. "The boys will be back soon—don't let those bitches outta your sight. Stan's gonna take me on a little hike."

O'Leary inspected the stillness of the valley, then pushed himself from between the pillars. Struggling to find a handhold, his fingers slipped across a syrupy warm trickle, oozing between the blackish rocks. The detective scrutinized the palm of hand, streaked with a red smear stretching towards his wrist. He wiped his hand on some dry leaves, then stripped Mood Deer's pistol from his holster. He scanned the basin a second time, then scaled the wall, using saplings and cracked boulders for footholds.

After inching along for several minutes, O'Leary flopped over the edge of a granite outcropping, landing against a slumped gunman, wheezing in a pool of blood. "Shit," he said. "This looks bad, real bad." He holstered his gun, shoved the gunman's rifle aside, and rolled the body over for a closer look.

The detective felt for a pulse, then sighed as he peeled back the hood of the gunman's blood-soaked sweatshirt. "Hmm, boy," he said, shaking his head. "Just had to go dressing like me, didn't ya?" A chilling breeze stirred the acrid scent of blood, mixing it with the faint essence of an ocean spray. O'Leary nodded and said, "Felt it from jump. You had your eagle eyes on us this whole time."

The gunman groaned as O'Leary propped her trembling shoulders against the lightning-scarred trunk of a crooked cedar. "Why?" He asked, leaning in to assess the gaping wound under her arm. Then he sighed as he shook his head. "The hell are we doin' here?"

She turned her face towards the quiet mountain lake, its ripples shimmering purple ahead of the setting sun. As the radiance faded from her watery eyes, she mustered a feeble shrug, then asked, "My boys alright?"

The detective whispered with a nod. "Safe and sound." She reached out and grabbed his hand, giving it a sodden, meager squeeze. O'Leary scooched closer, feeling the broken woman gasp and shudder. Then, without warning or fuss, Samantha's head drooped forward, sinking her chin into the crimson sluice that soaked her chest. O'Leary settled back and spent the next minute watching a majestic red-tailed hawk circle high against a cloudless sky, screeching to the heavens.

Dale Sommers curved the bill of his baseball cap and shifted in the pilot's seat, trying to shield the salmon-colored sun warming his windshield. He poked a crooked thumb over his shoulder and pointed at Jack Hughes, who sat focused, skimming his scribbles. "Well," Sommers said. "What did she say?"

Jack Hughes signaled with his index in the air, flipping through pages and circling some words and numbers scratched across his yellow pad. After watching the pilot fidget, Hughes chuckled, then cleared his throat. "Like almost every red-blooded woman between here and Yosemite, she wants to jump your bones."

"C'mon, man. You don't need to be like that?"

The lawyer leaned forward, tapping his pen on the armrest. "Hardesty's a sharp cookie, holding some face cards, but not showing her hand. I can't tell if she's looking out for you or trying to drop a piano on your head."

Sommers straightened the yolk, then stirred the air with his finger. "Cut to the chase, wouldja?"

Jack stuck the pen into the corner of his mouth and flipped to a different page. "She said the EPA's had their sights set on acquiring the Norman property for years. Something about watershed management and the American Rivers Restoration Act."

"I'm familiar with the program—good intentions, mediocre results. What's that got to do with me?"

Jack poked Sommers' shoulder with his pen. "On a hunch, Hardesty requested her own water tests after learning of Tommy Fulgham's disappearance. Susan Norman told her we've been snooping around, and she knows you threatened Colin Stroud about the DNR's missing water samples."

Sommers sputtered through his lips. "Woman covers her bases, doesn't she? I wouldn't consider my message to Stroud a threat, more like encouragement."

"Okay, whatever," Jack said, rolling his eyes. "Anyway. She said no one's seen Edward Norman for weeks, and Susan's no longer returning her calls. More pertinent to us, Hardesty knows you made a ridiculous, albeit informal, offer to buy Norman Farms. She asked me if there's something going on between you and Susan Norman, financial or otherwise? I told her she'd have to speak with you about that."

Sommers scratched at the back of his neck, then pulled a framed black-and-white picture from a cockpit cubby and passed it back to his lawyer. "If I gave you enough time and guesses, you'd be able to ID everyone in that picture." Sommers sipped from his water bottle and cleared his throat. "That's my father leaning against the barn. He and Jerry Reynolds hand-cut the posts and beams that bolstered that sturdy barn—a marvel of traditional engineering. See the trees and the native prairie in the background? No signs of flooding, no stinking piles of muck."

Sommers scanned the assorted gauges scattered across the instrument panel. "I'd like to restore that acreage to its past glory," he said, tapping the fuel gauge with his fingertip. "Those fields need some TLC, not a massive excavation project. You're about to warn me there's no money in conservation, but that's where my head's at. Sounds crazy, huh?"

Jack studied the photograph without speaking, so Sommers cocked his head towards the white cylinder tucked behind Lucky Dog's seat. "Speaking of crazy, what's in the tube?"

Jack handed the picture back to the pilot. "We'll get to that later," he said, waving the big man off. "Hardesty said Oasis Financial was trying to fast-track a closing date on Norman's property. North Dakota put the kibosh on the deal after auditors exposed Oasis' affiliation with China. Apparently, there's another bug in the soup."

Sommers reached back and ruffled Lucky Dog's ears. "Of course there is. Why am I not surprised?"

Jack exhaled as he rolled his eyes. "Keep your pants on there, partner. I'm just getting to the good stuff." He underlined an entry on his notepad. "During their title search, Oasis discovered a lien on the property, believed to be two point five million dollars."

Sommers adjusted his baseball hat and whistled. Lucky Dog perked her ears up, and Jack leaned forward in his seat. "That's right," he said. "For some reason, the lien holder's identity became classified, but Hardesty believes you have access to that privileged information."

Sommers sputtered and shook his head. "You know I don't," he said. "But I'll bet Greg O'Leary does." Then he remembered the modest, solitary man who lived in the tree-lined hollow along the river. He was certain Jack highlighted Jerry Reynold's name somewhere in his notes, but for the time being, the pilot held his tongue. "Who told Hardesty about the lien?" He asked.

"Maybe Norman. Hard to say for sure." Jack scratched at his chin, then tossed his yellow pad aside. Next, he grabbed his phone and began scrolling through his text messages.

Sommers peeked up at Jack through the convex mirror hanging above the windshield. "Anything from O'Leary or Moon Deer?"

Jack shook his head, then stared through the window for a long, weighty minute. "Things have gotten about as murky as that river down there," he said, puckering his lips into a pout. "One more thing, and Hardesty wants us to keep this under our hats. She says the Norman water samples are among the worst she's ever seen, bad enough to condemn the property for years. She's not pulling the trigger on shutting things down, at least not until after she sips coffee with you. My guess is there's some government grift at play here. Something she can't share over the phone. The clock's ticking, big man."

Sommers nodded, steering the plane south of an expansive cloud bank. He spent a quiet minute listening to the hum of the propeller while recalling his run-in with Susan Norman's monsters. The pilot looked over his shoulder and counted with his fingers. "First, call your wife. She's an expert at pulling strings. Ask her what she knows about the lien holder. Second, ask her to get Lindstrom's old bones outta that bed. And third, she's gotta convince Hardesty to get a Hazmat crew out to Norman Farms."

Jack circled some of his chicken scratch, then tapped a speed dial number on his phone and waited for a connection. He nudged the pilot's chair and shrugged. "Then what?"

The pilot twisted in his seat and locked eyes with his lawyer. "I know where they'll find Edward Norman."

Three hours later, Jack stirred from a restless slumber, his iPhone buzzing in his lap. He rubbed his eyes and cleared his throat. "Talk to me, Jules. Whatcha got?" He listened for a minute, then said, "Whoa, hang on a sec." Then he grabbed his notepad and felt around for his pen. Lucky Dog snored in the seat across from him. He pinched her nose and shushed her, then turned back to his phone. "Okay, got you on speakerphone. Go ahead."

Sommers caught only bits and pieces of their conversation as Jack's ballpoint pen kicked into overdrive, trying to keep up with Julie's intensity. Lucky Dog slinked from her seat and stretched, dispensing an offensive fart in Jack's direction. She twitched her tail, then stepped to the cockpit and curled up on the floor under the pilot's seat.

Jack waved the notepad in front of his nose. "The turbulence is something else up here," he said, scowling at the pooch, who cocked her eyebrows at him. After several minutes of frenzied note taking, Jack clicked his pen and said, "Okay, I'll tell him. Good work, hon." Then he signed off. "I will. Love you too."

Sommers shifted in his seat, reaching down to massage Lucky's bushy neck. Then he peeked in the mirror at Jack. "Whatever you're paying her isn't near enough. Gimme the skinny."

Jack forced a grin and pointed his pen at the pilot. "My wife's compensation is lavish and diversified in ways you could only imagine." He jotted another note, then leaned forward in his seat, pointing his chin at the dog. "She told me Lindstrom said you have questionable taste in women, but that doesn't make you stupid. I told her the jury's till out on that one." Sommers rolled his eyes and shook a fist behind his head.

Jack pointed the pen at his notes and nodded. "They're just bustin' your chops because you were right," he said. "Jules said it took a cadaver dog all of thirty seconds to find Norman's body submerged in the waste retention pond. Talk about a crappy way to go. Lindstrom says Edward wasn't sleeping alone. The feds have unleashed their hounds—got Susan Norman and Jerry Reynolds in their crosshairs."

The lawyer folded a piece of chewing gum into his mouth, then flipped the page. "But wait, there's more. Cops picked up three Venezuelan illegals in Moorhead. Surveillance cameras and GPS data have them linked to the Main Street Massacre."

"Drug cartel?" Sommers asked.

Jack shook his head, then underlined something in his notes. "Worse," he said. "Child traffickers. Jules said independent media outlets have these assholes connected to the Numbers Gang, the Dakota Sioux Syndicate, and Oasis Financial." Sommers adjusted his baseball cap and shook his head. "That's not all," Jack said. "ICE wanted to prosecute and deport the scumbags, but the locals let 'em go. ICE claims the sanctuary clowns ignored Miranda and gave those goddamn newcomers fresh cellphones and loaded debit cards, then said '*adios amigos.*'"

Sommers sighed and tightened his grip on the yolk. "I'm sorry I dragged you into this mess." He pressed the throttle forward and pointed the airplane's nose west, straight towards the shadowy hills looming in the distance. "Samantha's always been ultra-secretive," he said. "So deep in the woods, she couldn't see through the trees."

Jack's phone buzzed like an alarm clock seven or eight times. He skimmed through a new series of text messages, then opened a report from his wife. The lawyer read to himself for a few minutes. Then he shook his head, placing his hand on Sommers' shoulder. "Julie got into the files Lindstrom copied from the casino's database. She guessed right, because that's her superpower. Anyway, she cracked into Wenner's encrypted financial folder." He jotted another note on his legal pad, then shifted his attention back to the small screen. "Behind Edward's back, Susan Norman contracted with the DSS. Wenner facilitated the crypto transactions and laundered the money through his business accounts."

Jack swiped the screen up and furrowed his brow. "The files show Big Bill and his cronies profited from the sale of abducted children, natives, and detached illegals. Some documents mention a growing demand for child slaves and sex surrogates. Julie says DHS found Ro Lin Shui's laptop loaded with kiddie porn. Your guy, Colin Stroud, stars in the most explicit scenes, featuring Dirty Dean Rivers and the Chicken Man. On a side note, Julie says nobody's seen Peg McFarland since we took her to the bank."

Sommers furrowed his brow and pursed his lips. He sat speechless, staring through the windshield, connecting the heinous dots and arriving at some grim realizations.

Jack ran his fingers through his hair, then shook his head before picking at the whiskers on his chin. "The DSS voided their most recent contract with Wenner, saying the client's offer pales against a ransom windfall. Bottom line, Susan Norman, with Wenner's help, tried to purchase a unique child from the bad guys, but the whole shitty deal fell apart when the boy and his mother went missing."

Sommers reversed his hat, and his eyes grew wide. He slammed his fist against the fuselage, then with a low growl in his voice, he said, "Jack, tell me you're not talking about my boy. Tell me you don't mean Noah!"

Lucky Dog tucked her tail and slinked back to her seat. Across the aisle, Sommers' friend gazed out the side window, watching silvery drops of condensation dance by. He clicked his pen closed one last time and shook his head. "I'm sorry, partner. I can't."

Chapter 30
3 AM

"She said, "It's cold outside" and she hands me a raincoat."

"I need your phone," Dale Sommers said, reaching over his shoulder and feeling the weight of the world squeezing his chest. Jack Hughes sat staring at his yellow pad, oblivious to the pilot's request. The pilot snapped his fingers and Lucky Dog's ears perked up. "Phone, please. Now!"

Jack fluttered his eyes and rubbed the fatigue creases from his face, then slapped his iPhone into Sommers' cavernous palm.

Sommers checked his airspeed, straightened the yolk, then spent the next thirty seconds fumbling with his lawyer's iPhone. "Hey buddy," he said, at last. "You mind opening this stubborn gadget?" He passed the phone back, then exhaled a soggy, exasperated sigh. "And dial Grumpy's number, wouldja?" Jack made a rapid-fire series of swipes and taps, furrowed his eyebrows, and handed the phone back to his ham-handed friend.

The pilot extended the crackling speakerphone away from his face and heard an old man coughing and clearing his throat with a sloppy spit. After a few seconds of profane stammering, Grumpy said, "Either I'm being audited or that big fucker's dead. Which is it?"

Sommers glanced at the screen with disbelief, then rolled his eyes. His uncle, despite daily practice, never seemed to reach the depth of his crudity. In the background, he heard a dog barking, water splashing, and a child's infectious laughter. "Grumps, it's Dale. I've only got a minute or two, so listen up."

"We've got a dead pool goin' at DeRoxe," Grumpy said after making a whistling sound. "Shit, I guess this means I just lost five bucks."

"Sorry to disappoint you," Sommers said, shaking his head. "How's things at the lake?"

"Goddamn jet skiers are ruining the fishing vibe. I told the Peterson Boys to shoot a few of 'em so we can catch a basket of sunnies for a fry."

Sommers nodded, recognizing one of his uncle's superpowers was bossing people around with his outlandish demands. "What about Noah? Is he okay?"

"Heck, yea. Kid's like a rolling river—never stops stirring. He's swimming between the docks."

"Swimming?" Sommers asked, grinning and scratching at the back of his neck.

"Like a fuckin' fish," Grumpy said. "Your mother's been working with him damn near every day. Before long, the kid's gonna be one of them rescue divers with the Coast Guard." The old timer wheezed, then caught his breath. "Lemme tell ya, a ton of bricks is gonna drop on your noggin when you realize you missed the whole goddamn show. 'Sides, Gracie's not gonna be 'round forever."

After a moment of suffocating reflection, Sommers pursed his lips and shifted the phone to his other hand. His boorish uncle had a unique way of cutting him to the marrow. "Yea, well. Give 'em my love. I'll be home in two days, three days tops."

Grumpy snorted, then coughed. "Heard that one before—not holding our breaths here, partner."

"Grumps, I need you to focus for a minute," Sommers said, turning the plane left, then leveling off. "Joy's in trouble. Word on the street is that some evil men are holding her hostage. Jack and I are flying out to Spearfish to get her back."

"Hostage? The hell's that about?"

"Julie and Lindstrom uncovered evidence from a kingpin's computer. Apparently, Lilly foiled a kidnapping plot by dropping Noah in Lac Clair. The DSS killed her for it. Joy's one of only a few people who knows where Noah's been swimming. You know her as good as anyone—she won't talk. Plus, I think they've lured O'Leary into a trap."

After several seconds of weighty silence, Grumpy cleared his throat again. "Okay, big guy," he said, gravel in his voice. "What do you need from me?"

"Keep Noah under wraps. No trips into town, no cinnamon rolls or ice cream cones. Keep your eyes peeled for strangers, shifty-eyed migrants who look out of place—Venezuelans covered in tattoos, Somalis camping on the bluff. Don't be a hero. Call Sheriff Williams if you see anything suspicious. And whatever you do, don't alarm my mother. She'll twist herself into knots if she hears Noah could be in danger."

"Lucky for you, the boy's surrounded by avid backers of the 2nd amendment, and Phelps the Wonder Pup never leaves his side." Grumpy waited for some static to clear the line. "Bob and Al just got back from a gun show in Crookston. The fuckin' illegals gonna need nukes 'cause those hayseeds have armed themselves to the hilt. They're itchin' to blast the shit outta anything that moves."

Back in seat one, Jack nodded. "I like the sound of that."

Sommers waved him off, then brought the phone closer to his mouth. "We're not playing around here. No craziness, no stupidity. I know how you guys get sometimes."

"Don't go gettin' your panties in a bunch," Grumpy said with a snarl. "The boy's safe. Now, what you need to do is get blood-spittin' mean. Kick some redskin ass and fetch our girl. And for cripes' sake, get back here in one piece, wouldja? The evergreens 'round the cemetery need trimming."

"That's the plan," Sommers said as he slipped the old photograph from the center console. "Say, one last thing. When was the last time you saw Jerry Reynolds?" The phone's static-filled lull spoke volumes, and the focused pilot nodded to confirm his hunch. "Grumps, you there?" He asked, but the old timer clicked off the call amidst a cacophony of grunts and coughs. Sommers shrugged as he tossed the cellphone into his lawyer's lap.

"Piece of work, that uncle of yours," Jack said with a half-hearted chuckle.

Sommers reached back and ruffled Lucky's ears. "Thank heavens, the Good Lord broke the mold after him." He tapped the fuel gauge and adjusted his hat. "Do me another favor, wouldja? Call Black Hills Aero—get Otto Schuler on the line."

"Aye, aye, captain." Following another fit of swipes and taps, Jack waited for the call to connect, then handed his phone back to the determined pilot.

Sommers peered at a reddish sun sagging towards a dark band of rocks and trees. He thought about the striking terrain and the warm, leathery feel of the old west. Then he shook his head, realizing the grand scenery didn't carry the same luster it had just a few days earlier. Otto picked up after three rings. "Schuler here."

"Otto, it's Sommers. We're running on fumes, but coming in hot with a moody nose wheel. 'Bout twenty minutes out. Can you have a car ready?"

Schuler muttered some tangled complaints, then exhaled a deep sigh. "Runway 31 is clear until tomorrow morning," he said. "Set your GPS coordinates for one-three-five. PM updrafts are gonna rattle your nuts a bit. Taxi back on 13 to my service bay. I've got your struts." Schuler fumbled with the phone and snarled at someone walking too close to his tool racks. "Sommers? I'll alert Ellsworth—we'll be watching for you." Then he clicked off the call.

Seventeen minutes later, the pilot saw the sleepy Clyde Ice Airfield resting against the northern footholds of the Black Hills. The plane's engine sputtered once, then twice, and Sommers felt his propeller skip a beat. He glanced over his shoulder to see Jack's long face pressed against the window. The engine missed again and Sommers tapped his thumbs on the yolk. "C'mon baby. Just a few more miles."

The small Cessna shuddered as the engine loped and grunted through its last few revolutions. Sommers reversed his hat and adjusted the microphone on his headset. "SPF Ellsworth. This is Sommers, C1690. Two minutes out. We're experiencing engine failure, not gonna make 31. Please advise, over."

Jack leaned forward in his seat, watching the propeller slowing to a lazy whirl. "Are you fucking kidding me? Safer than driving, my ass!" Lucky Dog paced circles in her seat before curling into a ball and flipping her fluffy tail over her eyes. Sommers waved Jack off, and with a flurry, pushed buttons and flipped switches along the plane's instrument panel.

"Copy C1690, this is SPF Ellsworth. Brooks speaking. We've got eyes on you. Are you able to control the plane? Over."

"Copy that Brooks. Besides airspeed, yes," Sommers said. "Heavy controls. We're in a glide. Short on time. Over."

"Copy that Sommers. Change heading to zero-nine-two. Follow the Interstate—come straight in on runway eight. Over."

"Copy Brooks. Isn't eight a turf runway? Over."

"Copy that. Affirmative. Schuler informed us of your situation. Emergency crew's standing by. Over."

"Copy that Brooks. Not very reassuring, but here goes nothing. Over." Sommers furrowed his brow and pushed the yolk forward, increasing their speed and angle of descent. He aligned I-90 with the center windshield post and shot the gap between Elkhorn Ridge and Moonrise Mountain.

Through some white noise, Brooks said, "You're doing fine, Sommers. Negligible headwinds. Keep the nose light, the runway is in good shape. No end markers, dig in with your brakes or you'll end up in shit's creek. Over."

"Huh, copy that," the pilot said in closing, his voice fluctuating from the harsh vibrations.

Sommers peeked over his shoulder to see Jack tucking the hairy pooch under a blanket, then cinching the seat belt around the trembling bundle. "Back in your seat, Jack!" Sommers jabbed an angry finger at the vacant spot in the first row. "Strap in and cover your head. This ain't no drill—do it now!"

"Damn, you sure get bossy when things go haywire." Jack said, crouching in his seat and clasping his hands behind his head. "Have I ever told you how much I hate flying?"

Sommers shook his head, ignoring his friend's satirical remarks. "I thought you didn't care for dogs."

Jack, his voice muffled between his knees, said, "Never said that. I said bitches don't like me."

Lucky peeked from beneath her blanket, and Sommers nodded. "Okay, guess I'll buy that. But I gotta tell you, dogs are excellent judges of character." The pilot pressed back in his seat and tightened his harness. "Hang on, gonna get bumpy. Five, four, three…"

Two protracted seconds later, the single-engine Cessna bounced with an explosive slam, jostling every single one of its rivets and screws. A second bounce rattled Sommers' teeth and shook the headset from his ears. The tires howled, fighting to find their bite. Sommers feathered the brakes, and the plane shuddered and shimmied along the short runway. Flashing emergency lights loomed ahead, and the pilot leaned harder onto the brakes. Duffle bags and flight gear tumbled into the aisle and a lone white cylinder flopped on the floor, rolling to a stop under the pilot's seat.

The quaking G-forces subsided and Sommers' trusty bird lurched to a stop just a few feet from the uncut banks of False Bottom Creek. Jack sat up, looked around, then let out a whoop. Lucky Dog popped her head from beneath the blanket and let loose a spirited woof.

Sommers grabbed the framed photograph from the console, then looked up to see Otto Schuler standing before the motionless propeller with his arms folded across his chest, and a gnarled yellow pencil hanging from the corner of his mouth. Sommers flashed a two-fingered salute along the bill of his hat, then allowed himself a small grin. Schuler stood like an angry boss, puckering his lips and shaking his head.

After a few minutes of scuffling and packing, Lucky bounded down the steps with her tail wagging. She circled and sniffed the small gathering, then turned away and squatted over a clump of wilting weeds. Sommers stepped onto the grass runway, carrying two canvas bags and a well-traveled cardboard tube tucked under his arm. He shook hands with Schuler as Jack tiptoed his way onto the air steps, stretching his arms out wide. "Terra fucking firma," he said with a shout that carried across Spearfish Basin.

Schuler lifted his chin and asked, "What's his problem?"

Sommers shrugged while gazing at the scrub-lined runnel flowing just beyond the landing strip. "Lawyer."

Schuler tucked his pencil behind his ear, then nodded. "Ahh, I see."

Then, without warning, the front landing gear let out a groan and crumpled, sending the plane's nose collapsing to the ground. Jack stumbled and staggered down the remaining three steps, landing hard on the turf with a painful-sounding grunt. Lucky Dog trotted over and licked his forehead. After a curse-filled moment, Jack sat up, shaking his head and clutching his lower leg. "I hate goddamn airplanes. I really do." He extended his hand and peered up at the overgrown pilot, silhouetted against a high, fading sky. "Can we go home now? I'll even drive."

Otto waved his hands at the rumpled airplane, then stopped to scribble a note into his pocket-sized notepad. "Leave it. I'll get 'er later." He nudged Sommers' hip pocket. "Gonna cost you."

"Already has," Sommers said, scrunching his nose. "Know anyone who wants to buy an airplane? Low hours, professionally maintained."

Schuler rolled his eyes, and they lifted the defeated lawyer to his feet. They carried him and his sprained ankle to the waiting SUV. Jack whined and complained every strep of the way. The big man opened the back door and Lucky Dog jumped into Jack's seat, curling up and settling in for another ride. Schuler glanced over at the pilot and winked. Sommers nodded and bit his lip to keep from laughing.

A majestic red-tailed hawk swooped in close, then circled high over Iron Creek Lake and soared away. From his lookout above Pettigrew Gulch, Greg O'Leary watched Flannel Stan and the Sniper Monster back from the campground store in Stan's shiny new pickup. They rolled away, windows down, north and then east on Tinton Road. The two kidnappers left Porter behind, kneeling in the crushed gravel, ratcheting a spare tire onto his creepy delivery van. O'Leary held his breath and extended his index finger across the trigger, training the front sight of Samantha's rifle at the back of Porter's greasy head.

The detective exhaled and shook his head, then glanced over his shoulder at Samantha's blood-soaked body slumped against a twisted cedar. He shifted his gaze to the cabin tucked in the woods and lowered the gun's barrel from harm. O'Leary turned away and leaned against a pitted boulder, listening to the faint sounds of the breeze and water trickling from the valley's northern rim.

With daylight running short, O'Leary scouted the area above the hiking trail, squeezing himself through chasms and crawling under the brush. All of a sudden, he froze after coming face to face with a rattlesnake that was warming itself on a sun-drenched sill. Five feet long and coiled to strike, the leery rattler twitched its curly-q tail and flicked its forked tongue eighteen inches from O'Leary's nose. The detective backed away, inch by inch, giving a wide berth to the stealthy serpent and its balmy roost.

O'Leary slinked a safe distance from the venomous fangs before bumping into a moss-covered slab dripping with cool mountain runoff. He craned his neck and discovered the entrance to a narrow cave hidden behind the limestone chunk. After clearing debris from the opening, the detective scrambled back to his perch, where he watched Porter toss the car jack into the back of his rig. The grubby slasher slipped his knife from the glove compartment and slammed the door, then stomped off to the secluded cabin.

A streak of purple sunset provided just enough light for O'Leary to search Samantha's tactical pack. He found a P238 loaded with a six-round clip, boxes of extra ammunition, and a pair of night-vision goggles. Tucked into a side pocket, he discovered a Swiss Army knife and a small envelope with Sommers' name written across the flap. O'Leary sniffed the card and studied the meticulous calligraphy, then packed everything away. He heard scurrying footfalls and a man's pain-filled shouts, followed by the firecracker-like pop from a handgun that echoed below his sightline.

Wasting no time, the detective hefted Samantha's bloodstained body into a fireman's carry. He tucked her rifle under his opposite arm. Weighed down and focusing to keep his balance, O'Leary clambered back to the narrow cave. He knelt and brushed a lock of red hair away from Samantha's pale blue face, then he winced as he wrenched her stiffening shoulders and hips through the narrow opening. The evening gloom closed in as he concealed the entry with some rocks and broken branches. Then O'Leary backtracked, sweeping the dust and grit with a pine bough, erasing Sam's blood trail.

The angry shouts trailed off through the canyon and O'Leary muscled his way onto a ledge overlooking the hiking trail. He slid the pack and the rifle away from the edge, then stretched out flat on his stomach, catching his breath. A full moon scaled the eastern peaks, and an owl hooted from high in the pines. O'Leary, yielding to his weariness, folded his arms under his chin and let his heavy eyelids sag.

A short while later, and without warning, from somewhere rooted in the shadows, a huge hand gripped O'Leary's face, covering his nose and mouth. The hulk pinned the detective's arm behind his back, grinding his chest into the cool limestone slab and squeezing the last of his breath from his lungs. Fighting against the weight and the murk, O'Leary thrashed and kicked until a voice, deep and familiar, whispered in his ear, "Shhh, don't move—not one sound. There's a couple of bad guys with guns combing the area. Two more—right below us. One of 'em's snakebit, and I mean that literally."

"You're lucky," Greg O'Leary said with a whisper, manipulating his jaw with his fingers. "Two more seconds, I would've busted outta that hold and kicked your ass." Sommers nodded without speaking, peering over the edge, surveying the valley in the burgeoning moonlight. O'Leary gave him a lighthearted shove. "How the hell did you find me? Where's Jack?"

"Some of Moon Deer's tracking skills must've rubbed off on

me," Sommers said with a wink. "Jack and his bum wheel are back at the house with Lucky Dog. He's churning through his notes and making calls—moving the chess pieces 'round. We're bringing this thing to a close. And right soon."

O'Leary patted Sommers on the back and nodded. "Well. Never was much for eyewash, but I'm sure glad to see you."

Sommers sat up and pointed towards the park road. "Look. We've got company." Helped by the moonlight, they watched a black pickup truck pull in and park in front of the campground store. Lefty Porter stepped from the cabin and greeted two Native men, one tall and one short, with animated hand gestures and profanity-laced shouts. Porter's tirade soon ran out of steam, and the three men leaned against the porch railing, smoking cigarettes.

A few minutes after that, Flannel Stan and the Sniper Monster returned empty-handed. The store clerk dragged his injured leg along for a few strides before collapsing in the gravel turnaround. Porter scrambled to his van and rummaged through the back, producing a first aid kit. The giant sniper motioned to the rocky ridge where Sommers and O'Leary hid in the shadow of a red cedar.

They watched the two natives wave Porter off before flicking their cigarette butts into the weeds. Then the tall Indian grabbed Stan by the collar, lifted him up and shook him as the short Indian motioned towards the cabin. The short Indian pulled a pistol from the small of his back. He shot Stan in the chest, then in the head from point blank range. Acting as if nothing had happened, the two natives climbed back into their truck and drove away. After another minute of complaining, Porter and the giant sniper heaved Stan's lifeless body into a garbage dumpster behind the campground store. Their argument continued as they trudged into the woods.

"Snakes?" Sommers asked.

"Goddamn barbarians directing a freak show," O'Leary said, nodding his head. He tapped Sommers' shoulder and pointed to the cabin. "Joy's in there—gotta be. Hope to hell she's alive. Could be another woman in there, too. I've been over this a million times and still can't figure out their motive."

"There's a ransom demand floating around here somewhere. We just haven't found it." Sommers pointed his chin at Porter's van and said, "They couldn't break Moon Deer and they tried to grab you for leverage. Think about it, they wouldn't have left a numskull behind to look after dead bodies."

O'Leary nodded with his lips puckered. "Circumstantial evidence is all I got, but that numskull cut Bud Wolcott to ribbons with a filet knife."

Sommers dropped his head, then took a deep breath and turned to look past his shoulder. The ivory moonbeams washed over his partner, and the big man noticed large splotches of blood staining the detective's hoodie. "Jeez, did I do that to you?"

O'Leary inspected his clothing and shook his head. "Blood's not mine." He reached in and felt around the satchel, then handed Sommers the small envelope. "Mistaken identity. I should've told you straightaway. I'm sorry, man."

Sommers surveyed the campground before turning and inspecting the rocky ridge stretching above his head. He began piecing things together as he flipped the card and read his name in the moonlight. He waved the paper under his nose and took a sniff. Then, after looking up and searching the stars, he nodded and asked, "Where is she?" O'Leary pointed his thumb over his shoulder at the dark crevice splitting a towering monolith. Sommers pursed his lips and nodded again before opening the envelope and removing the scented card.

The big man read the words in silence, then looked out across the valley, gazing at the moon and stars reflecting off the glassy surface of Iron Creek Lake. He'd admired the heavens in this way countless times before. He turned and squinted his eyes at the ridge rising above his head, its ghostly face looking angular and familiar. Then he leaned out over the edge and shuddered against a chilling breeze.

Not surprised and not distraught, Sommers recalled Moon Deer's gruesome warnings. He searched the depth of his heart and felt disappointment, a sad realization his son might carry the same heavy water he'd lugged around for decades. Sommers waved the fragrant paper under his nose and closed his eyes, then sighed and passed the poignant message to his friend.

O'Leary tilted the card towards the light and whispered the handwritten words. *"We knew this would be a short flight, one way with plenty of chop. Come what may, I'll sleep sound, knowing my boys are safe."*

Sommers stood and fastened his tool belt around his waist. He pulled his American Ax from its sheath and inspected the polished hickory handle glinting in the moonbeams. The big lumberjack felt the grain of the wood as he flexed his grip, remembering the fire and the rain raging amidst the rugged Idaho Sawtooths. Then the big lumberjack ran his thumbnail along the razor's edge. He thought about life. And death.

Greg O'Leary extended his arm towards the valley and unfurled the fingers of his clenched fist. "Justice," he said, showing six bullets gleaming in his palm. "I believe it was Robert E. Lee who said, 'Ya don't wound a snake, ya kill it.'"

Sommers, following a somber moment of silence, sheathed his ax. "It was Harriet Tubman." Then he adjusted his baseball cap and lifted his chin towards the dark cabin, nuzzled among the trees. "Either way, we've got a score to settle," he said, and began climbing down from their lookout. "Time to finish this. How 'bout we get started?"

O'Leary glanced over his shoulder at the narrow cave, then shook his head as he packed his gear. "For real. How the hell did you find me up here?"

Sommers tried, but couldn't hide his smirk. "Stretched out on your breadbasket."

Chapter 31
It's All I Can Do

"One too many times I fell over you."

The offbeat sounds of the mountain evening made Lucky Dog restless, which put her senses on high alert. Agitated water surged along the bedrock of Spearfish Canyon and a fitful breeze pulsed through the porch screens. The vigilant pooch curled up on the sofa, crooking her nostrils and twitching her ears. She leaned against Jack Hughes' side, as he was the only warm bolster available. A throw pillow upon a coffee table propped up the lawyer's swollen ankle, and a bag of frozen peas chilled his bloated shin. Jack's .38 Special shimmered atop an end table, inches from his right hand. He glanced up at the muted TV, watching the Broncos and Steelers jog to their respective locker rooms, tied at half-time.

Jack, fighting fatigue, closed his eyes and pinched the bridge of his nose while his cell phone, charging cable, and dog-eared yellow pad rested in a stack on his lap. He'd placed a half-dozen calls, and despite the spotty reception, he was getting a clearer picture of the lawless viper's nest Sommers' posse had stumbled into. He felt an eerie quiet settle across the grid, no signals from Sommers, nothing but crickets from O'Leary or Moon Deer.

Jack's next call went to his wife, Julie, asking her to collaborate with D.T. Hardesty. He explained how modern Pembina County had become a financial cesspool, dripping with graft and corruption. Norman Farms sat smack dab in the middle of political infighting and corporate greed. Jack wanted Sommers' motivations communicated. The big lumberjack's lavish offer for Norman Farms wasn't driven by resource exploitation. Conservation and historical restoration occupied the core of his motivations.

Julie Hughes, already a step ahead of her husband, reported that Hardesty convinced the Department of Homeland Security to raid the offices at Oasis Financial. The investigators verified Ro Lin Shui spent the previous three years filling his hard drive with kiddie porn. Photographs and meta-data implicated Colin Stroud in an extensive human trafficking operation, preying upon Native American girls. Julie conveyed her cringe-filled disgust with a flurry of obscenities, saying there was tangible evidence the two pedofiles were lovers. Jack shook his head while he drew jagged arrows and scribbled unsavory reports in the margins of his notes.

Jack's next call went to Ted Lindstrom. The retired sheriff's post-concussion night vision remained spotty. Ted intended to spend the evening at Jerry Reynold's place, then drive down to Lake Victoria in the morning. Jack relayed Sommers' suspicions that ol' Jerry was sleeping in the hangar across the road from Grumpy's cabin. The solitary veteran likely parked both the notorious black pickup truck and his turquoise '66 Chevy in the Cessna's service bay.

Although an official statement had yet to be released, Lindstrom had seen dental records verifying the charred remains found in Norman's burn pile belonged to Tommy Fulgham and Manny Rodriguez. Lindstrom also summarized the county coroner's preliminary report. Edward Norman died from blunt force trauma, not from drowning and not from what everyone assumed, a drug overdose. Lindstrom said the North Dakota Bureau of Criminal

Investigation exhumed four corpses from Norman's waste retention pond. One agent told him the deceased would be impossible to identify, speculating the bones belonged to transient laborers who had witnessed too much.

After Julie and Lindstrom, Jack called Clayton Stearns. He informed the judge about his ties to Greg O'Leary and made calculated inquiries about the recent crime spree in Lawrence County. Stearns was reluctant to provide details over the phone, but felt confident about O'Leary's eventual exoneration. Stearns mentioned the feds had been snooping around Jo Douglass and Lefty Porter for months, but nobody could say why.

Lucky Dog's ears perked up, and a low grumble boiled in her chest. Jack tapped the remote, turning the TV off. In the darkness, he massaged the dog's neck, then sat up and grabbed his pistol from the table. Lucky let out another hushed growl as a stealthy intruder fussed at the back door.

A tall man took two steps onto the screened-in porch and Lucky let out a single high-pitched woof. The stranger stood silhouetted in front of the moonlight illuminating the backyard. Jack held the dog back with his left hand and aimed the gun with his right. "Take one more step. I'll let this beast loose. She'll gnaw on your legs while this .38 carves your skull into a salad trough. Show your hands."

The tall man with slicked back hair raised his hands to his shoulders. "Mike, Ike. That you?"

The dog curled her lips and let out another resonant growl. Jack shushed her, then asked the raider, "Who the hell's Mike and Ike, and for that matter, who the hell are you?" Jack waved his gun, making it glint in the dim light. "You better have a damn good reason for sneaking around up here. Let's hear it."

The tall man rocked on his heels and tilted his head towards the yard. "Name's Thorne. I'm meeting a couple of associates up here, looking for a fugitive. He's supposed to be wearing a monitor—dropped off the grid earlier this afternoon. This was the last place it pinged. I'm packing nothing but an iPhone. Can I lower my hands now?"

Jack shook his head. "Keep 'em where I can see 'em." Then he leaned forward, still holding the scruff of Lucky's neck. "Well, Mr. Thorne, you double dipping as a bondsman these days? Seems you know your way around here in the dark. Why is that?"

Thorne shrugged, then peeked up at his wristwatch. "I'm the executor of William Wenner's estate. I'm sure I have more right to be here than you, Mr. uhhh…"

"Jack Hughes. I represent Dale Sommers and Greg O'Leary. They're not here. But you knew that already, didn't you?" Lucky slipped from the sofa, and Jack smoothed the hair standing on the back of her neck, holding her close. "You're five minutes too late. I just had an enlightening conversation with Judge Stearns. I'm not letting you in here without a warrant—better call your boys, tell 'em the meeting's canceled."

Thorne shook his head and pointed at Jack. "I know why you're here. Four people are dead, maybe more by now. O'Leary and Sommers are gonna get the needle for 'em. You're outta your league here, Hughes. And your simpleton friends are way out over their skis. You're all going down. It's just a matter of when, not if." Thorne's cell phone buzzed in his pocket. "That's them. Mind if I take this?"

Jack stood, keeping his .38 pointed at Thorne's chest, grasping Lucky by the scruff of her neck. "Go ahead. Put 'em on speaker. This should be entertaining."

Thorne pulled the phone from his pocket and tapped his thumbs on the screen. He put the phone near his chin. "Are you on your way? We've got company." Jack furrowed his brow and thrust the gun's muzzle at the tall intruder.

The voice on the phone, raspy and irritated, said, "Well, shit. Cry me a river, why dontcha? We've got our own problems over here."

A second voice, deep and humorless, from the background said, "Goes without saying, Thorne. No truck, no kid, no fuckin' dice."

Then the first voice said, "Wenner promised us Hammer's truck and thirty-three percent. Times are tough, and with Numbers and the fat man outta the picture, let's make it an even fifty-fifty. Forget the goddamn truck. Let the pedos have the kid." A tense silence hung on the line. "Campground, one hour. Bring the cabbage—every fuckin' cent. Your boy Stan's got a splitting headache—won't be joining us. Don't be late."

Thorne snarled into his phone. "Problems? What fucking problems?" The call disconnected, and he glared at the small screen, shaking his head in its bluish glow.

Jack snickered, tracing a wavy line in the air with his pistol. "Snakes got you by the short hairs, don't they?" He cocked his head towards the dog, then pointed the gun back at Thorne's chest. "Neither of us wanna hear your whining. I suggest you haul your ass back to Spearfish, get your shredder fired up, then take a long last look around your office." Thorne wagged a finger, but Jack interrupted him, cocking the hammer on his gun. "Your boys are waiting on you, counselor."

Lucky let out a small bark. Thorne scowled at the dog for a second, then glowered at Jack for two seconds more. Then he backed from the porch and disappeared into the night. Jack lowered his gun and ruffled his companion's ears. "Guess we told him, didn't we? Simpletons? That's a new one." The protective pup looked up at the lawyer and twitched her tail.

———◆———

Sommers crouched in the woods above Pettigrew Gulch. He watched the truck's red taillights, like the devilish eyes of a serpent, creep away on Tinton Road. The big lumberjack thought about Jack and Lucky as he stood and cinched his tool belt. He turned and observed Norman's sniper monster, grabbing his rifle and stomping towards the campground store. Next, he watched the grimy bait man wander down to the boat launch, where he lit a joint and puffed his insolence towards a cloudless starlit sky. Thinking this was his best chance, Sommers signaled up to O'Leary's shadowy perch, then made his way through the trees, outflanking the kidnappers and the shimmering lake below.

A short time later, Sommers leaned against the cool, damp logs of the cabin, catching his breath. He closed his eyes and listened, allowing his other senses to absorb the subtle vibrations of life. Convinced he heard breathing. Sommers reversed his baseball hat and scanned the surrounding yard. Then he crawled across the porch, feeling for creaky deck boards, inching his way towards the front door left ajar by Porter.

After another fifteen feet, the big lumberjack crossed the threshold and closed the bulky wooden door with a light touch. He pivoted and let his eyes adjust to the gloom. The air hung thick with the stench of intimidation. Joy Moon Deer sat in an uncharacteristic stupor, mottled with cuts and bruises. The bad guys taped and lashed her to a wrought-iron chair. Susan Norman, her allure stripped away like a weather-beaten flower, sat gagged and blindfolded in an adjoining seat.

While Norman struggled against the biting cordage, Sommers peeked through the clouded windows, then felt for Moon Deer's pulse. Relieved she was alive, he went to work removing her bloodstained restraints. She let out a groggy moan as her body slumped to the rough, timbered floor. Sommers stretched her out and examined her for broken bones. Next, he pried her eyelids open and saw her dark pupils dilated and rolled back into her head.

Not wasting any time, he removed Norman's blindfold and held an index finger to his lips. Her eyes grew wide and tears spilled down her cheeks. Sommers sliced the ropes from her wrists and ankles, leaving the silver tape across her mouth. "We're getting outta here. Gotta hurry. Can you walk?" Norman flashed a thumbs up sign and nodded, then she threw her arms around the lumberjack's brawny neck.

Sommers stepped back and peeled himself from her grip. "No time for that," he said, glancing out the windows. He motioned to Moon Deer and shook his head. "She's unconscious. What'd they give her?"

Norman winced as she peeled the sticky duct tape from her face. She shrugged and said, "Don't know. I thought she was dead. Those fucking animals tied me up—scared the shit outta me. I tell ya, this whole goddamn world has gone insane."

Sommers adjusted his baseball cap, then he lifted his chin towards the door. "Car keys?" He asked, looking back at Moon Deer's ashen face. "How many men?"

"Four, I think," Norman said with a shakiness to her whisper. "One of 'em's got a crippled hand—psycho perv felt me up with it." She checked her pockets. "Beef's got my keys."

"Beef?" Sommers asked, biting his lip to keep from laughing.

Norman cocked her head towards the yard. "My soon-to-be ex-bodyguard. The big asshole carrying the sniper's rifle."

Sommers adjusted his baseball hat again and nodded, then surveyed the contents of the small cabin, considering his options. "Okay," he said, pointing his thumb over his shoulder. "I've got a spotter on the ridge, but we've gotta hustle across that valley. It's about a mile. I'll carry her, and we'll be double-stepping it. You gotta stay close and outta the light." Norman worked the kinks from her neck and jaw, then dabbed her tears with a sleeve. Sommers pointed to the windows. "Keep watch for two seconds. I'm gonna create a diversion."

Sommers grabbed a box of matches from a shelf above a dusty wood-burning stove. He shredded and crumpled the yellowed pages of some old newspapers, then tapped Norman's shoulder. "We good?"

Norman inhaled a deep breath and nodded. The big man struck a match and then another. In the flame's flickering glow, he scooped Moon Deer into his arms. "Let's go. Follow me to the tree line. No noise and no funny business. My marksman's gonna have eyes on us."

Norman shook out her blond hair and saluted Sommers. "C'mon, Dale," she said, unveiling the tiniest of grins. "Where's the trust?" He cocked an eyebrow before turning away from her diluted gaze. Smoke began filling the cabin, and the trio slipped out the door with Moon Deer's battered body folded over her guardian angel's shoulder.

They'd made the poplar grove in under two minutes. Sommers signaled to his partner on the ledge, then turned and held his hand up in front of Norman, who was breathing hard and struggling to keep pace. "Hold up a minute," he said, placing Moon Deer on the ground against a maple trunk. He stretched his back, then pointed his thumb over his shoulder. "We need to cross this clearing. The trailhead is below that crooked notch. Doesn't seem like much, but it's all uphill from here."

Norman bent forward, resting her hands on her knees, fighting to catch her wind. "Damn, I'm so outta shape. Can we just chill out here another minute?" She plopped to the ground on all fours next to Moon Deer, wheezing and coughing into the tall grass.

Sommers was about to offer Susan some brusque encouragement when he heard shouts echoing across the basin. He turned and watched Lefty Porter leap from his park bench, flicking his smoldering butt into the weeds. "Fff, fire!" He shouted as he dashed past his van towards the burning cottage. "Beef, cabin's on fire! Drop the sandwich and get your ass out here."

Sommers watched Beef, the shirtless monster, burst from the

store and sprint for the cabin, now engulfed in smoke and flames. The two men paced and circled, trying to approach the scorching blaze. Pops and crackles sent orange embers fluttering into the starlit sky. Beef wiped a mustard smear from his face, then thrust his finger at Porter. "You had one job, man. Now we're fucked. If Mike and Ike see this shit, they're gonna scalp our asses."

Across the valley, Sommers checked Moon Deer's pulse, then lifted her back over his shoulder. He nudged Norman with his boot. "Let's go. Now's our chance." She nodded and exhaled a hefty sigh as she labored to stand.

Four steps into their climb, Sommers watched the giant circling the yard, shaking his fists and yelling at Porter. "Shit, now the Mustang's melting." The big sniper pivoted towards the lake and did a double take, spotting the trio in the clearing, tracking across the open basin. Beef roared like a bear, then cupped his hands around his mouth. "Sommers, you sonofabitch. You're a dead man." Then he grabbed Porter by the neck and pointed towards the base of the rocky ridge. "Don't fuckin' lose 'em. I'm getting my rifle."

Norman's Mustang exploded with a thunderous whoosh, sending an orange ball billowing skyward. Susan stumbled, and Sommers grabbed her arm to keep her from falling. "C'mon now, let's go. We gotta pick up the pace. There's a ravine past that rise. It'll give us cover."

"Go on," she said, coughing and waving her hands. "I'll catch up." Sommers locked eyes with her, then shook his head and broke into a jog.

Seconds later, and just steps from the dry creek bed, a gunshot rang out. Sommers dove for the lip, sending Moon Deer tumbling into a brush pile below the edge. Hearing the crack of a rifle, he scrambled over all-fours and shielded her body under his own. His perception of time slowed to a crawl as he peeked over the rim and watched Susan Norman clutch her chest, then sag to her knees. Her palms awash in crimson, she reached for Sommers before collapsing face-first into the leggy fescue.

Sommers slid Moon Deer next to a large rotting tree stump, then bear-crawled to Norman's side, ducking as a second gunshot whistled across the valley. Sommers looked up in time to see the side of Beef's head explode into a mist of pink and white. From eight hundred yards, O'Leary's single shot toppled the furious beast, delivering death's savage blow in the blink of an eye.

The bait man stood in shock for a long, slack-jawed moment, staring at Beef's headless body before circling the yard like a crazed chicken. Soon he ran out of breath and out of options. Lefty hit the dirt and crawled under his delivery van. A second shot from Samantha's rifle obliterated the spare tire Porter had serviced earlier that evening. Sommers glanced up towards O'Leary's lookout, then rolled the bleeding woman onto her back.

A gaping exit wound the size of a fist flooded Norman's ravaged chest. Blood trickled from the corner of her mouth as her last words sputtered from her quivering blue lips. "Leave this madness." Sommers brushed a lock of golden hair from her face and braced her neck in his hand. He watched life fade from her eyes. Susan Norman heaved her chest as she squeezed the big man's hand. "Go. Save your boy."

Norman's head lolled to the side, and Sommers dropped his chin to his chest. Pain and suffering consumed him and he'd lost count of the bodies piling up all around him. He lifted his eyes and squinted, peering up at the shadowy ridge skirting the moonlit valley. From atop the scabrous peak, The Watcher stood tall, spinning a mocking tune and warning the deepest cut was yet to come.

Sommers glared at the rocks, letting The Watcher feel the full weight of his determination. Then, from over his shoulder, he heard a sound that didn't quite register. Alarms chimed deep in his reptilian brain. With his thumb, the big lumberjack flipped the snap that secured his tomahawk. He gripped the handle and, quick as a flash, swiveled on his hip.

Moon Deer's body twitched, and she whimpered with a feeble sob. A pair of nasty rattlesnakes searching for a warmer roost slinked from the tree stump and began coiling against the oblivious woman's side. Without thinking, Sommers fired his ax at the trailing snake slithering from the hollowed cottonwood stump. The snake's rattle buzzed with ferocity, even though the hatchet's blade found its mark, splitting the serpent's head from its curling body with a mushy chop.

The first snake raised up, hissing and flashing its lethal fangs. Sommers said with a whisper, "I get it. I'd be bitter too." He stripped a second ax from his belt and slid himself closer to the ravine, working for better light and a better angle. Moon Deer stirred, and the snake's tail vibrated, announcing an imminent strike. Sommers shifted to his knees, dug his toes into the ground, and cocked his right arm.

The two adversaries sized each other up like a pair of Deadwood gunfighters engaged in a mortal duel. Moon Deer sparked their battle by waving annoying bugs from her face. Fangs dripping, the snake hissed, then lunged. Sommers furrowed his brow and fired. Across twenty feet, his blazing ax sizzled like a bolt of lightning. The sharpened blade split the rattler's head between the eyes, intercepting its bite inches from Moon Deer's exposed neck.

Sommers adjusted his baseball hat, then sank back and sighed. He glared at the lifeless snakes and wagged a finger over his head. "Not today, demon. Not today."

Moon Deer groaned as she rolled to her back. She flared her nostrils and cleared her throat with a convulsive cough. "Stinks like goat piss," she said with a garbled voice. "Where the fuck am I?" Then she ran her fingers across her face and cracked her eyelids open. "Sommers?"

After letting the rush pass, Sommers flipped the snake carcasses into the ditch, knowing scavengers would devour them by morning.

He retrieved his hatchets, then turned from the flames before scooping Moon Deer into his arms. She grumbled and complained as the big lumberjack scaled the rise towards the Iron Creek Trail.

"Damn," she said through her bleary sniffles. "What the hell is that stench?"

Sommers scrunched his nose and afforded himself a small chuckle. "Hey, don't look at me," he said. She gave him a playful tap on the chin, then shook her head while pinching her nose.

A short time later, Greg O'Leary, catching his breath, met the pair on the trail. Moon Deer squirmed to her feet, ran a few steps and stumbled, falling into his outstretched arms. After kisses and a lengthy embrace, O'Leary picked up Samantha's rifle and cocked his head towards Spearfish Creek. "Jack."

Sommers' eyes tracked towards the top of the ridge, its craggy face grimacing in the light of a full moon. O'Leary tapped the big man's shoulder, breaking his distant stare. The detective pointed his thumb at the crumbling van sagging in the turnaround. "You two get going. I'll catch up."

Sommers raised his palms in a questioning shrug, and Moon Deer frowned and shook her head. "Seriously?" She asked her sweating fiancé. "What's left for us back there?"

O'Leary rotated the rifle in his hands, studying the stock and barrel, wiping the bolt and trigger with a frayed towel. He shouldered the gun and looped the black tactical bag over his arm. Then he lifted his chin at the bloodshed spanning the valley and said, "Plausible deniability."

O'Leary, dodging any more fuss, turned and jogged away. Sommers, once again, scooped his wobbly friend into his arms. He looked up and nodded, gazing one last time at the makeshift tomb overlooking moonlit Pettigrew Gulch.

Chapter 32
Harmony Hall

"We took a vow in summertime. Now it's late December."

In the moon's silvery light, ninety minutes after tipping his hat goodbye to his son's mother, Sommers secured Joy Moon Deer in the back seat of their rented Tahoe. During their hike back to Bill Wenner's lodge, she'd complained about lightheadedness, nausea, and shortness of breath. The big lumberjack suspected internal injuries, and Moon Deer was in no mood to argue his layman's diagnosis. Between her alarming symptoms and Sommers' insistent persuasion, an immediate trip to the emergency room advanced towards mandatory.

Next, Sommers hefted Jack Hughes into the passenger seat. "Maybe Doc Parsons will give us a two-for-one deal," he said with a half-hearted chuckle.

Jack sputtered his lips and shook his head. "That's funny. This may come as a shock, but I've grown to despise hospitals almost as much as airplanes."

Lucky Dog jumped in and curled up on the seat next to Moon Deer, who ruffled the pup's floppy ears. With weakness in her voice, she asked, "What about Greg?"

Sommers climbed in behind the wheel and turned the key. "First things first," he said, catching Moon Deer's droopy eyes in the rearview mirror. "We left him a note and he said he'd catch up with us. Let's get you guys to the clinic, then I'll circle back and fetch your man."

Jack tapped messages into his phone as Sommers backed from the driveway. Moon Deer reached up, tapped the back of Jack's neck and said, "All the fucking troubles aside, I really like this place." Jack elbowed Sommers and winked before flipping a page and scribbling a note onto his yellow pad. Moon Deer exhaled a gurgling, feeble sigh, then leaned her head against the window and closed her eyes.

Sommers caught his lawyer's subtle suggestion and nodded. They drove for a half mile along murky Victoria Lane, then turned right on the dark twisting two-lane the locals called 14A. A few seconds after accelerating from the stop sign, Sommers slammed on the brakes, bringing the SUV to a jarring halt. Jack lurched in his seat like an oversized bobblehead doll. "What the hell, man?"

Sommers peered into the rearview mirror and poked a thumb over his head. "Her boyfriend's back." Jack turned and looked over his shoulder, watching Greg O'Leary running up the road, chasing the reddish glow of their taillights. Jack reached back and tapped Moon Deer on her leg, but she remained unresponsive, slumped against the door with the dog's head in her lap.

O'Leary climbed in and tossed his tactical bag in the back. Lucky Dog stirred and licked the man's sweaty chin. "Nice try, you guys," he said, catching his breath. "If I was any slower, you'd be long gone. You know, in the Army we used to say…"

Sommers interrupted him with a wave, then lifted his chin at Moon Deer. "She's hurtin' bad. Gotta get her to the hospital ASAP. Your buddy Doc Parsons is waiting for us."

O'Leary scooched in, then reached across and felt Moon Deer's neck, checking her pulse. "Okay then, better step on it—those two BIA dudes are pissed, and not far behind."

Jack asked, "As in the Bureau of Indian Affairs?"

"Yea, but not really," O'Leary said, popping a piece of chewing gum into his mouth. "They're DSS operatives posing as BIA officers. My DHS contact says they're nothing but a couple of goddamn snakes."

Jack flipped to a page on his notepad and circled one of his entries. "Mike and Ike, snakes who turned on their chief and double agent, Jo Douglass. Does that sound about right?"

Sommers rolled his eyes and shook his head as he checked his mirrors and steered the Tahoe off the shoulder. "We should've looked deeper into Douglass—my bad there." He pressed harder on the gas pedal, making the engine roar. "What about Porter? He asked, fidgeting with his baseball hat. "And where's her rifle?"

O'Leary dabbed sweat from his face, then massaged Lucky Dog's hairy neck. He reached into his pocket and tossed a sleeve of one-hundred-dollar bills into the front seat. "Rifle's in the cave with its rightful owner," he said. "Lefty was a psycho hatchet man for the DSS. His guilt must've been overwhelming. I'll bet it felt like three tons weighing on his chest." O'Leary gazed out the side window, watching the rocks and trees float by in misty obscurity. "All four tires going flat within a matter of seconds. I mean, what are the odds?"

Jack flipped a page and jotted another note. Sommers nodded and pursed his lips, then looked up and spotted a pair of headlights in his rearview mirror, closing fast. "Looks like we've got company, gentlemen." Jack checked his side mirror and slipped his .38 from the glove compartment. O'Leary followed suit, snapping Sam's P238 from his shoulder holster.

Sommers took another peek into the mirror and pressed on the gas pedal. "Hang on, guys," he said, adjusting his mirrors. "And hold your water here. We don't know who's behind us. Let's assume it's the snakes. How would they know this car?" He peeked over his shoulder at Moon Deer. "I've gotten enough people hurt already. I mean crimony. When is enough enough?"

O'Leary shifted in his seat, watching the mysterious headlights gain ground. "It's not on you, brother." He checked and re-seated the nine-shot mag in his pistol, then tapped the driver on his shoulder with the muzzle. "Ford grill emblem, three men inside, can't make out their faces, but it sure feels like them."

Jack nodded as counted on his fingers. "Mike, Ike, and my buddy, Travis Thorne."

Sommers caught a flash in the mirror and jerked the steering wheel left, crossing the double yellow centerline. A split second later, the passenger side mirror exploded in a wash of glass and plastic. Jack ducked away and said, "Shit, I think they just stated their intentions."

Sommers chewed his lip as he floored the accelerator. "What do we do? I can't shake these guys."

O'Leary tapped Sommers' shoulder again and pointed his pistol at the winding road ahead. "Take a breath, big man. We got this. You're passing the Devils Bathtub Trailhead on your right. See the fork at the top of the hill? Hang right and let 'em see your brake lights. I want those assholes to follow us."

Sommers leaned forward with both hands on the steering wheel. "Then what?"

"Be ready to slam them brakes," O'Leary said, motioning with his gun. "The road will split north south before the dead end, and I mean right away. Stay right and take it around the bend, then kill your lights."

Jack looked over his shoulder and lifted his chin. "Are you sure about this? We could get boxed in."

O'Leary nodded, then motioned ahead. "Trust me. It's where they shoved Lilly's truck into the drink. I asked Joy to check it out during one of her road runs. Turn here, now!"

Sommers cranked the steering wheel and pumped the brakes, spraying gravel into the ditches. Lucky Dog curled up against Moon Deer as O'Leary shouted his commands. "Again, turn right. See those boulders? They mark the end of the line. Pull over in front of 'em and shut us down."

While they were still rolling, O'Leary jumped out and rolled into the leafy ditch with his gun drawn and his arms outstretched in front of his face. Jack lowered his window and leaned out. "Damn," he said, aiming his gun at the chalky fork in the road. "He must have a death wish or something."

Sommers shook his head and brought the Tahoe to a sliding stop. He cut the lights and the ignition, then reversed his baseball hat and held an index finger to his lips.

Sommers' team waited in the darkness, watching a black pickup fishtail across the gravel as it raced east on Cleopatra Lane. As the truck approached the abrupt split, Sommers heard a distinctive pop echo through the canyon.

Moon Deer groaned, and Lucky Dog barked a little yip. Jack ducked his head, and Sommers tightened his grip on the steering wheel, leaning towards the windshield, watching another calamity unfold thirty yards away.

The Ford's front tire exploded, sending the teetering truck careening into an enormous boulder. The impact flipped the truck end over end, before it burst into a ball of flame and toppled over the canyon's craggy rim. Sommers stepped out to hear twisting metal shredding the mountainside, crunching over rocks and smashing through trees.

Moments later, Lucky Dog joined the three men in studying the smoky swath leading to the bottom of the canyon. In the moonlight, they watched the demolished truck bobbing belly up in Squaw Creek. The steaming wreck hissed as it jounced in the whitewater churning towards Spearfish Creek. O'Leary reared back and heaved

Sam's pistol into the depths below. Then he turned away, placing his hand on Sommers' sturdy shoulder. "Well. I'd say they had enough."

Two hours later, Doctor Cody Parsons clipped a pen to his clipboard. He lifted his chin at Moon Deer, who slept in her hospital bed with an assortment of tubes and wires stuck to her skin with medical tape. "She's tougher than a two-dollar steak," he said with a grin. "She'll be fine after a couple day's rest. Hydration and meds, of course." Then he tapped O'Leary on the shoulder. "How's that wrist?"

From the chair he'd dragged to her bedside, O'Leary lifted his right hand from the armrest and smirked. "Never better, Doc." Then he pointed to his side. "Your stitches made me itchy. I took 'em out with a pair of pliers."

The friendly doctor shook his head, then flipped a crunchy treat into Lucky Dog's waiting mouth. He leaned in close to O'Leary and sniffed. "I'm assuming you're staying. We've got a room where you can get cleaned up."

O'Leary looked up and scrunched his nose. "That bad, huh?"

Parsons pursed his lips and nodded his head. "I'll give you all a few minutes." He slapped Jack's thigh with his clipboard, then chuckled to himself as he stepped towards the hall.

Jack pouted at a corner table with a gray walking boot adorning his right foot. He tapped the small screen, then pocketed his cell phone. "Well, Stearns is pissed about us dragging him outta bed. He's gonna call the sheriff. Smooth things over for us." The lawyer pointed his pen at O'Leary. "Judge expects to see you in his office first thing tomorrow morning."

O'Leary held Moon Deer's hand and slouched back into his chair. "Kinda what I figured."

Deep in his thoughts, Sommers hadn't uttered but two words since they arrived. Lucky parked her back end near the big man's feet as he stood from his chair. "I'm worn to the nub and stinking like Grumpy's old biffy. Time for me to get on home."

Jack raised his palms and shrugged. "What? You mean now?"

Sommers nodded. "Yep. My son needs me."

Jack cocked an eyebrow and scratched at the back of his neck. "You driving?"

Sommers gave Moon Deer a kiss on the forehead and shook hands with O'Leary. "I owe you one, buddy." Then he nodded at Jack. "Got no choice. Otto stripped the Cessna down to her frame. Ya coming with me?"

Jack jumped up, snatching his coffee cup from the table. "Does Smokey Bear poop in the woods?" The lawyer couldn't contain his excitement as he hobbled for the door. "Jules' patience goes only so far—says she misses me. Can you imagine that?" Then he waved his arms like a hyped-up drummer. "C'mon, big man. Let's roll."

Chapter 33
Should've Been a Cowboy

"I bet you never heard ol' Marshall Dillon say..."

Thanks in part to a crisp, quiet morning, and no small thanks to eight hundred horsepower under the hood, Ted Lindstrom barnstormed the chasm between Lake Bronson and Gary's Corner Market in under two hours. Southbound Route 59 didn't strike him much differently than North Dakota, more trees and more lakes, perhaps.

After rolling up to the gas pumps, the retired sheriff climbed out and stretched his back, then floated in the aroma of Gary's delectable cinnamon rolls. Two minutes after swiping his credit card, Lindstrom stuffed the nozzle back into the high-octane pump and grabbed a dripping squeegee from a trough of soapy blue water. He soon realized the tattered brush would be no match for the hundreds of bees and mosquitos squashed across his windshield.

Lindstrom drove around the back, parking in the nearest of three self-service car wash bays. He stepped out, peeled three singles from his wallet, and squared off with a stubborn-looking change machine. The uncooperative contraption spit back Lindstrom's first single, so he moistened his fingers on his tongue and smoothed a second bill.

Once again, the stubborn machine mocked him, accepting, then rejected, his dampened currency.

Lindstrom leaned to the side and watched a pair of eighteen-wheeled grain haulers round the corner and rumble away on Highway 5. Then he turned back to see the change machine teasing him with its flickering "out of service" light. He shook his head, locked his car with a click of his key fob, then trudged towards the storefront, his growling stomach sending a reminder he needed a sack of fresh-baked pastry with his roll of quarters.

All at once, Lindstrom heard a series of gunshots ricocheting around the front of the convenience store. He covered his head and ducked, then sprinted back to his car and snatched his service revolver from the console. With one of his chromed pistols in hand, Lindstrom squatted behind the hissing air pump and watched a white SUV squeal around the corner. The berserk driver plowed through a band of bearded yard gnomes before correcting the skid and racing north on Highway 11.

Lindstrom dashed between the gas pumps and burst through the front door, his revolver in one hand, and his security badge in the other. He discovered Gary Johnson, a blue-haired cashier, and a Latino fry cook huddled behind the ice cream counter. Gazing around, Lindstrom saw the looters had ransacked a beer cooler and a snack food aisle. "Anybody hurt?" He asked, crouching into a shooter's stance as he investigated the remaining few aisles of the cozy corner grocery. "What the hell happened here?"

Gary Johnson peeked above the pint freezer, then stood with his .44 pointed at Lindstrom's chest. Johnson glanced down and cocked his head. "Doris," he said, pointing with his thumb. "Crawl to the kitchen and dial 9-1-1. Molo, you too—back behind the grill." Then Johnson lifted his chin at the weathered intruder. "Who the hell are you?"

Lindstrom smirked and held his badge closer to Johnson's face.

"Ted Lindstrom, private investigator—retired sheriff, Barnes County." Then he motioned with his gun. "Are we gonna shoot each other now?"

Johnson glanced down at his .44 and then pointed its muzzle at the shiny pistol in Lindstrom's hand. He sputtered through his puckered lips. "I'm thinking I'll win."

"I wouldn't bet on it," Lindstrom said, shaking his head. Then he shouted towards the back. "Doris, honey. Is Sheriff Williams on the way?"

Doris Greene, her voice trembling through some sniffles, said, "I sure hope so. Dispatcher's trying to get him on the horn. But all the first responders are in town, something about a bomb threat at the middle school. Are you gonna shoot me? 'Cause I really gotta pee first."

Lindstrom rolled his eyes and snorted a small laugh. Johnson glanced out a side window, then slipped his gun into a drawer and fetched a dustpan and broom from behind the mangled cash register. He pointed the broom handle at three gnarled holes in the ceiling's corners and shook his head. "Goddamn Mexicans shot the security cameras out."

Morales Lopez shouted from the back. "C'mon boss, they said they was Venezuelans." Doris peeked through the doorway, then tiptoed towards the ladies' room, side-eyeing Lindstrom as she passed.

"Not that it matters much," Lindstrom said, tucking his gun into the back of his pants. "Think they were illegals?"

"No doubt," Johnson said, nodding his head. "One of 'em swiped a fresh debit card at the pump. They recorded each other with their fancy new phones, dancing around while they trashed the place." A concerned-looking crowd gathered in the street with their cellphones held high. Johnson stepped around a spray of broken glass and flipped the window sign to "closed." "Shit," he said before expelling a thick sigh. "This tomfoolery has gotta be all over TikTok by now."

"They's givin' away cars in the cities," Lopez said, marching up and down the aisles with a push broom, shaking his head. "Jus' gotta show 'em your migrant app. I should leave and come back—new name, new phone, new ride. Jus' like dem guys."

Lindstrom squatted and plucked a king-sized Snickers bar from the floor, tore the wrapper open and bit off half of it. After some onerous chewing, he placed a rumpled dollar bill on the counter, then picked a thread of caramel from the gray stubble peppering his chin. "Don't your gas pumps have cameras in the pay screens?"

"They do," Johnson said before shrugging his shoulders and pursing his lips. "But they're not connected to our security system."

Doris returned from the bathroom, wiping her hands on a paper towel and shaking her head at the mess. "I'm just glad everybody's okay."

Johnson patted her shoulder and then continued sweeping shards of glass into a pile.

She rolled her eyes and huffed as she extended her hand. "Here, gimme that. I'll take care of it."

Lindstrom mumbled after stuffing the rest of the candy bar into his mouth. "Any idea where those assholes went?"

"As long as they're not here," Johnson said. "I couldn't give two shits."

Doris nodded, emptying her dustpan into a garbage bin. "Ya got that right."

Molo, pushing an assortment of potato chips, M&M's, and beef jerky sticks into manageable heaps, stopped and leaned on his broom's handle. "¡Niño pequeño, niño pequeño!" He said, waving one hand over his head like a bronco buster.

Lindstrom stepped over one of Molo's snack piles and lifted his chin at the cook. "You sayin' they're looking for a small boy?"

The cook nodded, and the investigator turned and flipped his wrapper into the garbage can. Then he grabbed Johnson's arm and cocked his head towards Highway 11. "Dale Sommers' place up that way?"

Johnson pulled his arm free and pointed through the pick-up window beyond the gas pumps. "That's right. About ten minutes from here."

Lindstrom dug the Charger's key fob from his front pocket and wheeled for the door. "Shit, man. Gotta roll."

Johnson tossed his baker's smock on the counter, then retrieved his .44 and a box of shells from behind the counter. "Wait up, man! I'm comin' with you." Then he turned back to Molo. "You're in charge—lock the door behind me. Nobody gets in here unless they're wearing a badge."

Doris huffed, balling her hands into fists and grinding them into her hips.

The two gun-wielding men sent the street crowd scattering. Johnson shouted through the drive-thru window as he chased after Lindstrom. "Stop pouting Doris, you can be in charge next time!"

Seconds later, Doris and Molo pressed their noses against the smudged drive-thru glass, watching Lindstrom's Hellcat, still encrusted with bug guts and river muck, burn rubber as it exploded from the wash bay onto Highway 11.

With the push of a button, Jerry Reynolds opened two pairs of oversized hangar doors, inviting streams of natural light along with a refreshing lake breeze. He heard a distant logging truck muscle its way up a nearby fire road, and from somewhere below DeRoxe Road, he heard a child's laughter mixing with a dog's playful barks. The wrinkled old man pivoted towards the north opening and watched the Peterson Brothers harvesting corn from a rolling field west of Sommers' runway.

The moment passed, and he smiled while collecting an assortment of gadgets from the pilot's well-appointed tool chests. He reached up and tuned the stereo to a classic country station out of Fergus Falls. A block of Toby Keith songs poured from the overhead speakers and Reynolds turned in a circle, appreciating the down-home comfort of this tidy Quonset Hut. Across the shop, his '66 Chevy gleamed in the morning rays, parked atop the decaying car trailer he borrowed from Valley Auto Body.

The warhorse slid his glasses to the bridge of his nose, then hunched over a workbench, skimming the dog-eared page of a Ford chassis manual one last time. During the past few days, he'd memorized the factory clearances and assembly markings. This fine morning, he thought, was the perfect time to roll up his sleeves and get to work. He groaned as he crouched on the concrete floor and stretched out on his back. Then Reynolds shuffled his feet, wheeling a mechanic's creeper under the spurned black pickup.

Using a micrometer and a set of feeler gauges, Reynolds measured the gaps and allowances of the side panels and the cargo bed's floor. He hummed along with the music as he inspected the broken body welds and a few wayward inspection marks. He spritzed some WD-40 and went to work removing a row of nuts and bolts with an impact driver.

Next, he used a long screwdriver and a mishmash of wood shims to pry the floor panel from the inner wheel well. Reynolds shined a flashlight into the opening and craned his neck for a better view. After dabbing sweat from his eyes, he took a second look and nodded with a grin. "Kinda what I thought."

Seconds later, the music stopped playing, and Reynolds dropped his pry bar. "What the…?" He said, with his voice trailing off. As the tool clanked across the floor, Reynolds grunted and twisted to his side.

He straightened his glasses and watched three pairs of dusty hiking boots marching towards him, coming for Hammer's loot, he assumed.

Doris Greene bolted from the drive-thru window, stiff-arming and bowling over the pint-sized fry cook. Back in a cramped office, she grabbed the handset from a dusty, age-old rotary telephone and flicked the switch hooks.

Northwestern Bell installed the Lake Victoria party line in the early 1900s. The shared telephone service stretched along the south and west shores of the lake and extended to a few select locations within the county, including Gary's Corner Market. Then, in the early 1970s, following a series of regional takeovers, AT&T removed the obsolete infrastructure. Over the years, the technology improved and most users did away with their landlines. But two or three of the original connections survived.

Gracie Sommers answered after a series of blaring rings. "Hello, hello? I thought this ancient thing was just for decoration."

The cashier cocked an eyebrow and sputtered at her phone before she said, "Gracie. It's Doris Greene. Is Grumpy around? I need to speak with him—it's urgent."

"You sound kinda stressed, Doris—everything okay?"

Doris huffed a sigh and clenched her jaw. "I'm fine, Gracie. I just need to have a word with that old snapper. Can you fetch him for me, please?"

Gracie dropped the handset, and a minute later, Doris heard Grumpy coughing and wheezing between his obscenities. He fumbled with the receiver, clearing his throat. "Grumpy here. The hell you want, Doris?"

Doris inhaled and lifted her eyes to the ceiling, then she exhaled and described the robbery and the situation in Lac Clair as coolly as she could. "I don't want to alarm Gracie," she said. "Is she eavesdropping?" Then, without waiting for an answer, Doris's voice cracked. "They're coming for the boy—kidnappers. Round up the Petersons, and grab your guns. You gotta stop 'em, Grumps. These hooligans are ruthless animals. They plowed right through Molly Crick's gnome garden—that's hit-and-run for cryin' out loud."

Grumpy looked over his shoulder, watching Phelps and Noah playing fetch with a stick in the front yard. Then, without warning, the loud clap of a gunshot echoed through the trees. The crusty fossil flinched and dropped the handset before limping to the porch, where he snatched his brother's vintage rifle from the corner. Grumpy nodded after confirming Gracie kept the piece loaded, then turned and pressed it into her arms.

Confusion and the onset of panic drained the rose from her cheeks. "What is it? What's going on?"

Grumpy glared at Victory Bluff, then surveyed the quiet south shore. "Damn, he said, shaking his head. "Scooter and Rosie are in Moorhead today." He adjusted his baseball cap and pointed to the far side of the lake. "Tell you what, use the fishing boat—take Noah and Phelps. Buzz on over to Sandy Point and drop anchor behind the cattails. There's bug spray, bottled water, and life vests under the seats. Go!"

Gracie's lower lip quivered, and she shrugged her shoulders. Grumpy furrowed his brow and snarled at her with sand in his voice. "We're not fuckin' around here, and this ain't no drill. Any chicos come lookin' for you, wait 'til you can smell their taco breath, then blast their asses straight to hell. I'll signal when it's safe to come back. Now go!"

Ted Lindstrom's Charger roared along Highway 11 at one-hundred miles per hour, catching air over the Spring Creek bridge. Gary Johnson pointed his gun through the windshield. "Got some blind hills and curves ahead. I'd prefer the last earthly thing I see not to be the ass end of a manure spreader."

The driver peeked into his rearview mirror, then downshifted and glanced across at his passenger, seeing him struggle to load fresh shells into his revolver. "Say, cowboy," Lindstrom said before jerking the steering wheel to dodge a roadkill turtle. "Seems you enjoy waving that howitzer around. Let me tell ya, I've carried an FFL for darn near my entire life. If any shooting's gonna happen, better let me handle it."

"Self-defense and retribution, brother," Johnson said, smacking his lips as he tucked the small box under his seat.

Lindstrom wrung his hands around the steering wheel and rolled his eyes. "I get it. But you know how the politics work in this state. You wanna lose your livelihood over a few goddamn gangbangers?"

Johnson shook his head and pulsed his palm downward. "Better slow down. Erikson Road's at the bottom of this hill—sharp left."

"Shit!" Lindstrom said, downshifting, pumping the brakes, and cranking the wheel. The g-forces pressed him hard against the center console, and the driver willed his mighty Hellcat into a jarring four-wheeled slide that churned the washboard shoulder.

After straightening out and bumping along some orange-colored gravel for another mile, the pair idled into the DeRoxe Club's vacant parking lot. They climbed out with their guns drawn and surveyed the placid surroundings. Johnson shielded his eyes and pointed with his gun. "Sommers' place is down that lane, through those trees. Feels too quiet—only a handful of fishing boats on the water."

Lindstrom turned and pointed at an ATV kicking up dust as it raced north towards a cluster of farm buildings. "Who's that?"

Johnson got up on his toes, looked and said, "Grumpy Sommers,

Dale's cranky uncle. He's rounding up the calvary, I suspect. Best keep your head down. The Peterson Brothers will shoot you dead for breathing on their fence posts."

Lindstrom nodded, turning and scanning the lake and its surrounding forests and fields. "Good to know. Ya think they scared the bad guys off?"

Johnson shrugged, then turned and did a double take at the Quonset Hut glimmering across the road. "That's strange. The doors are open—we better check it out."

Soon, with their pistols leading the way, the pair stepped into the shadow of the oversized garage. Lindstrom lifted his chin at a bullet hole in the windshield of Jerry Reynold's turquoise Chevy. He tiptoed over and peeked inside, finding it clean and empty.

Johnson whispered after holding an index finger to his lips. He crept around the pickup truck, looking inside and underneath. "You hear that?" He asked. "Something inside."

The truck bed had a latched hardcover, so Lindstrom trained his gun towards the opening as Johnson dropped the tailgate. "What the hell?" Johnson asked, stepping back, but still leaning forward for a closer look at the surprising cargo.

Lindstrom shook off his momentary disbelief and holstered his gun. "Jerry, that you? Can you hear me?" Reynolds, muzzled and lashed to the creeper with duct tape, flexed his toes and wiggled his fingers.

After rolling him out and cutting the sticky tape from his face and limbs, Reynolds sat up, shook himself off, and guzzled bottled water. "Thanks, guys," he said, catching his breath and wiping his mouth with the back of his hand. "Another two minutes. My thermometer would've popped." Then he pointed his thumb and shook his head. "Look what those jerks did to my Impala."

His voice shaky and feeble, Reynolds outlined his journey and described the crude visitors that shot his car while threatening his life. "Those hooligans were hard to understand," he said before chugging more water. "They kept saying, 'muchacho, muchacho'. I offered them this truck instead, but they just laughed while they stuffed me in the back. I think they were drunk."

Lindstrom clutched Reynolds' arm, helping the old timer to his feet. "Where's the boy?"

Reynolds shrugged as he shuffled for the door. "Don't know—heard him playing with Phelps between the docks a short time ago."

Johnson patted Reynolds' shoulder and turned for the opposite door. "You did good, Jerry. I'm gonna jog over and check the house." And in a matter of seconds, the baker dashed across the road and down the south woods trail before the others could stop him.

Lindstrom sat with Reynolds on a bench set outside the hangar's double doors. "Say, Jerry," he said, unfurling a note from his pocket and pointing his thumb back towards the old Chevy. "We found your floor safe, one-nine-six-six." Reynolds grabbed the yellow slip of paper and studied his modest handwriting. Lindstrom slid closer to him and asked, "Is t-w-o some kind of clue?"

Reynolds pursed his lips and nodded. "Where's my old picture of the Holstein barn?"

Before the sheriff could answer, a pop-pop-pop burst of automatic gunfire echoed through the north woods. The two men flinched, then locked eyes on each other. Lindstrom stood and asked, "How well do you know your way around here?"

Reynolds braced himself as he struggled to stand. "C'mon, Sheriff. We can take the truck." The pair climbed in and Reynolds shifted the Ford into four-wheel low as they chugged north towards Dorfman Road. Lindstrom, clutching his pistol in both hands, leaned out the passenger window, sniffing the woodsy air as he surveyed the shady western shore.

A mile later, Reynolds pumped the brakes and slid to a stop at the base of the north woods fire road. They found Grumpy Sommers hog-tying a man to the back of his ATV. A trickle of blood dribbled between the dark tattoos on the unresponsive Latino's face. Lindstrom tapped Reynolds' arm. "Wait here a sec." Then he climbed out, showing his gun and his badge. "He dead?"

Grumpy coughed, then shook his head. "Shit no. Now why the hell would I be wasting rope on a goddamn stiff?" Reynolds climbed out and waved as Grumpy cocked his head towards the trees. "This greasy beaner ran smack into a tree limb—knocked hisself out."

Reynolds leaned in for a closer look. "Not the guy that shot my car, but I say let him bleed."

The retired sheriff stepped closer and shook Grumpy's hand. "Ted Lindstrom. We heard there were three of 'em. Any sign of the other two?"

Grumpy cinched his ropes, then peeled off his hat and waved it over his shoulder. "Only seen two—Peterson Boys are following a blood trail. I think Al winged the other guy."

Both Lindstrom and Reynolds nodded, then ducked their heads as another flurry of gunshots rang along the hilltop.

Lindstrom scanned the forest that skirted the north shore, then asked, "They're after the boy. Where is he?"

Grumpy lifted his chin towards the lake. "Fishing. His best buddy's in the crow's nest and Grandma Gracie's working the tiller. She's got Jake's rifle, but if that asshole makes it past the bluff, they're sittin' ducks."

Lindstrom searched his pockets and tossed his key to Reynolds, then cocked his head at the airplane hangar. "You guys head on back. My phone's in the car. See if Sheriff Williams can spare somebody, anybody. They need to be on the lookout for a white Ford Explorer, bald tires, and a temporary tag."

Gary Johnson met Grumpy and Reynolds back at the hangar. They sipped bottled water and compared notes as their groggy captive stirred on the back of the cart. The throaty rumble of C.J. Hunter's Harley interrupted their patchy conversation. The burly biker coasted into the shop, then slid his tinted goggles to his forehead as he climbed from his bike. "Doris called me in a fever," he said, his voice rough and booming. "The hell's going on out here?"

Johnson caught Hunter up to speed while Reynolds slapped a strip of duct tape over the burping kidnapper's mouth. Grumpy peered over his shoulder at the ghostly face of Victory Bluff as the scattered reports of gunfire continued beyond the lake. Hunter shook his head and pointed his thumb over his shoulder. "Third guy's no longer a problem."

Johnson pursed his lips and asked, "And how the hell would you know that?"

The retired firefighter rubbed his gloved hands together and clapped. "That white Ford you mentioned is belly-up in Spring Creek, right where Sommers found Andie Hansen a few years back." Hunter stepped in a circle, motioning past the south woods. "String Bean was in hot pursuit when the SUV hit a guardrail and flipped into the drink. Beer cans and tortilla chips strewn in every direction. Believe you me, nobody's walkin' outta that mess."

Reynolds leaned against the truck's fender, watching the kidnapper bleed in the back of Grumpy's ATV. "String Bean?" He asked, rubbing the bruises appearing around his wrists.

Hunter swatted a horse fly away from his motorcycle seat then rolled his eyes. "Nathan Bean, Community Service Officer—thinks he's Marshall Dillon, but acts more like Barney Fife. I stopped to lend a hand when Doris buzzed my cell. The sheriff is tied up in town and Sommers ain't answering his phone."

Johnson stood from his seat on the open tailgate. "Here come the mercenaries," he said, pointing at Bob and Al Peterson tromping from the north woods, each with a black AK slung over his shoulder. "They're arguing again. Go figure."

Hunter huffed as he slipped his pipe and a MAGA-themed lighter from his vest pocket. "Bitchin' is what they do best."

Grumpy coughed and nodded as he hobbled towards the door. "I better call the fishing party back."

Hunter snapped the lighter closed, tucked his pipe away, and waved. "Climb aboard, soldier. We'll ride over." Grumpy shook his head and sputtered through his lips.

Johnson motioned to the battered kidnapper, beginning to fuss in the back of Grumpy's cart. "What about this guy?" He asked.

Grumpy pointed to the bed of the black pickup and winked at Reynolds. "We'll toss him in the back. Then it's up to you, JR. You can dump his ass by String Bean's cruiser, or…"

Reynolds cocked an eyebrow and nodded. "Drop him at the train station."

Chapter 34
Graceland

"The Mississippi Delta was shining like a national guitar."

Six hours out, Dale Sommers pushed his rented Tahoe as hard as its headlights and windshield wipers would allow. Lucky Dog snored in the back seat and Jack Hughes' face twitched against the passenger window as he worked his way through a choppy dream. Hours earlier, the trio stopped for gas and a dozen pre-packaged burgers at a truck stop west of Dickinson, North Dakota. An isolated thunderstorm over Jamestown freshened the pre-dawn air and Sommers thought eastbound Interstate 94 stretched like a glossy ribbon unfurling towards his hopeful reprieve.

The big lumberjack shifted in the driver's seat and became mesmerized by the rush of the wind and the hum of the tires wheeling between those continuous white lines. From across the grassy median, he watched a parade of eighteen wheelers, their amber trailer lights touting the nomadic guild as their procession roamed westward like the wagon trains of a bygone era. Sommers scratched at the stubble on his chin, pondering the truckers' countless miles and their solitary days.

As the last rain drops gave way to moths and mayflies, Jack sat up and rubbed his face. "Still raining?" He asked, yawning and stretching his arms. "Where the hell are we?"

Sommers pointed through the windshield, sullied with splattered bugs. "The lights of Valley City. Navigation says we're ninety minutes out, but we're rolling fast. Sun's gonna be coming up soon."

Jack reached under his seat and pulled out his rumpled legal pad. "I like the sound of that. Starbucks nearby?" He asked, while unveiling a hopeful smirk. "I'd do cartwheels for a piping hot cup right about now." Jack waited for a response, then shook his head as he ran his fingers through his mussed-up hair. "How about a business meeting instead?"

Sommers signaled and passed a slow-rolling horse hauler with Oklahoma plates, then shrugged. "Do I have a choice?"

"No, not really." Jack grinned as he clicked his pen and flipped to a page filled with his chicken scratch.

Sommers adjusted his baseball hat and nodded. "Ah, just as well. My mind's been doin' flip-flops for the last hundred miles. Let's start with the South Dakota chapter, shall we?"

Jack clicked on an overhead map light and flipped to a different page. "Okay, go ahead."

"Even though there's some ugly history there, I want to buy Wenner's lodge for O'Leary and Moon Deer. I owe 'em big time and they're looking for a fresh start," he said. "I don't recall Big Bill having any kin—Lindstrom can confirm that. You mind looking into it for me?"

Jack tapped his pen on the pad, then underlined a few lines of text. "Way ahead of you. I've already requested a survey map and the property tax records. Yesterday, I asked Judge Stearns to put a good word in with the county commissioner. Stearns says he's got a special investigator's opportunity waiting for O'Leary once he's acquitted. A quick and easy formality—those were his exact words."

Sommers nodded as he drummed his thumbs on the steering wheel, lost in the murmur of the open road.

After unplugging his phone from a charging port, Jack checked the notification pop-ups and sputtered through his lips. "My scanner app says state cops found the wreckage in Squaw Creek. No survivors."

Sommers shook his head and reached back to ruffle Lucky Dog's ears. "Guess the bad guys found out, didn't they?" He wrinkled his nose and sniffed, then cracked the driver's window open for a gust of fresh air. "Let's shift our focus to North Dakota," he said, following a sigh. "Jerry Reynolds has endured decades within the eye of Hurricane Norman. Once this storm passes, he'll be exposed and he'll need some help. I'm gonna put a call into Judge Abbott. He's reeled nothing but bad luck into my fishing boat from time to time, but he's got a great legal mind—carries a big stick."

"I like your thinking," Jack said. "Immunity cases are his specialty." The lawyer flipped the page and drew circles and arrows on the yellow paper. "Julie has hitched her wagon to Hardesty. Are you good with the EPA acquiring Norman Farms as long as they clean things up and take care of Reynolds? If not, we can submit an official offer next week."

"Your wife and D.T. Hardesty—now there's a dangerous combination." Sommers licked his chapped lips and began counting on his fingers. "The EPA needs to resolve Norman's lien and guarantee Jerry's homestead. They also need to pave an access road from his place out to Highway 5. Like we discussed before, it's about natural restoration for me, and I'm pretty sure Jerry Reynolds feels the same."

Jack scribbled a series of notes, then pointed his pen at Sommers. "That old timer could be the perfect guy to manage our ghost town project—knows the history, lives only a few minutes away, and it's obvious he's a handy dude." Jack turned and gazed out the passenger window, watching miles of high-tension lines sag between an endless series of lanky towers. "By the way, there's still no sign of Peg McFarland."

"Tell you what, let's get Reynolds settled first," Sommers said as he tried rubbing the fatigue from his eyes. "Peg's disappearance shouldn't surprise anyone. She's lost darn near everything she's ever cared for. I've felt that pain, and I believe she's taken off." Sommers studied the horizon in silence, then pursed his lips and shook his head. "Ya know, you guys still haven't explained what's in that cardboard tube. Darn thing has got some real miles on it by now."

Jack cocked an eyebrow and skimmed through a thread of accumulated text messages on his phone. "We'll get to that later. We've got more pressing matters this morning." The lawyer studied a lengthy passage, then cleared his throat, shifted in his seat, and turned off the map light. "Ya know what? You buried the lead as if I wasn't paying attention. Wanna talk about her?"

The contemplative driver massaged his aching shoulder and watched the boundless fields of wet prairie grasses glisten and sway in the burgeoning morning light. As the pavement dried to chalky gray, he looked skyward and tracked an exquisite bird of prey floating on the morning breeze. The solitary hawk circled high above the Buffalo Creek Preserve, then flapped its wings and sailed away. Sommers scratched at the back of his neck, adjusted his hat, and sighed. "I suppose we should."

Jack held his index finger to his lips as he listened to a voicemail message on his cellphone. He tapped the screen and said, "Julie's been burning the midnight oil—says volunteer firefighters found Flannel Stan, Lefty Porter, and a nameless behemoth with no head. She said Park Rangers tripped over Susan Norman's body, searching for the shooter. That's seven bodies in one night—might be a record for the county coroner."

Sommers exited on Highway 52, avoiding a road construction bottleneck west of Fargo. "Beef."

"Beef?" Jack asked.

"Susan called him Beef—the headless giant."

Jack snickered as he shook his head. "Yea, well. Thanks to an unknown sniper, he's ground beef now."

Sommers rolled his eyes and adjusted his rearview mirror. "The body count should be eight. She got anything on Sam?"

"Not in the way you'd expect," Jack said, shaking his head and jotting a fresh note. "No body, no blood—Sheriff's got a cadaver dog chasing its tail."

Sommers looked across and cocked an eyebrow at his lawyer. "Seriously? Didn't they talk to O'Leary?"

"Don't know. But here's the kicker. Jules scoured through an online database and came across a death certificate, Samantha Stevens, Lawrence County—signed and stamped last week. Julie's smart as a whip. Everyone knows that. But even she can't wrap her head around this one." Jack tapped the pen on his front teeth, then turned towards the driver and wagged his finger. "Thing to remember is, thanks to Sam, Noah will never have to work a day in his life. That's a darn good gig if you can get it."

The trio rode in a stifling silence, crossing over the swollen, muddy Red River, then wheeling straight towards a golden Minnesota sunrise. Jack's phone vibrated on the dashboard, interrupting the driver's hushed introspection. "Now what?" Sommers asked with a half-hearted chuckle, trying to hide his soupy disappointment sprinkled with renewed apprehension.

Jack glanced across at his uneasy friend. "Sheriff Williams."

Again, Sommers adjusted his baseball cap and shook his head. "This early? Gotta be bad," he said as he set the cruise control and checked his rearview mirrors. "Put him on speaker, wouldja?"

Thirty minutes later, Lucky Dog flopped around the back seat as Sommers wrenched the grimy Tahoe into a sharp turn onto southbound Highway 11, its tires howling past a sun-faded Hunter's Marine billboard. Jack Hughes cinched his seat belt, then latched onto the grab handle and the dashboard with both hands. "You've taken years off my life. You realize that, don't you?" Then he pointed his thumb over his shoulder. "Route 59 is faster this time of day, at least three decent coffee shops over that way."

Sommers reversed his baseball cap, then gripped the steering wheel with both hands. He peeked into his rearview mirror and shouted over the engine's roar. "Last thing we need is a freight train bogging us down. Besides, if you were paying attention, Williams said first responders are blocking every road into town." Sommers glanced into the mirror and lifted his chin. "Hang on back there, Lucky Pup."

The weary SUV muscled up a hill and lumbered over a rise above gurgling Spring Creek. Sommers jerked the wheel and swerved around a parked police cruiser and a gathering of men standing beside a mangled guardrail, gazing down into a shadowy ravine. The flashing emergency lights and the smell of burning rubber reminded him it was the same treacherous stretch where Henry Two Horse ran Andie Hansen off the road just a few years earlier. Sommers considered stopping, but just sputtered through his lips and shook his head.

The three men spun on their heels and staggered to the shoulder as the Tahoe thundered past. Jack craned his neck and looked out the back window. "Whew, that was close. I see String Bean and CJ Hunter—don't recognize the other guy."

"That's Jerry Reynolds," Sommers said, wringing his hands on the wheel. "Our friends from the cartel have done their research. Although it seems they're having a tough time assimilating to our midwestern ways."

"Struggling with the driving too, obviously."

Sommers feathered the gas pedal, coasting around a swooping, tree-lined curve. "Williams said String Bean's got one of 'em in the back of his cruiser. Counting the reckless driver, that's two down, one to go."

"Got thoughts on número tres?" Jack asked, side-eyeing the driver. Sommers clenched his jaw and nodded without speaking, turning left on Highway 6, and a minute later, careening right onto County 15. Again, the driver jerked the steering wheel and crossed the double yellow line, passing a dawdling tractor towing a crusty disc plough.

Moments later, after streaking past Fog Lake, Sommers pressed hard on the brakes, bringing the Tahoe to a skidding stop in a gravel wayside short of South Beach Road. Lucky Dog fussed and barked as her new master stepped out and scanned the wooded area below Victory Bluff's backside. "Okay, girl," Sommers said, opening the back door, then buckling his leather tool belt around his waist. "Let's take a walk, but you gotta promise to keep quiet."

Lucky bounded out, then wagged her tail as she sniffed the weeds surrounding the wayside.

Jack leaned from the window and asked, "What's your plan?"

Sommers pointed his thumb over his shoulder. "No plan, just a hunch. Lindstrom and the Peterson boys are chasing gangster number three through the North Woods. We're heading up top to get the bird's-eye view."

Jack grabbed his .38 from the glove box and inspected the chambers. "I'm coming with you."

Sommers shook his head and raised a calloused palm to his lawyer's face. "I need you to gather everybody into a defensible spot, the hangar or the wood shop should do. Tell the posse to keep their powder dry. Today's not the day to get caught in a crossfire. Besides, we've had enough hospital visits to last us a lifetime. With a smidge of luck, Ted will drive the migrant right into us and we'll end this thing."

Jack offered his gun, then shrugged at the stubborn lumberjack. He climbed behind the wheel and drove west towards DeRoxe Road. Sommers ruffled Lucky's floppy ears before ducking into a stand of aspens bordering the lower trailhead. With a gentle breeze at their backs, the pair jogged up the winding trail leading to The Watcher's towering lair.

A murder of crows rustled the treetops above the pair as they trudged along, searching the forest while swatting pesky mosquitoes. A quarter-mile in, Lucky Dog turned and froze, perking her ears and lifting her snout to the air. Sommers slipped a hatchet from his belt and crouched behind an old hickory tree, its enormous truck blackened by a lightning strike. He pulled the pooch closer and whispered in her ear. "Somebody there, girl? Who's it?"

Lucky twitched her tail, then tiptoed from the dirt path, creeping and crouching between the trees like a stalking cat. After several paces and just beyond the gnarled roots of a fallen cottonwood tree, the pair came face to face with the muzzle of Ted Lindstrom's revolver. Seated with his right arm hanging loose at his side, he cocked his head and whispered as he lowered the gun. "Get your asses down here. There's a trigger-happy nut job out there wielding an AR-15. Damn thing is fitted with a bump stock."

Lucky sided up and leaned into Lindstrom, licking his face. Sommers climbed down and squatted behind the massive mossy trunk. "Glad to see you, too," he said, sheathing his ax and pointing with his chin. "You shot?"

Lindstrom shook his head. "Jus' shrapnel, I think." Then he pointed at his ankle. "Fell into a goddamn hole dodging a spray of bullets—might be broken. Just our luck, eh?"

Sommers unwound a length of gauze from his pocket and dressed Lindstrom's oozing wound. "Hang in there, partner. We'll get you outta here soon enough." Then he turned and peeked over the top of the fallen cottonwood, surveying the dusky hillside. "Where's the shooter?"

Lindstrom shoved Lucky aside and pointed with his gun. "Up top. I think one of the Petersons winged him. They had him dead to right, but that desperado escaped into the trees—young punk with crazy eyes." He pointed the gun at his bandaged arm. "Friendly fire, I'm guessing. That gangbanger couldn't hit water falling out of a boat."

"Yea, but ten rounds a second affords him some leeway. Where's Bob and Al?"

"Lindstrom coughed and spit a bug from his mouth, then winced and shook his head. "I sent those two boneheads back because they were slowing me down. Besides, I couldn't handle any more of their bitchin'—crusty old bastards almost killed me."

Sommers cocked his head towards the lake. "And Noah?"

"Not sure," Lindstrom said with a shrug. "Last I heard, he was in a fishing boat with your mother—anchored off Sandy Point."

The trio flinched and ducked as the popping sounds of gunfire reverberated above their cover, reverberating through the trees. "Hold tight," Sommers said, tightening his tool belt. "I gotta get up there."

Lindstrom struggled to stand. "Not without me," he said, pointing his revolver up the gloomy slope. "You're a good guy, tough as boot leather. But you're no killer. I'm goin' with ya."

"Yea, well," Sommers said. "Sometimes good guys have to do bad things. Stay here with Lucky, wouldja? Keep your heads down."

Like Jack, Lindstrom offered Sommers his revolver, but the big lumberjack was already gone, scrambling up the hillside on all fours.

After a few minutes of crawling and climbing, Sommers

crouched beside a boulder, catching his breath. He lifted his nose to the sky, inhaling the familiar scents of home. Within the depths of this aroma, he caught a whiff of smoke that took him back to the fire in Peg McFarland's cornfield. He searched the ground near his post and discovered blood spatters on the stones lining the hiking trail.

Without warning, Lucky bounded from the trees, startling the big man as she plowed into him, wagging her tail and licking his face. Sommers pulled her close and put a finger to her nose, trying to quiet her enthusiasm. He looked around, then slipped John Thompson's ax from his tool belt and studied the shiny, sharpened blade. The hulking woodsman recalled his Idaho adventures, but the smoke, the flames and the Hotshots' heroics were just fading memories now.

With Lucky Dog on his hip, Sommers crawled the next twenty yards uphill through thorny brambles and swarming bugs. Inches from the top of Victory Bluff, he shushed a muted growl percolating in his sidekick's chest. He gave the pooch a stern look as he ruffled her ears, then took a moment to focus his thoughts and catch his breath. The unruly crows, scattered by the gangster's gunshots, moved on as Sommers propped himself on his elbows and peeked over the ledge.

Thirty feet beyond the upper trailhead, Sommers saw the Venezuelan stretched out on his stomach with a black semi-automatic rifle tucked under his arm. The stealthy teen, dressed in camouflage-colored fatigues and brown boots, snuffed his joint on a flat rock. Sommers watched him flick his smothered butt over the edge while he scrutinized the lake from one-hundred feet above the depths of Townsend Drop-off.

Sommers held Lucky by the scruff of her neck and watched the Latino shift to his side, slipping a cellphone from his pocket. The shooter held the phone skyward, trying in vain to get a cell signal. Then the big lumberjack saw something grab the boy's attention, and the shooter pivoted, taking a photo of the lake. The teen double-tapped and studied his small screen while Sommers and Lucky Dog crept their way towards the upper trailhead, steeped in bright sunshine. The gunman, showing heightened urgency, pocketed his phone, then sat up, aiming his rifle towards the south shore.

Late summer sun warmed Sommers' back and a shifting breeze off the lake cooled his face. He plucked a golf ball-sized stone from the dirt and tossed it into the trees beyond the gunman's lookout. Sommers watched the shooter scramble from his seat, then fire a torrent of bullets into the woods.

Lucky Dog broke loose and charged from the trailhead, snarling and growling at the surprised shooter. Sommers stepped from the trail and watched the crazed gunman, no older than eighteen, falter and stumble with the rifle, waving it between his two attackers.

Beams of sunlight, creased by the treetops, washed the shooter's face as a silhouetted giant stepped from the shadows with a hickory-handled ax hanging from his seasoned right hand. Lucky Dog bristled and barked to the shooter's right.

Ted Lindstrom, from out of nowhere, emerged from the trees below the boy's left flank. "¡Déjalo, ahora!" Lindstrom said with a scratchy growl. The sheriff leaned against a decaying tree stump, pointing his revolver at the boy's chest.

Sommers felt the campaign play out in slow motion as his instincts and reflexes took over. The Venezuelan sneered as he pivoted and swung the gun's barrel across to Lindstrom. Recognizing the shooter's deadly intent, Sommers leaped up and fired his hatchet with all the speed he could muster. In the fraction of a second, the whirling blade struck the rifle's handguard at the shooter's grip and a stream of bullets splintered the limbs above Lindstrom's ducking head. The sheriff fired a wild shot into the trees as he toppled backwards down the hill.

The Venezuelan, shaking his injured hand, stumbled as he

struggled to find his footing. Sommers saw his chance and charged the boy as the gun's barrel swung back in Lucky Dog's direction. Sommers' broad shoulder and Lucky's front paws smashed into the gunman's midsection at the same time. The crazed gunman latched onto the lumberjack's tool belt for balance, but then staggered and slipped over the rim of Victory Bluff.

Sommers, defying the laws of physics and any reasonable explanation, latched onto the base of a two-inch sapling with his right hand, his feet dangling over the edge of the one-hundred-foot precipice. The battered gunman, showing gold-capped teeth through his wry smile, clung to the big man's tool belt with both of his bloodstained hands. Sommers' mighty left hand clutched the scruff of Lucky Dog's hairy neck as the shooter's rifle splashed into the dark water far below.

The big lumberjack, his face dripping with sweat, could feel his shoulder pulling from its socket. He gnashed his teeth and grimaced, fighting mass and gravity with all his might, fighting to keep his grip. The strain became excruciating as Sommers heaved the eighty-pound pooch over his head and onto the rocky ledge. Lucky Dog landed with a thud and a yelp, then scuttled to her feet, circling and barking at the two men suspended high above the lake.

From the corner of his eye, Sommers spotted his mother and his son motoring from Sandy Point in Grumpy's aluminum fishing boat. Gracie held her grandson close, shielding his eyes from the terrifying battle upon the brink. Then, without warning, the big lumberjack heard the tiny tree crack. He felt the roots giving way. He reached down for the shooter with his free hand. "Your hand, gimme your hand!" Sommers watched the gleam in the boy's eyes change from zealous to panicked.

The defeated Venezuelan, weakened and pale, with tears welling in his eyes, shook his head and let go of the big man's belt. Sommers looked away, then reached for the edge as the tiny tree gave up the ghost, roots and all.

Lindstrom, covered with cuts and scrapes, arrived a half-second too late. He sprawled along the rim and watched in horror as the big lumberjack's hand slipped between his outstretched arms.

Pulled by gravity, but suspended in time, Sommers' mind raced through snapshots of his life, recent and distant, many joyous and others dreadful. He saw glimpses of baseball games, fishing trips, and backyard barbecues. He saw the smiling faces of his family and friends. Then, in the blink of an eye, he fixated on a memory of canoeing with his father, watching a pelican dive for fish.

Through the cleft in Victory Bluff, the biting sunshine blinded the falling man and shook him from his dream. Wasting no time, Sommers straightened his legs, tossed the broken sapling aside, then thrust his hands towards the heavens, making himself as true as a diving bird.

The impact hit him harder than anything he could've ever imagined. Stunned and engulfed in chilling darkness, Sommers felt pain, like lightning, shocking his extremities. Breathless and paralyzed, tiny bubbles fluttered past his face, and he relaxed, realizing he was missing his hat and just maybe, he was still alive.

The big lumberjack fumbled for his belt buckle with his left hand, then surrendered to the water, allowing the swells to raise him towards the light. During his passage across a cool and timeless sea, Sommers remembered The Watcher's malice and thought, *"If this is my penance, then it's a fitting end."*

Seconds, minutes, or perhaps even hours later, floating on his back with Victoria's small reassuring waves kissing his cheeks, Sommers blinked his eyes and cracked a grateful smile. *"My boy is safe."*

Chapter 35
Rainy Day People

"Rainy day people always seem to know when it's time to call."

It was a festive fall evening, and Mother Nature displayed hues that were fitting and quite striking. Halloween was just days away, and the setting sun cast an orange cloak across the glassy water. The surrounding forests and fields, a spectrum of yellows and reds, melted into a rolling sea of blue-black obscurity studded by random yard lights glowing amber and white. Dotting the water, the last of the walleye fisherman. Those gritty diehards hauling their bounty to shore for cleaning and frying before sundown.

On the western shore of Lake Victoria, where bikini tops, yoga shorts, and sandals were in abundance, the DeRoxe Club was bursting at the seams from a boisterous Saturday night crowd. One hundred bikers, maybe more, from the tri-state H.O.G. Riders Club, rumbled in and set up camp in the parking lot above the boat launch. Led by Clayton Stearns and C.J. Hunter, the leather-clad Harley riders rode all day, paying respects to their fallen comrades.

Many of DeRoxe's hungry patrons arrived early, not just for Rosie's world-famous fish tacos, but to see with their own eyes the larger-than-life, death-defying lumberjack. Dale Sommers, never one for the spotlight, gave in to Joy O'Leary's raw demand, and stood in front of the bar, waving his left hand, requesting everyone's attention. His right arm bound in a sling, the big lumberjack, despite his reclusive back woods reputation, commanded the assembly like an accomplished professor. A hush fell over the room, and the willing crowd obliged Sommers with a sober moment of silence, honoring Tommy Fulgham, Bud Wolcott, and Lilly LeBlanc.

The mesmerized throng watched as Sommers raised his Coca-Cola bottle above his head and side-eyed the craggy face of Victory Bluff, blushing high above the eastern shore of Lake Victoria. Sommers, at least for the time being, kept The Watcher's vengeance at bay. He broke his fleeting stare-down and scanned the hundreds of faces holding their collective breath for the giant's stirring words. He saw it in their wanting eyes. These were his people, modern-day revolutionaries, craving something patriotic, honest, and free.

"How 'bout this weather?" Sommers asked before clearing his throat and quelling his emotion. "My Pop used to say Indian Summer was like hitting the jackpot with house money." He swept his beverage above his head as if he was tickling the heavens and spotted his tireless son seated atop Ted Lindstrom's broad shoulders. Sommers turned and motioned towards the lake's golden ripples. "Ahh, water," he said with a nod and a smile. "Everything ends as it begins, with water."

Then, following a lengthy pause, the legendary woodsman lifted the bottle to his lips and swallowed the dark nectar down in a single gulp. Sommers smothered a belch, then wiped his mouth with the back of his hand. He adjusted his baseball hat and once again studied the curious crowd. "It's heartwarming to see so many happy faces here tonight. As you've heard, I'm a simple man, a private man. All this attention is surprising, and honestly, it's got me shaking in my boots." Back in the kitchen, a food tray fell and rattled across the tile floor. Morales Lopez's profane rant, a peculiar Northwoods rendition of Spanglish, rose to the rafters, and a concerted chuckle reverberated across the cozy pub.

"Molo's the best," Sommers said with an affirming smile. "As I was saying, you're lucky because there are actual heroes among us tonight." He stood up on his toes and pointed out his valiant team members one by one. "These workaday folks stand for truth, justice, and of course, the American way. Veteran servants like Ted Lindstrom and Jerry Reynolds, Gary Johnson and CJ Hunter. Look, that's Wes Duncan standing at the end of the bar. You all know my mother, Gracie, and my uncle Grumpy. And let me tell you something about Doris Greene. She didn't wilt under pressure. She made the call, used our old party line to mobilize the troops. These brave souls saved my son. They protected us from hostile invaders. I mean, who in their right mind would take on the Peterson Brothers when they're in a sour mood?"

Grumpy whistled, then shouted from the back, "Shit, man! They're always in a sour mood. Look at 'em, they're fighting right now—bitchin' over who's gonna pay for their beers." The crowd laughed in agreement, and the crusty farmers swiveled on their barstools, holding their middle fingers high overhead, letting everyone know Grumpy was still the ace.

Sommers rolled his eyes and waited for the gathering to hush before finishing his introductions. "I'd be remiss to not acknowledge my good friends, the best legal team this side of the Supreme Court, Julie and Jack Hughes. I see Phelps and Lucky Dog, man's best friends, chasing their tails on the patio. And how about our gracious hosts, Rosie and Scooter Carlson? Last but not least, let's give our best to these daring newlyweds, Spearfish's newest power couple, Joy and Greg O'Leary."

After a long clamorous cheer, Sommers raised his empty bottle to the receptive congregation. "Here's to family and friends."

From behind the bar, Scooter rang a brass dinner bell and

shouted, "Sommers for governor!" Then the eager horde, craving a celebration, erupted with chants, shouts, and whistles.

Sommers grabbed Noah from Lindstrom's shoulders and carried him under his arm across the crowded tavern. He lifted his giggling son up to the Wurlitzer jukebox, and the boy's small hands fed quarters, one after another, into the glowing Bubbler. The boy pushed a random array of numbers and letters, then clapped his hands as the bar crowd cheered and sang along with his selections.

Rosie dashed from table to table, singing and smiling as she welcomed her customers with trays of tortilla chips and fresh-made salsa. Gary Johnson, after closing his convenience store early, helped Molo in the smoke-filled kitchen behind the bar. Sommers knew before long the food and the beer would run out and all but the most devoted locals would parade south to Zorbaz's pizzeria on Pelican Lake. Noah scampered off to find Phelps, and the big lumberjack waded through a sea of fist bumps and backslaps, searching for a quieter place to sit.

Sommers broke stride when the barroom exploded in a cacophony of whistles and catcalls. He couldn't help but shake his head and laugh as he turned to watch Rosie, Joy, and Julie Hughes dancing and singing atop DeRoxe's oaken bar. At last, the big man backed his way onto the veranda and pulled up a chair between Greg O'Leary and Ted Lindstrom. He found the grizzled pair comparing their battle scars in between their sips of light beer. Sommers lifted his chin at his uncle Grumpy, seated at a corner table with Jerry Reynolds. Grumps cursed under his breath, shuffling a rumpled deck of playing cards. The big man saw they were sharing a pitcher of Old Style, waiting for Gracie and Doris to join them in a game of pinochle.

Lucky Dog sidled up and leaned into Sommers as Phelps chased Noah around the patio. Sommers watched the vigorous tot sprinting in circles with a toy airplane clutched in his outstretched hand. Jack Hughes arrived with a round of drinks from the bar. He pulled up another chair after doling out the beverages. The men clinked their frosty bottles and Jack savored his tasty suds. "Ahh, to good times," he said, following a muted burp.

Sommers acknowledged his lawyer by raising his pop bottle in a subdued toast. "Best enjoy 'em while we got 'em."

After watching the ladies finish their dance, Greg O'Leary pointed his longneck bottle at Sommers' sling. "How's the shoulder?"

Sommers looked down at his right elbow and shrugged. "Three more weeks of immobilization, then six months of PT. Doc Abrams said I can start throwing in the spring. My left's getting stronger, so who knows? I may end up switching to the other side."

Lindstrom, wearing a walking boot on his left foot, leaned in and snickered after sipping his beer. "The other side has no interest in a sad sack like you." Then he cocked his head towards the lake and motioned back to Sommers. "Abrams told me the odds of surviving a fall like yours are one in four. And for you to bob up with nary a scratch—you should buy yourself a few scratch-off tickets, my friend."

Sommers adjusted his baseball hat and smirked, knowing he had beaten the odds once again, if only by the narrowest margin. He gazed across the water at the jagged cleft running down the middle of Victory Bluff and wondered how long his luck would hold out.

From out of nowhere, Julie Hughes danced over and sat in her husband's lap. She planted a kiss on Jack's cheek, then pointed her bottle at Noah, who has hit some headwinds and appears to be running low on fuel. "Look, his wheels are down," she said. "Someone better clear the little crumb-cruncher for landing." Then she swiveled to face the big lumberjack. "Speaking of pilots, what's happening with your Cessna? Did Jack mention I'm interested in taking flying lessons?"

Jack rolled his eyes before Noah puttered over and flopped across his father's legs. Sommers rubbed the boy's back, then peeled the small toy from his sticky fingers, giving the die-cast biplane a close inspection. "Otto's got the nose wheel and prop fixed. He's gonna tune the engine and install new hydraulics after that." He motioned to his sling. "I told him to take his time, since I'm grounded for a while."

Jack wiped a trickle of beer from his chin and said, "Sounds to me like you're keeping her."

Sommers scrunched his face and shrugged. "Yea. I think so." Noah cracked open his sleepy eyes and looked up at his father, flashing a bright smile between his rosy cheeks. Sommers flew Noah's plane past Julie's nose. "Listen, once that little bird's back in the hangar, you take 'er up anytime you want."

She swallowed her beer and smiled, then smacked her lips as she poked Sommers in his ribs. "Ya know. She'd be here tonight if she could."

"Who?" Sommers asked, craning his neck to survey the rowdy, but thinning, barroom crowd.

"You know damn well who," Julie said, rolling her eyes. Then she stood and strutted for the jukebox with her arms outstretched like a pair of wings. Sommers' face flushed, and the other men enjoyed a hearty laugh at his expense.

Jack stood from his chair and motioned with his beer. "Looks like the old-timers got stood up. I'm crashing their game. Wanna bet I can get more than two words outta Ol' Man Reynolds?"

"Good luck with that one," Lindstrom said as he shifted in his seat, propping his gimpy foot on a dog-eared milk crate. "Beware, my gambling friend, those guys are sharks. You should leave that fancy watch with me. Gimme them keys, while you're at it." Jack, feeling the effects of several beers, waved him off and wobbled for the card table.

The party paused, feeling DeRoxe's floors and walls shake. Everyone turned to watch one hundred mighty motorcycles thunder from the adjacent parking lot. Phelps, shaken by the noise, slinked over and sat beside Lucky Dog at Sommers' feet. The big lumberjack fished a pair of dog biscuits from his pocket, assessing his situation as the two slobbering pooches munched on their treats. "Seems I'm landlocked here."

Lindstrom stood with a smirk on his face. "Yes. I believe you are. And you wouldn't have it any other way." Then he pointed with his thumb. "Heading to the boys' room. Something from the bar?"

Sommers shook his head, and Gracie appeared in the doorway. She tilted her head and curled her lower lip into a pout. "Isn't that cute?" She said, reaching for her grandson. "C'mon, stinker. Grandma's had enough partying for tonight. Let's get you to bed."

Sommers stood and draped the droopy toddler over his mother's shoulder before kissing the back of his sweaty head. Noah, on the verge of sawing logs, reached one lethargic hand for his toy airplane and the other for his furry companion. Gracie, with one arm around Noah's waist, pivoted to the card table. "Grumps, our show starts in ten minutes—got pints of mint chocolate chip in the freezer. You comin' or not?"

Grumpy downed the rest of his beer, belched, then teetered as he stepped from the table. "No need to be bustin' my chops like a pigheaded matron. I'll be along soon enough." The wrinkled warhorse tipped his hat to Jerry and Jack before he limped for the door. "Here, gimme the boy," he said, his voice full of grit and vinegar. Then, with Noah dangling across his back, Grumpy ruffled Phelps' ears. "C'mon you hairy varmint, let's roll."

Sommers kissed his mother on the cheek, then walked to the screen door and watched this cherished foursome step from the patio and traipse onto the well-worn path for home. He waited for his family to fade into the woods, then looked over to find Lindstrom and Lucky Dog at the card table with Jack, Greg, and Jerry.

Sommers examined the barroom and scratched at the back of his neck. He tried not to show it, but the entire evening was a bittersweet challenge for him. As he predicted, most of the party fled in search of late-night pizza and beer. What the big man wanted most was to slip away unnoticed, escaping to his dock where a St. Croix fishing rod and a big landing net stood at the ready.

Sommers reached for the door, but Joy O'Leary grabbed his arm and shoved him into an empty corner booth. She chugged one of her two beers dry, then wagged a finger in the big man's face. "What the hell were you thinking? Wenner's place must've cost a fuckin' fortune."

Sommers sat up and tightened his sling, grinning at his longtime friend. "I'll take that as a thank you. Say, despite your advancing age, married life looks pretty good on you." Joy punched his good arm and Sommers laughed because it felt good. Felt like old times. "How are you settling in?"

"Heaven on earth, definitely a different vibe out there," Joy said, sipping from her second bottle. "We had that fuckin' bathroom remodeled, for obvious reasons." The pair soaked in a delicate moment of silence as she picked at the paper label on her bottle. Then, following a minute of quiet contemplation, she locked into Sommers' patient blue eyes. "Ted told me you've been having bad dreams—visions that are weighing on you."

Sommers adjusted his baseball hat and nodded, knowing there was no escaping one of Joy's healing sessions. He searched the room, seeing his friends, his lifeline, entangled in cards and conversation. Then he looked back at her and exhaled a weighty sigh. "I have this recurring dream where I'm roaming an open plain, lost in a snowstorm. The wind's howling my name and the blowing snow piles into drifts all around me. I'm naked, but covered with frost. The blizzard stings my eyes and burns my skin. There's no escape, then…"

Joy set her bottle on the table and grabbed Sommers' left hand. "When you've lost all hope, and you've surrendered to your destiny, a great beast appears."

"Yes," Sommers said, turning away to glare at the moon-washed crag towering ten stories above the shimmering water that has buoyed him time and again. "A white buffalo."

Joy smacked the table hard enough for the others to turn and gawk. "Tatanka. I fuckin' knew it," she said with a throaty whisper. "I've seen it too." She pulled out her cellphone and began tapping and swiping the screen. "Get a load of this, wouldja?"

Sommers took her phone and skimmed an article posted by the Rapid City Gazette. The story detailed a hiker's claim of spotting a white bison calf south of Wind Cave in the Buffalo Gap National Forest. The hiker's grainy photograph of the calf seemed to validate the legend. Sommers passed the iPhone back to Joy and pivoted to face the ghostly cliff. A warm breeze that smelled like ocean mist whistled through the window screens and the big man realized the date of the bison sighting was the same day he left Samantha overlooking Pettigrew Gulch.

Joy tapped Sommers' shoulder to regain his attention. "C'mon, let's take a walk." She stood and blew a kiss at her tipsy husband before the duo stepped from the patio and strolled past the deserted boat launch.

A harvest moon lit their way, and the amiable pair, walking arm in arm, entered the south woods trail, rounding tiny Fish Lake under a canopy of rustling cottonwoods. The big man glanced over his shoulder, and out of habit, scanned the twilight beneath the trees. "Where are you taking me?"

"Andie Hansen's old place," she said. "My Jeep's parked in the driveway." Then she stepped faster, pulling the wary man along. "Roarke skipped town with Spooky after she heard about me and Greg. I think she ran off to Texas with a pipefitter."

They walked in silence until the trail split towards South Beach Road. Sommers pondered Joy's relationship with Jenny Roarke until she nudged his hip. "I know what you're thinking, but rumors are just that. Your uncle thinks he's got dirt on everybody, but he don't know shit about me. Truth is, I loved that cat."

As they wandered through the woods, Joy explained how her people, the Lakota, revere the tatanka. She detailed how the Lakota believe the rare arrival of a white bison signals the onset of a great upheaval. For many, a sighting brings a period of peace and prosperity, but for others, the nonbelievers, the white bison is a harbinger of pain and suffering. The couple rambled along before entering a clearing along the lake where Sommers glanced up at the moon and asked, "These visions of mine, what do you think they mean?"

Sommers watched Joy cross her arms and shrug as if she caught a chill. She peered across the lake, and Sommers knew she was expecting to see their nemesis perched high atop the bluff. "Hard to know for sure," she said. "Unearthing one's understanding is a personal odyssey. And let me tell you, the meditative waters can get rough. But don't worry, I'll keep you afloat." She latched onto his left arm. "Let's go."

Soon thereafter, they stood in the shadow of a birch tree behind Joy's Jeep. She clicked the fob and paused, looking around, reaching for the door handle. "When Jo Douglass started talking about shapeshifters and divine sisterhoods, I thought she was fuckin' nuts. But after those goons killed her, my visions became more frequent. And more fuckin' real."

Sommers leaned against the car with his hand in his pocket, listening as Joy went on. "After I got outta the hospital," she said, opening the door. "I asked Greg to take me to her. He thought it was a bad idea, but I made him take me, anyway. You know me, I don't take no for an answer. Besides, I just had to see for myself."

Sommers watched as Joy motioned to a backpack and a hunting rifle resting in the Jeep's cargo bin. He scratched the stubble on his chin and considered the repercussions of holding these pieces. He knew what she was about to say, and he believed her conclusions would be hard for any rational person to understand.

Joy turned away, grinding her fists into her hips and pointing her chin at the haunting face of the rocky wall. "I couldn't find her body, Dale. I scoured that entire hillside and couldn't find one fuckin' drop of blood." Joy turned back and waved her hands over the incriminating artifacts like they were toxic. "She wants us to finish it. The white tatanka will lead us from the storm."

Sommers nodded without speaking, then rambled across the yard and stepped to the end of Hansen's dock. He slipped off his boots and sat at the edge of the weathered planks, staring through the moon's golden reflection into the calm, sable water. His eyes penetrated the depths, and he challenged Victoria, wondering if she'd reveal her deepest secrets. A warm gust washed over his face and he closed his eyes. Soon, he heard Joy treading along the creaking wooden boards. He looked up to see her holding Samantha's backpack and rifle. Sommers owed his friend a favor, and he knew she came to collect.

Before Joy could utter a word, Sommers waved his index finger above his head, setting his sights on the depths below Victory Bluff. He thought about Townsend Drop-off, ominous and deadly for some, cool and liberating for others. "I needed a moment out here," he said over his shoulder. "I had to establish a few ground rules."

Along the south shore, a bullfrog croaked from the lily pads, and an owl hooted from high in the poplars. Small ripples lapped the seawalls as parched leaves fluttered from the maples like giant snowflakes. The night grew eerie and still. Joy smirked and shook her head, hearing her husband collapse on the screen porch's old couch.

She surveyed the lake before kicking off her sandals and sitting beside her friend. "For the longest time, you frustrated the hell out of me," she said as she leaned into him. "I didn't hear you. Tried like hell, but I didn't get you. Tonight, when I have every reason to be happy, this water speaks to me and it sounds like a fuckin' warning."

Sommers draped his arm across her shoulders and pulled her close, offering his simple reassurance. They sat as they did many times before, watching the brilliant colors of Aurora Borealis glimmer over the north woods where Sommers' family garden lies in wait for both of them.

Later, well past midnight, the big lumberjack vanished into the south woods with a rifle and a daypack hanging by his side. He watched Rosie and Scooter dim the lights at the DeRoxe Club, and soon, he heard their pontoon boat chugging for home. Sommers reached the lower trailhead, where even in total darkness, he knew the way. He looked back, watching Joy swirl her toes in the lake. Sounds travel uninhibited across open water and her cries carried like a sad song. Sommers remembered her journey was arduous, and despite her warrior-like toughness, he knew she had many miles to go. Life's just that way for some.

Within minutes, Sommers stood at the brink, catching his breath and kicking at the rocks where he uprooted a pathetic sapling just weeks ago. The scene captivated him in a way he'd never felt before, and he dropped to a knee, absorbing this lake's rare bouquet. He listened as a refreshing updraft carried the word of God, and the humbled lumberjack took a moment to share his gratitude and request some forgiveness.

After taking a deep breath and scanning the horizon, Sommers did as the legendary beast demanded. He let go. Soon, a resounding splash, followed by another, from far below, delivered Lake Victoria's promise of finality. The big lumberjack stepped back and admired the ripples spreading towards the western shore. The shimmering sparkles pointed the way, leading to his family nestled in their cozy cabins. Then, after brushing some grit from his hand, Sommers recited Plato as he turned for home. "The sea cures all ailments of man."

A short time later, as Sommers stepped from the lower trailhead, he heard a red-tailed hawk screech. The glorious bird took flight on a chilly gust that whooshed across the treetops. Sommers saw his breath and acknowledged winter was just around the corner. Then he heard a grand spruce, alone in a clearing, relay the bird's soothing refrain. *"Our boy is safe."*

The big lumberjack adjusted his baseball hat, then nodded, wearing a knowing grin. From beside that whispering tree, he looked up and watched the graceful bird circle twice, then sail away.

Chapter 36
Alive and Kicking

"You turn me on. You lift me up."

A habitual early riser, Dale Sommers settled back on his haunches and caught his breath as he watched the rising sun pierce the lofty cleft splitting Victory Bluff. Sweat poured down his face and soaked his sleeveless shirt as he surveyed the azure waters of Lake Victoria. A gentle breeze carried the songs of birds, and he knew the fine folks along the southern and western shores would soon stir from their slumber. He heard Grumpy clanging pans and shouting obscenities over his cookstove, and before long, Sommers smelled sizzling bacon and percolating coffee, those mouth-watering bouquets of daybreak.

After a vigorous hike and pitching two hundred bulls-eyes, the big lumberjack sat with his family in the shadows of the north woods cemetery. He tended to their markers and the surrounding gardens with meticulous care. As the morning's rays washed over the top of the eastern crag, Sommers ruffled Lucky Dog's ears, then crawled to the last marble plaque and brushed away the cobwebs and grass clippings. He stood back and folded his arms across his chest. Then, in a whisper, he recited the simple sentimental inscription for Lucky. "My boys are safe."

Almost a year had passed since Sommers took his treacherous plunge into the chilly depths of Townsend Drop-off. He noticed the deciduous leaves were showing signs of turning. Hundreds of trees decorate these northern hillsides; white pine, sugar maple, red oak, and quaking aspen. The big lumberjack knows each one of them better than the callouses lining his muscular hands. Despite his advancing years, Sommers has remained a chiseled giant of a man, and there were many who believe he has defied the laws of nature.

The big lumberjack cinched his tool belt around his waist and turned his attention back to the western shore, where his sleepy son, wearing cut-off shorts and a Harley Davidson t-shirt, joined Grumpy and Phelps at the outdoor breakfast table.

Noah, having just enjoyed his fourth birthday, is maturing into an eating machine, growing taller and stronger by the day. Sommers wiped his brow and watched Noah lift his face from his plate long enough to wave to his "uncle" Ted, who has emerged from Hansen's screen porch wearing nothing but his boxer shorts and a cowboy hat. Sommers watched the retired sheriff amble for the dock, gripping a fishing pole in one hand and the wooden handle of an old minnow bucket in the other.

Ted Lindstrom is the closest thing to a brother that Sommers has ever known. With the help of Julie and Jack Hughes, the retired sheriff purchased the Hansen cottage for back taxes. This was after an extensive search for Andie and Abbie proved fruitless. These days, Lindstrom provides security for his newfound friends at the lake. In return for his surveillance and protection, he receives a modest salary from Sommers. Lindstrom also gets complimentary car washes from Gary Johnson, along with free food and beer at the DeRoxe Club.

Ted's cozy lakefront cabin sports a new dock, a covered boat lift, and a heated garage for his Hemi-powered Hellcat. C.J. Hunter has been pressuring him to buy a bass boat that's been sitting on his showroom floor for the past eighteen months. Lindstrom has told Sommers he's grown weary of the harsh winters, but he tells everyone else Lake Victoria security is the best gig he's ever had.

Seconds later, Sommers watched Gracie Sommers step from her cottage wearing denim overalls and a floppy hat embroidered with daisies. She's clutching a coffee mug in one hand and a dog-eared peach basket in the other. There's work to be done in her vegetable garden, and Sommers heard her call out for Noah, requesting his help. There's no need to bribe the boy, but she promises him cinnamon rolls and a dozen minnows from Gary's Place for a job done well. The boy sprang from the table, wiping pancake syrup from his chin with his shirtsleeve. Sommers watched him dash across the dew-covered lawn with Phelps nipping at his heels.

This is how many sunny mornings have gone, and Sommers has grown at peace with it. The coming days will be different. D.T. Hardesty, who he hasn't seen in more than a year, has invited the big lumberjack to a dedication ceremony in Pembina County. On the surface, there was no reason for the big man to feel anxious. But he was.

At Sommers' request and with the EPA's expeditious approval, the twenty-five hundred acres that comprised Norman Farms will become part of the Red River Wildlife Refuge. A multi-state coalition under Hardesty's direction, bolstered by tribal and Canadian backing, guarantees the sanctuary will have protection from unfettered mining and commercial development. Work on the wetland restoration, made possible by Jerry Reynolds' generous donation, has already begun. Sommers asked Reynolds to join the festivities, shake hands with a few dignitaries, then cut a ceremonial ribbon.

Reynolds, who is driving a new Silverado these days, has commissioned the Forest River Hutterites to restore Norman's dilapidated farmhouse and rebuild the historic barn number two. The buildings will serve as welcome and education centers for the refuge's visitors.

Along the glistening south shore, Lindstrom, armed with an ultralight spinning rod, has hooked into something big. Sommers watched Grumpy toss a landing net into his fishing boat and putt-putt over to lend a hand. Lucky Dog, sensing the excitement, led the way along the north woods trail. Sommers let his mind wander as he took in all the lake-life splendor. Fifty-three years ago, he was born in a modest log cabin, one of only three dwellings on this entire lake. From early on, he knew someday, with a bit of luck, he'd rest in the shade of this northern slope overlooking the girl he loves with all his heart.

Scooter Carlson's proclamation from last fall has grown legs. The conservative lobbyists, encouraged by Judge Abbott, continue to hound Sommers, wanting him to throw his hat into the gubernatorial ring. But the big lumberjack has felt the sting of Minnesota politics first-hand. He ruffled Lucky Dog's ears. "Lesson learned," he said, adjusting his baseball hat. "I'm staying right here where I belong." The loyal pooch wagged her tail as they continued their hike along the rocky north shore.

The pair reached the boat launch in time to see Ted and Grumpy hoist a feisty forty-inch northern from the water. Sommers snapped a few pictures with his phone, then signaled thumbs up to the two sweaty fishermen, who were smiling ear to ear over their catch. Sommers zoomed in on his photo and realized Grumpy's jovial expression looked more remarkable than the trophy fish. Noah and Gracie popped their heads from the garden to see the monster the proud anglers pulled from the lake.

Sommers watched Grumpy and Lindstrom take special care, releasing the mighty fish back into the water. Then he tramped across the yard and pulled a white cardboard tube from the back seat of his timeworn Blazer. As he made his way to the picnic table, he remembered Julie and Jack Hughes wanted to meet for dinner, after Julie logged two hours of flight time in Sommers' Cessna. In short order, her piloting skills have advanced, surpassing both Sommers and his flying mentor, Jim Thompson. Gary Johnson, at Sommers' request, painted a Barbie-doll wearing a pink bikini beneath the pilot's side window. Julie Hughes considers the sexy graphic a badge of honor.

Seated at the picnic table, Sommers unrolled the spool of papers, wanting to refresh his memory of the long-lost town of Robbins, Minnesota. Core samples and remote sensing data suggest there's a few buildings buried under the residue left by years of seasonal flooding. Decades ago, the people of Robbins decided they didn't want to deal with the rising waters any longer, and they left their small town behind. As Sommers unfurled a large terrain map of the Two Rivers valley, Noah raced across the yard, carrying a half-eaten cucumber. The boy kneeled on the bench seat and asked, "Cha doin', Pop?"

"Studying these maps."

"Why?" Noah asked as he leaned in and chomped another bite.

Sommers flipped a treat to each of the attentive dogs, then pointed his finger near the spot where he and Lindstrom rescued Lucky Dog the previous year. "Mr. Hughes thinks there's buried treasure right there."

Noah spit a cucumber seed into the grass, then cocked an eyebrow as he studied his father's face. "What do you think?"

Sommers studied Grumpy and Lindstrom, watching the pair motor across the lake towards Sandy Point. "Hard to say," he said, turning back and scratching at the stubble on his chin. "Jack's a smart man. I think he may be right."

Noah climbed down from his seat and scampered for the garden, with Phelps bringing up the rear. Sommers threw up his hands and asked, "Where ya goin'?"

"Getting Grandma's digger!"

Gracie emerged from the garden, brushing dirt from her work gloves. She wiped sweat from her face with a handkerchief. Soon after her whistle and a nod, Sommers carried the overflowing basket to her kitchen counter. He gnawed on a radish the size of an apple and returned to find Phelps supervising Noah on the beach. The boy had dug several holes in the wet sand bordering the foaming ripples. Sommers joined in the mining, and before long, Noah's shovel struck something solid.

Noah rinsed the heavy bauble in the water like a racoon washing a mollusk, then lifted it to the golden rays spilling across the lake. "What is it, Pop?" He asked, beaming with pride and unadulterated curiosity.

The big lumberjack turned the black stone in his hand. It was the size of his fist, blunt on one side, with a dulled edge on the other. He appreciates its history and timeworn craftsmanship, then nodded as he passed the bounty back to his son. "I believe it's a harbinger of things to come."

The boy scrunched his face, showing his confusion, so Sommers patted his son's head and grinned. "It's a tomahawk blade. The nicest one I've ever seen." Noah let out a whoop, then rushed off with Phelps to share his carrot with Grandma Gracie.

Sommers nodded, then turned away from the glowing face of Victory Bluff and ruffled Lucky Dog's ears. The pair returned to the picnic table and settled in with their charts and maps. A moment later, Sommers' cell phone rang and the big man checked the caller ID—Greg O'Leary was on line one. After a few minutes of small talk about sports and weather, O'Leary changed the subject. "My guy ran the data from Lucky Dog's chip. Are you sitting down?"

"Yep. And she's leaning into me. So go easy, wouldja?" Sommers scrutinized his screen because he heard O'Leary jostling his phone at the other end.

"Her real name is Misty Mae," O'Leary said with an uneasy laugh. "She's a retired service dog, decorated like crazy, about four years old. Your vet couldn't run the chip because the data is encrypted—most of her missions, classified. Sad to say, her handler was killed in Afghanistan a few years back."

Sommers caught the attentive pooch studying his face with her ears perked and her head tilted. "That explains a few things," he said. "How the heck did she end up in a Kittson County flood?" The big man exhaled a heavy sigh as he stroked the scruff of her neck. Then he removed his cap and asked the million-dollar question. "Is anyone looking for her?"

"The Army put her in the Warrior Dog program. Looks like she got passed around a bit—therapy dog. As far as I can tell, Misty just kinda slipped through the cracks." O'Leary paused and Sommers heard him leafing through some papers. "Seems the last veteran went off the grid. I've seen it on social media, pet abandonments are a sad reality these days. That's the only explanation that makes any sense to me. Anyway, I explained your situation and highlighted your service with the USDA. I'm gonna send you some paperwork. Have Julie notarize the signatures and return a copy. Doggone it. It's your lucky day, big guy."

Sommers laughed at Greg's silly pun and conveyed his gratitude while ruffling his dog's ears. Then, after discussing a recent fishing boom, he asked about his longtime friend. O'Leary said, "She just walked through the door. Hold on a sec." While he waited, Sommers waved to Noah and Gracie, who were heading over to Gary's Place for a bag of minnows and fresh-baked treats. Phelps wandered over, his droopy ears signaling his disappointment at being left behind. Sommers slipped another pair of dog biscuits from his pocket and flipped one to each of his watchful friends.

A second later, Joy O'Leary got on the phone, catching her breath after a morning road run around Devils Bathtub. Sommers listened as she thanked him for orchestrating such a gratifying career opportunity. Joy, with emotional intensity, described her new job with the U.S. Department of Justice. She can't provide many details, but her primary responsibilities involve tracking and locating missing Native American children. "Most of the outcomes are pretty fuckin' devastating," she said with a snort. "But the good guys win one every so often, and that makes it all worth it. Plus, I've got the authority to shoot evil motherfuckers anytime I catch 'em in the act."

"Sounds like the perfect job for you," Sommers said with a nod of his head. "I can hear the satisfaction in your voice."

"Got that right. I'm on the road a lot, but Greg loves the attention when I get home."

Sommers laughed as he pivoted towards the lake. "I'll bet he does."

After a long, clumsy pause. Joy said, "Listen, Dale. There's something I've got to tell you."

"Okay, sounds like I should be sitting down for this," he said, remembering Joy only used his first name when she expected trouble.

"Have you started digging around Two Rivers yet?"

"Reynolds has arranged for the equipment. Excavation begins next week if this weather holds."

"Okay, well, my visions have returned, and they're pretty fuckin' morbid. I've had deep conversations with a few of the Lakota elders, and I gotta tell ya, Jack's a smart man, but in this case, he doesn't know shit from Shinola. You need to tap the brakes on this one, temper those expectations of yours."

"You're being dark and kinda vague here." Sommers scraped at the sandy soil with the heel of his boot. "What are you saying?"

"I'm sayin' be careful. If my visions are any indication, you won't like what you find. You'll be unleashing a goddamn shitstorm nobody wants to deal with."

Minutes later, after their brief and gloomy phone conversation, Sommers rolled his maps and flipped the cardboard cylinder into the back of his rusty old Blazer. Then he strolled to the end of his dock, where he locked his eyes on the shadowy crevice that split the gnarled face of Victory Bluff. Sommers realized, after many years, he had misjudged the massive gray stone. No longer a sinister threat. The craggy ridge appeared tired, like an ancient titan straining to pull the two halves of the universe together.

Sommers shook his head and sputtered through his lips as he watched Grumpy and Lindstrom troll the weedline surrounding Townsend Drop-off. His curiosity took hold and the big lumberjack grabbed his walleye rod, sliding it into the hull of his boat. After whistling for his two hairy friends, he reversed his hat and stepped out to unwind the mooring ropes.

Sommers hummed a cheerful tune as he watched the eager pups playing in the shallows with their tails wagging. Then he heard the pitter-patter of footsteps creaking the dock's weathered planks. "That was fast," he said without looking up. "Got anything sweet for me?"

Crouched at the end of the dock with his back to the shore, Sommers heard a muffled giggle just before a hard shove sent him flopping into the water.

Bedlam rattled the western shore as the big lumberjack hopped up and shook himself off. He stood soaking and astonished in four feet of water. "What the heck?" He asked, wiping the cool drops from his face. He blinked his eyes and soon recognized his mischievous attacker smiling in the morning sunshine. Sommers huffed as he tossed his wet t-shirt and hat onto the dock. Then he looked up at her and grinned. "C'mon in," he said, waving an inviting hand. "The water is nice."

Sommers watched her pucker her lips and cock her head, considering the big man's proposition. Then she snickered as she kicked off her sandals and shimmied out of her faded blue jeans. She sang a bouncy tune and unfurled her shiny hair from a scrunchy band. "From the moment I laid eyes on you," she said, dancing as she stripped out of her camo-colored hoodie. "I knew you were a Pisces, or maybe an Aquarius."

From his pontoon boat anchored near the south shore, Scooter Carlson whistled and cheered. The lovely siren countered, signaling V for Victoria signs with her fingers. Then she sashayed to the end of the dock and creased the lake's surface with a graceful dive. As she glided through the water, Sommers took a deep breath and looked around, soaking in the ambience of this extraordinary fall morning.

Before long, the enchanting mermaid executed a skillful flip and swam towards him. The big lumberjack muttered to himself, recalling a verse he found spray-painted across a boulder high atop Victory Bluff. "In time and with water, everything changes."

He watched her breach the surface with hundreds of droplets, shimmering like diamonds, trickling along her freckled sun-tanned skin. A rosy smile stretched across her face as she reached up and threw her arms around his neck. Phelps and Lucky Dog circled them like frisky dolphins, and he lifted her up. Sommers explored the depth of her eyes, and he knew their lives were about to take a dramatic turn.

As she pressed into him, Sommers asked, "Do you think we're wading into dangerous waters here?"

She flashed a peace sign with her fingers before splashing his face and wriggling from his grasp. "Trouble times two, big guy." Then she gave him a wink and laughed. "And twice the fun."

An instant later, from over his shoulder, Sommers heard someone shout, "Cannonball!"

The big lumberjack turned in time to catch a face full of Noah's rollicking splash. He grabbed his giggling son under one arm, and the ticklish woman under the other. After roaring like a jolly sea monster, he gave them each a playful squeeze. "Twice the fun?" Sommers asked, spinning around as he gushed a hearty laugh. "Well, heck. Who couldn't use more of that?"

The End

Appendix One
Troubled Water, Song Credits

https://spoti.fi/45Pymwi

Chapter	Song Title	Artist
1	Last Kiss	J. Frank Wilson & The Cavaliers
2	It's Late	Ricky Nelson
3	Fire Lake	Bob Seger
4	Problems	The Everly Brothers
5	What Is Life	George Harrison
6	Fantasy Girl	38 Special
7	Gone	Montgomery Gentry
8	Highway Patrol	Junior Brown
9	Learning to Fly	Tom Petty & The Heartbreakers
10	S.O.S.	ABBA
11	I'm Moving On	Johnny Cash & Waylon Jennings
12	Straight Shooter	The Mamas & The Papas
13	Livin' Thing	Electric Light Orchestra
14	Don't Look Back	Boston

Chapter	Song Title	Artist
15	A Little Less Conversation	Elvis Presley
16	Lucky Penny	JD McPherson
17	It Don't Come Easy	Ringo Starr
18	Simply Irresistible	Robert Palmer
19	Gimme Some Water	Eddie Money
20	Trouble	Lindsey Buckingham
21	Solitary Man	Neil Diamond
22	Rock'n Me	The Steve Miller Band
23	No Time	The Guess Who
24	Here Comes the Rain	The Mavericks
25	Goodbye Yellow Brick Road	Elton John
26	Run to You	Bryan Adams
27	Hold Back the Rain	Duran Duran
28	Across the River	Bruce Hornsby & The Range
29	One Tree Hill	U-2
30	3 AM	Matchbox 20
31	It's All I Can Do	The Cars
32	Harmony Hall	Vampire Weekend
33	Should've Been a Cowboy	Toby Keith
34	Graceland	Paul Simon
35	Rainy Day People	Gordon Lightfoot
36	Alive and Kicking	Simple Minds

Appendix Two
Troubled Water, Character Glossary

Character	Description
Lilly LeBlanc	Young nursing student, Noah's nanny
Mike and Ike	DSS henchmen
Dean Rivers	Farmhand at Norman Farms
Manny Rodriguez	Former convict, laborer at Norman Farms
Ozzy Rodriguez	Manny's brother, Fargo drug dealer
Tommy Fulgham	DNR Field Officer
Dale Sommers	Larger than life lumberjack
John Thompson	Owner of Thompson Mill & Lumber, Idaho
Danny McBride	Idaho Hotshot firefighter
Joy Moon Deer	Deputy Sheriff, former B.I.A investigator
Jerry Reynolds	Army veteran, handyman at Norman Farms
Grumpy Sommers	Dale Sommers' cantankerous uncle
Gracie Sommers	Dale Sommers' mother, Noah's grandmother
Noah Sommers	Dale Sommers' son
Samantha Stevens	Noah's mother, former DSS operative
Conrad Kelly	Dakota Sioux Syndicate Chief
Stuart Barnes	Dakota Sioux Syndicate Chief
Ted Lindstrom	Retired sheriff, casino security officer turned investigator

Character	Description
Jack Hughes	Dale Sommers' lawyer and friend
Julie Hughes	Jack's wife, law student, legal investigator
Bud Wolcott	Manager at Black Hills Harley Davidson
Cody Parsons	Doctor in Rapid City
Otto Schuler	Airplane mechanic at Clyde Ice Field
Edward Norman	Bossman at Norman Farms
Susan Norman	Edwards estranged wife, aka Numbers
Big Bill Wenner	Crooked kingpin, car dealership, casino owner
Duane Rivers	Dean's son, drug-dealing flunky
Jose Guyton	Body shop worker, drug dealer
Angie McCormick	Bartender at Silver Wolf Casino
Clayton Stearns	Powerful judge in Lawrence County, S.D.
Travis Thorne	Crooked District Attorney
C. J. Hunter	Dale Sommers' friend, retired firefighter, owns a boat shop
Alan Peterson	Militant farmer, Robert's twin brother
Robert Peterson	Militant farmer, Alan's twin brother
Greg O'Leary	Former Army Ranger, retired cop, private investigator
Colin Stroud	Corrupt DNR executive
Ro Lin Shui	Corrupt Water Commissioner, CCP operative
Peg McFarland	Boss at McFarland Farm, drug dealer
Gus McFarland	Peg's husband, aka The Chicken Man
Jo Douglass	S.D. State Police Officer, special investigator
Joe Colletti	Disgruntled FBI agent
Donald Wagner	Disgruntled FBI agent

Character	Description
Scooter Carlson	Co-owner of the DeRoxe Club, Dale Sommers' friend
Rosie Carlson	Co-owner of the DeRoxe Club, Scooter's wife
Schmitty	Drone pilot, Dale Sommers' friend
Betsy Robbins	Friendly nurse, knows all the gossip
Wes Duncan	Army veteran, manager of the Gateway Motel
Lefty Porter	Bait delivery man, crooked henchman
Flanel Stan	Manages the Iron Creek Lake camp store
Beef	Susan Norman's bodyguard and enforcer
Morales Lopez	Cook at Gary's Place & the DeRoxe Club
Doris Greene	Cashier at Gary's Place, Gracie's friend
Cesar Flores	Porter at Wenner Motors, drug dealer
Gary Johnson	Owner of Gary's Place, Dale Sommers' friend
D. T. Hardesty	Attractive & mysterious Regional Director, E.P.A.

Also by Robert T. Schuetz, **"Uncommon Ground"**. The first book in the Dale Sommers series.

Milton Keynes UK
Ingram Content Group UK Ltd.
UKHW042113111124
451073UK00015B/351/J